M

Jane Gordon wa:
ITN until the bi
then returned to _____ launch
of the newspaper *Today*. She wrote a weekly
opinion column, 'The Heart of Today', until
she left the paper in 1993 to write her first
novel, *Hard Pressed*, which was followed by
her second novel, *Stepford Husbands*.

Jane Gordon now lives in Chiswick with her
family. She writes regularly for *The Times*, the
Daily Telegraph, the *Daily Mail* and the *Mail
on Sunday*.

Also by Jane Gordon

HARD PRESSED
STEPFORD HUSBANDS

JANE GORDON

My Fair Man

HarperCollins*Publishers*

HarperCollins*Publishers*
77–85 Fulham Palace Road,
Hammersmith, London W6 8JB

A Paperback Original 1998
1 3 5 7 9 8 6 4 2

A catalogue record for this book
is available from the British Library

ISBN 0 00 651100 7

Typeset in Sabon by
Palimpsest Book Production Limited, Polmont, Stirlingshire

Printed in Great Britain by
Caledonian International Book Manufacturing Ltd, Glasgow

ACKNOWLEDGEMENTS

Andy Jacobs, producer of *Fantasy Football League*, who taught me about the soccerati, the game and the trainee system.

Carol Busch, clinical psychologist, who advised me on my heroine's professional life.

Carole Malone, who gave me her memories of North Shields in the seventies, and guided me through Jimmy's childhood.

Mr and Mrs Malone, who allowed me into the West Allotment Working Men's Club.

George Todd, whose knowledge of Geordie idiom was invaluable.

GLOSSARY OF GEORDIE WORDS
AND EXPRESSIONS

bait-box – lunch box

babby – baby

doon – down

droothy – thirsty

gan canny – be careful

grafflin – searching

haddaway – go away

Haddaway an' bowl yor gord. – Go away and bowl your own hoop.

hinny – expression of endearment of indeterminate meaning

hintend – backside, as in 'Aa'll tyek me byut ti yor hintend.' (I'll kick your backside.)

keek – look

mam – mother

reet – right, as in 'Aaim reet an' yor wrang.' (I'm right, you're wrong.)

shuggyboats – swingboats, a regular feature of beaches in the North East

skelp – to smack as in 'He wants his hintend skelpin.' (He needs a good smack on the backside.)

tab – cigarette

pittle – urinate

Provy cheque – an insurance scheme where people pay in a few pence each week and receive, at the end of so many months, a cheque that is redeemable at certain (usually very cheap and nasty) stores

stottie-kyek – a large flat bun indigenous to Newcastle

starvin – freezing

tettie – potato

Whey ye buggor mar! – expression of delight or amazement

I shall make a duchess of this draggletailed guttersnipe
George Bernard Shaw, *Pygmalion*

For Jack

Chapter One

It was raining when they came out of the Opera House. A misty but insistent drizzle that soaked through Hattie's clothes. She shivered and Toby took pity, ordering her to wait with the others beneath the protective canopy of the theatre whilst he went in search of a cab.

Hattie hated opera. She had never understood why so many of her friends regarded it with such reverence. Try as she might she had never managed to progress beyond the *Opera Made Easy* CD that Toby had bought for her at the beginning of their relationship. It seemed to her that most of the three-and-a-half-hour so-called great works could be condensed into one memorable three-and-a-half-minute track (Pavarotti singing 'Nessun dorma' was her favourite). But this particular evening's epic – *Aida* – didn't contain a single moment that could move her.

In the interval, as she and Toby had stood sipping drinks with Jon and Claire in the opulent bar, Hattie's mind kept slipping back to the child she had seen at work that day. Opera, she had long since concluded, had no place in the real world.

'It's all so élitist,' she complained, 'and I don't just mean the £100 seats and Princess Michael in the royal box and all these awful Radio 4 types pushing and shoving their way to the white wine. I mean the storylines. Why do operas fall for the same old class clichés? Why is there always some peasant love interest who will eventually be exposed as an aristocrat? Why can't a peasant be a peasant and not the noble son or daughter of some exiled king?'

'Because, Hattie,' Jon had replied in that tone that made her want to slap him, 'despite all your fantastic socialist theories the truth is that life is like that. If Aida had been a real slave girl no one would have cared what happened to her.'

'Why should where she came from – who she was – matter?' said Hattie, rising, as usual, to Jon's taunts.

'Class, Hattie,' said Toby. 'It wouldn't have worked, would it, if they had been from different social classes?'

Class had always been a great divide between Hattie and Toby, the subject of some vehement arguments. She had always managed to hang on to the notion that all men were equal. What separated them, she passionately believed, was not their DNA make-up, or their genetic heritage, but the place and the circumstances in which they were born. And the way in which, during their developmental years, they were nurtured and cultivated by those closest to them. Lord knows, she had seen enough evidence of the damage done to the human pysche by neglect, cruelty and irresponsibility. In her work she had come to understand that what really mattered was not money, or privilege, or the cultural claptrap that Toby so revered, but love. Although of course Verdi – and the rest of tonight's enraptured audience – didn't see it like that.

Even now, as they fought for territory outside the Opera House amidst the teeming crowds and the relentless rain, she still felt angry about their interval discussion.

'Let's shelter over there,' said Jon. 'We'll never see Toby through all these people . . .'

They moved across the street and huddled in the deep doorway of a branch of the Halifax. While they waited, the constant fine rain spraying onto them as cars and cabs swept past, Claire turned to Hattie.

'You're too sensitive,' she said gently. 'You always want to see the best in people. I mean, I understand what you

2

are trying to say about opera – it has become a kind of symbol of cultural and social superiority. But Toby and Jon are right – you take things too seriously. It's not real, it's just a silly musical fairy tale. Besides, I don't think that even you – with your high moral principles – really believe all that nonsense about nurture ruling over nature . . .'

'Of course I do, Claire,' Hattie protested. 'I don't just believe it, it's what I've spent the last ten years of my life trying to *do*. I don't want to be boring, I know I take things too seriously, but I do wish that sometimes you would listen to me. I know what I'm talking about. I've seen the way in which kindness and consideration can made an abused, tortured child blossom—'

'What the hell has that got to do with a night at the opera, Hattie?' said Jon, glancing over at Claire and raising his eyebrows. 'Why don't we leave the discussion for dinner? That's if they hold on to our table. If Toby doesn't hurry up and find a cab we're going to be half an hour late.'

'I'm sorry,' Hattie said contritely, 'but I've had a terrible day . . .'

She knew – because of patient confidentiality – that she couldn't tell her friends the distressing details of her day or attempt in any way to justify her mood this evening. Instead she smiled at them and tried to swallow her pride – and her principles.

Then, as the three of them backed further into the darkened doorway, a piercing yelp erupted behind them.

'Christ Almighty, I've trodden on something!' shouted Jon.

'What was it?' said Claire, clearly alarmed.

'A bloody dog.' Jon jumped clear of the doorway.

Seconds later they heard another noise – a gutteral explosion that was definitely human – from behind them.

'Haddaway, man . . .'

'Pardon?' enquired Jon.

'Haddawayanshite,' came the reply in what Hattie thought might be some northern provincial accent.

'I think,' said Hattie in her clipped, cut-glass English, 'he is telling us to shut up and leave him and his dog alone.'

'For God's sake,' said Jon irritably as his eyes made contact with the shape that had emerged from a pile of old bags and clothing behind them. 'Why doesn't *he* move on?'

There was, Hattie noticed as the man came closer to them, a horrible smell in the air that she sincerely hoped came from the dog skulking beside him. The figure's hair hung in dreadlocked clumps around his face, obscuring his features and making it difficult to discern his age, though Hattie suspected he was very young.

'For heaven's sake, Jon, have you no compassion?' she whispered, anxious not to offend the poor misfit before them. 'Can you imagine what it would be like to be homeless?'

'Oh spare me any more social comment this evening, please, Hattie.'

The man seemed unconcerned by their presence. In fact, Hattie realised as he slumped back against the cash-dispensing machine, he seemed oblivious to everything but the mongrel dog he was now comforting.

'Perhaps, Hattie, he can't get his card in the machine. Maybe his swipe's gone,' Jon whispered.

Hattie was incensed by Jon's sarcasm. Moreover, the contrast between this sad, stinking stranger and the splendour of the Opera House over the road heightened her feeling of alienation from this whole evening.

'Maybe he is trying to tell us something about ourselves,' she muttered, bending down to stroke the whimpering dog but recoiling quickly when it snapped angrily at her.

'Are you trying to imply that he's making some kind of political statement, Hattie? Homeless man living in the doorway of a building society?' said Jon.

4

'For God's sake, you two, stop arguing. Here's Toby with the cab,' said Claire impatiently.

Hattie held back as the others ran towards the taxi, unsure now whether she could bear to sit through dinner this evening.

'I'm so sorry,' she said plaintively to the figure propped up against the wall. 'I wish I could do something to help you . . .'

'Bugger off,' he spat back at her.

'Here,' said Hattie, searching in her bag for some money to give him, 'take this . . .'

She was aware of his surprise at the generosity of her offering. He looked closely and steadily at her from large, unusually bright, blue eyes and then began hunting through a series of carrier bags that were situated, she could now make out, beside his sleeping bag.

'Ha this, hinny,' he said, thrusting a dog-eared copy of the *Big Issue* at her.

'Hattie!' screamed Toby from the cab. 'Will you hurry up? We're late enough as it is.'

She jumped in the back of the cab and pulled down one of the little seats. As the taxi moved away from the kerb she glanced back at the man, crouched down and gently stroking his dog, and wondered what tragedies in his life had led him to that doorway.

Even Hattie was cheered by their arrival at the restaurant. She wasn't sure what had chilled her more this evening – the relentless rain, the pathos of the homeless boy or Jon's behaviour. But warmed by the bright lights and the prospect of food she determined to forget about the incident in the doorway.

It was the kind of place that Toby loved, not for its food, but for its fashionableness. On the way to their table he had been acknowledged by several people – fellow lawyers, and political contacts Hattie presumed – whom he knew.

As they sat down Jon turned to Hattie and smiled in a placatory way. 'Hattie, let's forget our differences for the rest of the evening.'

She smiled back at him even though, however amusing he might be, she knew she could never forget their differences. Jon was a partner in one of the most successful advertising agencies of the moment – Riley, Toppingham and Futura – with a reputation as one of the best creative brains in the country. But despite his *apparent* political affiliations – he had been responsible for a recent highly praised campaign for the Labour Party – Hattie was wary of him. She disapproved of his professional devotion to what she saw as the brutal business of manipulating the public and she found his bleak cynicism depressing. But as he was Toby's oldest – and probably only – friend she made an effort to tolerate him.

Hattie was rather fond of Claire, Jon's companion this evening, despite the fact that she too made her living out of hype – or at any rate out of securing good publicity for a series of rather dubious clients. She was far preferable to any of the other empty women that Jon usually had in tow. Claire – an ex-girlfriend whom he had somehow managed to turn into a friend – had only joined them this evening because the latest woman in Jon's life was, somewhat typically, married.

Hattie was very hungry, and eager to see the menu and order. There had been no time for lunch that day and she was not even sure that she had eaten breakfast, but her companions were more intrigued by the other diners and the décor.

Hattie, who had no curiosity about the famous, or infamous, was becoming aware of the dampness of her hair and the rain-spattered state of her clothes. Muttering her excuses she made her way down the brightly lit steel stairs to the loos.

She stood and looked at her reflection in the mirror for a second and pondered on the differences between herself and the sleek females who surrounded her. She didn't really belong in this chic place, or rather she didn't really want to belong. She was as uncomfortable here as she had been in the Opera House. And as much an outsider as the man camped in the Halifax doorway.

Not that Hattie wasn't vain, in her own way. It was just that it wasn't the way of these women. She didn't really care about clothes or make-up, and she certainly wouldn't put herself through the agony of wearing the kind of shoes – curious spike-heeled mules – that she had noticed a number of the women struggling to walk on.

Pushing a comb through her hair and putting a touch of Lipsyl on her dry mouth, she straightened her dress, sprayed herself with scent and made her way back up the slippery steel stairs.

As she moved towards the table several other diners nodded in recognition.

'Hattie spends so much of her time worrying about life's underdogs that I always forget she has such a splendid pedigree herself,' Jon said as he watched her dodging between tables.

'Give her a break, Jon. It's not as if she has ever really bothered with all her good contacts,' said Claire equitably, 'and nor has she profited by them.'

'But Hattie doesn't need to profit by them, does she? What with the trust fund and—'

'Jon!' said Claire, darting him a warning look as Hattie sat back down at the table.

At this point the food arrived and the distribution of the various designer dishes ('French Vietnamese,' declared Toby in an authoritative manner) prevented further argument. Hattie ate hungrily as Claire attempted to lighten the atmosphere with the kind of gossip that she loved.

'Did you see Nigella's review of this place in *Vogue*?'

'I am sure that Hattie doesn't read *Vogue*,' interjected Jon with a wicked little smile. 'In fact I'd say that the copy of the *Big Issue* that Hattie has peeping out of the top of her bag is much more to her taste. While all the other women here spend most of their lives searching out things that will confer on them the kind of exclusivity that Hattie was born with, she chooses to carry – not, what is it now, a Prada handbag? – but a battered old briefcase and a magazine that clearly signals to the world that here is a woman with a social conscience.'

'That man gave it to me. The man we disturbed when we were waiting for Toby,' said Hattie a little defensively.

'I bet he bloody did. It's my own personal belief that there are more people selling the *Big Issue* than there are homeless. There must be two dozen in Kensington High Street alone just waiting to trip you up. It's brilliant marketing, though. You have to admire the way you can package guilt . . .'

Claire, in an effort to deflect Jon's comments, continued to give them a potted version of what Nigella had thought about the food at Vong. Undeterred, Jon continued with his diatribe against the *Big Issue*.

Hattie shifted uncomfortably in her seat, determined this time not to rise to the bait. She had often wondered if Jon's shocking comments and his black sense of humour were something of an act, designed to cover up a deeper sensitivity. Part of her suspected that he was as bored as she by Nigella and *Vogue* and all the idle chatter that seemed to fascinate Toby and Claire. Then, perhaps unaware of just how much the incident in the doorway had upset her, Jon began a diatribe on homelessness and the 'underclass', many of whom, he said with a provocative glance at Hattie, somehow 'defied Darwin's theory of evolution'.

'Do you know, Jon,' said Claire quickly, 'just for a minute I thought you were talking about your ex-girlfriend before last – you know, the blonde with the frontal lobotomy . . .'

'You'll have to remind me which one you mean,' said Hattie, grinning. 'I thought all Jon's girlfriends shared those characteristics – lots of blonde hair and one brain cell. Apart from you, Claire.'

'You know I'm the only intelligent woman Jon ever went out with. Nowadays he's hopelessly drawn to women whose vital statistics add up to more than their IQs,' said Claire, exchanging a smile with Hattie.

'Anyway, Jon,' said Hattie with gathering courage, 'I don't go along with all this business about an underclass. If there is a growing number of people who are slipping through the net educationally and socially it's because of lack of opportunity and poverty. If any of us around this table had been born into different circumstances we too might have become a part of your underclass.'

'Not with our genetic advantages,' said Jon, smiling patronisingly at Hattie. 'All those things we have got – our intelligence, for example – are locked into our genetic make-up waiting to be passed on to the next generation.'

'No, Jon. Let me quote Professor Steve Jones, *the* man on genetics, on this one. "The single most important thing that a child can inherit from its parents is money," he says. You might like to think that you have the kind of genes that could triumph over poverty but in fact I doubt that they are any more interesting – let alone superior – to those of that man we stumbled across tonight. *All men are born equal*,' said Hattie.

'But some, thanks to their genes, are born more equal than others,' said Jon with another one of his infuriatingly patronising grins. 'People are either born with good genes, like mine and like yours, Hattie – if, of course, yours aren't too inbred – or with a DNA of doom. Why do you think that man's on the streets while we are in this restaurant?'

'Money,' Claire said. 'Your parents bought you the privileges you enjoy. The best education that money can buy. And the right contacts.'

'Meanwhile,' continued Hattie, 'his parents were probably living on Government handouts and threw him out when he was no longer eligible for child benefit. If he had been given your advantages I dare say he'd be doing something more intelligent than you are now – attacking the defenceless—'

'Here we go again, back to Hattie's charitable mission. Do you really believe that that vagrant in the doorway could, in any circumstances, be transformed into a useful member of society?' Jon asked.

'Why not?' Claire and Hattie said in unison.

'In my work, Jon, I am only too aware that it is perfectly possible to take even the most desperate, desolate and destitute being and help them to achieve their potential,' said Hattie earnestly, thinking of the little girl she had encountered that day.

There was an uneasy silence, during which Jon looked intently at Hattie.

'If you really want to impress me, prove me wrong. I bet that you couldn't redeem that man we tripped over tonight,' he said.

'What do you mean?' said Hattie, sitting up in her seat.

'What I say. I bet you couldn't redeem that man – as a kind of wager. You can walk into a betting shop and put money on anything from man walking on Mars to England winning the World Cup. I'm prepared to bet you that you cannot change that man. That it wouldn't be possible to take him off the streets and turn him into someone who could join us at this table for dinner. That it wouldn't be possible to transform him into a man of worth.'

'A real bet? A financial bet?' Claire asked, as suddenly interested as Hattie.

'Well, I know money's not important to Hattie – or you really, Claire – but I'm sure it's bloody important to that man. So yes, let's do this properly. Let's put some money on it. Prove to me that I am wrong about him in – let me see – three months from today, and I'll pay him £5000. If you don't then I'll have this month's interest from your trust fund,' he said to Hattie with another of those grins that made her want to hit him.

Hattie glanced at Claire, unsure whether Jon was sober enough to be serious.

'What is your definition of worth, Jon?' asked Claire.

'Someone you could pass off in polite society.'

'You mean at the Royal Opera House and a pretentious restaurant? Someone that the chattering classes would perceive as one of their own?' said Hattie sneeringly.

'Yes. But more than that. He'd have to be employed, or at any rate employable. He'd have to be able to carry out a civilised conversation. He'd have to have an appreciation of the finer things of life and be able to satisfy me that he is intelligent. He would have to look, behave and react as if all this were natural to him. And he would have to pass a test that I would devise,' said Jon, swinging back confidently in his chair.

'God, you are so arrogant,' said Claire sharply. 'It would give me so much pleasure to prove you wrong that I would happily risk losing any amount of money. What kind of test would it be?'

'He'd have to be able to prove to a room full of people like this – the chattering classes if that's what you insist on calling them, Hattie – that he was the genuine article. A man of worth.'

'Three months?' mused Claire

'Your chance, Hattie,' said Jon with a slight sneer, 'to put into practice all your wonderful theories of nurture ruling over nature. And your chance, Claire, to get back at me . . .'

'Just twelve weeks,' said Hattie doubtfully.

'So you don't believe it's possible *either*?' said Jon with glee.

'Of *course* it's possible!' Hattie exclaimed, glancing at Claire for confirmation that she was still on her side.

On the back of a menu Jon began to write out, in fountain pen, his version of a betting slip.

'I promise to pay £5000 if in three months from this day, 16 May, Claire Martin and Hattie George can transform a tramp into the talk of the chattering classes, signed Jon Riley.'

'Take it or leave it,' he said.

'We'll take it,' said Hattie.

'Then write out your response,' he said, passing the pen across to Claire.

'Claire Martin and Hattie George promise to pay Jon Riley £5000 if, in three months' time, they have failed to prove him wrong . . .' she said aloud as she wrote the words beneath those of Jon. 'Here, Hattie, now you sign.'

Hattie took the menu from Claire and signed it. Then, very carefully, she placed it inside her battered briefcase where it lay nestled against her still damp copy of the *Big Issue*.

Chapter Two

The strip of light that had worked its way through the crack in the shutters told Hattie that it must be morning. That and the fast breathing of Toby who had been too weary and drunk to make love the night before and was now attempting to redress his usual balance (it *was* Saturday after all) with some fairly basic foreplay.

She wished he would stop. She didn't like sex first thing in the morning before she had brushed her teeth or showered. But then she probably didn't like it that much last thing at night either. She was, though, far too kind to upset Toby by telling him that she didn't want him. Or to break it to him that the earth had never really moved for her, that in fact when it came to sex she was a founder member of the flat earth society, unable to imagine that, even on its axis in space, it could ever achieve motion.

Claire had recently confessed how she had once told some man, *in flagrante*, to get off her and go home. He had sat weeping into his wilting manhood at the bottom of her bed. But she had not relented. If Hattie were as honest as Claire she would probably have told Toby on more than one occasion to go away and leave her alone. But Hattie approached her partner in rather the way that she approached her patients. The only kind of passion she really felt for him was the occasional bout of *compassion*.

It wasn't that Toby was unattractive. He was good-looking in a clean, smooth-skinned, bookish way. He wore little round steel-rimmed glasses that had made her think, when she had first met him, that he was sensitive and deep.

Now she thought that one of the main reasons she had been drawn to him was the fact that he was physically more boyish than manly – his thin, underdeveloped body was entirely hairless – which made her feel that somehow she would be safe with him.

How long, she wondered idly, would he go on this time? Aware that he was waiting for some indication of her own abandonment she muttered something he might take as an endearment. Then she went back to making out her imaginary Sainsbury's grocery list – her own reason for making a strong connection between sex and shopping. When Toby made love to her – at least on Saturday mornings – she would take a mental trip down the aisles of her local superstore: Two kilos of Coxe's Orange Pippins, a bunch of small bananas, one kilo of seedless grapes, butter, a pack of Yakult . . .'

'Yes, yes, yes . . .'

She lay still for a few minutes after he had finished. She was always impatient, after sex, to get up and off but she knew that sexual etiquette decreed that she lie for a while panting and looking sated – even if she was, in her mind, just making her way down aisle 10 towards the bakery. She was always amazed when Claire, at the outset of some new affair, would admit to having spent two or three whole days in bed. She didn't mind sleeping in the bed next to Toby but lying next to him in a conscious state was terribly taxing for her. Particularly when, as today, there was so very much to do.

It was at this moment, almost as she had reached the checkout in Sainsbury's with her imaginary trolley, that she remembered the bet. Had Jon really meant it or had he been joking? Grabbing her robe from the chair by her bedside she got up and made her way down the flight of stairs and through to the kitchen, the only closed-off part downstairs of her otherwise open-plan loft apartment.

And there, at the very top of her Samsonite briefcase, tucked alongside that copy of the *Big Issue* was Jon's hand-written wager.

'Do you think he was serious?' she asked Toby as he joined her.

'The terrible tragedy is that even when Jon's joking he's serious,' commented Toby, 'and he's always been a gambler. He'll bet on anything. Years ago he had a bet with Chris and me on the number of orgasms he could achieve in one night with a dreadful slapper we all knew. She had to swear an affidavit before we gave him the money . . .'

Hattie looked at Toby and realised that after six years together they barely knew one another. It genuinely surprised her that the word 'slapper' was one he was – well – familiar with.

'Toby, you know I really want to do this. It would be like the ultimate sociological experiment for me. I might even write a paper on it. Profit professionally as well as getting considerable satisfaction proving that dreadful fool wrong,' she said as she made her way through to her minimalist bathroom.

Minimalism appealed to Hattie because she had grown up in a dusty, cluttered, overdecorated stately home which was a virtual shrine to hereditary possessions. Every nook and cranny of her childhood home had been filled with rare antiques, paintings and *objets d'art*, most of which – despite her father's assertion that they were 'priceless' – were all about money and the ostentatious presentation of their family wealth. The fact that her own choice of living space – almost entirely empty of possessions – was now fashionable was not important to her. What she loved most about her bare white surroundings was the way in which it contrasted so totally with her ancestral home. It fitted perfectly with her general philosophy on life – which had caused such grief in her teenage years – property is theft.

Jon's favourite joke at Hattie's expense involved him saying that when it came to her own apartment that ridiculous phrase was true – the 3000-square-foot loft-style property, he would say, had been absolute daylight robbery when she bought it three years previously.

Sitting on the edge of her sandstone bath Hattie picked up her portable phone and rang Claire, who agreed that she thought Jon had been serious.

'Toby tells me Jon always wins his bets,' Hattie said carefully to Claire who had, after all, once lived with the man.

'Not this one he won't,' said Claire confidently, 'although I think that we will have our work cut out. For a start we have got to find that man again. And then we'll probably need Rentokil and an intepreter when we do,' she finished with a giggle.

It wasn't going to be as easy as Hattie had thought. The woman at the customer service desk inside the Halifax had been most unhelpful. They had absolutely no idea who – or what – lay in their doorway after closing hours, unless, that was, they happened to know his account number. Why didn't madam try the Salvation Army?

Hattie was disconsolate.

'For Christ's sake, Hattie, it doesn't have to be *that* homeless man. It could be any old vagrant. Let's go down to cardboard city and find another one,' said Claire.

'No, Claire, it's got to be that young man. Jon specifically said *that* man. And anyway I believe it was somehow fated. I've just got to find him . . .'

'But you probably wouldn't recognise him if you did stumble across him. It was dark and I certainly only remember the smell of him.'

Hattie didn't say anything but she knew that she would instantly recognise the man. His eyes, even in that dingy doorway, had a quality about them she knew she would never forget. And however much Claire might sneer she felt increasingly there was some, well, some cosmic link between him and herself.

'We have two options open to us. We either come back here tonight and hope that he turns up or we could go down to the mission and see if he's there.'

But he wasn't at the mission either and they had so few clues as to his identity that there was precious little more they could do. An earnest young man on duty suggested they try a couple of haunts that were frequented by the homeless young.

'Otherwise you could try the offices of the *Big Issue* on Monday. If he sold you a copy he must be registered with them,' he said.

Claire was all for this latter course but Hattie wouldn't think of it. And when Hattie made up her mind about something they were both generally carried along by it.

It was, Hattie said later, a depressing day on a number of levels. They trudged around soulless cafés and drop-in centres encountering, along the way, a new awareness of the meanness of the city they lived in.

By late afternoon Claire was ready to give up.

'Look, Hattie, I'm going to some dinner tonight. I'm going to have to get back to get ready.'

'Someone special?' said Hattie, who was always rather intrigued by Claire's relationships.

'No, only some friend of mine – another PR – who has lined up this man she just *knows* is right for me. As if I haven't heard that a million times before. His CV sounds hopeful though – good-looking, intelligent, divorced, successful . . .' she said wistfully.

'Sounds like the prototype of every man I've ever known you get involved with,' said Hattie. 'Take care, won't you, and er, take it slowly . . .'

'If I took it slowly, Hattie, I'd never take it at all,' answered Claire, kissing her friend on both cheeks as she prepared to leave her. 'You going home to cook dinner for Toby?'

'No actually, he's got some squash thing tonight. I think I'll carry on looking for a while. I'm not ready to give up quite yet,' she said.

'Well, be careful. The streets are no place for a nice girl like you,' warned Claire as she climbed into a cab, wondering, not for the first time that day, if this whole business of the bet hadn't been a terrible mistake.

There were ten of them at dinner. Three couples and four 'singles' as Antonia insultingly called anyone without a live-in lover and a joint mortgage. Claire was rather hopeful about the man who had been placed beside her at Antonia's long, bleached wood table. But then when it came to men she was a hopeless optimist.

'Hi,' she said as they took their seats, 'I'm Claire Martin.'

'Chris White,' he replied.

He was tall enough, she reckoned, and if not quite as good-looking as Antonia had promised, he wasn't unattractive. He had mid-brown hair and grey-blue eyes and very good cheekbones so that when he smiled, as now, he looked really rather fanciable.

The only vaguely worrying thing about him was his goatee beard. Claire wasn't very keen on facial hair. But, hey, she reminded herself, you can't have everything.

'Antonia talks about you a lot,' Chris said.

'She does?' Claire looked across at Antonia with surprise; they were not exactly close friends.

'Yes, she's always saying how you would be perfect for me.' Chris was also looking across the table at Antonia.

'She mentioned something similar to me,' Claire replied.

He poured her a glass of wine, and then another of fizzy mineral water.

'Are you a friend of Steve's?' she said, unsure of Chris's connection with Antonia.

'I was best man at their wedding. Known him since I was a child.' he said.

He was very attentive, filling her glass – just that little bit too often really – and virtually ignoring the woman on his other side. He wasn't particularly witty or overly fascinating (he was, after all, an accountant) but he seemed pleasant enough.

And when the meal was finished he sat next to her on one of the sofas in Antonia's living room, one hand, very casually, slipped behind her. Signalling, she thought, some kind of intent.

It was going well, Claire decided. He was successful and established – he had one of those lovely little Georgian cottages in that network of streets between Notting Hill Gate and High Street Kensington – and he had been divorced for just about the time a man should be before he considered remarriage.

At the end of the evening, as the other couples tumbled out into their cars, Claire asked Antonia, within earshot of Chris, for the number of a local cab company. Antonia looked at Chris meaningfully.

'I'll take you home,' he said. 'It's not far out of my way.'

She smiled, thanked him, and nipped into the loo on her way out to retouch her lipstick and check that she looked OK. In the car they talked a bit about the other guests and when he drew up outside her mews house he stopped the car and turned off the ignition (another sign of intent, she thought).

'Can I come in?' he asked.

She remembered Hattie's advice, earlier that evening,

about taking it slowly. But Claire had reached an age –
and if she were honest a state of desperation about ever
finding a man she could really love – when caution was
pointless. If she said 'no' she would probably never hear
from him again. And if she said (as she probably would
later) 'yes, yes, yesss' she would probably never hear from
him again. There was nothing to be gained, and nothing
to be lost, in being coy.

He didn't waste any time. Within seconds he was passionately kissing her. Telling her, whenever he surfaced to
take in a gulp of air, that she was *beautiful, hot, wild, the
best* – the usual gamut of meaningless compliments induced
by male sexual arousal.

She broke off for a second, as she considered only proper,
to offer him a drink. She didn't want him to think that she
was inhospitable (which, of course, he didn't).

'Is there anything you want . . . wine, brandy . . . ?'

'Just you,' he said, falling on her again with a ferocity
that rather overwhelmed, not to say irritated, her. What
was the hurry?

'Well, I'll just put on some coffee,' she said, struggling
free and rushing into the kitchen, pulling the zip up on the
back of her dress as she went so that it didn't fall off her
completely.

Claire hadn't lived with anyone since she had broken up
with Jon five years ago. In truth she hadn't really had what
you might call a regular partner for three of those five years.
There had been a few married men with whom she had
enjoyed brief affairs that would involve a couple of weeks
of frenzied clandestine sex (what she called her fort*nightly*
men). And there had been two complicated relationships
that had – over a period of a couple of months – never
quite come to anything.

For some reason she didn't seem to meet men in the way
she had a few years ago – at parties, through friends, in

clubs. Most of her female friends (and she didn't have many) seemed to be caught up in long-term relationships so there was no one to go clubbing with, and anyway she was so caught up in her work that really, finding time to develop relationships – let alone draw up some strategy on how to meet decent men – was almost impossible. Of late she had got rather used to snatching, as it were, whatever sexual action was on offer. She had a strong, growing feeling that this Chris was not going to be the love of the rest of her life, but what the hell? She wanted sex, even if she wasn't sure if she wanted him – and that horrid little goatee.

By the time she got back to the sofa he was so sexually charged that she wasn't sure there would be time to guide him up the little staircase to her bedroom. If she didn't hold him back for a minute it would all be over before the espresso machine had finished.

'Chris, Chris . . .' she said, pushing him back a little, 'let's go upstairs . . .'

They part walked, part stumbled, part fucked their way up the stairs.

'Oh GOD!' he cried within seconds of reaching the bed and fully entering her. 'Oh GOD!' he screamed again. And then there was silence apart from the ticking of her bedside clock and the beating of her own disappointed heart. Then they lay there in what she could only describe as postcoital gloom for several minutes.

'Are you going?' she asked, astonished at the speed with which he had then got out of bed and dressed.

'Yes, I think it's best,' he said. 'Look, I'm sorry about this. I never meant it to happen . . .'

Oh that's nice, she thought, so what did he think would happen when he asked to come in for a drink and then jumped on me?

He sat down on the bed and put his head in his hands.

'What is your problem, Chris?' she said.

'Antonia,' he replied.

'What's Antonia got to do with this?'

'Everything. We've been having an affair for two years. It's the only way we can get to see each other socially without Steve catching on. If she invites another single woman . . .'

'How many of her *single* friends have you fucked in the cause of perpetuating Antonia's marriage to Steve?'

'Oh, you're the first,' he said, looking at her with what he obviously thought she would interpret as sincerity.

I've heard it all now, she thought, 'Oh, you're the first.' She wondered if it weren't innate in men to come out with that phrase whenever they were caught in an awkward situation with a woman. It seemed to spring to their lips as automatically as a yelp if they were kicked in the balls or, in Chris's case, the name of the Lord when he reached his sexual climax (if you could call it that).

But then, she thought, perhaps she had been the first of Antonia's decoys to fall for the cheap lines Chris had thrown at her. Probably he never thought she would invite him in and when she did some automatic male instinct had taken over. However much in love he was with Antonia he wasn't actually going to turn down ten minutes (or was it five?) between the sheets with another woman. Men are like dogs, she thought as she watched him shuffling awkwardly beside her bed, that eat every meal regardless of their hunger just in case it's their last. Chris had approached her like an extra tin of Chum that fortune had thrown his way. And now that he had partaken of her he looked as if he were going to be sick.

'You won't say anything to Antonia about this . . . ?' he said hesitantly.

He had a nerve.

'Perhaps it would be more relevant if I talked to Steve,' Claire said coolly.

'Oh Christ, no!' A tone of real desperation entered his voice. 'He's my oldest friend.'

'Isn't he the lucky one?' Claire turned over in the bed and closed her eyes, hoping that when she opened them again he would have gone.

After an hour or so of tortured self-examination she finally fell into a fitful sleep that was punctuated by odd, recurring dreams of Jon in that brief period of her life years ago when she had felt in some way emotionally fulfilled.

Hattie had no intention of giving up on her mission, even if it took her all night. She spent the evening drifting round a savage network of streets in King's Cross, trying to get a better idea of the world the homeless man inhabited. She felt strangely diminished by the experience, as if she, in walking through this sad nether world, were somehow homeless herself. And that feeling made her all the more determined to find the man whom fate had placed in her path on the previous evening.

At nightfall she decided to return to the beginning, the doorway where the argument resulting in the bet had started. In almost every entrance she passed there were bodies in sleeping bags and boxes. She wondered if these people came to the same place each night or if they selected their pitch by chance. If so, she thought as she approached the Halifax, it was unlikely that she would ever find him. There were three bodies lying amidst a clutter of carrier bags and clothing, and her heart began to race. Moving into the entrance she peered down to see if she could identify the boy.

'Thank goodness I've found you,' she said aloud, relief and hope flooding through her as she recognised him, his hand clasped round a length of blue rope on the end of which was his thin, nervous dog.

They both flinched when Hattie approached them, the

dog setting up a high-pitched squealing bark designed, she supposed, to protect his master. The boy didn't recognise her at first and when he did he thought she had come for her change.

'Yous give me a tenner,' he said, taking a few coins from his pocket and holding them out to her. At this the dog began to growl and jump up at Hattie, a menacing look in his eyes.

'Doon, boy, doon,' the boy said firmly yet gently to the insistent dog.

'I meant you to have that money,' she said.

'But it's only 80p . . .' he said, looking at her suspiciously.

She realised now, as she stood before the boy, that her interest in him must seem, at the very least, odd. She couldn't possibly tell him about Jon's bet because, she realised, it was insulting and patronising and would, in any case, make her seem like some rich, bored socialite looking for a diversion. There was a silence between them – punctuated only by the squealing of his dog – whilst she searched for a way to appeal to him.

'The thing is I want to help you. I really do,' she stuttered. 'My name is Hattie George and I want to help get you back into the real world . . .'

He looked her up and down, wondering if she had any conception of what the real world was like but he didn't say anything. One of the other figures camped by him sniggered loudly. Hattie felt ridiculous.

'My friend and I – well, we want to get you back on your feet. Find you somewhere to live, a job, new clothes, you know the kind of thing . . .'

There was a huge guffaw now from the two other men but her man still didn't say anything. Her tone of voice became more beseeching and desperate as she continued with her plea. She realised that she must seem hysterical and maybe even a little deranged. But she was determined to convince him.

'I'm on the level, honestly. Please don't think this is some kind of trick,' she said.

The two men beside him, friends of his perhaps, made some comment she couldn't quite make out. But the man she had come to see ignored her and began to spread out his sleeping bag.

'Aren't you listening to me? I want to help you,' she said despairingly.

'Listen to her, man,' said one of his friends.

'Why?' he said, looking at them and then back at her with haunted and uncomprehending eyes.

'Because I can help you,' she said again, faltering a little for fear of offending him.

'Why me, like?' he said in his surprisingly strong and rich accent which, she thought now, was a little like that of that footballer who was always making a fool of himself.

'Look, why don't we go and have a coffee somewhere and talk about this? It's very important to me that you understand,' she said.

'Coffee?' he said blankly.

'Well, I don't know – can't we sit and talk somewhere?'

'This is me home, like. Sit doon here,' he said, indicating his sleeping bag on which the growling dog was now sitting.

Hattie crouched down beside him, self-consciously aware of the enquiring stares of passers-by and the inquisitive attention of his two friends. Behind the three men, nestling next to a rucksack, there were several cans – some empty and overturned – of Special Brew. Seeing her glance at them he took hold of one and passed it to her. She shook her head and then thought that it was probably rather impolite to refuse so reached her hand out and brought the half-empty can to her mouth, wondering if he would be offended if she first wiped it with a tissue.

'What's your name?' she asked as she handed him back the cold can.

'Why d' ye wanna know?' he said in the lilting tones that she now found oddly attractive.

'Because if I am going to help you I will have to know everything about you.'

He laughed at that, laughter that was echoed by his incredulous friends.

'I don't want your help, hinny.'

'Of course you do. You can't want to go on living like this,' she said.

'Why not?' he asked.

'Because it's such a waste. Because I – we – my friend and I – we can give you the life you have always wanted.'

'And how do you know this isn't what I've always wanted, like?' he said.

There was something very proud about him, Hattie thought as she sat watching him. Despite the grime that covered him, and that awful smell, he had an unmistakable dignity. And she had been right about the eyes – they were astonishing. Brilliant – almost turquoise – blue with long black fringed eyelashes that were almost beautiful. She was curiously excited by the idea of getting to know him, if he would let her. But she was aware of his ambivalence towards her. How could she convince him to allow her into his life?

'Look, please come with me and meet my friend and listen to what we have to say,' she said, reaching out to stroke his dog, which snarled and spat at her.

The boy leant over to grasp the dog.

'Doon, boy . . . Na, hinny, I don't want your help,' he said, turning away as if to indicate that this was the end of the matter.

'Look, you must have had dreams, you must have had hopes. You surely didn't imagine that you would spend your life sleeping rough in dirty doorways?' she said plaintively.

'There's worse than this, pet,' he said, an edge creeping into his voice.

She went quiet then because she felt foolish. How could she have expected to put her own values, her own aspirations, on to this man who had led a life of such obvious deprivation. Why had she imagined that she could impress him with talk of clean sheets, hot meals and a regular job? She had no idea how he had got here and no conception of the suffering he had seen.

'You can help me, darlin,' slurred one of the other men, hopefully. 'You can take me home with you . . .'

'Nah,' said the other man, 'it's Jimmy she wants. It's always Jimmy they want . . .'

'Jimmy,' said Hattie, pleased to learn his name. 'Look, Jimmy, here's my address, my phone number, my name. You can reach me any time on my mobile, and there is a day office number and a home number. Think about what I've said and call me . . .' She handed him a card, which he reluctantly took.

As she left she heard his friends begin to tease him about her interest and she wanted to cry. For the tragedy of his life and her own stupidity in imagining she could save him from it.

Chapter Three

In the days that followed, Hattie made it a habit, on her way home from work each evening, to detour via the streets of Covent Garden on the off chance of running into the boy called Jimmy.

But he seemed to have moved on or moved pitch because although she saw many other homeless people camped out in doorways near the big theatres she didn't see him.

She did, though, encounter one of the two men who had been with him on the day of her ill-fated proposition and she attempted to persuade him to pass on a message asking Jimmy to contact her.

But still there was no sign or word from him. In desperation on the Thursday afternoon she took two hours off work in order to visit the offices of the *Big Issue* in the hope that they might be able to help her to reach him. But they were very nearly as suspicious of her motives as Jimmy had been himself, although they did eventually agree to leave a message pinned on their notice board.

Her mood of desolation was beginning to irritate Toby who was, in any case, totally against the idea of her rising to the bait of Jon's bet. Her tender-hearted concern for others had been one of the things that had drawn him to her when they had first met, but nearly six years on, at a time when he was beginning to enjoy unexpected professional acclaim, he regarded her continued devotion to lost causes as naïve and unrealistic. Lord knows he was himself a devoted socialist – well, at any rate an ardent supporter of the ideals of New Labour – but he did not relish the idea of cluttering their lives – let alone their flat – with this latest sociological experiment of hers.

Besides, he was in the middle of a major case involving one of the biggest corporations in the country and he felt that he was in far greater need of support and sympathy than Hattie. Although they enjoyed what he claimed to be an equal relationship he secretly retained many of the attitudes and values of his own middle-class parents and believed that the female role in a partnership should be far more domestically rooted and nurturing than that of the male. He shouldn't have to come home, as he had tonight, to an empty flat and fridge. Some innate sense in him thought that Hattie's priorities were wrong, that she should put his comfort before that of the redemption of some hopeless stranger, and that his life should be more like that of his father's – a man whose role at the head of a respectful household Toby now privately envied.

He recognised, of course, the dramatic difference between his father's circumstances and his own. Their flat did, in fact, belong to Hattie, having been bought, several years before, with some of the income from her trust fund. His own flat – kept on but rented out after they had moved here – was a substantially less impressive property, so unimpressive that currently he was having trouble finding a tenant for it. So while his own mother had been dependent on his father (which probably did encourage a greater degree of respect) Hattie was a woman of independent means. But just because she wasn't dependent on him for a roof over head didn't mean that she could ignore, as she persistently did, the domestic details of their life. That weekend he was hosting, at Hattie's apartment, a small dinner party for the more important people involved in the important case at work. And although the food was being prepared by discreet caterers – Hattie had no interest in cooking – he was concerned that in her present distracted state the dinner would be a disaster.

This feeling of doom was compounded by her arriving home, that Thursday night, at nine thirty with a bleak expression on her face, after having been on yet another hopeless search for her homeless boy.

'Oh Toby,' she said in a dejected voice, 'it breaks my heart to see all those poor people with nowhere to go. I must have spoken to a hundred of them tonight and some of them looked so lost.'

'Hattie, at the risk of sounding like Jon I really do think it's time you gave the homeless issue a rest. I appreciate your concern, I know you're anxious to prove him wrong, but for Christ's sakes can't you just get a life?'

'I have a life, Toby,' Hattie said coldly as she made her way through to the stainless steel kitchen in search of food.

'There's nothing in the fridge, Hattie. It might have been nice – after the day I've had – to have come home to something. A piece of hard cheese, a crust of stale bread, a rotten apple . . .' he sulked.

'Look, Toby, I just haven't had time for any of that this week. And actually I haven't had such a brilliant day either. I've got a particularly difficult case on my hands at the moment,' she said, thinking of the little girl, Lisa, who had – when she wasn't searching for the homeless man – occupied her thoughts in the past week.

'Spare me the details, Hattie. The only way I could have got your attention in the last few days would have been to turn up at one of those soup kitchens with a sign round my neck saying "Homeless and hungry". That way you might have offered me a little sympathy and I'd have got a hot meal . . .'

It wasn't difficult for Toby to make Hattie feel guilty and inadequate. And even though it did flash through her mind that Toby himself might have nipped into M&S on his way home from work, she turned to him with a remorseful expression and put her arms round him in a placatory way.

'I'm sorry, Toby.'

'Look, Hattie, I'm going through a bad time myself at the moment. Saturday night's very important to me and I want you to help me with it—'

'Saturday night?' Hattie asked blankly.

'The dinner, darling. For the Chairman of UCO and all those involved in the case. You know how important it is to me – the first time I've hosted something for business at home. Surely you haven't forgotten?'

'Of course not. I'm sorry,' Hattie said, although, in fact, the events of the last week had put his dinner completely out of her mind.

'I want you to be the perfect hostess on Saturday, Hattie. In the morning we'll have to go shopping – flowers, candles, a dress that will fit the occasion. You will be co-operative, won't you?'

'Of course,' she said, offering him her most radiant smile.

Toby ordered a takeaway and they ate it whilst he gave her brief biographical details of the guests he had invited to the dinner and offered her – in a ten-point note he had carefully written out – various suitable topics of conversation. Hattie looked at the list with growing alarm. She knew very little about any of things Toby had deemed acceptable – the Millennium Dome, the redevelopment of the Opera House, EU economic policy, cars, Bill Gates, cricket, rugby, shooting (hadn't they banned shooting?), skiing and trout fishing.

'I'm not sure I'll be able to say a great deal, Toby,' she said.

'Well, try and read up on those things. The Chairman is

a member of Lords and heavily into field sports,' he said commandingly.

He was very relieved that Claire was going to be there, in her capacity as the corporate PR for UCO, to help him keep an eye on Hattie. He had also invited Jon, not as a partner for Claire (heaven forbid) but because he had, of late, become something of a celebrity in business circles. He was the current *enfant terrible* of advertising, responsible for a series of shocking campaigns – most famously the nineties relaunch of a fifties-style uplift bra that had featured a number of provocative posters that had been outrageously successful. His presence round the table would impress the Chairman (who would probably also be happy to talk about uplift bras).

Toby was a little worried that Hattie might get into some awful philosophical debate with Jon that might cause problems but he felt sure that Claire would be able to deflect any trouble.

Hattie was so keen to make amends for her behaviour that week that she offered, when they had finished their meal, to run him a hot bath and give him a massage. Whilst he sat in the bath she warmed some aromatherapy oil and turned down the lights in their bedroom.

Sensuality did not come easily to Hattie. She had been, her mother had always said, a late bloomer sexually. Her periods had not started until she was nearly sixteen and she had never had the kind of teen crushes enjoyed by her female peers. Toby had been her first serious boyfriend. Her obvious lack of experience and confidence – she had grown up in the shadow of her mother's legendary beauty – had never really left her, and at times like these – massaging her man as an obvious prelude to sex – she felt as if she were only playing at being grown-up. She was doing – out of a sense of duty really – what she had read women should do in the women's magazines she occasionally, rather furtively, bought. It didn't give her any sense of pleasure. In fact she felt rather absurd, sitting astride Toby's back, working warm oil into his well-toned body. But even though she doubted the skill of her touch he seemed to like it and within a very few minutes he had turned over and grabbed her so that, feeling even more awkward and ill at ease, she was sitting astride Toby's front working his cock into her pale, slender body.

Because of the seriousness of the crime that Lisa had committed – the actual charge was attempted murder – Hattie was seeing her three times a week. It was, she thought, probably the most difficult case of her career. Generally her patients tended to be either adolescents involved in less severe criminal cases (referred on by juvenile courts) or young children who were the victims of some kind of abuse. It was unusual to encounter a child of Lisa's age – she was just nine – who had been involved in a violent crime.

They had already fallen into a routine in their sessions. The first half an hour or so they would sit together on the little sofa in Hattie's office and look at the books. Lisa loved books, probably because they had been denied her by her parents. Each time she came she would pick a book for Hattie to read. And then, if it was progressing well and Lisa was relaxed, they would try to talk about those things that might have a bearing on her behaviour – her parents, her siblings, their Church, her isolation at her school.

Today she had picked out a Roald Dahl book for Hattie to read – *The BFG* – and, as she had opened the first page, Lisa had crept up and sat on her lap looking uncertainly at Hattie, fearful that she might – like so many other people who knew the details of her crime – recoil from her.

Hattie smiled at her, eager to encourage the trust she was building up with the child. She had come to see Lisa as she might any other patient – as damaged, vulnerable and in desperate need of affection and acceptance. She put one arm around her as she read and Lisa laid her head against Hattie's shoulder.

She seemed genuinely absorbed in *The BFG*, smiling at the funny bits, looking a little concerned about the frightening moment when the heroine, Sophie, was snatched from her bed by a twenty-four-foot giant.

'He's like Goliath . . .' she said.

'Who, Lisa?'

'The BFG,' she said eagerly, 'and Sophie is like David.'

Lisa's allusion to the story of David and Goliath was the only indication in her reaction to Roald Dahl's sometimes sinister story that gave Hattie any inkling that she was at all different from any other child of her age. Most nine-year-olds had a fascination for the macabre, the gruesome and the grotesque. It was just that for Lisa the bloodcurdling stories that had ruled her early life had not been taken from the fairy tales of regular children's fiction. They had come from the Bible.

'I'll have to finish there, Lisa, because we have run out of time. But we'll read some more next time.'

'Oh please,' said Lisa, giving Hattie such a sweet smile that she was suddenly moved to hug her.

'Are they being kind to you at Linton House?' Hattie said gently.

Lisa looked down at the floor.

'Don't you like it there?'

'They don't let me play with the other children . . .' she said, tears falling down her face, 'and when Mummy comes to see me I don't want her to go.'

It was the first time that Lisa had cried and Hattie leant down and held her, and attempted to offer her comfort. After Lisa had left, led reluctantly away by a social worker, Hattie replayed the tape she had recorded of that afternoon's session.

Some days, and this was one of them, Hattie found her work emotionally exhausting. God knows, she thought as she prepared to leave the office later that evening, how she was going to cope with Toby's dinner party. As she put Lisa's notes in her briefcase to take home to study further, she wondered if she would be able to put aside her work – the fate of this little girl – in order to be that weekend the woman Toby wanted her to be.

Hattie emerged from the changing room wearing the dress Toby had chosen. The way in which she hunched her shoulders made it quite obvious – at least to the sales assistant – that she wasn't comfortable in the tight cream sheath, but Toby loved it. Although it would never have occurred to Hattie to buy such a dress (and she was nervous of looking at herself in the shop mirror) it was, in fact, perfect on her.

Hattie's lack of sexual confidence extended to her choice of clothes, and she felt now, as she finally examined her reflection in the softly lit mirror, like a little girl wearing her mother's clothes, a ridiculous impostor pretending to be a woman.

Claire, who spent a great deal of time, money and artifice on her own appearance, was often amazed at Hattie's disinterest in clothes and make-up and astonished by her lack of vanity. Claire had long since given up trying to persuade Hattie that she was beautiful. She understood that her friend had some deep-seated physical inferiority complex prompted by the fact that she was so very different from her infamously lovely mother and her celebrated sister.

While Hattie's mother had brilliant blue eyes and straight, shiny white-blonde hair (even now at fifty-seven) her younger daughter was born with brown eyes and thick, dark curls that she struggled to control. And while both her mother and her elder sister, Arabella, were tall but shapely (they had breasts where Hattie had the merest hint of pectorals) she was short and skinny.

In company her mother had referred to the teenage Hattie as 'the changeling' or would say, when anyone remarked on her daughter's looks, 'She is a genetic throwback.' And as a result Hattie had never been able to see her own particular beauty.

'It would look good with a high heel, I think,' the fawning shop assistant now said to Toby as they studied the embarrassed Hattie. 'Suede stilettos . . .'

Inwardly Hattie groaned at the thought of having to wear this dress *and* high heels. Had she been able to get away with a pair of black opaque tights and some loafers she might have felt happier but the idea of being forced to wear a pair of sheer glossy stockings and stilettos made her feel even more the child at a fancy-dress party. But she went along with Toby's wishes – and the awful sales assistant's advice – because she just wanted to get the whole thing over with.

As well as Hattie's dress, shoes and a selection of under-wear, they bought various props for her empty home: a vast bunch of long-stemmed red chillis to put into plain glass vases, new cutlery and crockery for the table and a number of large church candles. That evening, before their guests arrived, Hattie felt as if both she and their minimalist flat had been sullied and cheapened by the way in which Toby had chosen to adorn them.

'Put on a little lipstick and smile, darling,' said Toby when he saw her. And with a heavy heart she went into the bathroom, put aside her trusty Lipsyl, and painted her mouth the same scarlet colour as the chillis that decorated the table. When she emerged Toby was temporarily stunned by her beauty.

'You'll do . . .' he said, with so little enthusiasm or expression that instead of suffusing her with confidence his off-hand compliment compounded her conviction that she looked terrible.

She had decided, minutes after the arrival of Toby's client, Tom Charter, and his lovely second wife, that the only thing to do was to drink. That way, she thought, she might achieve a little of the sparkle Toby desired.

For once she was quite relieved to see Jon, who arrived a little later than everyone else. The other guests – a senior partner in Toby's law firm and the QC advising them on the UCO case, together with their partners – all seemed to know each other and made Hattie rather nervous. It was her own fault, of course, because she was rarely free to enjoy – or for that matter interested in – the social events that punctuated the working lives of these successful men. And Toby's own reservations about Hattie's ability to indulge in the right kind of small talk had made it easy for her to escape the dinners and cocktail parties that came with his now burgeoning legal career.

Toby had long since discovered that the name of his girlfriend – that is, her family name – was of more use to him in his career than the woman herself. Her inability to play the social game was a bitter disappointment to him because he knew that in the circles in which he now mixed – and in which he longed to become further enmeshed – Hattie's family connections would be an enormous asset.

Still, tonight she seemed to be more the woman he secretly wanted. He could tell that Tom Charter – who had played an important part in Toby's recent elevation within his firm – was taken with her, and he crossed his fingers under the table and quietly prayed that she kept to the list of subjects he had suggested the evening before last.

Claire was carefully installed on the other side of their most important guest so that she could deflect anything that might offend the great man. Tonight she was in full professional mode, partly because Charter's company – UCO – was one of her most important corporate accounts and partly because, following the events of the previous weekend, she had vowed (not, of course, for the first time) never to allow herself to be used by a man again.

'So tell me what you do with your days, Hattie?' Tom asked innocently and affably.

'Oh, I work at this and that,' said Hattie, aware that clinical psychology and the decline of the NHS was definitely not on Toby's conversation list.

Unfortunately, Jon, who was incapable of resisting a quick jab at Hattie, was not going to allow her to escape closer personal scrutiny.

'Yes, Tom, instead of being the kind of socialite her parents had expected, Hattie has turned into their family's social conscience. Instead of living up to their upper-class expectations, she prefers to devote herself to administering to the underclass.'

'Doing what, exactly?' asked Tom.

'I'm a clinical psychologist, specialising in children, although most of them nowadays tend to be teenagers. My patients are usually referred to me by the juvenile courts and I have to make an assessment of them. Jon says I have a social conscience but if I have a conscience about anything it is that I don't do enough, I can only go so far in my work . . .' she said, breaking off as she caught a warning glance from Toby.

'What did your parents want for you?' asked Tom.

'Well, I think ideally they wanted Prince Edward,' said Hattie, her face flushed by her unusually high intake of alcohol. 'They didn't really envisage my wanting to do anything much more than my mother or my elder sister had done. Which was, and still is really, to look good and party.'

'Which,' said Claire with enforced gaiety, 'is great work if you can get it.'

'And makes your choice of career all the more noble,' said Tom.

'Not to the nobility,' said Hattie with a bitter laugh. 'I am something of an embarrassment to them. They regard me as a sad eccentric.'

'But your family is famous for its eccentricity,' prompted Tom.

'My great-aunt's divorce case – the citing of the entire English cricket team – and my grandfather's insistence on sleeping in a silk-lined coffin for the last twenty years of his life – were what you might call conventional acts of aristocratic eccentricity. What I do – working with the mentally displaced and socially deprived – makes me a much more peculiar animal.'

There was an awkward silence.

'But surely your parents are at least proud of your academic achievements? Blue stockings match well with blue blood, don't they?'

'I think they are much prouder of my sister, whose only qualifications in life are her looks and her ability to attract the attention of the gossip columns.'

Tom Charter and his wife, rather like Hattie's family really, were far more interested in her sister, Arabella's, outrageous lifestyle than they were in her own rather dull existence. In fact Mamie Charter clearly found the subject of Arabella's love life – which only that month had involved an infamous ageing rock star – fascinating. Much to Toby's relief.

'You must meet Bella,' he said enthusiastically.

'You'd love her,' said Claire. 'She's an absolute hoot.'

Hattie fell silent. Her earliest childhood memories involved cruel comparison with her glittering elder sister. And although she had no desire to compete on any level with

Arabella she nevertheless resented the way in which her sister – and of course her mother – haunted her life and made her feel, at least in situations like this, wanting.

Curiously it was Jon who rescued her.

'Bella has always reminded me of those Persian cats that used to feature in carpet ads. A woman whose lush beauty – vast eyes, wide, full mouth and big hair – distracts the viewer from what lies beneath: a skinny, spoilt creature of very little brain.'

Hattie, rather pleased by Jon's unusually perceptive description of her sister, began to clear the table in preparation for the entrance of the main course. All in all, she decided when Toby smiled at her, things were going quite well.

Mamie Charter even complimented Hattie on the food, and although such dishonesty was foreign to her she smiled modestly as if in acknowledgement of her culinary skills. Clearly Mamie's husband, who had taken centre stage at the dinner and was relating a series of elaborate stories to an enraptured (if somewhat obsequious) audience, was enjoying himself enormously. Leaning back in the Bauhaus chair, puffing on a Monte Cristo No. 4, and laughing uproariously at his own punch line – which totally baffled Hattie but reduced the rest of the table to helpless merriment – he declared it a great evening.

It was at that point, as Hattie was beginning to anticipate the departure of her guests and relishing the thought of finally kicking off her horrid high heels, that the doorbell went.

'It's probably Tompkins,' said Mamie nervously to her husband.

'Didn't you tell him to just wait in the car?' said her husband, an edge of savagery entering his voice as he addressed his wife.

'I must have forgotten,' she said meekly.

'Well, let him bloody well wait,' said Tom before beginning on another of his long anecdotes.

The bell rang again and Hattie got up, despite Tom and Mamie's protestations. She made her way to the door secretly rather relieved by the interruption.

It was dark in the hallway outside the apartment door. Despite the fact that this was one of the most exclusive developments in west London, the communal areas were badly lit. At first Hattie couldn't make out the shape of the man who stood nervously before her, although she realised at once that it could not possibly be the Charters' poor oppressed chauffeur.

Opening the door wider to let the brilliant halogen lighting from her apartment flood the hallway she gasped with a mixture of delight and shock when she finally recognised the late night caller who was standing hunched before her.

'Jimmy!'

He didn't move for a moment and when he did pull himself up it was clear that there was something wrong. He was hurt or ill.

'What's wrong, Jimmy?' she said.

'Help me, hinny,' he said in an unsteady voice that indicated he was in some pain.

She moved towards him and supported him as he made his way into the flat, completely forgetting the guests who were straining to see what the commotion was all about.

'What is it, Hattie?' said Toby in alarm.

'It's Jimmy,' said Hattie, 'and he's hurt. Help me, someone . . .'

Claire rushed forward and the two young women led him over to the pure white sofa in the corner of the living area.

Tom and Mamie Charter looked on in horror as Hattie made her way past them, her beautiful Dolce and Gabbana cream dress covered in the blood of a grubby and dishevelled stranger. Trailing behind them, and whimpering pathetically, stood a thin, nervous mongrel on the end of a length of blue rope.

'Another eccentric relative?' enquired Tom as he stood up to leave.

As if on cue the rest of the guests scraped back their chairs and, offering the odd furtive glance in Jimmy's direction, made their excuses. Within minutes they had all gone, ushered out by an effusively apologetic Toby.

Chapter Four

It was Jon who attempted to calm a furious Toby on his return from helping Tom and Mamie into their chauffeur-driven Bentley. And it was Jon who drove Hattie, Claire and Jimmy to the Chelsea and Westminster Hospital and helped to carry him into Accident and Emergency – although it pained him almost as much as Jimmy to do so.

Even at this hour and in this place they made a curious bunch, he thought, as he noticed their reflection in the plate-glass automatic doors. The tall, good-looking sophisticated man accompanied by the two young women in the bloodstained designer clothes, carrying between them the dishevelled, wounded homeless boy.

The woman behind the reception desk eyed them all sceptically.

'Name and address?' she commanded.

Jimmy grunted uncomprehendingly.

'No fixed abode,' said Jon pointedly as they stood waiting for the woman to fill in the necessary forms.

'Well, where did you find him?' she asked, glancing at Jimmy with evident distaste.

'He came to my—' Hattie began but Jon quickly intervened.

'We just saw him lying by the road,' he said hastily.

'Good Samaritans,' said the receptionist cynically to Jon before turning her attention back to Jimmy. 'Social security number?'

'Why are you so obsessed with names, numbers and roll calls? This man needs to see a doctor urgently,' said Claire angrily.

43

'So does everyone else here. He'll have to wait,' the woman replied dismissively.

They sat down on the mesh metal chairs and waited, aware that even amongst the motley collection of people gathered here – many of whom seemed to be drunk or drugged or mentally challenged in some way – Jimmy was an unwelcome outsider. The ranks of waiting patients moved apart in disgust in order to let them have more space.

'We should have given my address,' said Hattie anxiously as they waited.

'I don't think that would be a very good idea. Although I have to say I think he might have been seen sooner if he had a fixed abode,' said Jon.

'Well, he'll have to come home with me after they've seen to him,' said Hattie nervously.

'You can't be serious,' Jon began.

'Of course I'm serious. He can hardly go back on the street in this state. And you know they don't keep you in hospital nowadays unless it's terminal. Where else can he go?'

'Some sort of hostel, Hattie. You can't possibly take him back to your flat. Toby would go mad.'

'Well, he can't come back with me,' said Claire quickly.

It became clear in the next couple of hours that Jimmy was very low down on the casualty department's priority list. A nurse did come over and attempt to take some more details but it was obvious from the expression on her face – somewhere between exasperation and contempt – that since Jimmy's injuries were not life-threatening he would just have to wait. Gradually the chairs began to empty as one after another the people were taken away for treatment.

It was gone four in the morning before the nurse returned with her clipboard and took Jimmy away to a curtained cubicle within the treatment area.

'I think we should go now, Hattie,' said Jon.

'I can't just leave him here, Jon.'

'Of course you can.'

'Can't you imagine how awful it would be to find yourself in Jimmy's position? No home, no life, no job, no family. And no compassion from your fellow human beings.'

'But I never would find myself in that state, Hattie.'

'Oh Jon, how do you know that? It could happen to anyone—'

'Hattie, let's not argue about this here and now. You know my feelings. And perhaps now you've seen the hopelessness of Jimmy's case – Christ, he can't even make himself understood – you'll forget our stupid bet. Let's call it quits and I'll take you home.'

'I wouldn't think of it. I'm even more keen now to prove you wrong. And to show these people that Jimmy does have some worth. But you can go home. I'll get a taxi when they've finished with him here.'

'Rather you than me,' said Claire, who was, with every passing moment, wishing that she hadn't got caught up in this whole bet business.

'I'll wait and see you home. And I'll try and find out how he is,' said Jon insistently, getting up at the exact moment that Jimmy walked back through to the reception area. Apart from a nasty cut above his eye – which required three stitches – the rest of his injuries proved to be superficial. He looked dreadful though, his face bruised and pale and his clothes spattered with blood.

'You're coming home with me, Jimmy,' said Hattie gently as she guided him through the door and back into Jon's car.

'Is Rex there?' he asked.

'Rex?' Hattie replied blankly.

'My dog, like. Rex . . .'

They had been in such a rush to get Jimmy to hospital that Hattie had scarcely paid any attention to the dog that had followed him into her flat.

'Yes, I'm sure Rex is back at the flat with Toby,' she said, although she rather doubted it. Toby hated dogs.

Toby was so angry that even when he was finally alone with Hattie and the prone figure on the sofa, he could barely speak.

'You're not leaving him and his bloody dog here?' he said.

'What else do you suggest,' said Hattie, 'that we carry him up and put him in our bed?'

'That we carry them both to the door and throw them out,' said Toby angrily.

'I'd rather throw you out than him,' she said with an unexpectedly hard edge to her voice.

'You might have to. If they stay, I go,' snapped back Toby.

At this Jimmy attempted to pull himself up as if to leave, but Hattie pushed him down, placing a crisp white pillow beneath his bruised and battered head.

'Well then, you'd better go,' said Hattie to Toby.

Shock took over from anger then as he realised that she meant it.

'I can't leave you alone with this man. He might do anything,' said Toby.

'I really don't think, Toby, that he will do anything more tonight but sleep,' said Hattie coldy.

'I must say that was a great finale to the evening, Hattie. Something only you could have thought of.'

'I didn't organise it, Toby, it happened.'

'Christ knows what Tom Charter thought,' said Toby, running his hands through his hair in a gesture of despair.

'I don't give a damn what Tom Charter and his ghastly wife thought,' said Hattie.

'You don't give a damn for anyone but yourself.'

'That's absurd, Toby. I spend my whole life bloody well thinking of others—'

'Sad strangers maybe, but not the people you should be concerned with. Not the people who love you. Not me or your family. All you care about are social inadequates like that creature on the sofa. You are incapable of showing any affection or consideration to anyone that you might consider your own equal. You spend your whole life administering to the poor and needy and deluding yourself that in doing so you are escaping from your élitist roots when in fact all you are doing is being the lady of the manor, albeit a bloody great big manor like London,' he said with disgust.

Hattie's silence informed him that he had hurt her.

'It isn't just the disadvantaged that need warmth and emotional comfort, Hattie. Or support for that matter. It might not mean anything to you but tonight was very important to me. My success didn't come easily to me; I was not born with your advantages. My daddy didn't buy me a £300,000 flat, I don't have a trust fund and no doors are opened for me at the mere mention of my father's name. My parents worked hard to get me a future that was denied them. You might dismiss their values as misplaced and middle class but, my God, you can afford to, can't you? You have everything, Hattie, and you have the nerve to arrogantly deny me the chance of achieving what I want. Which, compared to what you already have, is bloody nothing.'

But Hattie, partly because she didn't want to hear any more and partly because she was so absolutely exhausted, had turned away and was watching the now sleeping body of Jimmy.

'I'm tired, Toby, you're tired. Let's leave this now. We can talk tomorrow,' she said softly.

Hattie woke just before nine to sounds of distress from somewhere below their bedroom. Leaving Toby sleeping soundly she pulled on a wrap and made her way down the stairs. Jimmy was standing in the kitchen with a blanket pulled around his shoulders.

'Is anything wrong? Are you in a great deal of pain?' asked Hattie anxiously, noting the bruises that had emerged across his face during the night.

'Nh, pet,' he said, looking round the steel kitchen as if it were the futuristic galley of some strange space craft. 'Rex needed to go out and I thought I'd make meself some tea, like.'

'Peppermint, Camomile, Lapsang Souchong, Earl Grey, Darjeeling?' Hattie responded, helpfully pulling open one of the cunningly disguised cupboards to reveal the wide selection of specialist teas and coffees that she and Toby had accumulated. Jimmy looked so confused. She made a pot of her normal breakfast tea gestured to him to sit on one of the stools while it brewed.

'Owt for Rex?' he asked, indicating his dog, skulking beneath the table, and who was, Hattie thought, in very nearly as dreadful a state as his master. His coat – short and coarse-haired – was a salt-and-pepper grey through which you could clearly see the outline of his ribcage. Here and there across his body were sections of hard skin and small round patches of baldness.

'I'm not sure what I've got that he'd like. There are a few scraps from last night but it's not quite Pedigree Chum,' she said as she took from the fridge a plate of sushi and a bowl of linguine con cozze and scraped them together into a dish.

'Here, Rex,' she said.

Rex took one look at her, growled savagely and then retreated back beneath the table, whimpering pathetically and looking up appealing at Jimmy.

'Eee, man, I'd better give it to him,' said Jimmy, taking the dish from Hattie and placing it close to Rex under the table.

The dog cautiously sniffed at the offering and, with one wary eye on Hattie, eventually decided to eat.

'Now, breakfast for you, Jimmy? I think I've got pain au chocolat, brioche, pain au raisin and croissants,' Hattie said, eager to make him feel welcome.

He looked at her as if she were speaking a foreign language which, she realised with some embarrassment, she was.

'Ee, I'll just have a tab,' he said, pulling a pack of cigarettes from his pocket and lighting one.

Toby would be horrified. He didn't allow anyone to smoke in the flat. In fact, smoking had been a major issue in their relationship. When they had first met, Hattie had a twenty-a-day habit that Toby had insisted she give up. Now and again, when Toby wasn't around, she would sneak a cigarette – she kept a packet hidden at the bottom of her underwear drawer – but she had always been too anxious to smoke here. The only time Toby had relaxed his no smoking rule had been the previous night when his odious client had lit a fat cigar. Lord knows what he would say when he saw Jimmy smoking.

'Would you like some toast?' she asked.

Jimmy nodded as she pulled a loaf out of the fridge, sliced it and put it into the big Dualit toaster. Then she opened another cupboard and began to bring out a selection of expensive preserves, conserves and confitures.

'Any jam, pet?' said Jimmy, looking through the jars before him, most of which were labelled in a language (chiefly French) he was unable to decipher.

49

'I'm so glad you came, Jimmy. Did you get my messages?' Hattie asked tentatively as she sipped her tea and watched him devour five slices of toast covered in the entire contents of a jar of Toby's favourite Tiptree redcurrant jelly. She wished he would close his mouth while he ate. Her view of his masticated toast – and more unpleasantly, his stained and twisted teeth (one of which, the important front left incisor, was missing) – was repulsive.

'Noowhere to go, like, that's all. I'll not be staying long.'

'No, you mustn't go. You're not fit to go anywhere, least of all out on the streets again. You must stay here.'

'And him?' Jimmy moved his head to indicate the bedroom upstairs where Toby still slept.

'Oh, he doesn't really mean you any harm. He was just eager to impress those people that were here last night,' she said.

There was an uneasy silence.

'What really happened to you last night?' she said eventually.

'Some kids, looking for someone to kick aboot. It happens,' he said as he lit another cigarette.

'You mean they attacked you for no reason?' He nodded.

'Jimmy, that need never happen to you again. I can make sure of that, if you'll only trust me,' she said.

He looked at her with his astonishing eyes and she, for some strange reason, had to look away.

'Why me, though?' he asked.

She couldn't tell him about Jon's bet. It would hurt him and might even frighten him away. He couldn't think that she wanted to help him just in order to win a wager thought up over dinner in some smart restaurant. It was better, she persuaded herself, to make him believe that it was a professional matter, to do with her work. Which, in a way, it was.

'It's very important to me, Jimmy, for my research, and it could be life-changing for you,' she said, not daring to meet those eyes again and instead fixing her gaze on the series of earrings that punctured his left ear.

He was looking round the huge flat as if taking an inventory of her and her life. And if her range of teas, coffees and confitures had invoked in him some kind of culture shock her home was even more incomprehensible to him.

'Where's your telly?' he said.

'It slides away into the wall,' she said, moving across to the living area to demonstrate.

'Why d'ya wanna do that?' he said incredulously.

'Because, Jimmy, the person who designed this place suggested it. It's funny really but televisions – in the circles I mix in – are something rather shameful. We hide them away in the way that other people might hide things that they think might betray basic instincts in them that they would not like others to see – like pornography or Jeffrey Archer novels . . .'

'What?' he said, his face creased up with confusion.

'I like bare space,' she said, suddenly thinking how very pretentious the term 'minimalist' was.

'I like places to be a bit more cosy, like,' he said. 'No offence, mind.'

Gradually she began to talk to Jimmy in rather the way that Toby spoke to their Bosnian cleaning lady: very slowly, choosing her words carefully so as not to baffle or confuse him. It wasn't that she thought that he was stupid, just that he came from such a different world to hers that it really was as if there were some international barrier between them.

'Can I watch it, like?' he said, indicating the television.

'Of course. I'm going to get dressed and then we can talk some more.' Hattie handed him the remote control.

In the bathroom she rang Claire, who sounded a little grumpy, and insisted that she get herself over as soon as she could. When she emerged, bathed and dressed, she found Toby making himself some coffee in the kitchen. His mood, she instantly surmised, was no better for a good sleep, and she had to suppress a smile.

'He's still here then?' He nodded his head towards the figure of Jimmy who was flicking from channel to channel on the remote control, a fag burning in his other hand.

'Yes, and so are you,' Hattie said sharply.

'What's that supposed to mean?' he replied.

'Oh Toby, I haven't the energy for another row. Claire is on her way over to help me with Jimmy. If we get our way he'll be staying here for a while.'

'You aren't seriously saying you're taking Jon up on his bet?'

'Ssh, the boy doesn't know about the bet. He thinks that he's helping me with some research paper I'm writing,' she hissed.

'But does he have to stay here? Does he have to take up residence with us? Christ, Hattie, he's smoking in there!' A look of disgust and horror passed across Toby's already disgruntled face.

They were saved from further argument by the doorbell and the arrival of Claire, now in high spirits.

'Well, where is he, darling?' she shouted as she came through the doorway.

'Ssh,' said Hattie. 'He's watching television.'

Jimmy had given his channel hopping a kind of rap rhythm. With split-second timing he wove between terrestrial and cable programmes, oblivious of the two women who stood watching him or the irritation he was causing Toby, who was clearing up in the kitchen, washing up last night's glasses that would, he always claimed, be ruined in the dishwasher.

'Hadn't we better clean him up first?' said Claire, her enthusiasm dimmed by her first glimpse of Jimmy in daylight.

'I didn't know quite how to raise the subject,' said Hattie in a whisper. 'I didn't want to offend him.'

'Leave it to me,' said Claire, walking across to Jimmy and grabbing the remote control from his hand.

'Hi,' she said. 'I don't expect you remember but I was here when you arrived last night. I'm Claire. I bet you would like a nice hot bath, and a shave. I'll go through and run one for you.'

Jimmy's eyes lit up. 'I divvant know if she had one, like. What with the telly in the wall and all. I had to pittle in the sink this morning . . .'

'Pittle?' said Claire in a bemused tone.

'Eeee, you know – pittle, piss . . .'

At this Toby, who had been rinsing the last of the glasses, threw in the mop. 'Christ, I can't take any more of this,' he said, looking distastefully into the murky waters of the kitchen sink. 'I'm going out.'

Hattie was enormously relieved to see him go and smiled encouragingly at Jimmy whilst making a mental note to rewash the glasses that were standing on the stainless-steel rack in the kitchen.

Claire was organising things in the bathroom, pulling from the concealed cupboards an assortment of pungent bath oils, soaps, shaving foams and razors for Jimmy.

'Don't forget to clean behind your ears,' she said, glancing with disgust at his matted hair as he walked in, his face wide with wonderment at Hattie's bathroom.

'Eee, man . . .' he said as he looked around him.

'The towels are in the cupboard by the loo,' said Hattie in a maternal fashion as they closed the door on him.

The two of them stood cautiously outside as Jimmy

wrestled with the power shower that pounded down into the sandstone bath.

After what seemed like an age, but was probably closer to half an hour, the door opened and from the steamy interior Jimmy finally emerged with a waffle towel wrapped round his waist.

There was about him, the two women suddenly realised, an extraordinary beauty. There were, of course, physical indications of the life he led. A series of tattoos covered various regions of his body – girls' names entwined in hearts on both arms, a dagger in the centre of his chest and, across his back, a prowling tiger. And there were a number of vivid scars and bruises gained, Hattie guessed, during his time on the streets.

Hattie had noticed his eyes right from the start but the rest of his features had been obscured beneath grime and facial hair. With his dreadlocks shampooed and slicked back from his brow, and his chin clean-shaven it was as if one man had gone into the power shower and another had come out.

'My God,' whispered Claire breathlessly, her interest suddenly and dramatically aroused.

And if the beauty and sensitivity of his face was a surprise, exposed at last beneath the dirt and hair, his body was, well, a revelation.

Perhaps that had something to do with the fact that now he was holding himself upright – rather than crouching down as he had been when they had first seen him – and was no longer swaddled in the thick layers of filthy clothes that now lay, in a horrid heap, on the bathroom floor, destined only for the rubbish bin.

Hattie and Claire looked as blankly at him as he had looked at them when they had first disturbed him in his own mean quarters on the streets. As if it were now they who were inferior creatures, not him.

The silence was broken by a long laugh from Claire.

'Hattie, do you remember what you said that night with Jon? You said that you believed that all men were born equal. Well, you were wrong and Jon was right. Some men are born more equal than others. But not Jon or Toby . . .'

Jimmy suddenly became self-conscious and crouched down again to reclaim his old clothes.

'Oh, don't put those back on,' said Claire. 'You can wear something of Toby's, can't he, Hattie?'

Hattie went upstairs and retrieved a white Paul Smith T-shirt, some Calvin Klein Y-fronts and a pair of Toby's button-fly jeans, and handed them to Jimmy, who moved back into the bathroom to get dressed.

'I really don't think our task is going to be too difficult,' said Claire confidently when Jimmy was out of earshot. 'I mean, what was it the bet said: "make him a man of worth"? I think that most women would count him that after a simple bath. Just as long as he didn't open his mouth to reveal those teeth.'

Hattie was quiet for a moment as she took in the flushed face of her friend. It would be just like Claire to mess this whole thing up by bringing sex into the equation.

'I think you'll find that we will need a great deal more than soap and water to help Jimmy achieve his potential,' she said curtly.

'Oh Hattie, don't be so prim. In the right clothes, with the right props, with a few very cosmetic changes we could pull off this bet tomorrow. He's bloody perfect,' said Claire with a wistful smile.

'But he is lost, Claire. Can't you see that? I think he has had a very limited education and if he is to be more than a gigolo or a bloody rent boy he can't just rely on his looks.'

At this point Jimmy came out of the bathroom dressed

in Toby's clothes. They were too small – Hattie hadn't realised how tall he was – so that the jeans were far too short and the T-shirt was strained around Jimmy's unexpectedly muscular body. But the effect, despite the tightness of the clothes (or perhaps *because* of the tightness of the clothes) was devastating.

'We'll have to take him shopping,' said Claire in wonderment, 'and he'll need a good haircut and some radical dentistry . . .'

The two women continued to appraise him as they all made their way down to the kitchen, Claire making some mental notes on how she might – with her renowned taste and styling skills – effect a transformation.

'We'll start tomorrow. I'll try and clear some space in my diary and make some appointments. I know this wonderful cosmetic dental surgeon just round the corner from Harrods. He's done them all . . .' she named a couple of celebrities, taking command in a way that slightly irritated Hattie.

'That is, if Jimmy agrees to go along with all this,' Hattie said, glancing across at Jimmy who was beginning to look more at ease – at home even – in her flat.

'Will you help me with my research, Jimmy?' she asked.

'Aye, man, why not?' he said as he opened the fridge and surveyed the contents. 'Where d'ya keep the brown sauce?'

Chapter Five

Hattie and Claire spent most of that Sunday afternoon making lists and notes on how Jimmy's makeover would best be achieved. First of all he had to have somewhere to live. Hattie knew that his continued presence in her flat would agitate and alienate Toby – who had still not returned home – but she was unwillingly to allow Claire to take him back to her own cramped mews house. She wanted to be in control of what happened to Jimmy because she was a little suspicious of the motives of her friend, whose values were not always her own.

They agreed that if they were going to win Jon's bet they would have to be prepared to invest some of their own money in the project. Hattie agreed to put up half the figure wagered – £2500 – to cover the initial costs of buying clothes and making the cosmetic changes Claire deemed necessary.

But to win the bet it wasn't enough to have his hair cut, his teeth straightened and to buy him new clothes. If Jimmy were to fit in with Jon's definition of 'a man of worth' he was going to have to be able to make some sort of living. And whilst Jimmy himself was eager to continue selling the *Big Issue* on his pitch near the Opera House – 'so I can pay my way a bit, like' – Hattie wanted more for him.

Rather more, in fact, than Claire, who was even now hooting with laughter as she tried to understand Jimmy's Geordie idioms.

'Haddaway, man?' Claire said in mocking imitation of

Jimmy's pronunciation of his favourite phrase. 'What the fuck does that mean?'

He was clearly shocked by her language. In fact, Hattie had already discovered, he never resorted to using the guttural expletives that commonly punctuated Claire's conversation. The worst words in his albeit limited vocabulary were 'shite' and 'bugger'.

There was, as Hattie had hoped and suspected, something rather dignified about the man Jon would dismiss as worthless.

'"Haddaway, man",' said Hattie, 'means "Get away with you" or "Would you ever?" Am I right Jimmy?'

He looked across at her gratefully. She had become interpreter for him in this strange new world. For he found the language of these women totally incomprehensible. He was fascinated by Claire's transatlantic accent – and rather disappointed to discover that it was Canadian – but she spoke so fast that he found it difficult to keep up with her words. In fact there was little about either of the women that Jimmy understood. The women in his own life – those in his vast dysfunctional family – were very different creatures and whilst he was at times mesmerised by the attention of two such attractive and confident females, he didn't trust them.

He was sufficiently worldly, though, to realise that going along with Hattie's research could be of benefit to him even if, along the way, he had to endure their mocking patronage. And if he had to choose one of them as his protector, then it would be Hattie, even if it meant staying in this odd place and accepting the disapproval and contempt of her man. So he agreed to their plans, and to staying on in her flat.

When Claire departed for home late that afternoon Hattie set about creating Jimmy his own area within the vast living space. Although their home was the height of fashion – what estate agents now described as a New York loft – it was ill-suited to house guests. There were no doors on the ground floor except to the kitchen and just the one big bedroom and bathroom upstairs so that Hattie had to fashion Jimmy a room by putting together two Japanese screens and offer him a foldaway futon to sleep on.

'There is one thing, Jimmy. Toby really doesn't like smoking. I don't mind, in fact I used to smoke before I met him . . .'

'Aye?' he said.

'So when you want a cigarette, do you think you could go and stand outside the front door . . . so the smoke doesn't pollute the flat . . . ?' she said nervously.

Then she turned her attention to Rex. The dog, she explained, would need to be a little more house-trained if he were to live with them.

'But he pittles in street,' said Jimmy.

'I know he does but he, well, he smells rather dreadful, Jimmy. Couldn't we give him a bath?'

'Rex hates water,' said Jimmy.

Rex, Hattie was beginning to suspect, hated everything apart from food and Jimmy. He growled every time Hattie or Claire inadvertently went near him, and he barked in a shrill, neurotic fashion every time the doorbell or the phone went. Worse, he clearly had a digestive problem which – perhaps aggravated by the sushi he had eaten for breakfast – resulted in regular emissions of offensive ozone-eroding wind. Hattie had grown up with dogs – her father had always had a brace of Labradors for shooting and her mother was never parted from her beloved West Highland terrier – but try as she might she could find nothing about Rex that was remotely attractive. She accepted, though, that the dog represented the closest thing to family in Jimmy's life and she supposed she would have to establish some sort of relationship with him.

'We have to clean him, Jimmy. We've got to do something to try and remove the bad smell from under Toby's nose,' she said, although she doubted if pickling the dog in Chanel No. 5 or Eternity would make Toby more tolerant of him.

Hattie ran a bath filled with pungent bubbles and Jimmy carried the reluctant, whimpering dog and immersed him in the warm water.

There followed a terrible scene in which Rex fought, scratched, clawed and finally bit his way out of the bath, displacing gallons of water over Hattie, Jimmy and the floor, before disappearing back into his favourite place under the kitchen table.

Hattie was touched by the way in which Jimmy tried to calm him, singing to him and gently drying him with one of her expensive white waffle towels. When he had finished and the dog had calmed down enough to stop shivering and whining Jimmy turned to Hattie.

'I'll need me stuff, like,' he said, 'if I'm staying a while.'

'Your stuff?' said Hattie, who had assumed that all Jimmy had in the world were the clothes he had once stood up in, his sleeping bag and the couple of carrier bags she had noticed when she had first encountered him.

'Yeah, me bits an' pieces, like. They're in a left luggage box at King's Cross,' he said, pulling a key from the pocket of Toby's jeans.

'Well, of course we should get them,' Hattie said, smiling at him. 'Now, if you want.'

'OK,' he said, jumping up.

Outside in the street Hattie hailed a black cab, to the astonishment and wonder of Jimmy who had not, it quickly emerged, ever travelled in one before. On the journey to the station he was enchanted by the two pull-down seats and moved from one to the other in the excited fashion of a small child on a big adventure.

Indeed, Hattie thought as she paid off the taxi and followed Jimmy through to the dirty, depressing station interior, he had many of the more endearing qualities of a child. He was enthusiastic, questioning, responsive and direct. He said what he meant, even if on occasion she could not quite understand his dialect or comprehend the words he used.

'This is where I came when I left home, like,' he said thoughtfully, pointing up at the departure board on which a dozen or so inter-city trains – coming from Northern towns she had never heard of, let alone visited – were indicated.

'When was that? How old are you, Jimmy, and how long have you been in London?'

'Must be going on five years now. I'm twenty-three,' he said, lighting up his third cigarette since they had left the flat.

'And what did you think of this place when you arrived?'

'Big,' he said simply, drawing on his cigarette.

Hattie wondered what he had expected of London, and if he was disappointed by what he did find.

'Where did you go when you arrived? Did you know anyone here?' she asked him gently.

'Na,' he said.

'So what did you do?'

'I got by, did a bit of labouring, like, now and then. There's people, like, that offer you a place to stay.' He paused and looked across at Hattie. 'Not people like you, mind. Hard people, mean people, what pretend they're going to help you and just sook ya in, like . . .'

She was aware of the fact that the young and homeless were often preyed on by unscrupulous shadowy men who led them into desperate and corrupt lives. She wondered a little guiltily, too, if what she was doing – in going along with Jon's bet – wasn't just another form of the kind of exploitation Jimmy had encountered since he arrived here.

'But you didn't get sucked in by those people, Jimmy?' she said.

He looked at her with those penetrating blue eyes and shook his head. 'Not for long, hinny.' He glanced away quickly.

She sensed that he did not want to talk about his past and she stopped her questioning and followed him silently towards the left-luggage area.

Inside his box was a cheap black Leatherette holdall, a cardboard box that was tied together with string and a small zipped child-sized canvas case. Hattie was moved by his evident excitement at his reunion with this odd collection of possessions. She held out her hand to grasp hold of the black bag but he would only allow her to carry the small case, and then not before he had gravely warned her that its contents were 'breakable, like'.

In the taxi he was rather more subdued than he had been on their outward journey. He didn't attempt to open any of his luggage but he glanced at the three pieces that he had carefully placed on the floor of the cab as if their reappearance in his life was an unexpected piece of good fortune.

Hattie felt like an intruder and, when they were inside the flat, she left Jimmy stowing away his booty, and made her way to the kitchen where a dour-faced Toby was sitting reading the papers.

'Picked up the Vuitton cases, I see,' he said, raising an eyebrow sarcastically in the direction of Jimmy's Japanese screened room.

Hattie looked at him with contempt. She was beginning to think that Toby was even more insensitive to the feelings of others than she had ever realised (although, of course, their sex life had been a bit of a clue). The thought of Jimmy's few material possessions – probably worthless in Hattie and Toby's terms – being pored over in the corner of her elegant home had touched something deep within her. Perhaps even sparked in her, she thought as she remembered the childlike qualities she had noticed in him earlier that evening, some sort of frustrated maternal instinct.

In her work she regularly came across injured children who would arouse a strong need to nurture in her, but she was never able to indulge it. She could only go so far in helping them which, for her, was never quite far enough. At the end of their sessions she could only send them back to their foster homes or their families. With Jimmy it was different. He wasn't a patient; she wasn't restricted by the rules and regulations of her profession. She could go further, do more, nurture in the way she wanted.

She was already conscious that Claire's approach to Jimmy was, rather like Claire herself, a little superficial. She even suspected that her friend might have some hidden agenda in her own interest in Jimmy's transformation. But Hattie felt that she had a deeper and more profound reason for wanting this young man to succeed. He would be the means by which she proved – not just to Jon but to herself – that she was right in her theories. All men, she thought, as she glanced past Toby towards Jimmy, were born equal.

'I thought I'd cook us some supper,' she said, moving towards the fridge and taking out some pasta, some mushrooms, a large onion and a piece of fresh Parmesan.

'That'll make a change,' Toby said snidely.

Just because Hattie didn't often cook didn't mean she couldn't. She just wasn't focused on food. And besides, there was never any real need to feed Toby because he had a business lunch every day. But having Jimmy here changed that. She was overwhelmed by the need to care for him. To give him some decent food, clean clothes and a place of safety in which to live.

She sliced the onions and fried them in some extra virgin

olive oil that Toby had brought back from Umbria. Then she threw in the exotic mushrooms and some garlic and finally mixed the lot with some fresh penne she had boiled, sprinkling the finished dish with freshly grated Parmesan and chopped parsley. She even remembered to put some part-baked ciabatta in the oven so that when the pasta was ready she could serve it with crispy, hot bread. She laid the table in the kitchen for three and opened a bottle of red wine.

Toby, who had been looking on in wonder at the sight of Hattie happily cooking, put down his paper and came over to the table.

'And is our guest going to deign to join us?' he said, in the sneering tone he adopted whenever he referred to Jimmy.

She went to the corner of the room where he was camped and coughed gently. 'Jimmy?' she said softly. 'Supper is ready.'

'Oh aye,' he said, putting his head round the corner. 'I was just sorting me things out, like.'

Hattie glanced down behind him and noticed the array of possessions that littered the bed: a collection of Newcastle United programmes, a scrunched up and soiled Everton duvet cover, some rosettes, a silver-plated cup, some medals, a pile of photographs and, beneath them, numerous other half-obscured trinkets. She didn't ask him about them although she was aware of a growing curiosity. She wanted to know more about him, his family, his origins, but she smiled for now and went back to the kitchen.

She indicated that he should sit down – something she had noticed he didn't like to do when he ate – and he slipped onto one of the steel chairs next to Toby. Rex, who followed his master like a particularly distorted shadow, slunk beneath the table.

'Christ Almighty – he's got my fucking clothes on!' exclaimed Toby, who had, until now, not focused on the newly cleaned up and beautiful Jimmy. 'That's the last fucking straw . . .'

'Eee, man, I'm sorry,' said Jimmy, his wonderful face blushing with embarrassment.

'Don't be sorry, Jimmy,' said Hattie shortly. 'Toby has got at least a dozen pairs of jeans and, to my certain knowledge, over fifty plain white Paul Smith T-shirts—'

'That's not the point, Hattie,' said Toby, who was experiencing, Hattie suddenly surmised, stirrings of what was probably deep sexual jealousy.

His eyes ran across the face of the unwanted intruder and down his torso to the crutch of his tight Tommy Hilfiger jeans.

'Besides, Toby, they look much better on Jimmy – even if they are a little too small,' Hattie added with a merry laugh.

There was an awkward silence during which it seemed as if Toby might leave. But something – the idea of this beautiful stranger sleeping so close to Hattie, or the delicious aroma of the pasta – made him stay and eat.

Jimmy – who had been studying the food with a wary eye – watched Hattie and Toby begin to eat, in the mannered way that they did, with just their forks in their right hands. Picking up his own fork and his butter knife he began gingerly to taste the pasta on his plate.

Alone with the two women Jimmy had been far more relaxed, but in the presence of this hostile stranger he was obviously intimidated. He stopped eating, switched his fork into his right hand and slowly attempted to imitate the way they so expertly ate their food. Very carefully he managed to prod his fork through the pasta and lift it to his mouth. His progress was slow, painful and noisy.

'I've had enough,' said Toby, pushing his half-empty plate away. 'I think I'll watch some television and get an early night.'

'In the bedroom?' enquired Hattie.

'Well, I wouldn't want to intrude on our guest's space,' said Toby, moving to get up. 'JESUS CHRIST! That bloody dog bit my leg!'

'He's a wonderful guard dog,' said Hattie defensively.

'It's probably bloody rabid,' Toby said, moving quickly out of Rex's way. 'It should be muzzled.'

It occurred to Hattie that Toby and Rex had a lot in common right now. Both were behaving in a territorial fashion that was positively primeval. They both needed muzzling, growling and snarling as they sought to demonstrate their supremacy.

Toby's exit up the stairs had a liberating effect on Jimmy, who jumped up, reached into the cupboard and returned to the table clutching a jar of crushed sun-dried tomato paste, the closest thing to ketchup he had yet found in this strange, foreign kitchen. Standing up, with the plate in his hand, he began to eat the food – now covered in the rich, red sauce – with more enthusiasm while he walked up and down the room.

Hattie suspected that long before he was reduced to squatting on the streets Jimmy had got used to eating wherever and whenever he could. And almost never at a table. He was happiest, she had already noted, pacing up and down while he ate.

'Why don't you finish that in front of the television, Jimmy,' she said, 'while I go and check up on Toby?'

Putting her own plate on the sheet steel work surface she left him alone and went upstairs.

Toby was lying in bed channel hopping in a slightly less furious fashion than Jimmy had done earlier. He looked up at her with a cold hard face.

'How long is this going to go on, Hattie?'

'Well, I've got just under three months to achieve the

transformation,' she said gaily, 'so I suppose till about August.'

'That's ridiculous. I'm sure Jon wasn't really serious about that bet. He certainly wouldn't expect us to put up with this kind of upheaval for some bloody wager about a brain-dead bum like that.'

'It was you who said that Jon is always serious about his bets. And anyway, what makes you think he's brain dead?'

'Those teeth for a start.'

'You mean no orthodontic care when he was a child might indicate a low IQ?'

'Low life, Hattie. He's low life. Anyone with any sense could see that. Christ, he eats like a pig. He can barely speak, for Christ's sakes. And what he does say is virtually unintelligible.'

'He's limited by his education, Toby. He didn't go to Charterhouse—'

'It's more than that, Hattie. He's on the same evolutional level as his bloody dog. He's not even house-trained. He pees in the sink, he smokes and he can't sit still to eat. And it's quite clear from this evening that he's rarely come into contact with a knife or fork before.'

'You are so fucking bourgeois, Toby. All you are saying is that he is not what you would classify as civilised. But that's just conditioning. You can teach people to eat with a knife and fork and to pull the chain on the loo – which incidentally you forget to do every morning when you pee – but what you cannot teach anyone is sensitivity. It's insensitivity that makes a man into an animal, Toby . . .'

'You really are serious, aren't you? You'd really put that animal before anything else in your life – our relationship, my happiness. Can't you see it's intolerable for me to have to live with him in my home?'

'It's my home, Toby . . .'

'You always used to say *our* home, Hattie.'

'Oh Toby, you know this means a lot to me. It might strike you as absurd and selfish behaviour but actually I am trying to help Jimmy. To take the animal – as you call it – out of the man and give him a chance to be something else than a creature that skulks around the streets and sleeps in shop doorways.'

'Fine but not *here*, Hattie.'

'Do you know something, Toby, this boy has awoken something in me. Oh, I know that I have always had what you and Jon sneeringly used to refer to as a social conscience but I have never before been able to make the difference in the way I can with Jimmy. Every day I see people who are so damaged by what has happened in their lives that it is almost impossible to help them. But I can only do so much for them. With him I have the chance to really achieve something. I believe that beneath that animal you see there is a fine human being with the potential to achieve great things. It's as if he were new, do you understand, raw, waiting to be transformed into something special? If you don't like it you can go back and live in your flat for a while.'

'He could turn out to be Frankenstein's monster.'

'Oh, I hardly think so, Toby. Look at him. He has, apart from those teeth and tattoos, a quite extraordinary beauty.'

'So that's it then? That's what you see in him?'

'Don't be so stupid, Toby. I am not the slightest bit interested in him in *that* way,' she said with a giggle as Toby confirmed the jealousy she'd earlier suspected. 'I am just saying that he has outstanding natural grace and beauty. And more than that, he has got – I don't quite know how to express it – *something*.'

Toby's face softened as his fear of Hattie's attraction to Jimmy receded. His insecurity – so rarely expressed by a man who carefully controlled all his emotions – touched what was left of Hattie's love for him.

'Is that your only objection, that I might find him attractive?' she said, laughing and reaching a hand out to hold his in the comforting way you might take the hand of a small, unsure boy.

Toby leant across and kissed Hattie passionately, thrusting his tongue into her mouth in a way that he hadn't since they first met. Kisses had slipped out of his sexual repertoire long ago and she found herself unusually aroused.

Toby fought to unbutton her shirt and undo her bra, without releasing his mouth from hers.

'Do you want me, Hattie?' he said urgently. 'Look at me, look how big I am . . .'

He pushed her hand down to touch his penis and then started to grab at her jeans, unzipping them and pulling them down quite roughly. When she was naked he entered her and began to make love more powerfully than he had done since their first days together.

'I'm going to fuck you and fuck you and fuck you,' he roared.

'SSH! Toby, he might hear us . . .'

'I want him to fucking well hear us. This is our home, not his,' said Toby as he thundered into her, and the bed, unaccustomed to such frenzied action, banged against the wall in an unmistakable rhythm that she felt sure could be heard above the sound of the television in the room below.

Chapter Six

An hour or so later, after Toby had fallen into a deep and obviously contented sleep, Hattie got up, slipped on her dressing gown and went downstairs. She felt unduly anxious about Jimmy. She supposed her concern about his overhearing their noisy lovemaking was linked to the maternal instinct he had aroused in her. At any rate she couldn't think of any other explanation for the need to check if he was all right before she herself slept.

Since there were no lights coming from the big open space living area she assumed he was asleep and made her way to the kitchen. She turned on the dimmer switch and noticed that Jimmy had made an effort to clean up. The plates were washed and stacked on the draining board and the pans were soaking in the sink.

It wasn't Jimmy who lacked house-training, it was Toby. The real animal here, she thought as she made her way to the bathroom, was the man she lived with. Marking out his territory with that loud display of his sexual prowess. She shuddered in recollection and experienced an added pang of guilt for the fact that, for the first time in she didn't know how long, she had actually enjoyed sex.

She poured some oil into the bath and turned on the taps. She wasn't the kind of woman who had any particular beauty regime but she felt the need to deep cleanse herself tonight and she fished around in the big drawer for an old tube of face mask which she carefully applied. The effect was, she thought as she examined herself in the mirror, oddly depersonalising. The greeny white paste obliterated her features and held her face in a fixed expression.

She lay in the bath and thought about the ways in which she might be able to help Jimmy. She needed to establish what kind of education he had and obviously – professionally and personally – she wanted to know about his family and his upbringing. Then she could begin to find out if there was any latent talent in him that might be encouraged. Claire was masterminding his physical transformation, which would begin the next day with a massive shopping expedition. But that, as today's brief clean-up had proved, wasn't going to be a particular problem. Hattie had felt rather gleeful, earlier on this evening, when Jon had rung to ask what was happening. It had given her some pleasure to tell him – out of Jimmy's earshot – that not only was the bet on but also that they were now even more confident of winning.

She let the water out of the bath, put on a deep-pile towelling robe and made her way back to the kitchen to make a drink. As she filled the kettle at the sink, she heard a sudden noise behind her that sent a wave of fear through her.

'Oh Jimmy, you frightened me. I thought you were asleep.'

'I was outside having a tab,' he said, a look of shock and wonder on his face.

'Oh my God, my mask,' she laughed, realising how ridiculous she must look. 'It's a strange female ritual that probably has primitive roots. Neanderthal woman daubing her face with mud . . .'

He looked at her quizzically with his perfect blue eyes and she felt even more uncomfortable.

'Would you like a drink? I'm making some tea.'

'Aye, OK,' he said, watching her curiously.

'Tell you what, why don't you make the tea while I clear this stuff off my face? Then we can sit and talk.'

He nodded and she went back into the bathroom to rinse the dried mask from her skin and put on some pyjamas so that she would be properly decent beneath her robe.

When she returned he was sitting on the sofa with a pile of his things beside him and Rex lying protectively at his feet, growling. On the table there were two mugs of tea and a packet of cigarettes.

'Eee, man, that's better. Ya look reet pretty again.'

Hattied blushed unexpectedly and pushed her wild, curly hair back off her face in a gesture of unaccustomed vanity. She went over and sat next to him, Rex's growl turning to a low hostile moan, whilst Jimmy shuffled through his possessions.

'Your man doon't like me or Rex, does he?' he said.

'No really, it's fine. Toby will get used to you.'

He smiled at her and again she pushed the hair back from her face. She picked up her mug of tea – which was so strong the milk had turned it orange – and sipped from it.

'Do you think I could have a cigarette?' she asked, glancing covetously at the packet.

'Eee, man, in here?' he said, with a gleam in his eye.

'Why not?' she said with a smile. 'Toby's asleep.'

He gave her a cigarette and took one himself and they sat smoking together in a manner that Hattie found, well, almost clandestine.

'Tell me about your things,' she said, drawing on the cigarette as if it were some dangerous narcotic.

'Just stuff from back home.'

'And where exactly is back home?'

'Meadow Well.'

'Is that near any town?'

'It's the estate, Meadow Well . . .' he said, clearly amazed that she didn't know of it.

'Is it near Newcastle?'

'Naa, hinny. It's in North Shields. Must be six or seven miles away from Newcastle.'

'And do you have a family?'

He was silent and reflective for a moment. Then: 'There's me mam and me brothers . . .'

'Have you got a picture of them, Jimmy?'

He began to sort through the pile beside him and eventually picked out a couple of photographs and passed them over to her. The woman could have been aged anything from thirty-five to fifty-five. It was difficult to tell because her face was hard and quite starkly made up, and her luridly red hair was very tightly permed. Round her neck she wore a gold cross and three or four other chains. She had none of Jimmy's beauty. In one picture she was standing by a beach with the sun in her eyes and in the other she was dressed up with a flower in her lapel, perhaps for a wedding.

'And your father?'

'Never knew me dad,' he said, blushing slightly.

'Your brothers are older than you?' Hattie asked.

'No, me brothers are younger. Me mam had me when she was seventeen.' He paused for a second. 'She said me dad was a Norwegian sailor. She met him down The Jungle on the fish quay. It was love at first sight. Only he never came back . . .'

A Norwegian father would probably explain the astonishing blue eyes, the pale hair and the big, muscular body, Hattie thought as she looked from the pictures of his plain mother to Jimmy's own startling face.

'And your brothers? Are there photographs of them?'

He began to search through his pile of pictures and eventually produced three separate photographs. His brothers – five of them, aged between about four and seventeen – had the same mean, cold expression as his mother, although none of them looked quite like the other. It was possible, Hattie thought as she studied the photos, that they all had different fathers. And not that unusual, she supposed, nowadays.

Jimmy himself appeared in one of the pictures. It must have been taken when he was about twelve years old and he looked, surrounded by his rough and rowdy siblings, as if he were a changeling. Which of course she supposed he was. The family group was standing in the front garden of a run-down, grey, pebble-dashed house surrounded by inner-city litter – car tyres, bits of old metal, abandoned toys and disintegrating black rubbish bags. To the right of the picture it was possible to see the next-door house, which was blackened by fire and boarded up. It was the kind of place that Hattie had seen in newsreels and documentaries on urban decay but had never glimpsed at first-hand. One or two of her friends lived in small 'worker's' cottages – two-up, two-down, in places like Wandsworth, where the outside privies had been turned into conservatories – but with her own privileged background she had no experience of the kind of deprivation Jimmy was showing her.

'Do you miss them?'

'The littleun. He's nine now. I miss him a lot,' he said.

'Fourteen years younger than you?'

He thought for a moment, screwing up his eyes as if making a difficult calculation. 'I suppose . . .'

'How did you get to that doorway that night? Why did you leave your home and your family?'

He sighed and looked at her as if to say that the reasons were too plentiful and the story too long and painful to tell.

'Me mam got a new man and there was no room. Wha aboot you, like? What aboot ye family?' he said, clearly trying to deflect her from any further discussion of his own origins.

'I have a family, a sister. You might have heard of my sister, Arabella.'

'Is she famous, like?' he said in tones of awe, offering her another cigarette which she quickly took.

'Infamous more like. She's very, very glamorous and is always being photographed by the paparazzi on the arm of this or that celebrity. And she writes a column in one of the Sunday papers in which she relates her exploits of the week – which particular parties or press launches she has attended.'

'What's her name?'

'Arabella Sykes. She took our mother's maiden name when she started to model. Thought it was more influential,' said Hattie thoughtfully.

'And you have a mam and a dad?' he asked.

Hattie giggled at the very idea of her ever referring to her parents as *Mam and Dad*. Her mother and father had always insisted on a more formal term of endearment – Mother and Father – or when they were feeling skittish, Mater and Pater.

'Yes. Although God knows how or why they have stayed together. They have little in common. Except their joint love and reverence for money . . .' she said.

'Pictures?' he said, indicating his own pile and implying, in the shrug of his shoulders, that he had noticed the sad lack of family photographs in her clean, uncluttered home.

'My mother and my sister are famous beauties. There are so many photographs of them – every photographer you can name from John Swannell to David Bailey – that it probably wouldn't be possible to get them into this flat, let alone the average family album. But if you really want I'll find you something,' she said, jumping up and moving over to the study area where, in a giant wooden retro filing cabinet, she kept a few mementoes of her family.

She passed him a clutch of pictures – a recent cutting of Arabella and the rock star torn from the *Daily Mail*, several pictures of her mother and father cut from the diary in *Harpers*, and some childhood holiday snaps. She wasn't sure whether she should include the picture of the four of them posed – for a colour supplement feature on her father – in front of Whitehaven, their vast and rather awesome family home, but she did anyway.

He pored over the pictures, clearly fascinated, looking up every now and then to examine Hattie.

'Well? They are beautiful, aren't they?' she said, waiting for the usual declarations of wonder at the beauty of her sister and her mother.

'Nah, lass, it's you that's beautiful not them,' he said, putting out a hand and gently touching her mane of long, dark curly hair.

She was taken off balance for a moment. His compliment – nothing more than the simple observation of an unsophisticated eye, she supposed – was the nicest thing she had heard in years.

'Jimmy, believe me, in our society they have the real beauty.'

'Ye dad?' he said, indicating a picture of her father.

She nodded.

'Ye look like him.'

And don't I know it? thought Hattie as she glanced across at Jimmy who was carefully studying the exterior of Whitehaven.

'Hotel?' he asked.

'No, our house.'

Sensing his embarrassment and confusion she leant across him and picked up one of the medals that lay amidst his pile of treasured belongings. Rex, who had been sleeping deeply beside Jimmy, jumped up and barked viciously at her.

'Doon, boy,' ordered Jimmy. 'He's gentle really, it's just that he doon't like strangers.'

'How long have you had Rex?' Hattie asked as she

watched him stroke the coarse coat. Before she had come into direct contact with Jimmy she had been rather cynical about the homeless and dogs. She had assumed that a dog was a begging accessory – rather like a crippled child in a Third World country – designed to pull at the heart and purse strings of the passer-by. But it seemed unlikely that this dog – ugly, nervous and aggressive – could have in any way helped Jimmy to scratch his living on the streets.

'He found me, like, when I was dossing in a place near the station. Turned out that he belonged to an old man that died. He just started following me, like . . .' he said as Rex squirmed onto his back and indicated that he wanted his belly tickled. 'He does tricks, like.'

'Tricks?'

'He jumps up and begs for his Newkie.'

'Newkie?'

'Newcassle Brown.'

'Beer,' she said, watching Rex with a less wary eye.

'And he watches out for us.'

'What's this?' Hattie asked, indicating the medal that she was still holding in her hand.

He snatched it back and put it away with his other things. As he did so a small ornament tumbled to the floor. Hattie picked it up and looked at it. It was one of those plastic snowstorms – usually a winter scene but in this instance the snow falling onto Blackpool Tower. She shook it and they both watched the white flecks settle to the bottom.

'It was a present from me nan,' Jimmy said, his eyes shining, 'when I was a kid, like. It reminds me of her.'

'Is she still alive?'

'Me mam and me lived with her when I was little. She was more of a mam to me than me own really. She died . . .'

Hattie felt like an intruder again, as if she were prying on parts of his life that he could not, would not talk about. She needed to find some way to draw him out so that she could begin to repair the damage she guessed had been done.

'Jimmy, you know what I do, don't you? I'm a psychologist. I spend most of my professional life talking to children about the traumas they have experienced. I wonder if you would talk to me about your early life?'

'Is that a doctor?'

'Sort of, yes.'

He was enormously impressed by this.

'But I'm not sick, like.'

'No, of course you're not. But in order to complete my work – this paper I'm writing – I need to understand what happened when you were a child. If you'll let me, later this week I'll take you into my office and we can talk there, in a proper professional environment.' She felt rather bad about misleading him about her real intentions but unable to resist the challenge of probing back in his life.

He regarded her as though he really wanted to trust her but was still unsure about the strange new world in which he had found himself. For a moment she wondered if she shouldn't level with him, tell him about Jon's bet, but she was too frightened of losing what trust she had already established. Proving Jon wrong – even if it involved a little initial deception – would ultimately be more important for Jimmy than telling him the whole truth at this delicate stage of their relationship.

'Tomorrow Claire is going to take you shopping. She's good fun, Jimmy, and she means well. I'll meet you for lunch afterwards.'

'Will I be coming back here?'

'Of course, Jimmy,' she said, reaching across to touch his arm in a gesture of reassurance that, unexpectedly for them both, produced a sudden surge of static electricity.

Chapter Seven

Claire woke up that Monday feeling rather sick. She must have drunk more than she ought to have done last night but she had no recollection of where she had been or, for that matter, with whom. She looked at the clock, calculated that she still had another half-hour in which to sleep and, turning over, encountered something large and solid (rock hard, actually) in her bed.

'Christ, Eddie, what are you doing here?' she said in horror as she recognised the face of the sleeping form beside her.

Eddie opened one eye in apparent bafflement and then the other in an expression of cold and ruthless calculation.

'Since I am here, Claire, why don't we finish off what we've obviously already started?' he said, easing himself on top of her.

She wasn't in the mood for this but, God, it had been ages. Well, apart from that awful five-minute interlude with the man with the goatee. And Eddie had been in and out of her life – in rather the way he was now motioning in and out of her body – for years.

'I think I must still be drunk, Eddie,' she said as her body responded to his rather basic foreplay.

It didn't take long. Five minutes later she was standing beneath the pounding waters of the shower feeling as if she were washing in her own tears. Why did she do it? Why did male attention matter to her so much? Why couldn't she have told Eddie to fuck off rather than giving in to yet another fuck?

Halfway through the act that she had just endured she had recollected the reason why Eddie had come to sleep in her bed the night before. And it had not been unfinished business he was completing. She had simply taken pity on him at a long drunken lunch party and allowed him to stay. It had never been her intention to be quite as accommodating as she had been five minutes ago. She could remember quite clearly him saying that he would just lie next to her, that he wouldn't touch her but that he just didn't want to wake up on his own.

Why was she so stupid when it came to men? She had a Masters degree in English. She spoke five languages but none of them seemed to help her to translate what a man said into what he really meant.

She ought, she thought bitterly as she rubbed her body clean, to write a concise dictionary of modern English as spoken by men. A compendium of male clichés that would correctly identify the meaning of 'I'll-just-lie-next-to-you-I-won't-touch-you-I-just-want-to-be-close-to-you' as 'Once I get into your bed I'll more than likely break down your resistance and get my way.' A phrase book that could translate expressions such as 'I've-never-felt-like-this-about-anyone-before' and 'God-you're-beautiful' into their plain English meanings: 'I haven't felt like this about anyone for at least three weeks' and 'God, I feel randy.'

The list of trite phrases – said with deep meaningful glances over a couple of glasses of wine – that had catapulted her into unsatisfactory affairs was endless.

She wasn't naïve in any other area of her life, in fact she was sharp and cynical about almost everything but men. And she was quite able to recognise a bastard when she saw one in someone else's life. She could see right through the manipulative selfishness of Toby, for instance, or the awful way in which Jon treated his succession of girlfriends, but when a man came into her own life her critical faculties were suspended.

She was rather relieved, when she emerged from the bathroom, to find that Eddie had quietly disappeared. She probably wouldn't hear from him for another six months and then find herself giving in as she had this morning.

The trouble was – and it was a trouble she knew she shared with a lot of other intelligent and accomplished women in their early thirties – she just wasn't drawn to the kind of caring, sharing men who meant what they said. And as she got older and became less able to compromise anyway, the number of men who crossed her path that were genuinely eligible became fewer and fewer. She couldn't think of one man, in the last couple of years, who had been halfway decent. The only men she had encountered who had measured up to her blueprint of Mr Right already had a Mrs Right (and two ex-Mrs Rights). And although she had much in her life that gave her joy and satisfaction, she felt, deeply unfashionable though such a thought was, that she was in some way incomplete without a man.

It was her mother's fault. Claire had been raised with the belief that her looks were her greatest asset. She had thick, naturally auburn hair, a perfect oval-shaped face and although she was tall and thin she had a bosom that Jon – the only man in the world that she could truly count as a good friend – always said gave her the dimensions of a 'blow-up doll'. Her mother had high hopes of her making a good marriage. From early childhood Claire had been instilled with the belief that the only real goal in life for a girl was a union with a good man. By which her mother meant someone rich with a high social status.

'Love and marriage, love and marriage, they go together like a horse and carriage,' her mother would croon to her when she was a little girl.

Her evident disappointment at her daughter's inability to make such a match had been one of the things that had prompted Claire to leave Canada and settle in Britain. That and the fact, as she would sometimes say with a brittle little laugh, that she had worked her way through the five hundred most eligible men in Toronto. Although it was doubtful that her mother would have regarded any of them as desirable in her sense of the word.

Now, returning to the bedroom, she attacked her bed as she had her body in the shower, pulling off the thick cotton sheets and throwing them into the linen basket in the corner of the room. The phone rang as she was opening the windows to allow in the warm morning air. It was Hattie, reminding her that she was taking Jimmy shopping in less than an hour.

'I hadn't forgotten. It'll probably be the highlight of my week,' she said.

'It'll be like *Pretty Woman* in reverse,' said Hattie wickedly, 'you taking the pretty man through the London equivalent of Rodeo Drive.'

Claire's first thought had been to take him to Versace because she had a feeling that Jimmy would look wonderful in those big, over-the-top jackets. But she had heeded Hattie's warning that she was not to make a spectacle of him, and besides, their agreed budget – £2500 – had to cover more than just a jacket and a couple of shirts.

'We're not dressing him for a film premiere or a rock concert,' Hattie had reminded her. 'He's not Elton John or Eric Clapton. We're dressing him for a new life in which he should be accepted as a man of worth. Not a man desperate to prove he's worth the price of a ghastly Versace suit . . .'

In the end Claire had agreed to go to Paul Smith, where the clothes had a more classic cut and the price tags were not quite so fearful.

Jimmy was bemused. He had only ever been shopping for clothes twice in his life. And both times his choice had been restricted to those stores in Newcastle – usually vast cut-price shops – that accepted the Provy cheques that were his nan's only means of payment.

Like most of the other kids on the Meadow Well Estate he had been dragged up in second-hand clothes or items bought through a savings scheme that the poorest families contributed to, paying a few pence each week and eventually accumulating enough money to receive the cheques – nothing more than vouchers really – that could be exchanged for clothes in the cheapest stores: track- or shell suits that were the very antithesis of the designer labels most of the lads coveted.

But this was something entirely different. The interior of the shop looked a little like Hattie's flat, he thought as he glanced nervously across at the racks of grey and black clothes illuminated by the funny phosphorescent light bulbs like those that covered the ceiling of her home.

'Can you measure him, please?' said Claire to an effete assistant as if Jimmy were a small child being fitted for new shoes.

The man raised an eyebrow quizzically as he examined the strange creature before him. Jimmy, aware of the extent of Toby's fury at finding him wearing his clothes the previous day, had gone back to his own things. Not the ones Hattie and Claire had thrown away after his bath but the ones he had retrieved from the left luggage box at King's Cross.

He was wearing a thick, coarse lumberjack shirt – in a hideous mix of yellow, black and purple – over a navy fleecy tracksuit the hood of which was pulled up over his head. He was horribly overdressed for summer – even an English summer – but his time on the streets had made him habitually wrap up as if for winter warmth all year round.

There was about Jimmy the nasty, lingering, musty smell

of clothes that had been worn and put away unwashed. The beauty that the women had glimpsed the day before had all but gone and the assistant approached him as he might a large pile of dog poo.

'And what size are we?' he said to Jimmy distastefully.

'Haddaway, man?' said a flustered Jimmy.

'What size are you, 38, 42?'

Jimmy looked uncertainly towards Claire.

'He wants to know what size you are,' she said very slowly.

'Medium,' said Jimmy, blushing slightly.

The assistant took a big gulp of air, held his breath and then went to put the tape measure round Jimmy's chest.

'Would *sir* take off his shirt?' he said, putting a sarcastic emphasis on the word 'sir'.

Jimmy gingerly removed the lumberjack top.

'And the hooded thing,' said the assistant scornfully.

Jimmy reached up and pulled the tracksuit top off his head revealing, beneath it, a greying string vest.

'Oh my, your Calvin Kleins accidentally slipped in with your mixed coloureds,' said the assistant with a sneering laugh.

'And the vest, Jimmy,' Claire ordered.

Jimmy pulled off the vest and it was as if the whole shop now held its breath. The eyes of every man – and every accompanying woman – were drawn to Jimmy's magnificently toned, if overly tattooed, body.

Even their assistant had, by now, warmed to the sight of *sir* and approached him with a great deal more enthusiasm than he had previously.

'Not medium at all, sir . . . LARGE,' he said incredulously as he looked at his tape measure.

'He needs a whole new wardrobe, Tony,' said Claire, noting the name tag on the man's lapel.

'I'm sure I can be of help,' said their assistant, changing

his tone, as he took in the sight of the man beneath the clothes, from officious to obsequious.

'He needs a suit that can take him anywhere, at least two good white shirts, a couple of ties, socks and some casual stuff,' said Claire.

'I see sir quite clearly now,' said Tony with an ingratiating smile as he glanced down at Jimmy's lower half. 'Inside leg measurements next,' he added with relish.

'Off with them, Jimmy,' said Claire.

'Here, man?' said Jimmy.

Tony took him off into a little cubicle at the back of the shop and ordered him to remove the fleecy tracksuit bottoms.

'He's like a walking Michelangelo's *David*. Only better endowed, if you get my drift,' Tony whispered to Claire when he emerged from the cubicle to select a series of jackets and trousers for Jimmy to try on.

'Really?' said Claire, unable to prevent herself from craning her neck to see over the top of the swing door of the changing room.

Jimmy had now adopted the expression and demeanour of a tailor's dummy, allowing himself to be dressed and adorned by not only Tony but several of the other assistants, who had gathered round to witness his remodelling.

'I *looooove* him in the grey flannel,' Tony said.

'Black leather,' suggested one of the other assistants softly but meaningfully.

'Yesss!' exclaimed Claire, taking hold of an impossibly expensive leather jacket and draping it across Jimmy's magnificent shoulders.

'Fab!' exclaimed Tony.

'As long as he doesn't open his mouth,' whispered Claire conspiratorially.

It was at this point that Jimmy began to worry about who was going to pay for all the clothes that had been selected for him. A huge pile of garments had been amassed in the last hour. It was clear that they didn't take Provy cheques in this place and even if they did he was skint.

'How much, like?' he asked nervously, indicating the latest addition to the mound – the soft leather jacket.

'It's £500 – but worth it. It's what I call the ubiquitous leather jacket. You'll be wearing it for ever,' said Tony.

Jimmy's face fell. Tony might just as well have said £8000, or £80,000 or £8 million. Any sum over a hundred was unimaginable to Jimmy.

'Eeee, man,' he said in panic.

'It's all right Jimmy, we're paying,' said Claire, magically producing a gold card that seemed to work like a Provy cheque, and securing for him with it a suit, two white shirts, two ties, two pairs of shoes as well as the white T-shirt, jeans, black leather jacket and boots that he was now wearing.

'Anyway,' she said, 'it's an investment when we win—' The moment she had said it she froze. God, he didn't know about the bet. If he walked out now Hattie would never forgive her. But although the look on Jimmy's face – which had appeared rather dazed the whole morning – intensified to a kind of puzzlement, he didn't question her. He just watched in awe as Claire's card was whisked through some machine, and a receipt appeared for her to sign.

'That'll do nicely, madam,' said Tony, indicating with his eyes his approval of the remodelled man before him.

'Won't it just?' said Claire as she dragged a dazed Jimmy from the shop.

Hattie looked up and smiled when Lisa came into the room.

'How are you today?' she asked.

The little girl returned her smile and went over to the shelf on which Hattie stored her collection of books.

'I thought today, Lisa, that you might tell me one of your stories . . . the ones your father told you from the Bible,' Hattie said tentatively, noting a look of disappointment on the child's face.

'But everyone knows those stories,' she said.

'I might have done once but I have forgotten them. Tell me one you like.'

'There's a lot of them. I could tell you one of the first ones. About Sodom and Gomorrah and Lot and his wife.'

'What happened in that story?'

'Well, Abraham told Lot to go to the East and he went to this place called Sodom. And then God said to Abraham that he was going to destroy the towns of Sodom and Gomorrah because the people were wicked and cruel and worthless. But he said that Lot and his wife would be saved. And two angels went to warn Lot to leave and he did. Only as he left the town the earth began to shake, the hills on either side of the towns erupted and there was hot ash and rocks. And then lava poured down and killed everyone.' She paused

'But not Lot and his wife?'

'Lot's wife turned round to look and she caught fire. And one of the angels said to Lot that it was her fault, that she should not have looked back. So Lot escaped and she turned into a pillar of salt,' Lisa said.

'Do you think that Lot should have tried to save his wife?'

'No,' said Lisa with a slightly condescending smile. 'Don't you see, she didn't have faith, she deserved to die? And anyway she was a woman.'

'And is that the end of the story?'

'Oh no, the story goes on and on. Then Sarah – who was Abraham's wife – had a baby when she was old and had white hair. The promised son. And he loved the baby Isaac and he was happy. And then God told Abraham to take his son to a mountain and offer him as a sacrifice. A burnt offering. And Abraham obeyed God.'

'You mean he killed the son he loved?'

'No, because just as he was going to kill him God sent a ram instead. So he cut the throat of the ram.'

'They aren't very happy stories, are they, Lisa, or funny?' Hattie said gently.

The child looked at her thoughtfully and then shook her head. 'I think I prefer Roald Dahl.'

'So do I,' said Hattie.

Then they talked about Lisa's father and how he had reinforced the messages that came from the ancient tales from the Old Testament. Women, he had told Lisa and her sister, had been the devil's instrument to tempt men since Adam and Eve lived in the Garden of Eden.

'Why do you think he said that?' Hattie asked.

'Because it was Eve that wanted the apple. And because women are concubines,' the child said as if she were explaining something terribly obvious.

'So your father preferred the boys in the family?' asked Hattie, aware that they might be about to touch on something important.

Lisa nodded.

'In what way?' she prompted gently.

'Well, he made the girls do things for him. Because he was the master,' Lisa said, her bright blue clear eyes looking up at Hattie with a tender vulnerability.

'What things, Lisa?' she asked in little more than a whisper.

'Those things,' said Lisa, looking down at the floor, afraid to meet Hattie's eyes.

'I don't understand, Lisa . . .'

'Touching us and making us do things . . . you know . . .' the girl said, fidgeting awkwardly in her chair.

At the end of the session, when Lisa left, Hattie felt that

she had made a major breakthrough. She had uncovered a background of psychological and sexual abuse that had been hidden from the authorities for years. And she had no doubt that in the weeks to come she would find further evidence of the agonies that Lisa had suffered at the hands of her father. Cruelty that he covered with this awful sanctimonious hypocrisy, this nonsense about the Good Book. With such a harsh father – backed up by such a cruel God – was it any wonder that the child had grown up with a strange moral code? Was it really surprising that – in one awful moment – she had turned from being victim to aggressor?

Phase two of Jimmy's transformation took place in a hair salon that was as different from the barber's shops of his boyhood as BHS was from Paul Smith.

A young, pretty woman sat him in a chair in front of a mirror and gave him a copy of a glossy magazine called *FHM* that was full of big pictures of lager, aftershave, semi-naked women and a lot of poncy men in the kind of clothes he was now wearing. Ten minutes later someone that Claire reverently called Moosh came and began to run a wide-tooth comb through Jimmy's matted blond hair. Jimmy decided that Moosh must be a lad even though he had a head of hair on him a bit like his nan's old wig: thick, shoulder-length and flicked up at the ends like a lassie. Jimmy twisted uncomfortably in his seat.

'Natural!' Moosh exclaimed after a few moments as if, for all the world, he had discovered the Holy Grail on the head of a customer.

He then began to confer with Claire, talking in a language that Jimmy couldn't make out, and now and again resorting to numbers.

'I could give him a number two,' Moosh said pensively. 'Or,' he said after a few minutes' thought, 'I could do an early Brad Pitt – the *River Runs Through It* look: parted at the side, layered at the back and full on the top.'

Claire nodded meekly and deferred to Moosh as if he were the master. Which, in his way, he was.

'It isn't,' said Moosh as he studied Jimmy's face in the mirror, 'as if he couldn't take a number two or even a number *one*. His bone structure is so good he could stand alopecia.'

Claire laughed nervously.

'But,' added Moosh as he ran his hands through Jimmy's dreadlocks, 'with hair like this that would be a waste. Wash him please, Sindy,' he shouted to his assistant.

Jimmy was led across the salon to the basin and had his hair washed – like a girl – leaning back over a sink. Sometime later, after Jimmy had been shampooed, conditioned and steam-cured, Moosh returned for the cut. Claire looked on anxiously as the scissors snipped through the matted pale blond mass.

He was still snipping, but with less decisive moves, an hour later. The floor beneath Jimmy's chair was covered in little wet clumps of thick blond hair.

By the time Moosh had blown the geometric cut dry, Jimmy was almost unrecognisable. He looked, Claire thought, like something out of the magazine that was propped open in front of him. The beautiful – slightly homoerotic – image of the boy in the Kouros ad or the model in the full-page ads for Calvin Klein jeans.

'Eeee, man,' Jimmy said uncertainly when he looked up into the mirror and caught sight of himself. Several of the other hairdressers – assistants and stylists – gathered round and murmured enthusiastically about the cut. Watching their reaction Jimmy's confidence in this odd new look began to grow. Putting his hands up to touch his hair – which had emerged an even paler blond – he smiled.

'I could use him,' Moosh said to Claire over Jimmy's

gleaming head. 'He's got it. Get some pictures taken and go and see this woman at Models One. He could be big, very big . . .'

Claire took the card that Moosh held out to her and smiled at Jimmy's reflection in the mirror. 'My goodness, Jimmy, wait till Hattie sees you,' she muttered as she, Moosh and the other hairdressers admired the reflection before them.

Chapter Eight

Hattie said nothing when Claire and Jimmy joined her for lunch. She was already sitting at their table in Deirdre's when the two of them arrived and she didn't miss the effect that Jimmy's new look had on the ladies who lunched around them. Little titters, craned necks and sighs greeted his journey from the door to the table.

Jimmy's blank but beautiful face lit up when he saw her and although she smiled warmly back, inside she could have wept. How could Claire have done this to him? She had turned him into a sort of walking, talking male accessory. Jimmy had been transformed into Barbie's Ken. His gleaming pale blond hair was coiffed into a contrived style which, along with the awful clothes, gave him the look of a gigolo. And a gay gigolo at that, she thought.

And while she was relieved to note that the unclean, musty smell had gone, what had replaced it was appalling. He was like some undignified lapdog, some giant version of a miniature poodle, who had been clipped and was now sprayed with a very strong and pungent cover-up scent. Like the sort of thing that people sprayed in their loos – Neutradol she thought it was called. Claire had Neutradoled Jimmy.

'What d'ya think, like?' Jimmy indicated the soft leather jacket he was wearing.

'It looks good on you, Jimmy,' Hattie said, trying to sound sincere because she didn't want to offend him.

'Everything does,' said Claire. 'And you'll never guess, Hattie, Moosh has already said he'd like to use Jimmy

92

for his next show. And he's given us the name of a photographer he knows will just love him. He said if he signed on with a good agency he could be earning in four figures within a week.' Claire punched the air behind Jimmy's back to indicate privately to Hattie that the bet was already won.

'A model?' said Hattie incredulously, looking across at Jimmy.

'You'd be surprised. The top male models these days earn a good whack. And Jimmy has got something really special about him,' Claire added reflectively.

'But does Jimmy really want to work as a model?' Hattie asked sceptically 'I mean, there's more to life than money.'

'That's rich, darling, coming from you. It's all very well for you to turn up your nose at Jimmy being given the opportunity to be the dream double-page spread – money has never been a problem for you. Don't please forget where we found Jimmy,' said Claire testily.

'We can talk about that later. Let's order, shall we?'

A waitress came over with menus and Claire ordered a bottle of white wine.

'What do you want to drink, Jimmy?' Hattie asked.

He glanced round the room and noted that one or two of the few men present were sipping what looked like beer straight out of the bottles.

'I brought me own, like,' he said with a grin that revealed the missing front tooth and restored a little of his old character to his face. Delving into one of the carrier bags – the one containing his old clothes – he produced from the pocket of his lumberjack shirt a can of Newcastle Brown Ale. Ripping the ring off he raised it to his mouth and began to drink.

'Jimmy! They'll probably charge corkage,' said Claire with a derisory laugh.

'Ee, man, if they can sup from the bottle,' said Jimmy, gesturing towards the men he'd noticed earlier, 'why not straight from the can, like?'

He relaxed a little then, removing the black leather jacket and placing it carefully on the back of his chair. Beneath it, Hattie noticed with alarm, he was wearing a tight, white T-shirt that perfectly exposed his six-pack stomach and the elaborate tattoos on his arms.

'We've decided to keep the tattoos,' Claire whispered to Hattie. 'Everyone has them these days. They have become very déclassé for the lower class and very classy for people like us.'

There was, Hattie thought, something rather, well, homo-erotic about this new Jimmy. If the women around them had been interested in his muscled, tattooed perfection, the men in the restaurant – several of the waiters and a few of their fellow diners – were clearly entranced by his appearance. He looked rather like those men who appeared, often naked to the waist, in aftershave ads that appeared in the more iffy of the men's fashion magazines.

Their waitress came back and put on the table a small ceramic bowl filled with flavoured oil and a basket of fresh ciabatta. Jimmy watched with fascination as Hattie and Claire dipped pieces of the bread in the communal pot of oil and then ate it. It must, he thought, be some funny southern version of bread and dripping, a particular favourite of his from home.

'Eee, man, this is reet good,' he said, trying it.

'And it's free, Jimmy,' said Hattie.

'Free?' he said incredulously.

'Although of course there is no such thing as free when you lunch at Deirdre's,' said Claire. 'It'll be on the bill somewhere.'

'Are you ready to order now?' asked the waitress, her eyes never leaving Jimmy.

Hattie was immediately aware that as Jimmy now examined the pretentious – and mainly Italian – menu he was experiencing fresh waves of the culture shock he must have been suffering all morning.

'What would you like to eat, Jimmy?'

He looked blankly from the menu to Hattie and shrugged his massive shoulders.

'Red meat, probably,' said Claire. 'Northern men like meat, don't you?'

'Aye, man,' said Jimmy.

'There's a fillet of Hereford beef served with ginger and onions,' said Hattie helpfully.

'Is there styek like?' he said.

'That is steak, Jimmy. It's hand-reared so that it isn't riddled with BSE,' explained Claire. 'I think I might have a buffalo mozzarella salad.'

'Eee, man, *buffalo* . . .' said Jimmy, to the hilarity of Claire.

'No, Jimmy, it's a kind of cheese,' she said before turning back to the waitress to customise her order as was her rather tiresome way in restaurants. 'And could you make sure that there is no dressing – just a dash of fresh lemon juice. And no tomatoes. And then I'll have the plain char-grilled chicken without the roasted vegatables or the linguine.'

'I'll just have a main course – the pan-fried scallops,' said Hattie.

'What's that, then?' Jimmy asked.

'Fish, Jimmy.'

'What, with chips, like?'

'Well, not exactly . . . but we could have some fries on the side.'

He ordered it anyway, partly, she thought, because he trusted her choice more than that of Claire. He felt, she sensed, safer when she was around. She didn't scoff at him in the way that Claire sometimes did. And she didn't regard him – as Claire clearly did – as an amusing new plaything. Hattie was trying hard to look beyond the obvious at the real Jimmy. Who, she suspected, even without his striking good looks was very much a man of worth.

'Can I smoke, hinny?' he said, cautiously looking around him, already aware that the habit was – in Hattie's world – regarded as slightly obscene.

'If I can too,' she said, gratefully taking a cigarette and lighting up.

Then Claire began to tell Hattie about their experiences that morning, the way in which they had won round the camp assistant in Paul Smith. 'When we arrived he looked at Jimmy as if he were a bad smell beneath his nose and by the time we left he was like a fucking dog on heat,' she screeched as if Jimmy were not there.

Jimmy was clearly disappointed when the waitress brought his main course – the scallops artfully arranged alongside fennel leaves and finely chopped spring onions. But he cheered up when a big bowl of chips arrived, this time accompanied by a ceramic pot filled with what looked to him to be salad cream but was, Hattie said, 'aïoli'.

He looked so hungry at the end that Hattie suggested pudding, ordering, for both of them, slices of mascarpone torte which, Jimmy declared with satisfaction, tasted just like 'stottie-kyek'.

'What's stottie cake, Jimmy?' asked Claire.

'I think it's a dish that is indigenous to the North East,' said Hattie.

Ten minutes later, thankfully just after they had asked for the bill, Arabella walked into the crowded restaurant. The very last person in the world that Hattie wanted to see.

'Hat darling!' she shrieked as she abandoned her friend – another trust fund babe with a similar media profile – and rushed over to their table. 'How the hell are you?'

There was a brief silence as Arabella's eyes focused fully on Jimmy.

'Introductions, Hattie?' Arabella said. 'Who's this gorgeous creature you've got with you?'

'Arabella this is Jimmy, Jimmy – er . . .' It occurred to Hattie then that none of them had any idea of Jimmy's surname.

'Ryan . . .' supplied Jimmy.

'Jimmy, this is Arabella Sykes, my sister,' Hattie said quickly.

'I seen your picture in the paper, like,' said Jimmy.

'And you, Arabella,' interjected Claire, 'will soon be seeing Jimmy's picture in the paper.'

'I don't doubt it,' said Arabella, picking up Jimmy's big butch hand and raising it to her lips in a gesture that made Claire shriek with laughter. 'Where *did* you find him?'

'In a shop doorway in Covent Garden,' confided an animated Claire. 'We just tripped over him.'

'Aren't you the lucky ones?' said Arabella with a tinkling, insincere laugh that set Hattie's nerves on edge. 'And aren't you the dark horse, Hattie?'

'It's actually quite a serious project I've taken on professionally,' said Hattie, a little pompously. 'Jimmy is the case study for a paper I am doing.'

'Shall we join you?'

'No, actually, Arabella,' said Hattie in a rather territorial manner, 'we're just leaving.'

'Another time then.' Arabella gave another tinkling giggle. 'I'll catch up with you *later*.'

Not if I can help it, thought Hattie. The idea of her sister – whose motives would be even more suspect than Claire's – getting her manicured hands on Jimmy was so appalling that she decided to accelerate their departure by paying the bill in cash.

''Bye, Bella,' she said less that three minutes later, as she ushered Claire and Jimmy out into the street.

''Bye, Hattie,' Arabella replied, wondering why her sister was in such a terrible hurry to get her odd new male friend out of the restaurant.

Jon decided to drop in on Claire on his way back from a meeting at a hotel a few hundred yards away. He still felt, quite inappropriately he supposed, that he could call in on her whenever he wanted. She ran her PR business from her mews flat and he comforted himself with the fact that she was usually as pleased to see him as he was her.

It was five years since they had been a couple. They had lived together for two years, the longest period that either of them, before or since, had stayed with one person.

Claire was, in fact, his only true female friend, probably because (as Claire herself always claimed) she was the only woman he had ever gone out with that was his equal. All the women – or to be more precise, *girls* – that Jon had subsequently been involved with conformed to a dreadful dumb bimboesque stereotype. He was, he now acknowledged, drawn to women for all the wrong reasons. The biggest wrong reason being their looks, the second biggest their unavailability – he was a magnet to married women.

Time and again he would fall into a liaison – few of them lasted long enough to be affairs – that would offer him a brief period of excitement followed, rather speedily, by a terrible disillusionment.

Claire was the only woman who was constant in his life. And the only one in whom he could confide, he thought, as she answered the door and led him into her kitchen. He had never managed to build a rapport with any other women – not Hattie whom, he sensed, disapproved of him; not his female colleagues; not one of the countless girlfriends he had been involved with since he had split with Claire.

'Do you want to stay for supper?' she said, noting in his face his need for company.

He nodded and she handed him a bottle of white wine and told him to open it whilst she rummaged round for some food.

'It'll be pot luck. I've not got much in,' she said, pulling from the fridge an assortment of leftovers which she proceeded to throw into a giant caesar salad.

'What's wrong, Jon? You look even more doleful than usual,' she said as they sat opposite each other at her little kitchen table.

'Life, I suppose. There's this woman I've been involved with and as usual she wants me to *commit*. You know it's funny, isn't it, how the word "commit" is usually associated with bad and negative things – commit a crime, commit suicide, commit murder? Yet women seem to think of it – when it involves a relationship – as a positive thing. For me it's a terribly negative word. I'm not going to commit to Alison any more than I am going to commit suicide or murder.'

'But if the avoiding of commitment makes you so suicidal maybe you should bow to the inevitable,' said Claire. 'What's this Alison like, then?'

'Young, pretty, slender, sweet-natured . . .' Jon said.

'BUT,' said Claire, who secretly delighted in Jon's inability to commit. Deep down, although she didn't like to examine her motives too closely, she couldn't stand the idea of Jon finding a woman to whom he could commit.

'Exactly, Claire, BUT she bores me. BUT she doesn't make me laugh. BUT she doesn't stimulate me.'

'Or is it just BUT the timing is wrong?'

'The timing will always be wrong. I can't envisage ever finding my perfect woman.' He looked moodily at Claire.

'Instead of a Miss Right a series of Miss All Right Buts . . .'

'Apart from you, Claire, there's never really been a woman who has touched me,' Jon said, noting how attractive she looked bustling round her kitchen this evening.

'That's dangerous talk, Jon,' she said sharply, remembering the situation she had got in the night before with Eddie. She had been very careful to keep Jon as her friend.

There had been moments over the years since their breakup when they had found themselves on the verge of falling into bed again. But Claire had been determined not to spoil the friendship they had established. In an odd way Jon was the most important man in her life, more important to her than the men with whom she became temporarily besotted. She couldn't risk what they had over something as unimportant – if temporarily all-encompassing – as sex.

'Is there someone special at the moment then?' he said, wondering, as he watched her clearing up their plates, how he would feel if she had found someone. He knew it was selfish, childish even, but he didn't like the idea of Claire being seriously involved in a relationship. There was something reassuring about the fact that she seemed as incapable as he of finding a permanent partner. At least, that was what he told himself.

'I'm thinking of taking the pledge,' she said.

'You mean you've had another unsatisfactory affair?' he said.

'Not quite affair. Let's just say I've been used again.'

'Want to tell me about it?'

'Oh, I met this man at a dinner party and I misinterpreted his signals. Thought it would be OK, ended up in bed and then discovered I was nothing more than a decoy duck – or perhaps I should say a decoy fuck – for an affair he was having with the woman who gave the dinner party . . .' She paused for a moment and then ploughed on, 'Which would probably have been all right if I hadn't found myself in a similar situation this week.'

'You're always telling me that I'm drawn to the wrong women. I suppose it wouldn't be possible that you had the same trouble with men?' Jon suggested.

'Jon, I don't need you to tell me *that*. I've decided from now on that I'm going to break the mould. I'm going to go for a different kind of man.'

'But I thought you thought all men were the same: cowards, liars, cheats, amoral bastards?' he said with a smile.

'Perhaps they don't start out like that; perhaps that happens later on.'

'Meaning?'

'A younger man,' she said.

'And have you got one in your sights?'

'Sort of, yes. Jimmy, you know, the homeless boy,' she said, glancing at her reflection in the mirror as she ran her hands self-consciously through her thick auburn hair. 'You mustn't say anything to Toby or Hattie but I find him dreadfully attractive.'

'Jimmy?' Jon was incredulous.

'God, Jon, it's fascinating to see the changes in him,' Claire said. 'And the extraordinary thing is that I am gripped by the whole business. It is rather like moulding our own man. I can't really explain it but it is something rather alien to women, something I never imagined I would be part of. I mean, you are always hearing about older men taking ignorant young girls and turning them into the perfect mate. But generally women don't aspire to doing that with a man. Sure, they sometimes want to change a man – tame him, as it were – usually because he's a total bastard. But the idea of a blank canvas that you could paint to order is not something I had ever thought to do.'

'What on earth do you mean? Are you planning to turn him into some kind of toyboy?' said Jon, feeling rather alarmed by Claire's tone. The bet, after all, had been about turning that destitute boy into a man of worth, not some kind of sexual plaything.

'Oh Jon, don't be silly. I'm not quite old enough for a toyboy yet, and anyway he's only nine years younger than me. But being involved in changing Jimmy has made me begin to understand why exactly older women get involved with younger men. I think it's got a lot to do with the fact that older men are such awful chauvinists. I think they find men younger than themselves more caring and sharing than their own contemporaries. And more available, of course, because of all those demographic changes. Half a million more men under thirty than women. But I don't think the idea of teaching a man is as much a part of female physiology as it is for men to want to teach – to form – women.'

'I suppose it's more of a male fantasy. To find some beautiful young thing that you could educate and form into your perfect mate. And maybe, like everything else, it's a male fantasy that you postfeminist women are now ready to reverse and buy into – only I can't believe that Jimmy could possibly be the subject of any woman's sexual fantasy,' Jon said, feeling, for the first time in he didn't know how long, a little jealous of the idea of Claire's interest in a man.

'Do you remember that friend of yours Charlie, the one who picked up that young girl, Susie, on holiday? Do you remember how I could never understand why he did that? Well, all of a sudden I can relate to him,' said Claire.

'I meant to tell you, he's marrying her.'

'That doesn't surprise me at all,' Claire answered thoughtfully. 'She probably has the same innocent appeal as Jimmy. And she's certainly got a body to match his. Do you know, today when we were having lunch there wasn't a woman in Deirdre's who didn't desire him. Charlie probably gets the same reaction from other men when they see him dining out with Susie and I dare say it's made him determined to keep her for himself.'

'Are we talking about the same man here? You can't seriously be saying that you've transformed him into the male equivalent of Charlie's Susie in just a couple of days?' Jon felt unaccountably irritated by the idea. He had certainly never bargained for this kind of reaction when he had challenged Hattie and Claire to the wager.

'Of course not, but there is *something* there, Jon, and it isn't just his face and body,' Claire said.

'And Hattie? Is she as starry-eyed about this boy as you?' he asked, his face betraying his disbelief.

'Well, you know Hattie. Her emotional life is a bit of a mystery. She's stuck with Toby for all these years and they seem to have such a plodding, cold relationship. I don't think that Hattie is a very sensually aware person, do you? No, I think it's me that will have to teach Jimmy how to appreciate the erotic pleasures of polite society,' she said with a wicked laugh.

Jon stood up and put his empty glass on the worktop. It was time, he thought, that he left. For some reason their conversation that night had disturbed him and he departed feeling even more depressed than he had been when he'd arrived.

There was a dreadful smell pervading the flat when Hattie and Jimmy got home late that afternoon. A putrid, awful rotting odour that hit her the moment she turned the key in the door and walked over the threshold to be greeted by a barking and snarling Rex.

'Doon, Rex, doon boy,' said Jimmy.

Hattie's first thought was that she had been burgled. The whole of the open-plan area was in a state of devastation – books, papers, cushions, plants all messed together on the hardwood floor.

But it wasn't, of course, burglars, it was Rex. In his desperation to get out of the flat he had not only pulled down blinds and upset furniture, he had ripped fabrics and broken the few china and glass ornaments that had adorned her home. Worse, he had clearly eaten something that had upset him – the feather stuffing from the cushions, perhaps, or the large wax church candles – and subsequently left several dark and stinking piles of mess dotted around the flat.

'He's reet upset, he is,' said Jimmy, concerned more for his pet than Hattie's beautiful flat. 'I should never ha left him aloon, like.'

'We'll have to clean it up before Toby gets in,' said Hattie, panicking at the thought of her overly neat – Claire called him anally retentive – partner coming across this terrible mess. She had no doubt that if he saw the havoc the dog had caused he would throw him and Jimmy back on the street. And although she had, in her more assertive moments, told him that if he didn't like it he could leave she was, in truth, terrified of making the break with Toby. He represented her security in much the way, she supposed, that Rex represented Jimmy's.

It took them a while to get the place in any sort of order. Quite a lot of the damage was superficial, but some of it was so bad that things had to be thrown away. Hattie removed several black bin liners full of chewed books, dismembered cushions and broken glass – carefully dragging them out of the flat to the service area in the basement so that Toby wouldn't discover the evidence. It occurred to her then that it would be better if Jimmy and Rex were not at home when her partner got back that night.

'Look, Jimmy, you go out and take Rex with you. Here, take a key so that you can get back in later,' she said before resuming her desperate cleanup.

By the time that Hattie heard Toby's key in the door

she was almost certain she had covered – and in some cases washed and disinfected – Rex's tracks. She had even managed to put on some lipstick. Her eagerness to ensure that he didn't look too closely at the slightly more minimal state of their minimalist flat had even led her to sling a chicken in the oven. So what greeted Toby's homecoming was not the foul smell of the dog's accidents but slowly roasting juices.

'Hello, darling,' she said. 'Good day?'

Toby looked at her, a little taken aback by her unusual enthusiasm at his arrival home. 'So-so. I think Tom Charter has taken against me since that dinner. He was looking at me in a very strange manner today,' he said as he went to the fridge, pulled out a bottle of white wine and poured out two glasses.

'I'm sure you're imagining it. I think he enjoyed the evening, even if the ending was a little, well, sudden,' said Hattie with an uncharacteristically ingratiating smile.

Toby walked into the living area and sat down on the sofa. 'There's something different, Hattie. What is it?' he said.

'Well, Jimmy's out,' she said with another sweet smile.

'Have you moved the furniture around or something?' Toby looked around the room as if making some mental inventory.

'Oh I expect it's Sandrino. You know what she's like. She's had another spring clean,' said Hattie nervously. 'Why don't you go and have a shower and I'll get the supper on the table?'

Toby looked across at her fondly. She was behaving, this evening, very much like his idea of the perfect partner. She had put lipstick on, which was unusual; she had made an effort to cook for him and the flat was so gleamingly clean that he thought he could almost detect the aroma of Parozone beneath the tempting smell of cooking chicken.

This was how it must have been for his father, he thought as he undid his tie and put his arm around her, coming back to an ordered home with a dutiful and respectful wife waiting expectantly for the master's return. Why, she was even wearing an apron over that dress he bought her in Italy last summer.

'OK, darling,' he said, ruffling her hair as he got up to make his way upstairs.

Hattie felt relieved. She had pulled it off, she thought as she went over to baste the chicken and put on some vegetables.

'Jesus Christ!' Toby screamed from upstairs.

It had never occurred to Hattie to check their bedroom. She ran up the stairs to find Toby standing by the open doors of his wardrobe looking in horror at what had happened within.

Clearly this was where Rex's handiwork that day had started. The dog had clawed down and chewed up Toby's Gieves & Hawkes suits, he had pulled his shirts off their hangers and lifted his leg over the resultant mess. Beneath this sopping heap – they discovered when they moved them away – Rex had left his most dramatic calling card in Toby's prize pair of pale tan suede Gucci loafers.

'God, they're ruined!' said Toby.

It was almost as if, Hattie thought as she began to clear up this second scene of destruction, Rex had deliberately tried to upset Toby. None of Hattie's clothes had been disturbed. In fact, almost everything that Rex had chewed up or fouled that day belonged to her partner. She knew that dogs had a very strong sense of smell and it occurred to her that it was just possible that the whole thing was, well, personal. That Rex had maliciously set out to attack Toby.

She worked hard that night to ensure that Toby felt no lingering resentment towards Jimmy and Rex. Having cleared up his wardrobe, loaded the washing machine with salvageable clothes and cleaned out the loafers as best she could, she then managed to serve up dinner with a welcoming and compliant smile.

After two bottles of wine and a great deal of placatory chatter she even managed to loudly seduce him, safe in the knowledge that neither Jimmy, nor the malevolent Rex, could hear.

Despite her exhaustion she kept herself awake until she heard – sometime after midnight she guessed – the comforting sound of the front door opening as the boy and his dog slipped back in the flat. She fell asleep wondering which was going to be the harder task of the next couple of months – transforming Jimmy and winning the bet or ensuring that she didn't lose Toby.

Chapter Nine

In Claire's native North America orthodontic work was an essential part of growing up. As a child she had been subjected to a series of torturous procedures – at one stage being forced to wear a steel brace round her entire head at night – in order that she might achieve the perfect smile.

And having spent the best part of two years with a mouth full of metal she was therefore familiar with the terms that dazzled Jimmy, a couple of days later, as he lay in the big chair in Barry Driver, 'dentist to the stars'', Knightsbridge surgery.

Barry had been in equal parts appalled and fascinated by the interior of Jimmy's mouth.

'Do you know it would probably be possible to write a sociology paper from looking closely at this man's incisors,' he said, following Claire's lead and talking as if Jimmy himself were not there.

'In what way exactly?' enquired Claire.

'Well, the decay is indicative of a bad, sugar-based diet, poor hygiene and, I suspect, the kind of grinding poverty that I don't see in this part of London. What's more, Jimmy is one of Thatcher's children: denied free milk in the early years of his school life – which would explain the calcium deficiency – and, with the onset of her cutbacks to the NHS, unlikely to have been anywhere near a dental surgery in his life. And to be quite frank with you I doubt he's even seen a toothbrush, let alone fluoride drops or anti-decay toothpaste. As a result you have the mouth of what could be medieval man. No fillings, enormous cavities, severe overcrowding and, at the same time, several missing molars. Christ, the Royal College would love a look at this.'

He was right: Jimmy had never been to a dentist before.

'Me nan pulled out me teeth when I was little,' he said by way of explanation.

'Including the front left incisor?' Barry asked.

'No, me mam knocked that out of me head when she caught me skiving once,' said Jimmy, dribbling a little from the effects of keeping his mouth open for so long.

He had been nervous when he arrived. Dentists were like bogey men in the North East, called in only as a last resort and regarded with fear, suspicion and loathing by most of the kids growing up on the Meadow Well Estate. But this man seemed OK and his surgery was a little like Jimmy imagined the interior of a space craft to look – all big machines, stainless steel and, in the middle, the chair that could double as a sleep capsule from a sci-fi movie: a vast perspex bed that rose, fell and tilted at the touch of Barry's foot. Above him, on the ceiling, there was a bank of TV screens showing cartoons to the accompaniment of loud rock music. Jimmy couldn't now understand why he had been so frightened.

'Can I used him as a case study?' Barry asked with mounting excitement as he prepared to take moulds of Jimmy's mouth.

'Of course,' Claire answered for Jimmy.

'No one will believe this. I could give an entire lecture tour on this mouth,' Barry added.

'So what are you going to do?' Claire asked.

'Well, it's difficult to know where to start. There's not much point starting on the fillings yet. They'll probably take days. I'll take this mould and work out what we can do to make the whole thing look better. And we'll start with a temporary front tooth. And then I'll get the hygienist to have a start at the cleaning process. You could leave him here for the rest of the day. Pick him up at about six – and please, take that dog with you.' Barry ushered Claire and an unwilling Rex out of the surgery.

Hattie was very apprehensive about meeting Lisa that day. She sensed that their sessions were edging closer and closer to the point at which they might finally be able to talk about the child's crime.

Hattie didn't want to hear the disclosures that she knew would come, she didn't want to address the awful details of what had happened. She had read the transcripts of the statements that Lisa had made to the police – in the presence of her mother and father – in which she had weepingly confessed to having led the little girl from the playground. But since then, in the weeks in which she had been seeing the child Hattie had somehow pushed that knowledge from her mind.

It had been so much easier to talk about Lisa's life. To discover – as she knew she would – the difficulties of her life within her enclosed family. The manner in which she and her siblings were prevented from mixing with other children. The rigid system of discipline administered within the home. The overbearing and perverted religious beliefs of the father that had been used to justify the sexual abuse he perpetrated against his daughters. And about the move the family had made from their native Leeds to a sprawling North London estate just a few months before the crime.

Lisa came in and smiled at Hattie. She was dressed, as she had been on every occasion that Hattie had seen her, like a model child from the past, a fifties vision of the perfect, prim, pretty little girl. Neat, ordered and sweetly smiling.

A number of things baffled Hattie: why, for instance, the teachers at Lisa's primary school hadn't picked up on her isolation; the absence of any previous acts of cruelty to other children – especially her siblings; the fact that any abuse had remained undetected over the years.

But then, of course, Lisa did not have the usual profile of an abused child. She was part of a traditional – not to say God-fearing – family: the mother staying at home to raise the four children – albeit in an austere, materially poor environment – whilst the father went out to work. Their upbringing had been nothing like that of the other kids on the estate they moved to, who had been been exposed to the worst aspects of popular culture, video nasties, cable TV, red-top tabloids. Lisa and her brothers and sister had not even had a television. And while their contemporaries spent their weekends roaming the streets looking for trouble, Lisa had been in prayer meetings at their church.

To outsiders – to school teachers, neighbours and social workers – Lisa's family must have seemed to have all those old-fashioned values that were horribly absent in the community in which they lived. But appearances, Hattie thought as she glanced again at the little girl, were sometimes very deceptive.

And when, finally, Lisa began to talk about what had happened on that day, all Hattie's theories about how and why this child had misinterpreted the difference between right and wrong were confirmed. It all led back, inevitably, to her father.

'Did you make any friends in your new home, Lisa?' Hattie asked.

'At church,' Lisa said.

'Yes, but outside the church – at school, the children who lived nearby – did you make some friends?'

'My father said they were heathens,' she said.

'Heathens?'

'Like the people in Sodom and Gomorrah, remember?' she said, looking at Hattie intently.

'But they were just children . . .' began Hattie.

'It doesn't matter. Don't you know about original sin?' said Lisa.

'Tell me about it.'

'Well, it means that even babies are sinners. They are born sinners,' said Lisa.

Hattie was silent, wondering where this was leading.

'Don't you see?' said Lisa. 'I tried to tell her about God absolving her sins. I tried to baptise her, to take away the sin. But she kept screaming and screaming.'

'And?' said Hattie gently.

'And then I got cross. I got so cross because she wouldn't stop screaming and it was like she was mad, possessed. And then I held her under the water . . .' Lisa said, and for the first time she was overcome with tears. 'I only wanted to save her for God . . .' she said, between sobs.

Hattie didn't know what to say, how to react to what Lisa had revealed. She looked at the child, at her pinched, pretty face and she wondered at the dreadful things that were done in the name of God.

When Claire and Rex arrived back at Barry Driver's surgery that evening, Jimmy was sitting waiting in reception with a clutch of accessories given him by the dentist: a packet of Flossettes – dental floss mounted onto sticks that could be slid between the teeth – some fluoride drops, two toothbrushes – one thick one for general cleaning and a thinner one for reaching into smaller spaces – some disclosing tablets and a large tube of Colgate Total.

He had been particularly taken with the disclosing tablets which, with the aid of a little hand mirror, enabled him to see how well he had cleaned his teeth. And as they left the building to make their way back to Hattie's flat he attempted to demonstrate to a startled Claire exactly how they worked.

'All the germs and, like, *plaque* that you can't see show

up,' he told her as if he were demonstrating a magic trick.

'Yes, Jimmy,' said Claire with an indulgent smile. 'We'd better get a cab back to Hattie's; we'll be late for supper.'

'A black cab?' he said with enthusiasm, insisting, when she said yes, on standing waving his arms in the street until a vacant taxi stopped.

'How was Rex?' he asked Claire when the three of them had clambered into the cab.

'I took him home with me and, really, he wasn't so bad. He was a bit territorial about one of my clients and he did need to go out every half an hour but actually I quite like him. What about you? Did it hurt at the dentist?'

'Nah, man,' he said, grinning so that she could see his dreadful teeth, now marginally less discoloured and disfiguring.

She was glad she had accepted Hattie's invitation to supper. She was totally engrossed in Jimmy's conversion from street boy to man of the world, and the more time she spent with him the more she liked him. She knew, too, that she was doing Hattie a favour since, in the days following Rex's disgraceful fouling of the flat, it had become easier for Jimmy and Toby to get along if a neutral person were around.

'Eee, man,' Jimmy said with a big smile of pride when an exhausted-looking Hattie opened the door for them. 'Barry said me mouth was great, like.'

'He said, Hattie,' said Claire, raising her eyebrows to her friend out of Jimmy's sight, 'that he had never seen anything like it. "The mouth of medieval man" were the words he used. He's going to use Jimmy as a case study.'

Aren't we all? thought Hattie as she made her way back into the kitchen to get on with the supper. Jimmy was, she supposed, emerging as the ultimate specimen of primitive man: unformed, barely educated and totally unused to the so-called niceties of contemporary society. And yet, for all that, there was a purity about him. For all the probable bleakness and brutality of his childhood and despite all the time he had spent on the streets, he was somehow unsullied by life. He was almost, and she hesitated to use the word, virginal.

She had no idea if Jimmy was a virgin. It was unlikely, given the nature of his upbringing and his undeniable beauty. But he was certainly naïve, and not once since she had first encountered him had he said anything coarse or vulgar about a woman. In fact, he seemed to have genuine respect for women. He would be, she thought with a jolt, the most wonderful lover.

She didn't want to dwell too much on Jimmy's sexuality. To her, his physical presence as she watched him talking to Claire was astonishing and somehow unnerving. She was a little frightened of the way in which Jimmy had emerged in the few days, and more than a little afraid of her own reactions to him.

She went to the fridge and got out a bottle of white wine and a can of Newcastle Brown – she had bought a crate especially for Jimmy – and went over to join them, pouring Claire and herself a glass of wine and handing Jimmy the can.

'Man, that's reet good of you,' he said, his face lighting up at the sight of his favourite beer.

'How does it taste, Jimmy?' said Claire in what Hattie thought was a rather coquettish manner.

'Try some, hinny,' said Jimmy, handing the opened can to Claire.

Claire raised the can to her mouth but her eyes did not leave Jimmy.

'Good,' she said provocatively, licking her lips and giving the can back. 'I think I'll pass on the wine, Hattie, and join Jimmy in the Newcastle Brown,' she added, pronouncing Newcastle Brown in an awful imitation of his accent.

'Get yourself a can then, Claire,' said Hattie wearily. 'There's a few in the fridge . . .'

By the time that Toby arrived home, a little over an hour later, Hattie was feeling quite anxious about the way in which Claire seemed to be moving in on Jimmy. And for once she was quite relieved to see her boyfriend and rushed over to greet him with a kiss.

'Supper's ready,' she said.

She looked beautiful, he thought, her face slightly flushed from cooking and her thick dark hair falling around her shoulders. However much he resented the presence of the dreadful duo, Jimmy and Rex, Toby was aware that this project of hers was doing her good. She had regained the enthusiasm for life he had found so appealing when he had first met her, which – he didn't know why – she seemed for the past few months to have lost.

He would, he decided, be more tolerant towards this Jimmy because doing so would make Hattie happy. It couldn't do him any harm to be a little less hostile to the bloke, even if he did find him irritating. And indirectly it could benefit him, he thought, remembering the way in which their sex life had picked up of late. And the suppers – when had Hattie last volunteered to cook him a meal before Jimmy arrived on the scene?

It was almost as if Jimmy were her child, Toby thought as he watched her bustling around in the kitchen. Perhaps that was what was missing from her life, some outlet other than her work for her maternal instincts. Maybe it was time they had a baby.

'Food's ready, everyone,' she called.

Toby sat down expectantly. He had always liked his food, and Hattie, whilst never usually that keen to cook, knew exactly the kind of things he liked. Nouveau international cuisine, he called it, an eclectic mix of all the different ethnic foods that had, in the last few years, become the staple diet of people of his age, class and financial status. Thai, Italian, French, Caribbean, Mexican and even – with its new fashionableness and political correctness – South African food. He was, therefore, rather surprised to find that tonight Hattie had reverted to what might be called old-style English cuisine.

'Sausages?' he said incredulously as she brought a frying pan to the table and began to prong out the big brown bangers, swimming in what was clearly *not* extra virgin olive oil, straight onto their plates. Worse, she then produced a large bowl of mashed potatoes – tetties Jimmy called them – which, with some pride, she claimed had come out of a packet.

'It's Jimmy's favourite,' she said by way of explanation.

'But Christ, Hattie, do you know what they make sausages from?'

'Pork,' said Jimmy, confident for once that he had got the right answer.

'But what part of the pork, Jimmy?' said Toby.

'The parts we normally don't reach,' said Claire with a girlish giggle.

And in place of the usual smart array of relishes and dressings there was, instead, an odd collection of mass-market condiments – Branston pickle, HP Sauce, Heinz tomato ketchup, salad cream, and some Colman's mustard.

'Toby, you are such a petit bourgeois,' said Hattie with feeling. 'If you didn't come from such a miserable middle-class family you wouldn't regard bangers and mash with such disdain. One of my greatest memories of my grandfather, the fifth Earl,' she added turning to Jimmy, 'was sharing a sausage and mash supper with him in the Great Hall . . .'

'Tastes good to me,' said Claire, raising her fourth can of Newcastle Brown to her mouth.

'Eee, lass, it's good,' said Jimmy as Hattie produced the final *pièce de résistance* to the meal – a piping hot pan of baked beans.

Toby had indigestion before he had even raised his fork to his mouth. It was one thing to be more tolerant of this cuckoo at his table – allowing him to share a civilised meal with them – but quite another to descend to his level. Besides, Hattie knew his stomach couldn't tolerate fried or fatty foods. And what they had here, he thought as he probed the contents of his plate, was both fatty and fried (with knobs of butter on).

'I think I'll pass on this,' he said, pushing the plate away from him.

'Toby, why are you so incapable of change or compromise?' asked Hattie in an unaccountably hard voice.

'Look, for Christ's sake, Hattie, I think I've done more than enough compromising since he arrived,' Toby replied, 'and I absolutely draw the line at this muck.'

'Please yourself, Toby,' she said as he got up, went to the fridge and returned with a crust of ciabatta (which had been replaced on the table that night by white, sliced Mother's Pride) and some goat's cheese which he began to eat with a martyred expression on his sour face.

'Iny more, hinny?' Jimmy asked enthusiastically.

'Well, there's Toby's plate,' said Hattie warmly. 'I don't think he touched any of his . . .'

Jimmy reached over and pronged two of Toby's sausages, at which point Toby threw down his knife and left the table.

'Ignore him,' said Hattie with a tense smile. 'I'll get the pudding.'

'Pudding!' boomed Toby, who was now incandescent with rage. 'When did you last serve a pudding?'

'Well, I know how much you like to watch your weight Toby so I don't usually bother,' said Hattie coldly, 'but since Jimmy isn't so neurotic about his, I've made something with apples.'

'*Tarte aux pommes*?' he asked petulantly.

'No, apple crumble, Toby, with custard,' informed Hattie.

'Custard?' said Toby, bewildered.

'Eeee, man,' said Jimmy.

'Is it possible for you to speak English?' Toby spat at Jimmy. 'You seem to have a vocabulary of about ten gutteral sounds: eeeee, aaaayyy, liiikke, mannn and hawayyy. I suppose it would be too much to expect you to be able to say please and thank you.'

Jimmy looked up at Hattie with a puzzled expression on his beautiful face while, from beneath the table, Rex sounded a warning growl at Toby.

'That's quite enough, Toby,' Hattie shouted more assertively than she had ever done in her life. 'How dare you be so fucking rude to our guest . . .'

Jimmy winced at her language. His might be gutteral but he had still not uttered anything stronger or more offensive than 'bugger'.

'Listen, darling, if Toby is so upset by Jimmy's presence,' slurred Claire, putting her hand on Jimmy's thigh, 'why don't I take him home with me?'

'NO! You can't do that,' said Hattie a little too forcefully. 'He's coming to my office with me tomorrow. We're due to make a start on the – on the research I'm doing . . .'

'Well, darling, don't panic. I can get him to your office, no problem. He can stay the night with me and give you and Toby a little space,' Claire said, standing up a little unsteadily.

'Claire, that's the best thing I've heard tonight,' said Toby spitefully. 'As long as you take that savage dog with you.'

'Done then, darling,' said Claire, turning to Jimmy and

adding, 'Get your jacket and Rex's lead and we'll be off.'

'But *really*,' Hattie said, horrified at what might happen if Claire got her hands – quite literally – on Jimmy. 'It just isn't practical . . .'

But Claire just ignored her, sweeping Jimmy and Rex out of the flat without so much as a goodbye or a thank you.

Although Jimmy felt more comfortable with Hattie he had to admit that Claire's home was much more homely. Her mews cottage conformed more closely to his – and Rex's – idea of affluence, filled as it was with big sofas, tables covered in ornaments and extravagantly draped curtains.

'Take your jacket off, Jimmy, and relax,' said Claire, making her way to her drinks cupboard and mixing herself a gin and tonic as Rex jumped up on a big wing chair conveniently placed by the fire. 'Drink?'

Jimmy shook his head, sat down on the deep chintz-covered sofa and wondered whether he would be allowed to smoke here and if he should risk telling her that she had consumed quite enough alcohol for one night.

She came to sit beside him, a little too close for his comfort. And Rex's. The dog looked up from his armchair and growled a little. Jimmy could smell her breath – a mixture of ale and gin – and he instinctively moved away from her.

'Jimmy, I think you're a little bit of a prude,' she said.

'Eh?' he said, putting on a deliberately vacant expression.

'I just want to get to know you a little bit. Don't you find me attractive?' she said, throwing back her luxuriant hair and crossing her legs in a fashion that he found, frankly, unseemly and which, from the chair opposite, Rex clearly thought – from his deep-throated growl – was threatening.

'You're reet pretty . . .' he said nervously.

'Show me how pretty,' she said, slipping her hand, to his horror, down the front of his new buttoned-fly Paul Smith jeans.

'Nay, lass . . .' he said, moving further back from her grasping little hands as Rex leapt from the armchair to take his place at Jimmy's feet. Jimmy found Claire a little intimidating and he was deeply shocked by what, he now realised, she was suggesting.

'What's wrong, Jimmy? Aren't you that sort of boy?' she said with a brittle laugh.

'Nay, lass, we've both had a skinful tonight,' he said.

'Can't or won't perform, Jimmy?' she questioned.

'I'm reet tired,' he said, yawning a little obviously to cover his shock and confusion.

'You don't have to sleep in the spare room, you know.' Claire's voice was wheedling.

'I think I'd better,' he said firmly, standing up and moving towards the stairs with Rex following behind him. She was pretty, he couldn't deny that, but she terrified him. Besides, she was drunk and if he went along with her wishes who knows what she might think when she was sober?

'Why don't you sleep with me in my room? I hate sleeping alone,' she said, subtler tactics having failed.

'Nay, lassie, what would Hattie think?' he said.

'Why should we care what Hattie thinks? You're here with me now,' she said, softening the tone of her voice.

'Because Hattie wouldn't like it.'

'You bet Hattie wouldn't like it,' Claire said, her seductive tone evaporating slightly. 'She likes to think that you are hers.'

Jimmy gulped. He was quite sure that Hattie would never, ever, behave as Claire now was even if he *had* heard her doing Lord knows what with that Toby the other night. She was decent, he thought, unlike most of her friends.

'Go on, Jimmy. I'll just lie next to you. I won't touch you, I just want to be close to you . . .' and it was as she uttered those words – words that had so recently been whispered in her own ear by the predatory Eddie – that she pulled herself together and gave up the fight.

As she got into her big cold empty bed she cursed her own clumsiness. She would, she thought as she turned off the light, have to take Jimmy's sexual education at a slower pace.

As soon as Claire and Jimmy had left, Toby launched into a full-scale argument with Hattie, in the course of which he threw at her every insult he could think of. She was a selfish, spoilt, cold, hard and uncaring rich bitch.

For once she didn't respond. She just sat watching him, wondering at his anger. Which only served further to enrage him.

'Don't you feel ANYTHING?' he shouted at her.

'I'm not sure that I do any more, Toby. Least ways when you behave like this. If you only knew the kind of day I had – and then you were so rude to Jimmy tonight,' she said very softly.

'It's always Jimmy, isn't it? Jimmy, Jimmy Jimmy. He's probably your perfect bloody man, Hattie. Someone you could control, someone you could look down on from a very great height and feel oh-so-superior to. Is that why you brought him into our home?'

'I don't think of Jimmy in that way but I suppose that would be the only thing you could understand, wouldn't it? You were bound to reduce something good and decent to your own disgusting level,' she said, her anger at last aroused by his references to Jimmy.

'Mind you,' continued Toby, apparently ignoring Hattie's outburst, 'I think you might find you've miscalculated with him. I can well imagine how he managed to survive on the streets with his baby blue eyes and blond hair. I shouldn't think women have come into the equation much with him.'

'What are you trying to say?' she said, suddenly alarmed.

'Just that you are so naïve, Hattie. You seem to think of Jimmy as simple and innocent. But how can he be? You don't live rough for years and not be corrupted and degraded by it. It's desperate out there, Hattie. Kids do whatever they can to get by – forced into a nether world of drugs and petty crime; trading on nothing more than their wits and, in his case very probably, his looks . . .'

'Are you trying to suggest that Jimmy is some sort of low-life rent boy or something? Can't you just accept that he's just down on his luck? Jimmy is a victim. You always have to put such a sordid, corrupt slant on everything.'

'Well, think about it, Hattie. Look what he's getting here. All those clothes, the food – he's even getting bloody Newkie Brown on tap – and the adoring attention of two attractive women. He's in bloody clover, isn't he? If anyone is a victim here it's me.'

'Oh, spare me the sob story, Toby. What I'm doing with Jimmy is really important to me. I can't tell you how badly I want to prove Jon wrong. And you,' she said passionately.

'Then you'll have to make a choice between Jimmy and me.'

'Why do I have to make a choice? Why can't we just go on? It won't be for ever,' she pleaded.

'It's intolerable for me, Hattie, living like this. Go ahead and carry on with your conversion of Jimmy. But do it without me. I'll move back into my own flat for a while. When you've finished with your wager we can think again about our relationship,' he said in the cold tones he always used during their arguments.

'OK then, perhaps it's for the best,' she said quietly, unnerved by the idea of his going.

She was torn between her relationship with Toby – built up over nearly ten years – and her determination to win the bet. She was, she knew, being a little hard on her lover. Hadn't she always stressed since she bought this flat from her trust fund that it was *their* home? And now here she was reminding him, on an almost daily basis, that it was *hers*; insisting that she could bring into it whomsoever she pleased (and his dog), regardless of what Toby thought or felt. Maybe she should have consulted him more; maybe she should have listened to him, compromised a bit more.

But she couldn't give up now. She was so caught up in the wager that – if she had to – she would sacrifice her relationship with Toby. It would be hard to let him go but much harder still to give up on Jimmy.

Chapter Ten

When Hattie arrived at work the next day Jimmy was already waiting for her. He was sitting in her office – on one of the two chairs that were pushed together, NHS style, to form a small sofa – looking at the special toys she kept for her younger patients. Over the years she had amassed quite a collection of playthings that helped to make children feel comfortable with her: a helicopter on a piece of wire that could be wound up to fly, a chrome-balled Newton's cradle that clicked in perpetual motion, several pull-apart puzzles, a teddy bear and the books that Lisa so loved.

'Jimmy,' she said enthusiastically when she saw him. 'And Rex,' she added a little less warmly when the dog snarled at her.

She was relieved on two counts. First because she thought Toby's behaviour might have put Jimmy off turning up for his appointment and secondly because, at the back of her mind, she feared that Claire might have turned his head.

'Were you comfortable at Claire's?' she asked as casually as she could.

'It was OK,' he said.

'She didn't, er, she didn't do anything silly, did she?'

'She tried, like,' he said with a sheepish grin.

'But she didn't succeed, Jimmy?'

'Nay, lass.'

Relief flooded through her. It would have been just like Claire to mess the whole thing up by seducing Jimmy.

'Tea?' she said with a smile.

'Aye,' he said, then added a hesitant 'please' as if he had taken to heart Toby's comments of the night before.

She left him for a moment and went to the little galley kitchen outside her office to make him a cup of strong orange tea and herself a cup of black coffee.

'So, Jimmy, this is where I work. Most of the time patients are referred to me by social workers, doctors or the courts. I see all kinds of children and young people. Most often they are victims but sometimes they are aggressors. Either way they are usually damaged. And I am supposed to help them or assess their chances of being helped.'

He was listening to her very intently.

'Obviously you don't fit into any of the normal categories of people I see. I mean, you are not a minor and you have come here voluntarily and you don't have any of the problems I am usually consulted on. But I think it would be very helpful if I could ask you some questions and find out a little more about you. And if you don't mind I'll record what you say. I usually do that, OK?'

'Aye,' he said as she switched on the machine on her desk. 'Can I have a tab, like?'

'Yes, if it helps.' She watched longingly as he lit a cigarette.

'So tell me about yourself, Jimmy. Let's go right back to the beginning – if that's all right with you – and talk about your earliest memory.'

He looked at her blankly.

'The first thing that you can consciously remember from your childhood?' she said.

'I'm standing on the Fish Quay watching someone – me granddad, I think – gutting fish,' he said slowly.

'Tell me about the Fish Quay.'

'It's gone now. But then – twenty years ago – it was busy, bustling, the centre of North Shields. The men would stand at big wooden benches and gut the fish. The heads and the innards would be thrown in a pile and the cleaned fishes packed in cases. Some days me nan would take us doon there. It was noisy and smelly but I liked it. The men used to make a fuss of us, like . . .' he said, surprised at how vivid this memory was.

'And your nan was always with you too?'

'Me nan never left us. And sometimes she and me granddad would take us up to the mission and we'd have a cup of tea and they'd give us a rock bun or a piece of bread and sugar.'

'Bread and sugar?'

'We used to have it for breakfast, like – bread spread with margarine and sugar.'

As he talked his speech became more fluent and less filled with the colloquialisms that sometimes made him unintelligible to Hattie. There was, she thought, a kind of beauty in the way he described his early life.

'And were they kind, your nan and your granddad?'

'Aye. Me nan, she was reet good to me. Treated me like I were her own. Me mam was working up at Welch's toffee factory and me nan had us all day. Took us with her to do her cleaning jobs, took us with her shopping. In summer she would take us down to Whitley Bay beach to play on the shuggyboats.'

'Shuggyboats?'

'Like big swings on strings that ya pull to make them go. They had them on all the beaches and the kids would play on them. They were free, like . . .'

'And are these memories happy ones, Jimmy?'

'Aye, they were good. Me nan and me granddad and me were a family, like.'

'But not your mam?'

'Nah,' he shook his head, 'she was young, like, and she didn't want me.'

'Because she wasn't married?'

'Nay,' he said with a cynical laugh, 'because she weren't ready to settle doon. Nan says she tried everything to get rid of me – falling down stairs and all sorts.'

'So you lived at your nan's?'

'Until I was four or five . . .'

'And then?'

'And then me mam met someone.'

'Just someone?'

'He was called Bob.'

'And did you and your mam go and live with him?'

'After a while. After she'd had Wayne. That's when we went to Meadow Well. That's when it started to go wrong. She couldn't cope with Wayne – he cried and Bob – well, he'd get drunk and that. And then she fell for Alan.'

'How old were you by now?'

'Six.'

'And did you see your nan much?'

'She fell oot with me mam. She didn't like Bob and he didn't like her. And there was only us to look over the little ones.'

'At six you were looking after your brothers?'

'Well, me mam worked. Bob was on the social, like. The work had dried up by then. The pits had closed and the shipyards were empty and most of the men were laid off. Bob spent his days doon the betting shop or in the pub. They kept me off school to look after me brothers.'

His upbringing was as dreadful as any she had listened to in this room. The only moments of happiness he had were those he snatched with his nan and granddad. For the rest of the time he had to endure the indifference of his mother and the anger of his stepfather. The work ethic was particularly strong amongst the men of the industrialised North East and during the period in which Jimmy was growing up most of the regular work had disappeared. Unemployment soared and many men – like his first stepfather, Bob – found themselves misplaced and angry. It was, Hattie thought as she watched Jimmy's proud face, the beginning of the end for so many of the young men of his generation. Even now, with the slow regeneration of the area, few of the men could be sure of employment. Jimmy, she realised, would have been the third generation of his own family with no job and no prospect apart from 'the social'. Even his grandfather – the one he remembered on the busy Fish Quay – had lost his fishing boat ten years ago, a short while before he might have retired with dignity, because of the introduction of new EU regulations. After that not one man in his family had a job and, as Jimmy said, in the North East 'a man wasn't a man if he couldn't feed his family'.

Lord knows what daily indignities Jimmy had to endure as he grew up in that forbidding and fearsome place. Hattie had done some research. The Meadow Well Estate was a notorious no-go area in North Shields, the place where every problem family found themselves in what eventually turned into a ghetto of despair and hopelessness. Every awful urban atrocity was committed within its environs and those who didn't conform to the norm were bullied and beaten. No doubt Jimmy's particular beauty – that pale blond hair and the startling blue eyes – had probably worked against him as well. Certainly in the pictures she had seen, his height and his obvious good looks had made him seem an outsider when he stood next to his brothers with their stooped shoulders and mean, haggard faces. By the time he was fourteen he had five brothers by four stepfathers. Each of his stepparents had brutalised him, but the third sexually abused him so that, at nine, he and his brothers were put in care to be released, a few months later, back to his mam and her latest man.

Hattie recorded his memories all that morning. At one thirty she turned off the machine and suggested that they went out for lunch. There had been something particularly gruelling about this session. She was used to patients with difficult histories but most of them were unknown to her before they entered her office. She so wanted to be able to redeem Jimmy's life for him, to make things right again, and she was not sure how much more of his miserable past she could take.

They went to a pub near her office. Several of the female staff raised their eyebrows as the two of them left, obviously perplexed by the odd young man and his dog who had taken up so much of Hattie's time.

She tried to order him a Newcastle Brown Ale but the pub didn't have it and he had to settle for something else. She had a gin and tonic, which was very unlike her during a working day.

'Well, Jimmy, how do you feel?' she said as they took their seats in the corner of the snug.

'Tired,' he said, lighting a cigarette.

Hattie delved into her bag and brought out a packet of her own. Her rediscovery of smoking – begun clandestinely in the flat with Jimmy – had now turned into a habit.

'It must be difficult going back over your past,' she said, lighting up.

He looked at her for a moment and then began to question her in much the way she had quizzed him that morning.

'What aboot yours, then? Were ya happy growing up?'

She smiled. 'My childhood was very, very different and yet . . .'

'What?'

'I think I can relate to some of the things you told me. Your mam, for instance, and her total lack of interest in you. I don't think my own mother showed me much affection. But of course she had the financial support to enable me not to notice too much: nannies, housekeepers and the like.'

'And did ya have a nan?'

'Yes, Jimmy, but not like yours. But I did have a father and at least he showed a little interest in me sometimes. Although of course Arabella was always the favourite. She looked so much like my mother and my father idolised her in those days.'

'And ya could be as lonely in that big hoose as I was in Meadow Well?' he said.

'And at boarding school. I think that was the worst. It wasn't exactly grinding poverty, but it was the rich person's equivalent,' she said with a hard little laugh. 'We were ritually humiliated, bullied and housed in appalling conditions. Some winter mornings there would be ice on the inside of the windows. We were allowed two baths a week – no more than two inches deep and usually in cold water. And we were fed a little like the kids on Meadow Well with cheap high-fat, high-sugar foods. Not exactly like your bread and sugar breakfasts but not far off. Still, I doubt that anyone would regard the inadequacies of my own upbringing in an English public school as anything like as hard to bear as yours,' she finished with a sympathetic smile.

Back in her office, with the recorder light on, they started again.

'Did you have any way of escape?' she asked.

'Aye, in the end.'

'And what was it?'

'Football . . .'

'You mean you used to go off and play with a group of friends?'

'Nah, I mean I got into a junior team, into a league and I got good. It came natural to us. I was reet good . . .' he said, his fine face animated for the first time since she had met him.

'How good?'

'Good enough to play for a top team. I was first boy from Meadow Well to make it oot,' he said.

'Those medals, the cups you have at home – were they won on the football field?'

He nodded. 'It was me way oot, like. I got all me School of Excellence medals. Then a scout saw us. When I was fourteen I joined Everton as a junior. Lived in digs and did the dirty work like. Cleaned the big players' boots, washed oot the changing rooms. But I got to train alongside them and I got to see where it might get us,' he said, his eyes alight with the wonder of the memory.

'And what about your exams, your schoolwork?'

He blushed, looked down and mumbled something.

'Jimmy, did you go to school?'

'I was going to be the next Gascoigne. I had a future all the other lads only dreamt of. Playing for Everton then a transfer back to the Toon. Even me mam were proud. I was different, me, and not because of the way I looked either for once. I was different because I was good . . .'

Being selected for the trainee scheme at Everton was quite simply the highlight of his short life. He had, of course, been different from the start. Beautiful where his brothers were ugly. Sensitive where his siblings had been hard. Tall and muscular where they were short and stooped.

But this difference, this ability to play, to score, for the first time in his life was a *better* kind of difference. One that, in some ways, made his ever going back to Meadow Well an impossibility.

'And then?'

'And then I had us an accident. Playing for second team. Me first real game,' he said, his face falling at the recollection.

They had sent him home to recover. Called him back three months later only to dismiss him for ever. He was useless to them now. His injury – a broken leg – had wiped out the only chance he had of getting out of the Meadow Well with any pride.

Abandoned, with no compensation, he went home in shame only to discover a new man in his mam's bed and – more appalling for him – his nan dying of breast cancer.

'And that's when you left?'

'Aye,' he nodded. 'I never saw her again, like. Never went to the funeral. Never paid me respects . . .'

They worked on into the early evening. At the end of the day Hattie had recorded over seven hours of tape. Jimmy's life story, while not especially tragic, was none the less a tale of his times. Rather like the inside of his mouth – the bite of primitive man that Barry Driver had noted – his childhood history represented a unique document of social change. It was, Hattie thought, an indictment of contemporary society, a horrific narrative that perfectly illustrated what happened if you robbed people of their pride and their right to work and offered them, instead, poverty 'on the social'.

When they got back to the flat Toby had gone. He had packed most of his clothes – and a few of his possessions – and moved back to his own flat.

'Was it my fault?' Jimmy asked, like the lost child in a divorce, when Hattie told him.

'Of course it wasn't. Toby and I need some space, that's all. Your arrival just made that a little more obvious,' she said.

She had a terrible headache brought on, she supposed, by Jimmy's heartache and her own sense of loss. Toby had played a major part in her life and she was frightened of losing him for ever.

She made Jimmy something to eat and then decided she would have an early night.

'Thank you for being so open, so honest with me,' she said as she left him sitting in the kitchen and made her way up the stairs to her empty bedroom.

'Nah, hinny . . .' he said with that particular smile that exposed his vulnerability and tugged so terribly at her heart.

On the big double bed that they had shared for so long Toby had left her a note.

Hattie,

Have taken most of my clothes but will probably come back in the next few days to get the rest of my stuff. I wish it didn't have to be like this.

When you have sorted out your priorities perhaps you will begin to understand all this from my point of view. You seem to have so much compassion for the rest of the world and so little for me. Take care.

Toby

It was typical of Toby to lay all the blame on her. In truth their relationship had been in difficulty long before Jimmy had come into their lives. They had different ideals, different interests and different goals. But she had loved him, lived with him, for so long that letting go was painful. And he had been, in the early days of their relationship, so nurturing, so supportive, so gently encouraging of her.

She crumpled the note in her hand and wondered if she weren't quite mad in sacrificing her own happiness for the sake of what had been – at first at any rate – little more than an idle challenge.

But it was much more than a wager now and there was no way she could give up on Jimmy at this stage. She wanted to win so much, not for herself and not to prove Jon wrong. Now she wanted to win for Jimmy. It wasn't, she knew, going to be easy. There was a lot to do in such a short time. But if at the end of it all she could make Jimmy happy, free and employable then it would be worth the struggle and the loss. She lay down on her bed, still clutching the note, and wept for Toby, for herself and for Jimmy.

Chapter Eleven

'Football?' said Claire thoughtfully, putting down her fork and listening attentively to Hattie.

'Yes, football,' Hattie said. 'Don't you see, it's what makes him special? His childhood by itself didn't make him what he is. Thousands of kids endure that sort of upbringing. It's just regular horror. What made him special was that he found a way out. For a while his hopes were raised so high that he could see and smell the fame and fortune that would be his. He told me he would sit in the first-team changing rooms just inhaling the game. It was like an apprenticeship really. The boys – the young hopefuls – would be expected to do all the dirty work for the established first-team players: wax their Mercedeses and their BMWs, polish up their Nikes, run errands for them. In return they would be allowed to attend all the training sessions. The hopefuls, the wannabes, would get to kick the ball with the greats. And there was none more hopeful, more promising, than our Jimmy. At least until the accident.'

Hattie and Claire were having a kind of council of war over supper at Claire's mews house. Four weeks on they had reached a stage in their mission – as Hattie referred to it – when they needed to sit down and work out what to do next without Jimmy himself overhearing. They had made some cosmetic changes that were effective (Barry was virtually restructuring Jimmy's mouth), but they had barely started the other changes that were necessary if they were to win the bet. Hattie was beginning to feel a bit tense about the fact that they had never told him the real reason why they had taken him off the streets. He still accepted that it was all to do with her research. He had no idea that he was part of a wager. It would hurt him terribly if he were to discover the truth.

'The easiest bit has been making the physical alterations. Changing his attitudes and his ambitions and reinventing him as a successful, intelligent, sophisticated member of the chattering classes is rather more difficult,' said Claire, pausing pensively before continuing, 'Moosh called me the other day to say that Models One would like to see him, but Jimmy seems a bit nervous about it and really I'm beginning to agree with you that modelling isn't the answer.'

'It might pay well for a while but it won't prove Jon wrong,' said Hattie, lighting a cigarette and inhaling thoughtfully.

'I'm sure that there must be some clever marketing opportunity for Jimmy if I could only think of it . . .' Claire said, pouring herself another glass of wine.

It might have been Hattie who had set this whole thing in motion, Hattie who had originally been keener than she to take up Jon's bet, but now Claire felt that she was the motivating force in the transformation of Jimmy. It was up to her to find the way forward for him. Hattie's approach to Jimmy was ideological rather than practical. She was so determinedly anti-materialistic that she kept losing sight of the fact that what he needed more than her well-meaning nurturing was a way to earn money.

There was, Claire felt, a growing element of competition in their joint relationship with Jimmy and she was beginning to feel resentful – not to say a little jealous – about the way in which Hattie monopolised his time, particularly since Toby had moved out. When Toby had been around there had been little likelihood of Hattie's relationship with Jimmy developing into an affair. But now there was something a little too cosy about their setup – just Hattie and Jimmy – and sometimes Claire felt as if she were being marginalised and excluded.

'Have you heard from Toby?' she said carefully, hoping that she might bring the conversation gently round to the state of Hattie's relationship with Jimmy.

'Not really. He rang about some insurance policy he'd taken out on my flat but we didn't really talk about us. Part of me wished that we had, Claire. I know we weren't getting on too well at the end but I always saw us together as a couple with the whole bit – children, dogs, you know. Even with all his faults I always believed he would make a good father. But it's over between us, there'll be no going back. And now I have to face the fact that I might never have a family.'

'What nonsense! You will have children, Hattie,' said Claire impatiently. 'Christ, you're only thirty-two. There's loads of time yet.'

'Is there though, Claire? Look at the two of us. In previous generations we would be married with one or two children apiece. But our generation have decided that having children is the last thing on our agenda. We are so intent on being independent, on establishing our careers, that we completely forget that procreating is the strongest urge a human being has. And by the time we do get round to acknowledging that fact it's often too late,' said Hattie despondently.

'The pity is that none of us can get our heads around having children without a regular man,' said Claire. 'I have been completely conditioned to want the whole package – rich, good-looking man, true love, children. But if you can't get the right man how do you get to the children? I can't think of one woman of my acquaintance who is happy with their man if they've got one. They're either too domesticated and caring – like Caroline's Nick – or they're frightened of commitment. Most of us are faced with the prospect of settling for a weak man whom we'll probably have to support financially and emotionally, or being stuck in a relationship with a shit. If, that is, we can find one,' she added, eyeing Hattie meaningfully.

'I always thought you were rather happy the way you were, Claire. I never thought you wanted all that – true love, children . . .' said Hattie.

'Of course I do. Why do you think I keep going back for more?'

'You mean that when you meet all those men – the ones like that guy you met at the dinner party the other week – you have all these romantic dreams about them?'

'Yes, Hattie, I do. And even when the signs are very bad – usually just after we've had great sex and he's making his excuses and leaving or when I find out he's married – I still can't help but wonder if he isn't *the* one.'

'Do you think either of us will ever find *the* one?'

'Do you know what I think's going to happen to a lot of our generation?' said Claire forcefully. 'We'll go looking for *Jimmys*. Younger men who can accept our success, who respect us. Younger men who have grown up seeing women achieve and therefore do not feel threatened by a woman who is clever, capable and physically attractive. Younger men you could teach and mould into some sort of ideal mate. People always have such a prejudice about older women and younger men – they assume the relationship is based on sex. But it isn't just about sex, it's about the way they communicate, the respect they show, their honesty, their vulnerability. Hasn't Jimmy made you feel that?'

Hattie felt a little uncomfortable under Claire's cold scrutiny. 'I don't think of Jimmy like *that*. My interest is more – well, I suppose you'd call it maternal . . .' said Hattie awkwardly as she lit another cigarette. 'And now that I know how hard it was for him when he was young, how little affection he got from his own mother, I feel an even greater need to nurture him.'

Claire felt so relieved she almost kissed Hattie. She had been absurd to imagine that Hattie's interest in Jimmy was in any way sexually motivated. Or, for that matter, that Jimmy would be attracted to Hattie.

'That's quite a habit you've developed there,' said Claire, indicating the cigarettes. 'Toby would be appalled.'

'Being able to smoke openly is the best thing that's come out of Toby's departure,' said Hattie, inhaling gratefully on her cigarette.

'You know, I think there could be something in this football thing,' Claire said thoughtfully. 'Have you noticed how obsessive most men are about the game nowadays? This bloody "France '98" thing has driven me insane already. There are two things you can sell to men: sex and football. But he'll get bored with the sex long before he tires of the football. Soccer is the last remaining male bastion. A few women might profess an interest but it remains, I believe, the last real symbol of masculinity in our society.'

'And the last outlet for all their primitive tribal instincts, which is probably why it has gained an even greater importance in their lives,' added Hattie with a grin.

'And the thing is,' Claire continued, 'it now crosses the class barrier. Not the playing – that's still primarily a working-class thing. You have to be hungry – as hungry as Jimmy – as well as talented to make it into professional football. But the game appeals to everyone from Melvyn Bragg to David Mellor. Did you know there is a Professor of Football at the University of East Anglia?'

'What are you trying to say, Claire?' asked Hattie.

'I'm trying to say there is a connection between Jimmy becoming a man of worth and football. Hattie, could you get me transcripts of those tapes you recorded?'

'There are over seven hours of them. It might be quicker if I just sent you copies of the tapes.'

'The longer they are and the more detailed, the better. I have an idea I think might just work,' Claire said.

Hattie raised an eyebrow.

'No, I'm not going to say anything yet. I haven't thought it through properly and it may yet turn out to be a waste of time.'

'OK, I'll wait, but meanwhile, what are we going to do about introducing Jimmy to polite society?' Hattie asked.

'How about taking him to the first night of Benedict's exhibition at the Serpentine?' Claire suggested with a cynical smile.

'As long as Jon isn't there. I think we should keep Jimmy well away from Jon. We mustn't forget that he wants to win this bet as much – if not more – than we do.'

Claire looked at Hattie thoughtfully. 'You're probably right. I wondered why Jon had been paying me so much attention lately. He keeps ringing up on some pretext or other, and leaving messages on my phone – which, of course, I don't bother answering. He wants to find out more about how we are getting on with Jimmy. I'll have to be more careful. But don't worry about Benedict's do – Jon is definitely not going.'

'Well, I suppose we've got to expose Jimmy to some contemporary chattering-class culture sooner or later,' said Hattie as she got up to leave. 'Although heaven knows what he'll make of conceptual art . . .'

Rex seemed almost pleased to see Hattie when she arrived home that night. Jimmy wasn't the only one to have undergone a physical transformation. His dog had positively metamorphosed, Hattie thought as she bent to stroke him.

He still wasn't a handsome or particularly appealing dog but his coat had lost that unkempt, mangy appearance and his manner was altogether less nervous. A change of diet – to one of the new 'scientific' dry foods – had brought his digestive problems under control (the ozone layer was under a lot less of a threat) and allowed a layer of fat to cover his ribs.

'Good boy, Rex,' she said encouragingly as the dog nuzzled her hand.

She could hear the television from within the big open living area and she smiled to herself at the way in which Jimmy had come to feel at home here. He had transformed his cubicle bedroom into his own little shrine, sticking up Newcastle United posters and pinning his soccer medals to the back of the Japanese screens. He slept beneath his Everton duvet cover – washed and ironed by Hattie's bemused cleaning lady – and he had fashioned himself a bedside table out of one of Hattie's high-tech chairs and arranged on it his Blackpool snowstorm, a photograph of his nan in a seashell-covered frame and his Junior Achiever's Cup 1990.

He had established his presence in the kitchen, too, with a corner of the big food cupboard devoted to his own foods. The day after Toby had left, Hattie had taken Jimmy shopping in Sainsbury's and the memory of it still made her smile. It had been so different from the fortnightly visits she used to make with Toby. In place of their usual nutritionally correct trolley she had reached the checkout with an array of high-calorie, processed foods that would have sent her ex-lover into a sugar shock.

The egg fusilli had been replaced by Pot Noodles, the pancetta by thick-cut smoked bacon and the extra virgin olive oil by Mazola. Toby's coarse-cut Cooper's marmalade had been thrown out for Golden Shred, his salt-free rice cakes had been banished in favour of chocolate Hobnobs and his bio yoghurts had given way to tins of thick, sugary condensed milk.

'Jimmy, I'm home . . .' Hattie called as she hung her jacket up on the big chrome rail in the hall and made her way into the living area, stopping still when she realised Jimmy was not alone.

'Oh Jimmy, you've got a friend,' she said, her face falling at the sight before her. 'I mean friends.'

There were three of them. Two men – perhaps the ones that had been with him the first night she had propositioned him – and one slight, waif-like blonde girl. It was clear from the way they were positioned – one man lying full-length across the cream sofa, draped in a sleeping bag, another sitting on Toby's Aram chair with his feet planted on top of a big antique Chinese vase, and the girl sitting on the floor next to Jimmy, rolling what looked to be a joint – that they had been here for some time. The table near the television was strewn with food, fag ends and empty cans of Newcastle Brown. The floor was littered with crisp packets, carrier bags and an assortment of grubby-looking clothing.

Jimmy made no attempt to introduce Hattie and she stood, rather awkwardly, in the middle of the room until the man on the sofa noticed her.

'I'm Scott,' he said, 'and that's Annie on the floor and Mick in the chair . . .'

Hattie nodded to them and then, feeling an intruder in her own home, retreated to the kitchen to make herself a cup of camomile tea.

The table in the kitchen was equally littered with dirty plates, cigarette ash and empty cans.

'This is dead good, this is,' said Scott, who had followed her into the kitchen. 'Landed on his feet has our Jimmy.'

She smiled, unsure how to deal with the situation. She should, she realised now, have expected that Jimmy would at some point want to re-establish contact with his friends. She supposed she had better try to be pleasant.

'Have you known Jimmy for a long time?' she asked.

'We go way back,' said Scott, eyeing her up and down in a way that she didn't quite like.

Jimmy wandered into the kitchen and Hattie realised that he was out of his head on drink or drugs, or both. A wave of disappointment overcame her. She knew it was naïve of her to think that Jimmy might not have been corrupted during his years on the streets, but she clung to her vision of him as an almost virginal victim of an awful upbringing. She supposed, as she watched him stagger towards the fridge, that she was now getting a glimpse of another Jimmy, maybe the *real* Jimmy, and she didn't like what she saw. She felt like the outraged mother of a teenager who suddenly discovers that her child has another life. Somehow she had never imagined his involvement with illegal substances.

'No more Newkie,' he said in slurred – and almost accusatory tones – to Hattie.

'Give us some money, love,' said Scott, 'and I'll go and get some more.'

Hattie nervously searched through her bag and drew out her purse which, in an instant, Scott had grabbed and emptied.

'That'll do nicely,' he said, leering at her in a manner she found terribly intimidating. 'Come on, Jimmy.'

They left then and it occurred to Hattie to wonder if they would ever return. But half an hour later they stumbled back in through the front door with several carrier bags from which they took cigarettes, six-packs and several bottles of vodka.

'Come on, Rex,' slurred Jimmy as he pulled the tab from a can of Newcastle Brown. 'Beg for ya Newkie . . .'

The dog had, Hattie noticed, resumed the skulking posture he had displayed when he and Jimmy had first arrived.

His ears were turned back, his head was down and he was whining in his old nervous manner.

'Oop, boy,' said Jimmy as he emptied the contents of the can into Toby's beautiful sculpted silver Alessi fruit bowl and placed it on the floor.

The dog seemed reluctant. He stood before Jimmy with a sad – well, a hangdog – expression on his face as if, for all the world, he wasn't in the mood for his tricks.

'Newkie, Rex!' Jimmy shouted in what seemed to Hattie to be an uncharacteristically harsh manner.

Finally Rex lowered his head into the bowl and lapped up some of the liquid before stopping, jumping up in the air, and barking twice.

'Good boy!' shouted Jimmy as Annie put her arms round him and pulled him down onto the floor next to her, her tongue thrusting into his mouth in a way that Hattie found disturbing.

'More Newkie for my friend Rex!' screamed Scott.

It was very late now and for the first time since Jimmy had arrived – and Toby had left – Hattie felt nervous about going up to bed. But it would be rude and patronising to suggest to him that his friends leave. Not least because, she realised, they had nowhere to go apart from the streets.

'Jimmy,' she said nervously, having waited for a moment when Jimmy emerged from Annie's embrace.

He didn't seem to hear her. Perhaps he didn't want to. He hadn't allowed his eyes to meet hers since she had come home.

'Good night,' she called as she went upstairs, but there was no response.

She locked the door of her room and sat, unable to sleep, on her bed. The sound of the television had been drowned out by CDs, played loudly. She must have dozed for a moment eventually but awoke with a start to the sound of a rhythmic pounding on her door.

It was Rex. The dog looked up at her with a pitying expression as if he, too, was as disturbed by the behaviour of his master as Hattie. She was rather relieved to have his company.

'Oh Rex,' she said, reaching out and ruffling his coat.

The dog pushed past her and leapt up onto her bed, then lay down with his head on his feet.

Perhaps he's had a little too much Newkie, too, Hattie thought as she relocked the door and followed Rex to bed.

The noise went on for most of the night. Toby's precious Bang & Olufsen hi-fi blaring out so loudly that neither Rex nor Hattie got much sleep.

She woke with a terrible feeling of disquiet. It was eight thirty and if she didn't hurry she would be late for work. Rex was stretched out across the bed in a deep alcohol-induced sleep. Creeping past him Hattie made her way to the bathroom for her shower. The dog was still sleeping when she had dressed. Patting him gently she left him there and cautiously went downstairs, fearful of what she would find.

Two of Jimmy's friends were stretched out on the pale sofa. Jimmy and the girl, she presumed, were tucked up in his futon the other side of the Japanese screens.

She looked around her at the mess. CDs were strewn across the floor, half-empty cans of Newkie were spilling across the table, a number of plates covered in congealed ketchup lay scattered around the big open-plan living area. Someone had been sick on the Persian rug.

Hattie was not especially house-proud; certainly not as fastidious as Toby had been. But she was furious at the way in which Jimmy had allowed his friends to behave in her home.

She got a bin bag from the kitchen and began to fill it

with empty cans, cartons of Pot Noodles, cigarette ends –
there must have been a couple of hundred fag ends dotted
around the room, one stubbed out on the upholstered arm
of a chair, even.

Jimmy must have heard her clearing up. He came into
the kitchen wearing just a pair of Calvin Klein boxer
shorts, his Everton duvet draped around his shoulders.
His eyes, she instantly noticed, were dilated and even from
a distance of about five feet she could smell stale alcohol
and tobacco.

'Oh Jimmy, you're up . . .' she said in a tone of voice
that she realised sounded priggish and superior.

'Aye, I'm oop,' he said aggressively, swaying from side
to side as he watched her.

'I'm very disappointed in you, Jimmy,' she said, sounding more like her old headmistress with every passing
moment.

'I'm very disappointed in you, Jimmy,' he said, contorting his face as he repeated her words in a ridiculous
high-pitched posh accent.

'I thought you were different,' she said as she began to
clear up the kitchen surfaces.

'From me friends, like?' he said, reverting to his own
voice.

'Yes,' she said, backing away from him.

'Why?' he asked. 'Why would I be different?'

She looked at him and realised that maybe she had been
mistaken. Maybe he was no different from the grabbing,
manipulative and thoroughly unpleasant Scott – or the
sluttish Annie.

'I believed in you, Jimmy . . .' she said, fighting back
the tears.

'Yous believed what yous wanted ta believe, hinny,' he
said coldly.

'I'm going to work now, Jimmy. When I get home do

you think you could make sure your friends have gone?'
she said equally coldly.

Then she turned her back on him and walked carefully
across the littered floor and out of the flat, slamming the
front door hard behind her.

Chapter Twelve

When Hattie did get home from work that night the flat was empty. Jimmy had kept his word. There was no sign of his friends. He had even made an attempt to clean up. Much of the mess had disappeared – beer cans, fag ends, bottles had been spirited away. There was, though, she thought as she made a mental inventory of the flat, still a lingering stale smell of alcohol and sweat. And there were still clues as to what had gone on the night before: an inch of Newkie in the bottom of the Alessi fruit bowl, for instance, and a worrying wet patch on the Persian rug.

It took her all evening to realise that it wasn't just Jimmy's friends that had left the flat, but Jimmy himself. At ten o'clock, when he still hadn't returned, she finally thought to look behind the Japanese screens. All his possessions had gone: Rex, the Blackpool snowstorm, the picture of his nan in the seashell frame, the Everton duvet, the medals, the Junior Achievers Cup 1990.

The only things that Jimmy had left behind were the clothes that Claire had shopped for with him: the suit, the shirts, the black leather jacket, the jeans. Everything – right down to his Calvin Klein boxer shorts – had been left carefully folded and laid out on the futon bed.

Hattie realised she had badly mishandled what had happened last night, and that she should have made more of an effort to talk to Jimmy that morning. She shouldn't have seemed so snotty and disapproving. After all, he'd only met up with a few friends for a few drinks. Her expectations of him had been unrealistic. She had, she realised, rather idealised him. She hadn't been able to see the real Jimmy. Her interpretation of him as some innocent victim was, she now saw, absurd. Maybe there was something – deep down – that was pure and good and innocent about him but considering the life that he had led, was it any wonder that from time to time he might behave badly? That he drank, that he inhaled the joints that his friends passed round and that, she thought with a jolt, he had sex?

Besides, didn't she deal with kids like Jimmy every day of her working life? Wasn't she used to the kind of behaviour she had witnessed last night? Imagining that Jimmy would be any different from any other of the deprived, neglected or abused children she dealt with in the course of her work was ridiculous. She had been treating him as if he were somehow above the corrupting forces that kids of his generation and background were exposed to.

And what had she done when she was presented with the evidence of Jimmy's human frailty? She had come on like some outraged hausfrau, scolding him like a small child, belittling and even humiliating him within earshot of his friends.

She decided she wouldn't tell Claire about his defection for a day or so; she didn't want her knowing how badly she had handled the situation the night before. She had thought, for some time, that her friend was trying to take control of Jimmy's future and she didn't want her to use their disagreement as a means of taking him further under her wing. It was better, Hattie concluded, to keep quiet for a while and hope that he would just turn up again

Claire wasn't at all sure it had been sensible to invite Toby round for supper. It smacked, she thought, of betrayal. And in a way it was. It would suit her very well if Toby and Hattie were to be reconciled, leaving the way clear for her to take the lead with Jimmy. She would try her best, this evening, to encourage some kind of a reunion between them. But she felt a little bit guilty about asking him round and she hadn't dared whisper a word of it to Hattie.

She was still working at her computer when he arrived. Business, in the last few months, had been going so well that she was reaching a stage when she would have to move into a proper office, rather than the little study at the back of her house. Hearing the doorbell she got wearily to her feet with little energy, after a long day's work, for the evening ahead.

Toby had bought her flowers, which was kind, and a bottle of good white wine – ready chilled – which he immediately offered to open. He knew the layout of her home pretty well. He had been here often with Hattie for dinner, and of course for the odd meeting with UCO. While he opened the bottle and found a couple of glasses she went to her fridge and got out the food.

'I'm afraid it's Marks and Spencer,' she said, thinking privately that poor old Toby would probably be grateful for whatever he could get. Hattie had never really bothered much with cooking and now that he was on his own he probably tucked in – as most men in Claire's experience did – to takeaways and cold tinned Fray Bentos pies.

'It's just great to be here,' said Toby.

'How's it going then, Toby?' asked Claire in the gentle, coaxing tones she usually reserved for heart-to-hearts with Jon.

'Oh, you know, it's always difficult adjusting to big changes in your life,' said Toby.

'You don't think there's any going back then?'

'Do you?' he said.

'Hattie's very upset,' she said tentatively, to test the water.

'Is she?' he said eagerly.

'I don't think she knows what she wants right now,' said Claire.

'Apart from that boy and that foul-smelling, vicious dog . . .' said Toby.

'Oh Toby, don't be ridiculous. She doesn't want Jimmy in that way. She feels maternal towards him,' said Claire.

'You don't think Hattie's sleeping with him?' Toby blurted out.

'Absolutely not,' said Claire, her face contorting at the very thought. 'No, she's just indulging her well-known nurturing instinct. She's only really happy when she's helping some poor unfortunate.'

'And she never quite saw me like that,' said Toby dolefully.

'You were so good together, Toby. Why give up so easily? Why not try and get back what you had?' said Claire sweetly.

'I'm not sure if I can, Claire. It's complicated now,' said Toby.

Claire pierced the film on the M&S pasta dish and put it in the microwave. Then she emptied a packet of their mixed salad into a bowl and bunged a baguette in the oven. Within ten minutes everything was ready to eat.

'This is good,' said Toby, smiling up at Claire, the effects of three glasses of wine finally reaching him and lifting his mood.

'So, Toby, why exactly is your life so complicated?' said Claire.

'You won't tell Hattie . . . ?' he said anxiously.

'What, Toby?'

'Oh, you know, I've been having this thing with a girl at work for a while now.'

'You mean long before Jimmy and Rex came along?' Claire said, privately noting the marvellous way in which

Toby had described his infidelity as 'having this thing'. That was another one for her man/woman dictionary.

He looked a little sheepish and nodded.

'So it was a good excuse then, getting out when you did,' she said, narrowing her eyes at him and noting that it was true. They were all bastards, even nice, dependable Toby.

'Oh, I don't know. I did want it to work with Hattie. I did love her and our life together – that flat, her family, you know the whole George heritage. But Chrissie is different, she's so . . .'

'So, so what, Toby? Good in bed, great at doing all the household chores, fantastic with food?'

'All three, actually,' he said, looking pleased with himself.

'And really those are the most important qualities a man looks for in a mate, aren't they? Even at the turn of the twentieth century. Even with all this talk about girl power, all this glorious success women are achieving. Men still judge them by those three qualities. The only three – I suppose – that you have decided Hattie doesn't have.'

'Hattie and I were having problems . . .'

'You mean she wasn't giving you blow jobs every night, bringing you breakfast in bed and ironing your Y-fronts?' said Claire.

'Oh God, Claire, you know what Hattie was like. She always put the poor and the needy before me – even before this bloody Jimmy came along.'

'Whereas this girl you were *having this thing* with put your comfort and sexual satisfaction first?' said Claire.

'No . . . it's just . . .' Toby said uneasily, putting down his knife and fork.

'And would you have ever told Hattie the truth, Toby? No, of course you wouldn't. Men are congenitally incapable of telling the truth. It occurred to me recently – just after some man had told me a particularly terrible lie –

that someone could make millions out of manufacturing portable lie detectors for women to carry in their handbags. Little machines that would be as marketable – and useful – as rape alarms, that would bleep every time he told you an untruth. I have to say though I'm surprised at you, Toby. I always thought you were the one man who was trustworthy and truthful,' she said, feeling, against all her instincts, suddenly very protective of Hattie.

He looked affronted at this, pulled himself up and started to justify his behaviour to Claire.

'Oh God, don't think I made a habit of cheating on Hattie,' he said, 'but you have to remember I had been with Hattie since university . . .'

'So don't go throwing it away so quickly, Toby,' she said sharply. 'Shall I open another bottle of wine?'

'Why not? I know you disapprove, Claire, but it's been really good to talk about things. It's been eating me up,' he said.

Poor Toby, she thought. He isn't really bastard material. One affair in ten years and here she was accusing him of being some sort of Jack Nicholson figure.

'Toby, don't worry,' she said a little later when they had moved into her living room. 'I won't tell Hattie.'

He looked at her with transparent gratitude. 'You're a wonderful woman, Claire,' he said.

'Not really. It's rather underhand of me to have asked you here at all. Hattie would be cross. I just wanted to try to get you two back together.'

'Do you think it's really possible?' he said.

'Anything's possible if you want it enough,' she said. 'You shouldn't let one indiscretion destroy what you had with Hattie. You are not really such a shit.'

'Was that meant to be a compliment?' he said.

'Yes,' she smiled.

He picked up the bottle of wine and came over to fill her glass. Then he sat down next to her on the sofa.

'A toast,' he said, his voice slightly slurred, 'to us . . .'

And then, just as she was beginning to believe that he was more a victim than a sexual aggressor, he jumped her, throwing himself on top of her – upsetting her glass of wine – and thrusting his tongue in her mouth. She wanted to scream, but obviously she couldn't, so instead she sank her teeth deep into his tongue, which produced a rather more effective response than a scream.

'Get out, Toby,' she said.

He didn't say anything – but then perhaps he wasn't able to. He just got up, his face flushed with pain or shame, and left.

Claire only had herself to blame. It had been stupid to try to meddle in Hattie's affairs. And however much it might have suited her to have the two of them disappear into the sunset together even Claire had to admit that Toby wasn't worthy of Hattie. She had only done it because of Jimmy. Everything in her life right now led back to Jimmy. As she collected their glasses and put the plates into the dishwasher she remembered the package of tapes Hattie had sent her. She went back into her office and took them out of the big Jiffy bag. They were numbered, and she took the first, put it in the tape deck in her hi-fi and sat down to listen.

'I'm standing on the Fish Quay watching someone – me granddad, I think – gutting fish. It's gone now, the Fish Quay. But then – twenty years ago – it were the bustling centre of North Shields. The men would stand at big wooden benches and gut the fish. The guts and the innards would be thrown in a pile and the cleaned fishes packed in cases . . .'

She listened to the first four tapes in one sitting, only stopping when she noticed the time and remembered how much work she had to do in the morning. They were incredible, mesmerising. She could have sat there all night listening to them. But more important than their effect on Claire was their potential effect on other people. The tapes, she thought with mounting excitement, were the means by which Jimmy would finally escape the terrible legacy of his childhood. And the way in which she and Hattie might win their wager.

Hattie was much happier dealing with her patients than attending the regular case meetings that punctuated the ongoing treatment of a child. She was in no mood today to deal with the aggression being directed at her by Tina Brooks, the senior social worker responsible for Lisa's case.

Hattie had written a preliminary report on the child in which she had, very carefully, alluded to what she believed to be the root cause of the girl's problems. She wasn't ready to reveal everything that Lisa had told her; she needed to do further background research before she made what were, after all, serious allegations against the father. But she had enough evidence – from the recordings of her sessions with the girl – to suggest that the family should have been subjected to closer scrutiny when they arrived in London. And it was this hint of incompetence that had incensed Tina Brooks.

'There is simply no way that this child was at risk in her home. The mother is intelligent, responsible, and loving. These were children, for goodness' sake, who went to church every Sunday, who were being raised in a secure and apparently happy environment. There was no indication of neglect, much less *abuse*,' Tina Brooks said.

'You mean that because they didn't display the usual signs of social decline that are present in so many of the cases we deal with you didn't think to look any further. Traditional family with a strong religious base. No need to worry about *them*,' said Hattie.

'I mean,' spat the social worker, 'that everything appeared to be OK. More than OK, in fact. They were a shining beacon of parental responsibility in a sodding desert of deprivation and despair. And I particularly resent your inference that my department is in some way responsible for what happened,' she finished, slamming her hand down on the case notes in front of her.

'You are misinterpreting my report. I am not trying to lay the blame for what happened on social services. I am trying to find the source of Lisa's problems. That is my job, Tina. And it is quite clear that this family was deeply troubled—'

'Clear? Clear? We are not the bloody thought police, Hattie. We can't walk into a family's home and question their religious beliefs. We can't go up to one of the few families on that estate that weren't giving us grief and say to them, "Your children are polite, well-behaved, hard-working, clean, neat and well cared for – are you abusing them?" How were we to know the family was deeply troubled?'

Hattie really had to win Tina Brooks on to her side. If she wanted to achieve anything for Lisa – offer some kind of defence in the form of mitigating circumstances – she needed to be able to influence some of the other people involved in the child's case. But it was clear that far from convincing Tina of Lisa's abuse she had, instead, made her overly defensive of her own position.

'Look, Tina, I know how difficult it is for you. I know that whatever your department does you will be first in the firing line. If you rush in too quickly you will be accused of overreacting. And if you don't react fast enough you will be regarded as culpable by the police and the public when something goes wrong. I appreciate that you simply don't have time to look behind the curtains of families that seem – on the surface – to be secure and happy. I understand that it would have been incredibly difficult to pick up on what was going on in the Price family . . .'

Tina relaxed a little and shrugged her shoulders to indicate, Hattie supposed, that from time to time she did come across a family where signs of trouble were almost impossible to discern.

'The thing is, Tina, I need your help. I need to know what you think about Lisa, about what happened. Have you ever seen a case like this before?'

Tina looked across the table at Hattie and ran her hands through her hair. 'I've never encountered a case exactly like this before. But, sure, I can remember instances where ostensibly loving and caring Christian families have inappropriately disciplined their children. But I am not totally convinced about your preliminary findings on Lisa,' she said.

'But you will be, Tina, when I've made my full, official report within the next two weeks,' said Hattie.

'For Lisa's sake I hope so,' said Tina, putting all her case notes and a copy of Hattie's report in her briefcase as she prepared to leave.

'We shouldn't be enemies, Tina. Surely we are on the same side?' said Hattie with a bleak smile.

'Actually in this case I feel more on the side of the other child, poor little Lindy,' said Tina as they parted. 'Now *her* family background of abuse and deprivation was far more of a worry than Lisa's.'

But Hattie wasn't listening. She was writing pencil notes on the bottom of her preliminary report, aware that if she was going to win others on to Lisa's side, she had a lot more work to do. She had to find more evidence – more precise details of the abuse the child had suffered – so that the crime she had committed, terrible though it was, would be more easily understood by a judge and a jury.

*   *   *

It was three days before Hattie heard from Jimmy. Or rather before she heard from Rex. On the Saturday morning she was woken by a commotion outside her front door: a scratching and whining punctuated by a single shrill bark every now and then. When she opened the door Rex was sitting there expectantly.

'Rex,' she said, unaccountably pleased to see him.

He followed her into the kitchen and stood looking at the big bag of dog food. She emptied some into his bowl and laid it down for him. He ate ferociously. In just a few days he had physically regressed, she noticed. His coat was matted and dirty and his ribs were beginning to show again. She wondered how his master was doing and if he, too, had deteriorated as quickly.

Rex's arrival was a good sign. The dog and his master had rarely been parted and Hattie felt certain that sooner or later it would occur to Jimmy that Rex might have made his way back to her flat. If, that is, something terrible hadn't happened to him.

He came early that evening. He looked awful. But not, she noted, as awful as he had done when they had first encountered him. He was dirty and dishevelled – back in his awful old lumberjack shirt – but he seemed sober.

'You've come for Rex?' she said, seeing the relief on his face at the sight of his pet.

'Aye,' he said as he took the full force of his dog's welcome. 'I thowt he might ha gan hessel here . . .'

She watched as Jimmy fussed over Rex, the dog lying down, twisting backwards and forwards in excitement.

'I'm sorry, like, aboot tha other neet,' he said after a while.

'There's nothing to be sorry about, Jimmy,' Hattie answered quickly. 'Perhaps I should be saying sorry. I shouldn't have reacted like that to your friends. He seems to like it here . . .' she said as Rex padded back to the living area and settled down on a corner of the Persian rug.

'Aye.'

'Do you want a cup of tea?' she suggested and Jimmy nodded.

She made him his tea as he liked it: loaded with sugar and a deep, dark tan colour, not the weak, beige, perfumed Earl Grey that she preferred. She didn't want to frighten him away but she wanted to sort out what had gone wrong.

'Why did you go, Jimmy?'

'Because ya said, like.'

'But I didn't want you to go.'

'But yer wanted me friends to go.'

'It was just the mess, Jimmy,' she tried to explain, unsure how she could justify throwing out his friends. 'You know that you and Rex could make this your home, don't you?'

He shook his head. 'Maabe it's for the good if I'm back oot there, like,' he said.

'Why on earth would it be better being back there?'

'It's wha' I know, like,' he said. 'I've got me nowt.'

'That's not true. You've got an awful lot, Jimmy. It's just that no one has ever taken the time to show you.'

He looked up at her as if he was frightened of believing she was telling the truth.

'What are ya eftor, hinny?' he said.

She didn't know what to say. 'What are you after, Jimmy?' she finally replied.

'What d'ya mean, like?'

'Apart from the football, was there anything else you wanted to do, or wanted to be?' she asked him.

'It's nay use people like us wanting. What we want we divvint ever get,' he said, shrugging his shoulders to illustrate the uselessness of his having any ambition.

'That may have been true but it isn't any more. Claire and I can help you be whatever you want, Jimmy.'

He looked at her sceptically. 'Boot whas in it for ya? I've got nowt that ya want.'

She wondered if now was the time to tell him about Jon's bet. He might understand why it was so important to her to rescue him if he knew that it was something she was trying to prove for a reason. But she wasn't sure he was ready to hear; it might frighten him off again. She would just have to convince him that she still needed him for her research and, more than that, that she now really wanted him to get away from his old life. In truth, the bet didn't really matter that much to her any more. What really mattered was giving Jimmy another chance, helping him to achieve the potential that she sensed, more and more as she got to know him, was there.

'It would make me feel good if I could help you. Not just because I need you for my work. It would make me happy if you would stay here and let me and Claire get you established. I promise you it'll turn out right. And if you move back in you can bring your friends here from time to time if you want. Have your girlfriend – Annie, was her name? – with you sometimes,' she said, although the idea of him cohabiting with Annie beneath her roof rather disturbed her.

'Annie's not me girlfriend, like,' he said, blushing a little.

Hattie felt absurdly relieved. It was going to be all right, she thought. He would come back.

'Will you stay, Jimmy? And let Claire and me help you?' she said.

He didn't reply, just lowered his head and carried on petting Rex.

There was still something bothering him, she could tell.

'Is there something else you want to tell me, Jimmy?' she asked

'Remember when we talked about me past, like?'

'Yes?'

'There's summat I didn't tell ya . . .'

'Yes?'

'I larned nowt at school,' he said, clearly embarrassed at the disclosure.

She had suspected as much. His tortured description of his early years had made her wonder if he had received even a rudimentary education. And in any case what incentive had there been to educate himself? There'd been no work around, no need to get any qualifications.

'I canna read or write properly, like,' he said, lest she had misunderstood him.

'I could teach you, Jimmy,' she said.

He looked up and smiled. 'I can write me name, like, and I know me letters and me numbers,' he said, pulling a piece of paper off her Post-it pad and picking up a pen to show her how clever he was.

'I'm not stupid, see . . .'

'I expect you're dyslexic, Jimmy. My sister, Arabella, is dyslexic,' Hattie said sympathetically.

'What?' He was baffled.

'Dyslexic. It's a kind of word blindness. It doesn't mean you are stupid although I dare say a lot of kids on Meadow Well might have been dismissed as stupid if they had a problem with their reading. Put to the back of the class with raffia, I think they used to say. But down here in the South it's almost acquired a smart status amongst the middle classes. All sorts of people have come out of the woodwork in the last few years to claim that they are dyslexic,' she said, glancing at him.

'Aye,' he said, not looking up from the painstaking progress his hand was making across the paper.

'If you stay we can make a start tomorrow,' she said with a smile as she looked at the paper in front of him. The tortured childish writing of the word *Jimmy*.

The woman in Waterstone's talked in hushed tones to Hattie as if Jimmy were, indeed, stupid. There were, she said, smiling patronisingly towards him, all sorts of adult literacy schemes.

But in the end, attracted to the sticker books and tapes in the children's section, they bought a reading system for four-year-olds.

'You don't mind that it's for little ones, Jimmy?' she said.

'Nay, hinny,' he said.

At home, free of the constraints that Toby put on her life, Hattie set about educating Jimmy.

She had bought phonetic ABC posters and friezes which she hung around her minimalist flat like bunting. She even put a chart in the bathroom so that he could practise the letters when he washed or went to the loo.

She quickly discovered that he wasn't dyslexic; he had no confusion over his letters. It seemed as if his problem was simply poor education – his continued truancy and the lack of parental interest during his childhood.

The most difficult part of her task was to increase his vocabulary without sacrificing his rich Geordie speech. The last thing that Hattie wanted to do was to dilute the richness of his language. In the weeks since he had arrived in her life she had gradually picked up the meaning of many of the words which, at first, had seemed incomprehensible. 'Cowp', she now knew, meant spill, 'tetties' were potatoes, a 'bummler' was a bee and 'keek' was look (as in 'Have yourself a keek at thon'). She had even taken to using certain words from his dialect in everyday conversation. Pet, hinny, canny and haddaway had now been absorbed into her own vocabulary, to his evident amusement. It was difficult to match the world shown in the books with that of Jimmy's own childhood. For although the characters in the books had been rendered politically correct – a white and a black family lived next door to each other and the fathers were pictured cooking food whilst the mothers cleaned the cars – nothing in them was recognisable from his own upbringing on the Meadow Well Estate.

'No pubs, like, no betting shops and no one on the social,' he said to Hattie with a shadow of a smile.

No domestic violence, no sexual abuse and no dysfunctional families either, she thought darkly as they worked that day.

Whether it was his diet or a natural tendency towards hyperactivity, Hattie couldn't tell, but Jimmy found concentration for long periods of time difficult. Although he was quick and responsive for the first few minutes, nothing could hold his interest for very long and there was a restless quality about his behaviour whatever he was doing that made their progress frustrating. He still preferred to eat whilst pacing the floor in front of the television – one hand on his food and the other permanently channel hopping with the remote control. His mind darted from one thing to another in such a way that even Hattie began to lose patience with him.

It wasn't, she decided, his fault. It was just that no one had taken sufficient interest in him as a child – apart from his nan when he was very small – to allow him to develop his mental faculties. No one had ever encouraged his interest in anything apart from football. Such was the emotional and physical poverty of his home environment that just surviving from day to day was enough of an achievement.

Besides, he was used to constant noise. The television was on from morning to night and the sounds that five boys made in a small house were such that it was hardly surprising he could not follow a thought through to its natural conclusion.

He and his brothers had grown up almost like pack animals, scavenging for food, for the means to live. It wasn't difficult for them to slip through the net at school. And while such a start had made Jimmy streetwise and perfectly capable of living – or perhaps more accurately existing – on his wits, he had never developed a capacity for learning. He had to take regular breaks from his work with Hattie so that he could make himself a doorstep sandwich or a sweet and sour Pot Noodle.

But in those few precious moments when he did concentrate Hattie realised that he was, in fact, bright. Very bright. She just had to help him to realise his own intelligence and encourage him to have a more positive attitude to his own education.

'Eee, man, I've had enough,' he said after one particularly gruelling session. 'I'll never get it, will I, hinny?'

'Of course you'll get it, Jimmy. In fact you've already got it really, you just don't believe you have. You *can* write and you *can* read, you just don't want to,' she said. 'But there's more to learning than all this. Claire is determined that we don't neglect another part of your education.'

He looked at her curiously. 'How d'ya mean, like?'

'You'll have to learn about the way people like Claire and I live. You'll have to learn to eat like us – not walking up and down while you watch television.'

'Boot that's how I've always di'd.'

'And you'll have to learn to appreciate the kind of food that we eat: the pastas, the breads, the sauces, the different regional French and Italian cuisines. Not to mention the ethnic restaurants – Thai, Vietnamese, Caribbean. And you'll have to have a nose for good wine,' she said, smiling at his confusion.

'And once you understand the food you'll have to learn to make conversation. You'll have to talk about what you

164

think and what you feel. Make comments about politics, the issues of the moment, that sort of thing,' she said.

'What else?'

'And you'll have to learn to appreciate some of the nonsense that people like us call art and entertainment.'

'The telly?' he said.

'No, absolutely not the telly. Apart, that is, from the occasional programme on Channel 4. No, I mean theatre, films, opera, ballet, art galleries. And what is oddly called The Season – which is actually a series of rather dreary sporting events that happen in early summer. You must have heard of Ascot and Henley? To start you off, tomorrow night Claire wants to take us to the opening of an exhibition of the work of a very controversial man. Benedict Wright makes free-form structures and sculptures.'

'Ya mean an artist, like?' he said.

'Yes.'

'Drawing and that? Me granddad, he was an artist, like. He could draw real lifelike.'

'Well, Benedict's not quite like that,' Hattie said. 'I can't wait to see what you think.'

It would, she thought as she glanced across at his eager, beautiful face, offer Jimmy a whole new – and quite literal – wave of culture shock.

Chapter Thirteen

It was difficult to see the exhibits for the people partying at the Serpentine Gallery. Charles Saatchi was there, and his ex-wife, Doris. In fact anyone who was anyone within the tight, select world of contemporary art was paying homage to Benedict Wright's – in Hattie's opinion – rather dubious talent. But then he *was* on the short list for this year's Turner Prize.

He was a particular favourite of Claire's and, over the years, she had dragged Hattie along to enough of his shows for her to have become immune to his shock tactics. He had made his name with some gruesome work that had caused a furore amongst certain sections of the tabloid press. His Organic Period, as it was now known, had involved his turning parts of the human body into bizarre and bloody works of art. *Broken Heart*, his most famous work, which was subsequently bought by the Tate, featured a real human heart with a large kitchen knife protruding from its scarlet centre. There had, of course, been a number of outraged responses to the exhibition of this work, principally because, at least according to the *Sun,* the heart had been used without the express permission of the donor.

Benedict had developed this theme in his subsequent shows which, bit by bit (as it were) had become more and more grisly and grotesque. *Five Finger Exercise*, for example, involved a dismembered hand clasped round a dumbbell and *Old Blue Eyes*, a free-standing sculpture that featured a pair of brilliant blue eyes oozing formaldehyde tears. But tonight the exhibits had taken a new twist. *Full Stomach*, for instance, consisted of a bloody, stretchy stomach lining filled with famous brand-name foods.

'What do you think, Hattie?' said Benedict, who liked to think that he shared her own political views and social conscience. 'The stomach is extended in the way that we are used to seeing in starving children in the Third World and its interior is full of processed commercial foods. It's a metaphor for the way we are: the greed of the First World and the hunger of the Third World . . .'

She smiled at him, rather than say what she thought. 'This is Jimmy, by the way, Benedict,' she said.

'Jimmy who?' said Benedict, gazing with interest at the tall blond stranger beside her.

'Jimmy Ryan,' interjected Claire quickly. 'He's something of an artist himself.'

'Oh?' said Benedict.

'Eeee now, hinny,' said Jimmy nervously.

'What do you work in?' Benedict asked.

'Life,' said Claire, darting a warning look at Jimmy.

They moved on to the next work, *Steak Ta Ta*, an oozing T-bone steak preserved in formaldehyde into the meat of which Benedict had stamped the letters 'BSE'.

'What do you think, Jimmy?' Benedict said.

'I might pay to eat it, pet. Boot hang it on the wall – never!' he said, rather loudly as it happened, so that several of the other guests heard.

Jimmy was astonished when Hattie showed him the catalogue with the prices typed neatly next to the names of the exhibits.

'The price is £60,000 for this,' she whispered to him as they reached *Smell's Good*, a pig's head mounted on a carton of Paxo sage and onion stuffing.

'What, £60,000 for a pig's sneck full a snot? Gerraway, hinny,' he said. 'I could do berra than that meeself.'

Claire screamed with laughter. 'That's it! Jimmy could become a conceptual artist. One of his sandwiches displayed on a plinth would have this lot slavering.'

'Eeee, man, or maybe a couple a cartons of me Pot Noodles,' said Jimmy, enjoying the joke.

Many of the crowd were listening to him now, to the evident irritation of Benedict. And his comments were being whispered from one little group of spectators to another.

'What's this then, hinny?' he said to Hattie as he stopped by a bottle of Spa water that was half-filled with an amber-coloured liquid.

'It says here that it's called *Bottled Water*. Sold – see the red spot there – for £20,000,' Hattie said. 'I think it's probably urine.'

'What?' said Jimmy, still not comprehending the contents of this particular exhibit.

'Urine, Jimmy. You know what urine is,' said Claire. 'Piss, wee wee, tinkle . . .'

'Pittle, man! He's selling pittle in a bottle!' Jimmy was incredulous. 'Whey ye bugger mar!'

By now many of the attendant art critics had heard about Jimmy. The whisper was that he was a new force to be reckoned with in the art world.

'What do you think of Benedict's work?' Nigel Reynolds from the *Telegraph* asked him.

'It's shite, isn't it?' he said. 'Or at any rate bluddy pittle . . .'

Hattie couldn't remember when she had enjoyed herself so much. Until, that is, she caught sight of Arabella lurking in a corner of the gallery.

'Daddy wants to talk to you, Hattie,' she said when, unable to avoid doing so, Hattie went across and they came face to face.

'Why?' asked Hattie.

'Well, he's heard about you and Toby. And he's found

168

out what's going on with Geordie Boy over there. He's not happy, darling. Thinks you've gone mad. Actually we all do. Not, mind you, that he isn't – in his way – delicious . . .' she added, glancing across at Jimmy, who was now surrounded by an entranced group of people.

'How many times do I have to tell you, Arabella, this thing with Jimmy is strictly professional? Why did you have to tell Daddy?'

'Who said I told him?' said Arabella, like a small child caught out in a betrayal.

'Who else knows, Arabella?'

'Only the whole of bloody London,' Arabella indicated the crowd around them.

'Anyway, it's got nothing to do with Daddy,' said Hattie defensively.

'Of course it has. Isn't Daddy paying for it? I'm sure you didn't buy his clothes out of your pathetic NHS wages,' she said.

'My wages may be pathetic, Arabella, but at least I earn them,' said Hattie.

'And you think I don't earn my money?'

'I think you have a lot in common with Benedict,' said Hattie, blushing with rage. 'He gets paid to piss on high society and you get paid getting pissed with high society. There's not much to choose between you. He's just got bigger pretentions than you.'

'You really think I'm stupid, don't you, Hattie?'

'No, Arabella, I don't *think* you're stupid, I *know* you're stupid. You are the most expensively uneducated person I have ever come across. That's your tragedy.'

'You've *always* been jealous of me, that's yours,' said Arabella.

'Oh, don't bring up that again, Arabella,' Hattie said, aware that their argument was now causing as much interest as Jimmy's reaction to Benedict's work. She sometimes forgot that in these circles her sister was a celebrity. Moving away from Arabella, who had, in any case, now become the focus of the attention of the paparazzi, Hattie made her way back to Claire and Jimmy.

'Hinny, where ya been?' said Jimmy.

'Hattie, let's get out of here and get something to eat,' said Claire.

'I don't think I could eat after that,' Hattie said, unsure if it was the sight of her own flesh and blood or Benedict's that had dampened her appetite.

'What did you think of Benedict?' Claire asked Jimmy as they went to get their coats.

'He wants his hintend skelped,' said Jimmy.

'What?' said Claire.

'He wants his bum kicked,' translated Hattie with glee.

'Don't give him ideas, Jimmy. He's created art out of the human body, and art out of the connection between the human body and food. I suspect what comes out of his *hintend* could be the basis of his next show,' said Claire.

'Haddaway and shite, man,' said Jimmy with a grin.

Hattie's father rang her in the office the following Monday and demanded, as was his way, that she have lunch with him. It didn't occur to her, as was her way, to say no. She came off the phone, having agreed to meet him the next day at his club, feeling nervous and jumpy.

It was curious, she thought as she sat through a particularly harrowing family case conference later that morning, that however privileged you were your parents still 'fucked you up'.

Of course, her father had never abused her; never raised his hand to her or taken advantage of her sexually. And he had not been absent from her life because of alcohol, drugs or – as in today's case – because of any criminal activity. Nor had he forced on her misguided religious beliefs and fearful punishments for imagined crimes against God, as Lisa's father had. He had been missing from her childhood because he chose to be.

His pursuit of success, his awful, overriding material ambitions, had prevented him from involving himself in the day-to-day life of his family. He had plugged the gaps with money – exotic holidays, expensive schools, ponies, and all the other conventional trappings of wealth. But Hattie never was a material girl and the only thing she had wanted, as she had grown up, was the approval and interest of her father. He had noticed her, briefly, when she had gone up to Oxford but when she had chosen to read psychology he had dismissed her, somewhat ironically she thought, as 'mad'. Had she followed him into business he might, just, have been impressed.

She had finally decided that his own brand of chauvinism was so deep-rooted that he simply couldn't understand women who did not conform to his own sense of the female ideal. If, that is, they were anything other than pretty and frivolous.

Her mother and elder sister were, quite simply, every-thing he thought a woman ought to be, whilst she, with her fine academic brain and her need to contribute to society – rather than to be the talk of it – was, in his eyes, odd.

Yet even now, years after she had come to terms with his disinterest, a simple phone call could bring back all that pain and longing from her childhood. Indeed, his shadow fell over her that day, as it had when she was a child, and she felt despondent, depressed and insecure.

On her way home, weighed down with her work and her misgivings about seeing her father the following day, she had arranged to meet Claire for a drink in a wine bar. As was usual when they met up, Hattie was the first to arrive. She ordered herself a red wine and sat looking at the report she had written after today's case conference. It didn't do much to lift her mood.

'Hattie!' Claire said as she reached the table and threw down a fat document onto Hattie's lap. 'Take a look at this.'

Hattie picked it up. In bold type across the cover page the words *The Final Whistle* were written and beneath it, in smaller letters, *A Lost Life Remembered by Jimmy Ryan*. She turned the page and began to read. It was a transcript of the tapes that she had sent Claire the previous week. Hattie's questions had been edited out so that it now formed a simple first-person narrative. And curiously, whilst Jimmy was limited by his vocabulary and his dialect, it was a compelling and moving read. There was, she realised now, a beauty and a wonderful fluent simplicity in his use of language.

She looked up at Claire with a questioning expression.

'I mentioned Jimmy's story to a friend of mine who works for one of the big literary agencies. She went mad for it. Said that it had all the criteria for a massive bestseller. Football – as you said, Hattie – is such a huge marketing force. Then, of course, you have to add in the fact that Jimmy is a Geordie in an age when publishing is absolutely obsessed by what she calls "provincial patois". If you want to get on the Booker short list you have to have language that is riddled with slang, swear words and colloquialisms that no one but a native would understand. Roddy Doyle, Irvine Welsh, James Kelman – they're all at it. Then there's all the political overtones: growing up in the age of greed: Thatcher's child denied an education, abused and then being offered a kind of mirage of a way out – The Game. Which, as we all know turns into just another trick of the light in his life so that, by the time he's twenty-one he's on the scrap heap, living on the streets and selling the *Big Issue* to strangers.'

Hattie listened to Claire's excited babble with a growing

disquiet. Her friend had somehow taken control of Jimmy's future.

'Anyway, Hattie, the upshot is that Jay Hector is crazed to sign up Jimmy. Wants a meeting ASAP. The icing on the cake as far as they are concerned is that our boy is bloody beautiful. The marketing is going to be a dream. He'll be on every chat show – *Start the Week*, *Room 101*, Frank Skinner . . . Everyone who is anyone in the bloody media is obsessed by fucking football. I've got the whole thing mapped out,' she finished breathlessly.

'But what will Jimmy say? What about patient confidentiality? I should never have allowed you to have those tapes, let alone to have them transcribed and edited into this. Because even if he didn't object to you seeing them he might not be that keen on having his life story marketed like a bloody soap powder,' Hattie said, her face flushed with indignation.

'Think of the bet, Hattie. Think of Jon's face when he reads in the *Telegraph* – as he will next week – that Jimmy Ryan has signed a two-book deal with HarperCollins for an undisclosed five-figure sum. We'll have done it. Jimmy will be the talk of the chattering classes. And, what's more, he'll be a man of worth. He'll have his independence. He'll genuinely have escaped from the hell of the Meadow Well Estate.'

'Into publishing heaven?' said Hattie. 'Look, I can't allow you to use Jimmy like this. It's not fair. We will have duped him, cheated him. When I recorded those tapes I did so because I was trying to help him. I needed to understand what it was that had led him to the point at which we met him. I should never have mentioned them to you, let alone allowed you access to them. I have never, in my whole working life, compromised a patient. What you are suggesting is unethical, wrong . . .'

'Oh, don't be so prissy, Hattie. I'm not doing this for my

own financial gain. I'm doing it for Jimmy. It will enable him to escape from the streets on his own terms. No more charity from you and me. He'll have his own money. And we'll have won the bet and proved Jon wrong. Don't let your precious principles come in Jimmy's way,' she added a little spitefully.

Hattie reluctantly admitted that probably Claire was right. This book would be the best possible way in which they could ensure that Jimmy became his own man of worth.

'He'd have to agree, though. We'll have to explain exactly what will happen, and what it's all about,' she said nervously. The irony of Jimmy, who could barely write, with a book contract and a literary agent was not lost on her, but it took a PR brain like Claire's not to let the facts stand in the way.

'I think Jimmy will love it,' said Claire, relieved that she had won Hattie round. 'He adored all that attention he got the other night at Benedict's show. This would just be an extension of that.'

'I'll have to prepare him very carefully. He'll need to be sure that the publication of this wouldn't in any way expose him,' Hattie said thoughtfully.

'Who'll ever know he can't *write*? People will take one look at him and it won't matter what he says, providing he says it in a strong Geordie accent. I tell you, Hattie, this book is dynamite.'

'I think you might be right,' she said, her face, for the first time that day, transformed by a glorious smile.

She didn't raise the subject with Jimmy when she got in that night. He was watching a Newcastle United match on television and she judged it wasn't the right moment.

'Sit with me, hinny, and watch. It's the Toon playing,' he said.

'I'm not that good with football,' she said. 'I thought I'd have a nice long bath and an early night.'

But he made her sit down on the sofa beside him and earnestly explained to her the rules. No one had done that for her before and, curiously enough, she began to enjoy the game. Within a few minutes she found herself urging on his team as if she, too, had been a life-long Toon supporter.

He clasped her hand when Tottenham were awarded a penalty kick. He screamed when they missed. Rex, infected with their enthusiasm, ran round them in circles, a big black and white bow (Toon's colours) tied round his neck.

'Eee, man, did you see that?' Jimmy shouted, throwing his arms around her.

And when Newcastle United scored he performed an odd little dance with Rex – distinctly tribal she decided – that made her cry with laughter. She even joined him in a can of Newcastle Brown.

'Whey ye buggor mar!' he shouted when they scored their second goal.

At half-time he made them both a Pot Noodle and they sat, with the television turned down, and talked for a few minutes. He told her about how his granddad used to take him to St James' Park to see the Toon play and how afterwards they would go down to the quayside and eat fish and chips while Jimmy watched the big cranes on the docks. She listened intently; Jimmy had so few good memories of his childhood.

'Hinny, did you notice . . .' he said after a while, offering her an especially wide smile.

'Oh Jimmy, you've got teeth. Perfect pearly white teeth,' she said, admiring the incredible work that Barry had done in the last weeks.

'Aye, man, and there's more,' he said. 'Close your eyes . . .'

When she opened them he produced a book – a proper

grown-up book – and began to read, quite fluently, the first few pages to her.

'It's brilliant, Jimmy, in only a few days,' she said, thrilled at the extraordinary way in which he was progressing.

She got a big tub of Häagen-Dazs from the freezer so they could eat it during the second half of the match, and Jimmy fetched two more cans of Newcastle Brown.

'Two nil, two nil, two nil,' he chanted.

The tension increased during the second half when Tottenham scored first one goal and then an equaliser.

'Eeee, man, the lads have lost it,' Jimmy winced.

With ten minutes to go, as Newcastle United were about to take a penalty, the doorbell went and Rex began his high-pitched barking.

'Shit, who on earth can that be?' said Hattie, dragging herself away from the television to the intercom.

It was Toby, standing in the pouring rain, wanting to be let in. She pressed the buzzer and waited at the door for him.

'I've come to pick up a few of my things,' he said, glancing across at Jimmy who was contorted in front of the television, watching the penalty kick. 'I tried ringing but I couldn't get through.'

'Give it a kloot, lads!' Jimmy shouted. 'It's a goal, hinny! It's a goal!'

Hattie wanted to shout too but she controlled herself in front of Toby.

'Well, you'd better come in, although it is a bit late,' she said.

'I'm sorry to disturb your evening,' he said, casting a cold eye at the mess on the table by the television: the Pot Noodles, the empty carton of Häagen-Dazs, the abandoned cans of Newcastle Brown, the ashtrays filled with fag ends. Not to mention the dog who sat eyeing him malevolently from the middle of his pure white sofa.

'Oh, Jimmy was just watching his team on television and I was cheering them on,' she said.

'Were you indeed?' Toby was looking at her meaningfully.

Hattie could feel herself blushing. Goodness knows what this evening looked like to Toby. She and Jimmy curled up together watching football which was, she thought now, probably the most intimate thing a man and woman could do.

'Look, is it possible we could have a word on our own?' Toby said rather tersely to Jimmy.

'As long as you don't clag her,' Jimmy said, narrowing his eyes at Toby.

'What did he say?' said Toby aggressively after Jimmy had left them.

'He was joking. "Clag" means to hit someone . . . I think he thought you looked a little dangerous,' Hattie said.

'Jesus Christ, what's come over you, Hattie? Are you planning to take a Masters in goddamn street slang?'

'It's interesting, his language. Some of the words are extraordinarily expressive. And it's not street slang.'

'It's always him, isn't it, Hattie?' Toby said irritably.

'Not like that it isn't, Toby. I'm just terribly involved with what I'm doing for Jimmy. It's consuming me. I can't remember when I've been involved in such an exciting project. So much of my work nowadays is depressing and hopeless and ruled by NHS bureaucracy. It's just so good to be hands-on again.'

'Well, that's an interesting phrase, isn't it – *hands-on*? Hattie, I think you have become obsessed by this boy and that you have lost your head. Look at you tonight – swilling beer and eating all that crap with him. I thought you were supposed to be turning him into a man of distinction, not lowering yourself to his level,' he said, feeling, he realised, jealous of the obvious bond between Hattie and the boy.

'What do you mean, Toby?'

'For Christ's sake, Hattie, can't you see yourself? How pathetic you are chasing after that boy – talking in his Geordie accent, pandering to his every whim? He must think he's bloody landed in heaven. No rent, as much ale as he can drink, as much food as he wants and you thrown in.'

'Toby, you are being stupid. I like Jimmy, he's fun to be with. He's opened my eyes almost as much as I have opened his. But it's not the kind of relationship I had with you.'

'You must take me for a fool, Hattie. Is he that bloody good in bed?'

'I have no idea what he's like in bed, Toby. But I do know what you're like in bed and I have to say that I shouldn't imagine it's possible for him to be worse.'

He had, she thought, been drinking and this final insult really hit home.

'How fucking dare you, Hattie?' he said, moving forward as if to hit her.

'Eeee, man, that's enough,' said Jimmy, reappearing and pushing himself between Toby and Hattie.

'Get out of my way,' said Toby, thrashing out at Jimmy.

At this Rex flew into action, growling and snarling and leaping up at Toby like some latter-day Lassie, desperate to defend his master.

Toby had never liked dogs. He had, Hattie suspected, been brought up to fear them, and the sight of this beast jumping at him brought out the coward in him. Backing off, darting a hateful glance at both Hattie and Jimmy, he ran for the door and left the flat without another word.

'I'm sorry,' she said as they heard the door to the street slam shut. 'You mustn't be upset by Toby's rudeness.'

'He's right, though, hinny, aboot me living here with you, like . . .'

'It's fine, Jimmy, it really is. Toby is full of hot air – blether,' she said, translating, as had become her custom of late, her language into his. 'Do you know, I can't remember when I had such a good time as I did tonight – before he arrived,' she said with a grin.

'But, hinny, I'm on the hard card . . . broke . . .'

'But you won't be for long. Take a look at this.' Hattie took from her briefcase the manuscript that Claire had given her earlier that day.

He took it and looked at it. 'What is it, hinny?'

'It's a book, Jimmy. Look at the name on the front page.'

He looked up at her with a puzzled expression as he read his own name.

'It's your book, Jimmy, your story. I was frightened to tell you in case you would be upset, but you know those tapes we recorded – in my office? Well, I gave them to Claire; she said she had an idea. It never occurred to me it would be this. But it's wonderful, Jimmy, she's edited out all my questions and what is left is a moving and disturbing tale of our times.'

'But I'm not a writer, hinny,' he said, looking doubtfully at her.

'Well, technically I suppose you are not. But in these pages you have spoken for your whole generation. There is this literary agent – he's quite famous actually – and he has gone mad about your book. He wants to call it *The Final Whistle*, and he wants to see you this coming week. And the thing is, Jimmy, he wants to give you money. A lot of money . . .'

'Eee, lass . . .'

'You don't mind, Jimmy, do you? About the world knowing your story?' Hattie asked.

'I don't want people thinking I'm stupid, like,' he said hesitantly.

'How many times do I have to tell you that you're not stupid? Quite the contrary in fact. You are clever, Jimmy, very clever. And by the time the thing comes out you'll be feeling much more confident anyway. No one will know you didn't exactly write it,' she said.

'Ya promise?' He looked at her for reassurance with such an expression of vulnerability on his beautiful face.

'I promise,' Hattie said gently.

Chapter Fourteen

Walking into her father's club was rather like walking back into the dark ages for Hattie. While part of her quite liked the attention she received – the old-fashioned courtesy that was shown her by the footman, the waiters, and by the club members – another part of her was aware that to these men, in this place, women were still inferior beings.

'I've come to meet Sir Jeffrey George,' she said to the dress-suited man as she signed the visitors' book.

'Lovely to see you again, Miss Henrietta,' he said.

Of course her father and his friends would vehemently deny their chauvinism, insisting, as they kissed her hand in greeting, that they did so because they liked to treat women like women. In truth, most of the men here were unaware of the true effects of the march of feminism.

So confident were they in their masculine superiority that it never occurred to them that women like Hattie were outstripping them in almost every area of contemporary life. As she walked up the sweeping stairs to the drawing room she repeated in her head, like a mantra, the statistics that proved that women were winning. It was no wonder that her father and his friends – the male establishment of the day – spent more and more time in this place. The In and Out was one of the few places left where they could bar the doors to women and pretend that it was 1958 and not 1998.

Her father stood up to greet her and she smiled at him sweetly. She had made a particular effort to look right for him. She was wearing her smartest suit, bought on Toby's instructions for a wedding the previous summer. It was pale blue, tight-fitting and, she thought, very Arabella.

'Henrietta darling, it is good to see you,' he said, smiling and putting his arm out to her, not quite daring to embrace her.

'Daddy,' she said.

'Shall we go through and eat,' he said.

Their lunches together – once every six months or so – always followed the same routine. He would order their food without even glancing at the menu and she would acquiesce to his choice even if, frankly, she would probably be happier with a carton of Jimmy's Pot Noodles.

The cuisine at the club, rather like the attitudes of the members, had scarcely changed in forty years. They still served the mix of nursery food and roast meats that men of her father's generation loved.

It was, Hattie thought as she glanced at the vast side of beef balanced on a giant silver trolley, about as palatable as a work of art by Benedict Wright. In fact her own plateful of rare meat, ordered by her father, bore an uncanny resemblance to his *Steak Ta Ta*. At first, as always, their conversation was cursory and formal. He told her about his latest business acquisition – his corporation was now one of the largest in the country – and she told him about her recently published research paper. Her father, whilst not quite a self-made man, had spent much of his life trying to live up to her mother's expectations. Lady Miranda Sykes, eldest daughter of the Duke of Cumbria, had been, when they had first met, the Deb of the Year, whilst he was the relatively humble half-Jewish son of a Tory MP. Their elopement had been regarded, by her family, with horror and in the years that followed his need to prove himself to the Duke had been the driving force behind his ambition.

'Well then, Henrietta, what's all this I hear about you and Toby?' he asked eventually.

'We've broken up, Daddy,' she said.

'Is that wise?'

Her father's obvious approval of Toby had been one of the reasons why she had struggled on in the relationship for so long. He had recognised, from the moment that he had met him, that Toby was a driven man who would, in time, achieve what her father would call 'great things'.

'We weren't really suited, Daddy,' she said.

'Nonsense, he was perfect for you. A good balance for all your mad socialism.'

'Daddy, you forget that Toby is a member of the Labour Party too.'

'I hear he's on a selection list for one of the by-elections.'

'Is he? I haven't spoken to him about that sort of thing for a while.'

'Arabella says you've been seen out with someone new.'

'No, I have been involved in a project with a young man and Arabella has assumed that there is some kind of romantic thing going on. But there isn't, Daddy, I promise you.'

'But this young man is *living* in your flat?' he said, looking down on her through his half-moon glasses.

'But not with me, Daddy. I've just given him a bed, that's all, not *my* bed. And just until he gets himself sorted out. Which, actually won't be long now.'

'And what does this young man *do*?'

'He's . . . he's a writer . . .'

'Ah, artistic, is he?'

'He writes about football,' she said.

'Football?' His voice held a hint of interest.

Amongst his many other business involvements her father was on the board of Tottenham Hotspur, and had been a supporter of the team since he was a small child. His aspirations for social advancement – he had achieved a knighthood and was well on the road to being created a life peer – had led him of late to show an interest in rugger but – at heart – he was a soccer man, much happier on the terraces at Tottenham than he was at Twickenham.

'He used to play Daddy – for Everton.'

'Did he now?' her father said.

'But an injury forced him out of the game.'

'Your mother and I thought you should come down for lunch on Sunday. With this new man of yours.'

'He's not my new man, and I'm not sure I'm up to being scrutinised by Mummy at the moment.'

'Come on, Hattie. It's your mother's birthday and we so rarely see you these days.'

'OK, I'll come . . .'

'And this chap?'

'If you insist. And if he agrees.'

'Good. What team does he support?'

'Newcastle United.'

'The Toon,' her father said. 'Bastards beat Tottenham last night . . .'

Hattie was beginning to worry about her sessions with Lisa Price. Every moment of her time that wasn't taken up with Jimmy or the rest of her work she devoted to Lisa's case. She had reread the case notes time and time again looking for clues to how she could further draw out the child.

She needed to get more out of the girl, to accumulate some solid evidence of the abuse and the cruelty Lisa had endured within her family home. And it was becoming increasingly difficult to get her to talk about her past.

She smiled as Lisa came into her office and went over to the shelf on which Hattie stored the books she loved. Now that Lisa had told her what had motivated her attack on Lindy she was trying to link the act back to the child's relationship with her oppressive, domineering, religiously obsessive father.

They looked at the books together for a while and then, very patiently, Hattie led the subject back to Lisa's home life, establishing that the mother – probably as fearful of George Price as his children – left all the discipline to her husband.

'How did he punish you?' Hattie asked gently.

'He would make us pray to God for forgiveness,' she said, judging Hattie's reaction before continuing, 'and sometimes he would not let us talk at all. We would have to be quiet all day.'

'But did he hurt you, Lisa?' she pursued.

The child nodded and looked down into her lap.

'How did he hurt you?'

'He hit us with a belt if we sinned,' she said softly, stopping again to see Hattie's reaction, 'and if we did something to someone else he would do it to us.'

'An eye for an eye . . .' Hattie muttered under her breath.

'Once he told me to make him some tea. And when I took it to him in his chair I spilt a little bit on the sleeve of his jumper . . .'

'And?' Hattie said.

'He jumped up and led me to the kitchen and he took the kettle and he poured boiling water all over my arm,' she said, pulling up the sleeve of her dress to expose the unmistakable scar of a serious burn that Hattie had noticed on the very first day that she had met Lisa.

'Oh Lisa . . .' she said.

'I didn't cry because it was God's punishment,' the child said, pulling down her sleeve.

When she got home from work that day Jimmy was locked in the bathroom getting ready to go out to the theatre with Claire. When he was a little boy his nan had once taken him to see a pantomime at the Theatre Royal in Newcastle and his recollections of it formed one of the most moving moments in *The Final Whistle*.

'It was all crimson curtains and men with violins and lights that blinded your eyes, like,' he had said.

Hattie was doubtful that the Donmar Warehouse would match up to his childhood memories of *Mother Goose* but Claire had thought it would form a useful prelude to his future exposure to the chattering classes.

Hattie had decided not to go because she needed to catch up on some work and because she was worried she was becoming too constant a presence in Jimmy's life. It was good for him to go out with Claire on his own. And it would be good for her to have some space tonight.

He emerged from the bathroom dressed for the first time in his new suit.

'You know it's quite casual in London, Jimmy. We don't dress up except for the opera,' she said when she saw him looking so stunning.

'Eee, lassie, it's Sunday best for the theatre,' he said.

It was, Hattie noted a little cynically when she arrived, Sunday best for Claire too. She had put a lot of effort into her appearance that night. Claire was wearing a high-fashion semi-transparent lacy dress beneath which you could see her (34DD) underwear.

Jimmy was clearly worried about her going out dressed like that. He took Hattie aside before they left.

'You can see next week's washing there,' he whispered, indicating Claire's black bra and pants.

'You're meant to, Jimmy. That's the fashion.'

'Man, I've seen everything now.'

'Not quite, Jimmy, but if Claire gets her way you will,' said Hattie a little savagely under her breath.

When they had left she poured herself a glass of wine, put on the television and fed an expectant and impatient Rex. She was tempted to make herself one of Jimmy's doorstep sandwiches or even a Pot Noodle but she resisted and instead took a loaf of ciabatta from the freezer and heated it in the oven. Toby, she thought as she looked at the illuminated contents of her sheet steel fridge, would be horrified by the way in which Laughing Cow and St Ivel had taken over from his usual selection of designer cheeses. But she was beginning to develop a taste for thickly spread processed cheese served with mounds of Branston pickle and topped with ketchup. Curiously the reverse was happening with Jimmy. Very gradually his tastes – in every sense of the word – were beginning to be influenced by his exposure to Hattie and Claire's world. He was becoming familiar with all manner of sophisticated foodstuffs in a way that Hattie privately found rather depressing. He now preferred the Singapore noodles from their local takeaway to the Pot Noodles that had been such a staple part of his diet. Heinz salad cream had been replaced – in his big sandwiches – by Hellmann's mayonnaise. He had even, she noticed, begun to develop a liking for crisp, dry white wine in place of his beloved Newkie. And although these changes were, she supposed, a necessary part of his transformation it sometimes seemed as if they were corrupting him. Taking away a part of his original charm and innocence.

It was Hattie, now, who kept their kitchen stocked with the things that had once been Jimmy's favourites. She made up a tray with her supper – her own version of Jimmy's doorstep sandwich (with the added concession of a few pieces of rocket) and a can of Newkie – and made her way back to the sofa just in time for the opening credits of *Coronation Street*.

Toby had always been a bit sniffy about television. But since his departure – and Jimmy's arrival – Hattie had begun to understand the allure of popular culture. It had become quite socially acceptable in Toby's precious circle of friends to watch *EastEnders* which was now, Hattie thought, positively New Labour in its appeal. But any other regular viewing habit (apart from *Newsnight* and *ER*) was rather frowned upon. In fact, Hattie had never actually sat through an epsiode of *Coronation Street* prior to Jimmy's arrival. Nor had she had any idea of the delights of *Blind Date* or *The Bill*. Now she began to plan her evenings – or at any rate her evening meal – to coincide with the programmes she most enjoyed. With Rex curled up at her feet, her supper on a tray on her lap, she sat mesmerised in front of the TV when, at a particularly inconvenient moment, the doorbell rang.

She toyed with not bothering to answer it. But whoever it was kept pressing the buzzer until, reluctantly, she put her tray down and went to see who it was.

'Hattie, I thought I'd pop in and see how you were getting on,' Jon said nervously as he hovered on the doorstep.

She had always found Jon's presence threatening. If she had been initially attracted to Toby because he had seemed so safe she had always recoiled from Jon because he was too smooth and cynical. He had the kind of dark good looks that she knew other women found irresistible but which she herself found almost repellent. He had an almost permanent five-o'clock shadow, and hairs on the backs of his arms that, she suspected, probably covered much of his muscular body. She couldn't, for the life of her, work out what he was doing here. Spying, she suspected – trying to find out something for Toby or attempting to gain information on how the wager with Jimmy was progressing.

'Did Toby send you?' she asked suspiciously.

'No, I haven't spoken to Toby for weeks,' Jon said.

'Oh well, come in then. Do you want to share my supper? It's just bread and cheese,' she offered, although she was privately rather irritated that she would have to switch off the TV and miss the second half of *Coronation Street*.

They sat down at the table in the kitchen and she went to the fridge to get a bottle of wine.

'I'll have what you're having,' he said, indicating her can of Newcastle Brown. 'I didn't know that you drank ale, Hattie.'

'I didn't. I'm something of a new convert,' she said.

'Brown sauce?' he said as he picked up the bottle of HP and poured it lavishly on his bread and cheese. 'I hadn't got you down as a brown sauce woman either. Christ, I love this stuff. Things have certainly changed around here.'

There was, Hattie noted, something changed about Jon too. He was more approachable, less critical. It was almost as if he wanted – after all these years of mutual animosity – to be her friend.

'Toby would have a heart attack if he could see us,' she said and, for probably the first time ever, they smiled conspiratorially at one another.

'How's the bet going?' he said, reverting to his old tone.

'I'm not sure I should tell you. But I think that you've probably guessed that the beer and the brown sauce are part of it.'

'You mean this boy has effected a greater change on your tastes and sensibilities than you have on his?' he said with a mocking laugh.

'Well, that's what Toby thinks. But actually I suspect that what has happened is that I've been opened up to an area of life that had previously been denied me,' she said.

'Like *Coronation Street*.' He indicated the television.

'And *Casualty* and *The Bill* and *Blind Date*,' she said with a grin, enjoying the fact that for once Jon wasn't sending her up or criticising her.

'And what about Claire? Is she equally taken with this boy and his populist tastes?' he said, trying to keep the concern from his voice. He was no longer bothered about losing the bet – in fact he had resigned himself to it – but he was very worried about losing Claire. He had only come here this evening to try to find out more about Claire's relationship with Jimmy.

'Well, you know Claire. I think it's rather more physical with her. She's grooming him in all the areas in which I can't. Teaching him about sex and shopping, that kind of thing,' said Hattie, a slight edge entering her voice.

'Literally?' said Jon.

'She's taken him to the theatre tonight and then out to dinner.'

'Has she?' Jon looked thoughtful, as if he were trying to make up his mind whether to confide in Hattie.

'In fact I don't think I've heard Claire talk about another man since we took on Jimmy. She says she's put all those bastards she usually falls for out of her life. She's quite taken with this new experience of being with a younger man, of being able to teach him,' said Hattie, trying hard not to display too obviously the resentment she felt towards her friend.

'She's very keen on him?' Jon asked as casually as he could.

'You should have seen the way she's dressed tonight. I never imagined Claire being interested in a man who couldn't bankroll her into a relationship. In fact I never imagined her being interested in anyone who didn't have all those trapping of status that she loves . . .' Hattie said, wondering a little anxiously what Jimmy and Claire were doing at that moment.

Jon shifted in his seat. Hattie had never seen him as reflective as he seemed this evening.

'And do you think that this boy is drawn to Claire?' Jon asked after a while.

'I wish I knew,' Hattie said ruefully.

'This is the first time since she and I split that I have

seen her like this. Other men have come in and out of her life but I've never seen her so abstracted before. I always regarded Claire as my best friend – at least my only proper woman friend – and suddenly I have this feeling that I have no place in her life any more.' He paused, looking across at Hattie to judge her reaction. 'And the thing is, Hattie, I don't like it.'

'You mean you're jealous?' Hattie said.

'I suppose I am. And the discovery has sent me mad. I wish I'd never had that ridiculous bet in the first place. It was just a game, just a way to aggravate you. I never imagined Claire would get so caught up in it.'

'Have you told her any of this, Jon?'

'No, not yet. You won't say anything to her, will you, Hattie?'

'Not if you don't want me to,' she said, feeling a little sorry for him.

'Do you think we could be friends now, Hattie?'

'Why not?' She smiled broadly at him. 'At least once I've won this bet . . .'

'Regardless of the outcome of the bet. Can we be friends? Can we talk again like this . . . about Claire and everything?' he asked tentatively.

'About the bet, Jon, have you decided what the final test will be?' she said a little smugly, changing the subject.

'No,' he said disinterestedly. 'Somehow the outcome of the bet isn't so important to me any more.'

'You said that first night that he would have to prove that he was employed or employable, that he appreciated the finer things of life and that he could hold a civilised conversation. I think I could prove all that to you tonight if you stayed around till he came home. But I dare say you would want more public proof,' Hattie said.

'I think I said something about polite society, Hattie. We

need somewhere, some venue or party or society function that we could use as his final test. Somewhere you can't buy your way into. The Royal Enclosure at Ascot would be no good – anybody can get in there these days. Glyndebourne would be wrong. It must be an event that is strictly invitation only.'

Hattie got up and cleared away their plates.

'It's your test, Jon. You'll have to decide where Jimmy proves he isn't pond life.'

'Henley Royal Regatta,' said Jon, and they both laughed. 'No, I tell you what: Frost's summer garden party. If your man gets an invitation to that – which of course he'll have to get on his own merit, not because you make a call to Daddy or Mummy – and if he is accepted by the other guests then you'll have won.'

'OK,' she said, reaching out her hand to shake his in agreement. 'We were always such opposites, Jon. You constantly delighted in disagreeing with everything I said. And although I resented you I never really believed you were as heartless as you pretended.'

'I just liked winding you up,' he said as he got up to leave, 'and it was always so easy.'

They smiled at each other. Some kind of bond had evolved between them. Born, Hattie supposed, of the fact that they were both feeling similar emotions about Claire and Jimmy. She hated Claire's obsession with their protégé almost as much as Jon did.

'Give my love to Claire . . .' he said a little pathetically as he left the flat.

As soon as the lights dimmed in the auditorium of the Donmar Warehouse Claire had known that Jimmy was disappointed. Two actors stood in jeans and T-shirts on a set that was completely bare apart from a single bent-wood chair.

'Where's the band, like?' he stage-whispered to her five minutes into the play.

'Band?' she said. 'This isn't a concert, Jimmy. It's a play . . .'

'But there's always a band in the theatre.'

'You mean an orchestra!' said Claire. 'Sorry, Jimmy, it's not that kind of production.'

'Ssh!' said the man immediately in front of them.

During the performance, to Claire's amusement and the irritation of the rest of the audience, Jimmy asked her repeated questions about not only the plot – it was an obscure but well-reviewed South African play about oppression in the townships – but also about the absence of those things he had considered essential to any theatrical experience. Why were there no plush red curtains, no scenery, no costume changes, no props and no ice creams in the interval?

Even Claire found the action – if you could call it that – hard to follow. And much of the piece was written in a mixture of Afrikaans and pidgin English which was, she thought, very nearly as difficult to understand as Jimmy's Geordie. Like him she was relieved when the harrowing final scene was over and the two actors moved forward towards the audience, raising their fists in the clenched salute of the ANC.

'Eeee, hinny, that's a bit rude, like,' Jimmy said so loudly that the man in front turned round as if he were ready to smash his own clenched fist into Jimmy's face.

Such was the enthusiasm of the audience that, as the actors turned to walk away, some of them began, in faltering voices, to sing.

'What are they doing?' he said as one by one the audience – few of whom were either South African or black – began to sing '*Nkosi Sike Lela Lafrica*', the ANC anthem.

'It's the South African anthem, Jimmy,' Claire said.

'Wha'evva happened to "Godsavethequeen", like?' he said.

She took him out for a meal afterwards. They went to Zen Central. He had, he said, never eaten Chinese food before.

'This then, Jimmy, will be a whole new experience,' Claire said, marvelling at the sight of him sitting opposite her.

Everyone had looked at them as they had arrived. She couldn't help but think that they made a striking couple. So what if he was a bit younger than she. It wasn't as if he were underage and she some middle-aged mother of three. The few years that separated them were, in the late nineties, really quite unremarkable. Besides, it was such a pleasure being the one who took the lead – ordered the food, the wine and instructed about which dishes were the most delicious.

Most of Claire's romantic life had been spent with men who – in every sense – dominated her. Men who picked the restaurant, recommended the food, chose the wine, paid the bill, selected which side of the bed they would sleep on. It was so wonderful to find herself in charge. Although, of course, she knew it would be a while before she would be able to risk raising the subject of sex with Jimmy. She wasn't going to risk rushing things again. Instead she would slowly work on him – as men had slowly worked on her – wooing him, flattering him, buying him the odd little gift, taking him out for meals, so that gradually he would fall in love with her.

He was, she thought as she ordered a selection of the most simple dishes, already beginning to respond. Already Jimmy had started to develop a taste for the finer things in life, such as the crisp, dry Chardonnay the waiter had poured.

When the first few dishes arrived, Claire picked up her chopsticks and, with expert grace, began to eat.

Jimmy was aghast. It was bad enough trying to cope with the various knives and forks Hattie put out for him. But sticks, man?

'I can't eat with those,' he said.

'You can. Look hold them like this,' she said, demonstrating how he should position the chopsticks. He picked his up and copied her. He was quick, she thought, much quicker than Hattie wanted to accept. Within minutes he had almost perfected the art. And not only was he quick, Claire thought as she watched him, he was much more inquisitive than Hattie liked to think. He was genuinely interested in the new tastes before him. Trying one dish after another and concluding that the food was 'reet tasty'.

Claire had guessed that he would like Chinese food because it was so sweet. The few children of Claire's acquaintance liked Chinese food for much the same reason, which was what had her made her pick this restaurant tonight. In many ways Jimmy was like a child. She would gradually expose him to new experiences, new tastes, new ideas. So that by the time he could appreciate fresh truffles he would, she felt sure, be ready to appreciate the woman feeding them to him.

'This is just the start, Jimmy. In the next few weeks we're going to try lots of new things. And we'll go and see more plays, and films. And the odd sporting event – polo and point-to-point, not football or dog racing. Will that be all right with you?'

He smiled at her and picked up his glass of Chardonnay.

'Aye, hinny, if it's all as good as this, like,' he said, draining the glass in one gulp.

Chapter Fifteen

Arabella's latest boyfriend had offered to pick up Hattie and Jimmy and drive them down to Whitehaven for lunch that Sunday. If Jimmy was nervous at the prospect of meeting Hattie's parents he didn't show it. But she did.

She always got anxious when she went home. But she was especially concerned at the prospect of letting her family loose on Jimmy. Claire had told her not to be silly, reassured her that their protégé was perfectly capable of coping with the snobbish scrutiny of the George family. It would, she had said, be a dry run for the Frost party. The new man in Arabella's life – she had split with the rock star after a much-publicised row in a nightclub – was the handsome owner of two of London's most exclusive restaurants. He was the kind of man who made Hattie's flesh crawl: smooth and confident, wearing the summer uniform of his particular set – a blazer, twill trousers, and shoes that she just knew would have been made on his own last at Lobb.

By contrast Jimmy seemed uncomfortable and over-dressed in his Sunday best suit. He looked as Hattie always felt herself when she had worn the clothes that Toby chose for her – as if he were a child dressing up in adult clothes. Moreover the suit, restricting and formal as it was, seemed to diminish his personality and his individuality. Jimmy was at his most stunning, Hattie decided, in jeans and T-shirt because they allowed him to be himself. The suit was, quite literally for him, fancy dress.

More poignant, perhaps, was the way in which Rex

(without whom Jimmy went nowhere) had been tidied up for the occasion. With his coat carefully brushed and his new collar and leash – a nasty black leather studded set that would have been more suited to a Doberman or an S & M dominatrix – he looked as awkward and displaced as his master.

In the car – Alistair drove his Range Rover with the same arrogant assurance with which he did everything else in life, with one hand on the steering wheel at a terrific speed – Jimmy engaged in conversation with Arabella who, from time to time, would turn to Hattie with a puzzled expression on her face.

'What's he saying, Hattie?' she would demand.

'"Scrafflin" means searching,' Hattie said, 'and "moothy" means mouthy, talkative.'

'It's a good thing he's brought his interpreter with him,' said Alistair, raising his eyebrows at Arabella, who collapsed into giggles.

Hattie was aware that today Jimmy would be the star turn at a command performance he would not understand. There would be, she had no doubt, many quickly exchanged glances, nudges and moments when eyebrows would be raised. She just hoped that their derision of Jimmy wouldn't be obvious enough for him to pick up on it.

Her mother came out onto the gravel drive to greet them, followed three paces behind, by her West Highland terrier and the two old black Labradors. She was, as ever, faultlessly elegant, wearing a cream dress and lots of pearls that softened her features and toned with her sleek, honey-coloured hair.

Alistair, as Hattie had expected, was all over her, kissing her hand and shamelessly flattering her. Establishing, within a minute of meeting her, an obvious rapport. Having embraced Arabella and twittered happily with

Alistair, Hattie's mother turned her attention to her other daughter whom she frequently referred to as the 'black-haired sheep of the family', a reference, Hattie had long ago decided, to the fact that she had inherited her long, dark, curly hair from her Jewish paternal grandmother.

'Hattie darling, you look lovely,' she said with the particular tone of insincerity that she reserved for her younger daughter.

'And you, Mummy, look beautiful. Happy birthday,' she said, going through the motions of kissing her mother on both cheeks although, of course, no physical contact was actually exchanged between them.

She had brought her mother a first edition of a book written by one of her Sykes ancestors, a gift that would probably be wasted on her mother, especially when she compared it to the magnificent present that Arabella would, undoubtedly, have purchased for her. She handed over the little parcel, noting, as she had expected, how inferior it looked next to the gift-wrapped, designer-ribboned offering of her sister.

Finally Lady Miranda's glance turned to Jimmy, who was holding on to Rex's leash with a firm, if nervous hand.

'And you must be Jimmy,' she said, graciously holding out a rather limp wrist to him.

To Hattie's absolute horror instead of clasping her hand Jimmy dropped her a clumsy curtsy.

'Ya ladyship . . .' he said, bowing his head and momentarily losing his grasp on Rex's leash, precipitating an even more humiliating scene on the gravel drive. Jimmy's dog, clearly aroused by the delicious scent of Lady Miranda's West Highland terrier, pulled himself up on the little dog's back and began to mount her.

'Get that thing off Jontie,' she screamed in horror.

'Eee, Rex, doon boy!' shouted Jimmy, regaining the lead and pulling him away from the furiously barking little bitch.

'You'll have to tie him up,' said Lady Miranda, offering Rex exactly the same look of disgust that she had given Jimmy.

It occurred to Hattie, as Jimmy took the dog and tied it securely against a wrought-iron gate, that her mother's disdain for both Rex and his master was in some way connected. It would be as appalling for her to find her precious Jontie impregnated by some horrid mongrel as it would for her to discover that her daughter was involved with someone like Jimmy (not that she was, of course). In her mother's eyes neither the dog nor the man had Kennel Club approval. Neither had what her mother regarded as proper breeding potential.

In the drawing room Hattie's father offered them all drinks and Jimmy repeated his strange little bobbing bow when he was introduced to Sir Jeffrey.

'Ya lordship . . .' he said this time.

'No, you've got that wrong, I'm *Sir* Jeffrey,' her father said a little irritably.

'It'll be another year or so till he's elevated,' said Arabella with a tinkling laugh.

'Elevated?' Jimmy was confused.

'My father is in line to be made a life peer, which would make him Lord George,' Hattie said, her own face flushed with embarrassment for Jimmy.

Alistair had already moved in on Sir Jeffrey and was regaling him with an anecdote about an outcast member of the royal family who was a regular customer at one of his restaurants.

'After six months of her just signing the bills we finally got the courage up to ask her for payment. She sent us a cheque a couple of weeks later that was returned to us by

Coutts with the immortal words "refer to drawer" on it. Which of course we didn't dare do,' he said.

'She's so very vulgar,' said Lady Miranda. 'Marrying into The Firm was like winning the lottery for her.'

'One of me nan's friends won the lottery,' said Jimmy. 'Bowt hersell a big hoose up Whitley Bay.'

'Oh really,' said Lady Miranda without pausing even to glance his way.

'Loved your column today, Arabella,' said Sir Jeffrey.

'Yes, darling,' said Lady Miranda. 'It's like a postcard home for me when I haven't seen you. Although I have to say I thought your Versace frock was cut a little on the skimpy side . . .'

Hattie was clearly the only person in the family who found Arabella's weekly diary column an embarrassment. A banal and shallow round up of the parties she had attended, and the frocks she had worn, it represented, to Hattie at least, an awful indictment of her sister's vacuous lifestyle. And was proof positive that Britain was no more a classless society at the turn of the twentieth century than it had been at the turn of the nineteenth.

By the time they sat down in the dining room for lunch Hattie felt sick. Jimmy was seated between her mother and her sister and she feared for his safety. Her father had already questioned him – like a high court judge – about his background, establishing within half an hour that he was, as Jimmy might say, 'a glaky nowt'. A person of no consequence.

'And where exactly is it that you come from?' said Lady Miranda, feigning an interest in Jimmy.

'Meadow Well, maam,' said Jimmy.

'And where is that?' she said.

'It is a large estate near Newcastle,' said Hattie quickly.

'Much shooting?' enquired Lady Miranda.

'More joy-riding and ram-raiding,' said Hattie under

her breath, 'but the occasional incident with an Uzi or an AK-47.'

'I see,' said her mother, looking closely at Jimmy. 'And how did you come to meet my daughter?'

'He was selling the *Big Issue* in Covent Garden,' Hattie said.

'Oh,' said her mother.

No one directed a single question at Jimmy for the rest of the meal. Instead they indulged in the sort of small talk that Hattie hated: idle and scurrilous gossip about people unknown to Jimmy. She had forgotten the reason why she so rarely came home to her family. But seeing them through his eyes – inhospitable, supercilious, patronising and cold – reminded her forcibly why she had become estranged from them.

'I think – if it's all right with everybody else – I'll show Jimmy round the place,' she said when the awful meal finally came to an end.

She took him back out of the big oak front door and onto the big gravel drive where – to their mutual relief – they lit up cigarettes.

'Can I show you the gardens, Jimmy and the stables?'

'Aye hinny,' he said, allowing her to take his arm and guide him round the vast grounds.

'Whey ye bugger mar!' he shouted shortly into their tour, pointing up a small path that led towards some greenhouses.

Rex had somehow managed to escape and was furiously mating with a more than willing Jontie.

'Leave them,' said Hattie, overcome with laughter.

When the dogs had finished – Jontie rolling on the ground in what seemed like a post-coital glow – they took Rex back and tied him more firmly to the old iron gate.

'Eeee, what will your mam say?' said Jimmy nervously.

'She won't know, will she?' replied Hattie gleefully.

Jimmy looked at her blankly.

'Don't you see, Jimmy? It's Rex's revenge on my ghastly family. His way of, as it were, sticking two fingers up at the lot of them. Or at any rate, leaving his mark on – or rather in – my mother's dog. Can you imagine her joy ten weeks from now when Jontie gives birth to six or seven coarse-haired mongrels?'

But Jimmy didn't see the joke. In fact he had become as distant from Hattie as her family were from him. It was as if, she thought, his opinion of her had been in some way tainted by his exposure to them. It had been a terrible mistake to bring him here.

She left Whitehaven that evening more convinced than ever that the only person of real nobility that day had been Jimmy.

She could tell from Jimmy's silence, when they were alone again in the flat that evening, that he had been hurt by the way in which her family had treated him. She knew for certain now that seeing Whitehaven and meeting her parents had changed his view of her. She tried to excuse their bad behaviour and their snobbery but she couldn't seem to get through to him.

'I'm sorry they were so offhand and rude, Jimmy,' she said.

'Nah, hinny, it's all right,' he said.

'No it's not all right, Jimmy. Do you understand now why I see so little of my family?'

'They're yourn, hinny,' he said softly.

'I wish they weren't sometimes, Jimmy.'

'We come from different worlds, pet.'

'We don't really, you know. You said to me that you sometimes felt like an outsider from your family – that never knowing your father made you feel separate, different from your brothers. Well, I feel like that about them. As if I were some kind of changeling, planted on them. My mother even calls me her "black-haired sheep". We don't come from different worlds, Jimmy. We were just *raised* in different worlds . . .'

'I'm tired, lassie,' he said, turning away from her.

'I have to leave early in the morning. But I've left you some work to do. Oxford Reading Tree Stage 6 Book 3. And some exercises with your letters,' she said. 'There's lots of food in the fridge. I won't be home late. Try and get through the whole book and we can work together on your letters tomorrow evening.'

'Aye, hinny,' he said despondently.

During the months in which she had been seeing him, Hattie had grown quite fond of Ben. He was, she was quite certain, irredeemable. At fifteen he had a police record that filled two foolscap files. He had committed every modern urban crime you could think of: joy-riding, ram-raiding, drug dealing, mugging, breaking and entering. He was a liar, a cheat, a coward and a bully.

In the course of his substantial criminal career he had become something of a celebrity. Achieving the status – in certain of the tabloids – of the nickname The Eel, not just because, under the Childrens Act it was not possible for them to identify him by name, but also because of his amazing ability to slip away from the scene of a crime. In seeing her he was just going through the motions, going along with the recommendations of the juvenile courts and his social worker, who hoped that the answer might be found in Hattie's assessment of his mental state. In truth, despite a fairly difficult but not particularly damaging childhood, she could find no signs of any particular disturbance that might have pushed him into his anti-social behaviour. Indeed, despite his reputation she had come to look forward to her time with him, perhaps because it represented light relief when compared to the sessions she spent with her other patients, most particularly Lisa.

There was, she had long since decided, an undeniable charm about him, a quality that – in circumstances other than those in which he was raised – might have taken him a long way in life. He was funny, self-deprecating, slightly overfamiliar and very likeable.

'Hi, Ben,' she said as he slumped down in his usual pose on the little sofa in her office, his legs sprawling and spread out in an overtly masculine manner. He raised one arm in what she took to be the latest street signal of greeting.

'How are you?'

'OK,' he said.

'You know, Ben, try as I might I can't really find any reason for the two of us to go on meeting like this.'

'You mean you've made your assessment?' he said.

She nodded.

'Are you going to recommend sending me on one of those expensive foreign trips?' he said with a big mocking grin.

'No, I don't think that you need a holiday, Ben. And I don't think that you need treatment.'

'So I'm, like, going to be sentenced by the court?' he said.

'Yes. But don't worry, you won't end up in a boot camp or a borstal.' She paused for a moment. 'At least you won't if the courts follow my guidelines.'

'Like what?'

'Like you going to a special school in Oxfordshire. I've mentioned in my report that I believe that you are highly intelligent, Ben, and that you have potential.'

'I don't want to go to any school,' he said.

'Believe me, you'll like this one. It's a boarding school,' she said.

'You mean you're going to send me to fucking Eton or something?' he said.

'If that were possible I would. You'd do very well at Eton,' she said with a smile.

She showed him the brochure for the school, set in acres of countryside, but he was clearly unimpressed.

'When you think about the alternatives, it won't look so bad,' she said.

It was unusual for Hattie to be able to suggest a solution that she genuinely believed might effect some change in a child. In Ben's case – although of course there was always the danger that he would run away and reoffend – the obvious answer was education. And while Overton House wasn't a public school it was just possible that in a controlled environment, with small classes and special coaching, Ben could achieve some of his potential. She left her office feeling, rather unusually, that she had done her best for The Eel. Even if he didn't see it that way.

When she got home from work that evening she knew immediately that something was wrong. There was no Rex waiting to greet her with his yaps, howls and – of late – enthusiastic embraces. And no Jimmy sitting at the table waiting for her to check his day's work.

His little cubicle bedroom behind the Japanese screens had been cleaned out again. The only things left, carefully hung on hangers, were the clothes they had bought him in Paul Smith, and his books. The manuscript of *The Final Whistle* lay on top of his Oxford Reading Tree scheme.

He had left a note written in his painstaking script and pinned to the rolled up futon: 'Gan canny, hinny, Jimmy.'

She rang Claire.

'Christ, Hattie, we were due to have lunch with Jay Hector on Friday. You'll have to find him and get him back. Why on earth do you think he's done a runner?'

'My family, Claire . . .'

'Your family?'

'We went to Whitehaven for lunch yesterday and they were unspeakably rude to him. I knew when we got home last night that he was upset but I didn't realise how much.'

'Where do you suppose he's gone?'

'I don't know.'

'Well, fucking well find him, Hattie.'

Hattie put the phone down and tried to work out where to look first. Would he have gone back on the streets? Was he with Scott, Mick and Annie in some doorway somewhere? She stood by the phone wondering what on earth to do first when it began to ring.

It was Arabella.

'Has he gone?' she said.

'What do you mean, Arabella?'

'Has Jimmy gone?'

'Why should he have done?'

'I came round to see him today while you were at work. To put him straight . . .'

'Straight about what, Arabella?'

'For goodness' sake, Hattie, who's being stupid now? I told him he had no future with our family.'

'Why should he have thought he had a future with our family, Arabella?'

'Oh, don't be a fool, Hattie. It was quite obvious to all of us yesterday that he thought he'd got a foot under the table. And a leg over somewhere else, I dare say.'

'How many times do I have to tell you, Arabella, there is nothing between Jimmy and me?'

'Anyway, I told him the truth, Hattie. That he was the latest in a long line of lame ducks that you had picked up. That he was nothing more than a challenge to you. That you really loved Toby and that he had got in the way. That the only reason he was here at all was because of a bet between you, Claire and Jon. That Jon

206

had put a wager of £5000 on your being able to turn Jimmy into something that passed for a decent member of society.'

'You said WHAT, Arabella?'

'He didn't seem to know anything about the bet. And I don't think he liked it either. Daddy told me to offer him some money. But I didn't have to. He began packing before I had even finished my little speech.'

'Where was he going, Arabella?'

'How should I know?'

Hattie slammed the phone down hard. When she had composed herself again she rang Claire back and told her the news.

'I said we should have told him about the bet right at the start,' Claire said in accusatory tones.

'But it would have offended him so. I mean, when you think about it, Claire, it was a horrible, arrogant thing to do, to try to make something out of Jimmy just for some bet.'

'You should have thought about the implications of that ages ago. It's too late now.'

'What am I going to do, Claire?'

'You are going to find him, convince him that he must come back and bring him to that meeting with Jay Hector. And then we are going to win the wager,' said Claire.

'But it isn't really about the bet any more, is it? It's about Jimmy. It isn't about proving Jon wrong now, it's about making things better for Jimmy.'

Claire's silence at the other end of the phone indicated to Hattie that her friend felt much the same. As they had got to know their social guinea pig – as they came to like Jimmy – their attitude and their motives had somehow changed. The bet was no longer something they had to prove for themselves, or to get back at Jon, it was something they had to do for Jimmy.

'Look, Hattie, I'm in the middle of a huge presentation this week. I can't drop everything and search for him. Can you take time out to find him?' said Claire.

'I think so. Last time he just went back on the street.'

'Last time?'

'Oh, I never told you but we had a row a few weeks ago and he ran off back on the streets. He returned in search of Rex,' said Hattie.

'Well, let me know what's going on, OK?' said Claire.

After they rang off, Hattie picked up the note Jimmy had left as if it might offer her some clue as to where he had gone.

'Gan canny, hinny – go carefully . . .' she said aloud to herself, crumpling the paper in her hand and throwing it into the bin.

Hattie told the cab to drop her at the Royal Opera House. It was almost as if she had travelled back in time, she thought as she paid off the driver, back to the night on which she had first stumbled across Jimmy's path.

It was raining as it had been the evening that they had seen *Aida*. It seemed so long ago. So much had changed in the intervening weeks. She crossed the road and made her way to the Halifax doorway in which they had sheltered on that fateful night. But there was nothing, and no one, there apart from a pile of burger cartons, newspapers and Coke cans. She began walking round the streets that bordered the West End of London, looking in all the doorways to check out the men – and the occasional woman – who were camped out that night.

There must have been close to three hundred of them in the network of streets that she covered over the next two hours. But none of their faces was familiar, and anyway she knew he wasn't here any more. She knew deep down that she wouldn't find him in London.

He had, she felt sure, finally gone home. Back to the Meadow Well Estate. More wounded, she suspected, than he had been when he had returned there after his accident.

Chapter Sixteen

Hattie was on the first train out of King's Cross the following morning. The office had been a little surprised by her sudden demand for a few days' leave but with her current low caseload they hadn't raised any objections.

She had never been to the North East before. Had never, she was shocked to realise, travelled across the country by train. She had been to Scotland several times but on each occasion she had flown, unaware of the geographical changes that took place as you progressed northwards.

Sitting at the window of the train, watching the changing landscape, impressed on her how terribly ignorant she was about her own country. There was, it seemed to her, a quite distinct visual divide between the North and the South. It didn't quite change after Watford, but almost. Within half an hour she began to notice the signs of industrialisation – chimneys, cranes, collieries – that signalled the difference between her world and Jimmy's. Even the countryside somehow mutated – the clipped and manicured meadows of the South turning to a wild, darker, richer moorland as they went north.

Under the arches outside Newcastle Central Station she got a cab. The city itself was bustling and prosperous-looking. Familiar chain stores dotted the streets, interspersed by the kind of restaurants, cafés and brasseries that you might find in corresponding cities in the South.

Even on the outskirts of the city there were indications of prosperity: big houses with high walls and large gardens set way back from the road.

'Where are we now?' she asked, curious to understand the geography of Jimmy's birthplace.

'Jesmond,' said the taxi driver, looking at her curiously in his driving mirror.

It was only when they were travelling down the Old Coast Road towards North Shields that Hattie started to notice the industrial decline that had shadowed Jimmy's childhood – the vast Wills factory, closed down years ago and now boarded up and covered in hostile Keep Out signs.

But all along the Tyne there were signs of regeneration: warehouse developments, office blocks and hotels being constructed or renovated along the river banks.

When they got closer to North Shields the driver asked her where she wanted to go.

'Meadow Well,' she said, noticing him flinch a little.

'Whereaboots?' he asked, examining her closely in his mirror.

'Avon Avenue.'

'Eeee.' He gave a sharp intake of breath.

She recognised the house from the photograph Jimmy had shown her. Its semidetached twin was still blackened and boarded up, and the front garden of number 23 was still littered with rotting rubbish bags, old tyres and abandoned toys.

'Gan canny, lass,' the driver said warily as she paid him off and walked up the little path.

She stood for a moment and took it all in before she knocked on the door. From inside she heard the sound of a dog barking – not the familiar high-pitched yowls of Rex but the booming, echoing voice of, she guessed, an Alsatian.

For some minutes Hattie stood there waiting for the door to open, hesitant to knock again. Then, just as she was bracing herself to rap one more time, the door swung open and a woman – Jimmy's mam – looked out.

'Whees yee?' she said, and it was impossible to believe that Jimmy's beautiful face could in any way have descended from her coarse features.

'Er, I'm Hattie George, a friend of Jimmy's from London.' she said, smiling warmly.

The woman looked her up and down for a moment a little suspiciously. 'Coome in then. Doon, Tyson, doon,' she said, guiding Hattie along the dark hallway, past the snuffling, sniffling dog – an Alsatian as she had guessed – and into the front room.

Its shabby décor represented a quite different kind of minimalism to that of Hattie's smart London flat. There was hardly any furniture in the room at all – just a Leatherette sofa, a stool and a huge television. The floor was covered in a fraying carpet the pattern of which was disturbed, here and there, by large, dark, ominous-looking stains. The woodchip-covered walls were bare apart from a single picture – cut from a magazine she supposed – of the Queen. The smell was terrible. Hattie had a feeling that Tyson might have marked out his territory, and although it was summer the steel-framed windows were clasped shut and the thin floral curtains pulled across so that what light came in was suffused in a yellow glow.

'Is Jimmy here, Mrs . . . ?' She wasn't sure what to call the woman so she just let the sentence trail off.

'Dawn,' she said, smiling at Hattie. 'And yissell?'

'Hattie . . . Hattie George,' she repeated

'Jimmy's roond the Co-op.'

Jimmy's mam – Dawn – brought her a cup of the dark orange tea that, Hattie thought, matched perfectly with the extraordinary colour of her hair.

'Aa'll gi ye a byut i' the hintend, Tyson,' she said, kicking the dog out of the room and sitting down next to Hattie.

Ten minutes later – ten minutes of stilted conversation that neither of them could fully understand – the front door opened and Hattie could hear the voice of Jimmy and what sounded like a child.

He walked into the front room and froze when he saw her – behind him a dark-haired boy of about nine and Rex.

The dog, to Hattie's absolute delight, threw himself at her, whinnying with pleasure.

'Rex,' she said, stroking him with genuine affection. In the corner Tyson began a hostile growl.

Jimmy said nothing, just looked coldy at Hattie.

'Jimmy,' she said, smiling at him.

He was wearing the same clothes he had worn the day Claire had taken him shopping – a fleecy tracksuit topped with a lumberjack shirt. But the deeper changes that they had made to his appearance remained. He looked as he had as a boy in the picture taken outside this house – too beautiful to belong to this ugly place, these plain people. His little brother was contorting himself to get a closer look at Hattie, and their mother, clearly feeling this was rude, pushed him back in rather the way that she had pushed back Tyson.

'Whaat are ye gaakin at, Sean?' she said to him, taking him out of the room and leaving Jimmy and Hattie alone.

'Whay are ya divvin here?' Jimmy began in the same cold tones.

'I came to see you, Jimmy. To persuade you to come back with me. I know Arabella said some terrible things. But she was wrong. What she said was not true . . .'

He shook his head angrily. 'It was all just a game for ye, wasn't it?' he said.

'No it wasn't, Jimmy. You must believe me—'

'It were all for soom bet. Like on the dogs or the horses. It were only about ye winning,' he said bitterly.

'At first it might have been. And I know that seems terrible to you. I wanted to show Jon that he was wrong. Even if I won, I stood to gain nothing – the money was always going to be paid to you. You must know I've never been interested in the money,' she said.

He gave a long, crushing snigger. 'Ya don't need to be frittlin about money,' he said.

'But then once I had come to know you, once Claire and I got to understand you, everything changed.'

'Why didn't ya tell me, like?'

'About the bet?' she said.

He nodded.

'Because I realised – very soon actually – that you would be insulted by the whole thing. And I was frightened that you would run away,' she said.

She didn't seem to be making any impression on him. He was looking at her now with a detachment she had never seen in him before.

'Don't give up on me now, Jimmy, just as we were getting somewhere. It may have hurt your pride to have discovered about this stupid bet but it would be mad to throw away the chance to start over again,' she said in beseeching tones.

'Maybe I divvint want to start oover agin,' he said despondently, looking down at her.

'Don't give up, Jimmy. I don't care if I win or lose that bet.'

'Divvint ya?'

'No, I only care about you.'

He gave her a little smile then.

'Wha'di ya think of me hoome, like?' he said, indicating the room they were in.

'I think it's rather nicer than Whitehaven,' she said.

'More cosy, like?' he said.

She nodded. 'I showed you my world, Jimmy. Will you show me yours?' she asked with a beguiling smile.

They walked to the end of the road – Hattie holding Rex on his leather-studded leash – and caught a bus down to the

Fish Quay. Along the way Jimmy pointed out landmarks from his childhood, many of which she recognised from *The Final Whistle*. The infamous Ballard Rat pub which, so the local joke went, was so rough they had 'plasma on draught'. And the betting shop, with thick metal grilles covering its windows, where, as a boy, Jimmy had taken his stepdad's betting slips.

The Fish Quay had been transformed in the years since Jimmy was a child. There was no sign of the bustling industry he remembered as a small boy when he had been brought down to watch his granddad gutting the day's catch. All the boats had been sold off now and the quay had been turned into a point of local interest with little cafés and fish and chip shops scattered along it.

And the old wooden jetty – from which on special occasions Jimmy had gone on day trips to Jarrow with his nan – had been knocked down and replaced with a modern brick and glass building.

They made their way into a small café and Jimmy ordered them some tea. His mood, she thought, had mellowed a bit.

'Stottie-kyek, hinny?' he said, smiling at her as he pointed at a glass-covered cakestand in which there sat several large, flat buns.

'I have to have a stottie cake,' she said, and he bought them both one.

'Wha'di ye think?' he said, indicating the place.

'I can imagine it as it was when you were a boy.'

'The mission's still here and The Jungle,' he said, looking out of the window.

'Claire rang to say that the meeting had been set up about the book,' Hattie said cautiously, trying to bring the subject back to his return to London.

'Aye?'

'This man – Jay Hector – has seen the manuscript of

The Final Whistle. He says he's already got five publishing houses fighting over it.'

He shrugged his shoulders.

'Why give up now, Jimmy?' she asked.

'Ya doon't know who I am. Ya doon't know the real Jimmy,' he said.

'I think I do,' she said gently.

'Nah ya doon't. I've finally come back where *I* belong. *I*'m hoome now,' he said.

'And what can it offer you, your home?'

He looked at her over the top of his teacup.

'The social, Jimmy, is what it can offer you.'

'Nah, they're building all sorts along the Tyne. I could get missel a job, like, no problem,' he said.

'Come back to London with me for just one more month and then you can return here with enough money in your pocket to do something – buy a café, a business . . .'

'And ya'll win tha bet?'

'I keep telling you, Jimmy, it isn't about the bet any more. It's about you,' she said, toying with the huge partly eaten cake in front of her.

'Eat oop then,' he said.

The cake was rich and sweet and heavy, and that bit of it that she had managed to swallow had stuck in her throat and was now weighing down her stomach. Try as she might she couldn't eat any more. Cautiously, whilst Jimmy was looking the other way, she manged to slip the rest of it into the pocket of her jacket.

Seeing her empty plate he got up and walked towards the door.

'Coom on, I'll show you the mission.'

She nodded and followed him meekly out onto the quay, Rex leaping before them both.

'Do you know what I want to see most, Jimmy?'

'What?'

'The shuggyboats on Whitley Bay beach,' she said, as Rex came sniffing up to her jacket, pushing his nose into her pocket and extracting – to Jimmy's evident disappointment – her uneaten stottie cake.

It wasn't a sunny day but it wasn't cold, and there were lots of people – families with children – sitting on the beach behind windbreaks. The shuggyboats were, she discovered, like the swingboats that they had at old-fashioned fairgrounds. You sat at opposite ends of the wooden structures and pulled on a coloured rope that served to move you back and forth.

They queued behind a group of children and then took their turn, Jimmy helping her in and showing her how to hold the ropes.

Later they bought ice creams and walked across the beach, talking. Instead of his telling her – on his home territory – about his own childhood, she told him about hers – hoping, she supposed, that the details of her upbringing might explain the way she felt about her family. If she could make him in some way empathise with her, make him feel that despite their different backgrounds they had much in common, then maybe she could persuade him to come back to London with her.

'I have no real memory of my mother before I was about eight. We were raised by a series of nannies, living very much in a nursery world, in a very old-fashioned traditional upper-class way. It would be a treat to see our parents briefly before we went to bed. My mother and father travelled a lot and we would be left alone with the staff at Whitehaven. They weren't cruel to us but my mother was difficult and the nannies changed so often that we were never able to form deep relationships with any of them,' she explained.

'Ya didn't have anyone like me nan to make ya feel special?' Jimmy asked.

'I had my paternal grandmother. She adored me because, I think, I looked a little like her and I inherited her interest in people and politics. But we didn't see her that often because she didn't get on with my mother. You have to remember that my mother came from one of the oldest, grandest families in Britain. And my grandmother was a Russian Jewess who had been, as she saw it, rescued by marriage to my grandfather. They had no point of contact. And anyway, I think my father was a little ashamed of his mother. So we saw less and less of her as we got older. But the warmest, most tender memories of my childhood are those I have of her.'

She told him about her school days. And how she lived in the shadow of her pretty, vivacious and popular elder sister. Her only escape, she said smiling up at him, was through her work, which only served to turn her into an even greater outsider.

'And Toby?' asked Jimmy.

'He was my first real boyfriend. I think I was just grateful that he was interested in me. And then my father and mother liked him, thought he was good for me. I never really had any confidence about my looks. My mother, you see, was one of the great society beauties of her day. And Arabella, of course, took after her. But I was always different . . .'

'Like us, hinny?'

'Yes. You don't look like your mother. Or your brothers. I think that something as simple as looking different can make you feel – all the time that you are growing up – as if you are in the wrong place, the wrong family . . .' She paused for a second and then brought the subject back to his own past life. 'And what of you and girls, Jimmy? Has there ever been someone like Toby in your life?'

They had never talked about Jimmy's sexuality before. He had made no mention, during the recording of the tapes that were now edited into *The Final Whistle*, of a woman in his life, but Hattie felt certain that – looking as he did – he must have experienced some female interest. Even if it were only empty fumblings in dark alleys behind the Ballard Rat.

'When I was aboot fifteen there was a girl called Linda,' he said, rolling up his sleeve to reveal, at the top of a group of five tattoos on his left arm, a dagger with her name engraved on it. 'And then there was a friend of me mam's, like, who saw to me . . .' He hesitated a moment, looking at her face as if he was unsure whether or not to continue.

'What happened to Linda?'

'I went away – for the football – an' she met someone else,' he said, looking away.

'Did you love her?'

He shrugged. 'Maybe . . .'

They sat in silence for a moment, Jimmy looking thoughtfully out to sea. Hattie judged it the right time to raise the subject of his coming back with her again.

'Jimmy, let's finish what we've started. Let's go back to London and get the book published.'

'Nay, hinny, it was a stupid idea.'

'But it would give you the money to do whatever you want. It's a dream come true. Like when your nan's friend won the lottery.'

'Nay, hinny, it wouldn't work, like.'

'Of course it would. Claire has set up the whole thing. You'll be famous.'

'Boot, hinny, ya doon't understand . . .'

'What don't I understand?'

'There's things aboot me ya doon't know.'

'Like what? Jimmy, you told me everything, that's what the book is about. Everything that happened to you.'

'Nay, ya doon't know the haf of it,' he said.

'Are you still worried about your reading and writing?'

'Hinny, howd'ya think I lived on the streets?' he said.

'You sold the *Big Issue*,' she said, 'and people always gave you extra for Rex.'

'Boot I didn't always . . .'

She was alarmed now. What other secret had he kept from her? She knew that some of the street boys traded on sex. Over the years she had dealt professionally with a number of underage boys who had run away from home and become enmeshed in prostitution. Suppose Jimmy were a rent boy?

'Was it men, Jimmy, for sex?' she asked hesitantly.

'What d'ya take me for?' he said angrily.

'I'm sorry . . .'

'They tried mind,' he said, 'when I first went on the street. Boot I wouldn't do that. It were drugs and thievin and the like.'

'To support your habit?'

'To live . . .' he said simply.

'What sort of thieving?'

'Cars, mobile phones, then mooney, then I got into trouble, like.'

'You mean you got caught?'

'I got caught agin and agin. In the end they put us away for a year,' he said, looking across at her to judge how shocked she was, not realising that with all that Hattie dealt with in her professional life she was not easily shocked.

'In prison? Was it bad?' she said gently.

He laughed again. 'No worse than the streets or the Meadow Well – or mabe your posh school. Chance to keep meself fit at least.

'And when you came out?'

'I got missel straight, like. Started with the *Big Issue*,' he said, still examining her face for signs of her disapproval.

'Why would that change anything, Jimmy?' she said

calmly. 'Why is that any more dreadful than the other things you talked about?'

'Wha' if they find oot?' he asked.

'It'll probably increase the sales of the book, Jimmy,' she said, aware that her answer had surprised him. 'At least as long as you never mugged little old ladies . . .'

He smiled. 'Nay, hinny, nothing like that.'

They caught the bus back to Meadow Well as dusk began to fall. She sensed now that he would probably come back to London with her. The balance of their relationship had changed. Here, in his birthplace, it was she who was unsure and vulnerable. She was no longer the teacher, the leader. For the first time, she realised, she and Jimmy were equal.

Hattie was aware that, for all its meanness and shabbiness, Jimmy's home was a more welcoming place than Whitehaven. His mam was more hospitable than her mother would ever have been to a stranger whose rank, class and income she didn't know. And Dawn's new man, Tom, seemed, at least on the surface, to be decent and caring and kind to the only two of Jimmy's brothers who still lived at home – nine-year-old Sean and fifteen-year-old Steve – even if he did wander about in his vest and trousers, asserting, Hattie thought, his status as master of the house by barking orders at them all and threatening, every five minutes, to 'skelp' them.

Dawn had prepared them a big tea which they ate at a table they had put up in the shabby living room. There were sausage rolls, tinned salmon sandwiches, fairy cakes, buttered malt loaf and then – served like a pudding – sweet, tinned fruit cocktail and evaporated milk.

With it they drank the now familiar deep orange tea from a big brown pot which was covered in a knitted tea cosy. They didn't talk while they ate – there was none of the inconsequential social interaction that there had been when Jimmy ate Sunday lunch at Whitehaven. But then the television – which was placed centrally like some religious shrine – rather dominated the meal. Hattie realised, though, that they had put on a show in her honour, and that she was being scrutinised by Jimmy's family as he had been by hers.

'Thank you, Dawn,' she said as she cleared away the plates.

'Alreet whey?' Tom said.

After supper Dawn went upstairs to change for the evening ahead.

'It's *turn* night at the club,' Jimmy explained.

Twenty minutes later Dawn came down the stairs dressed in a Lurex cardigan over a short, black skirt that clung precariously to her body. She didn't wear tights or stockings, just a pair of pointed, red stilettos. And jewellery – a lot of jewellery: big hooped gold earrings, four or five gold chains, rings on almost every one of her fingers.

Hattie realised that she was hopelessly underdressed in the plain white shirt and the black trousers she had arrived in, her only jewellery being her little platinum Elsa Peretti Tiffany necklace.

'Ha'ya noothing else to wear, pet?' said Dawn, critically appraising Hattie.

She shook her head.

'Well, ya'll have to do then,' she said.

They made their way to the end of the road and caught the bus to the little village – several miles away – to the club that was the centre of the social life of their community.

Chapter Seventeen

The West Allotment Working Men's Club was, Hattie quickly decided, a Northern working-class equivalent of her father's In and Out Club in London. If her father and his friends looked upon the quiet order of their club as a haven from the world of women so the men of the North regarded their UICs as places of safety where they could escape from their womenfolk.

Of course, it was an altogether louder, jollier place but, for all that, a place where the old order of things was firmly adhered to – where men were men and women accepted it.

The difference, Hattie decided – as Jimmy and Tom disappeared into the spit and sawdust of the men's bar, while she, Dawn and Jimmy's widowed Auntie Mary, with whom they'd met up at the door, were banished to the Big Room – was that while in London the In and Out represented the last bastion of chauvinism, in the North, the West Allotment was simply one of many, many outposts of a network of clubs that blatantly supported the ideals of male supremacy.

But then there were, Hattie had discovered, many things in the North that had long since been outlawed or abandoned in the South on the grounds that they were politically incorrect. Hattie could not remember, for instance, being at any function where the smoke hung in the air, as it did now, so thickly that within five minutes nonsmokers weren't just passively inhaling, they'd have a hundred-a-day habit.

Nor had she any recollection of consuming, as she had

today, so much sugar. Why, even the alcohol in this place was served sweet.

'Malibu-an-lemonade?' said Dawn, passing her a drink that she had to fight the urge to recoil from.

'Would it be possible to have a glass of house wine?' Hattie said and a hush fell over the crowded bar area of the Big Room.

'Eee, *hooose* wine,' said the barmaid in mocking tones as she began to search the bottles that were stacked behind her. 'We did have some like. I remember two yearn ago someone coming in here an ordering wine . . .'

Five minutes later she produced a dusty, half-bottle of screw-topped white Hirondelle and poured Hattie a cloudy glass. But even that was sweet.

'Gi's a tab?' said Auntie Mary, taking a cigarette from Dawn's packet, lighting it and passing it on to Hattie.

'Thanks,' said Hattie.

The Big Room was the place where, at 8 p.m. precisely, the acts would come on to do their *turns*. In the corner there was a small stage decorated in silver paper and dominated by a huge old-fashioned microphone stand. Beside it was the organist who would be the musical accompaniment to the acts and who was now warming up the audience with a medley of Lionel Richie songs.

There was, too, a small dance floor to the left of the stage over which hung a spinning silver ball and where, already, one or two of the women were swaying gently to the music.

Auntie Mary told Hattie that the women were sent in to the Big Room early so that they could be sure of 'keeping their seats'. Rather like German tourists round a Spanish swimming pool, the regulars at the West Allotment had their favourite positions on the smooth plastic banquettes that ran round the edge of the room.

'If we'd been five minutes later,' said Auntie Mary with

a knowing nod as she led Dawn and Hattie to their places, 'they'd have taken our seats.'

'Five minutes and they'll jump in ya grave,' Dawn said to Hattie.

What shocked Hattie most that night was the way in which the women went along with the idea that they should be subservient to the men. At no point during the evening did she hear a single word of criticism uttered by a woman about a man, even though many of them were now living in circumstances where they were the wage earners and their men were paid by the state to stay at home, or hover in the pubs and betting shops.

In her own sophisticated circle of women friends, in the wake of the All Men Are Bastards movement, the ritual humiliation of men had become a sport. In fact, for Southern women the superfluousness of the male had become a bit of a girlie joke, or at any rate a series of jokes: 'What do you call a man with half a brain? Gifted'/'Women who want to be equal to men lack ambition', and so on. One friend of Hattie's had turned her home into a shrine to the uselessness of men. Over the door of her kitchen, in large italic letters, she had inscribed the legend 'So many men, so few bullets' and in the back window of her car she had hung a sticker proclaiming 'A husband is God's way of proving a woman has a sense of humour'. But here in the North where all the men did seem to be bastards, no one dared say so. She wondered idly how Jo Brand and her famous advice to women, 'never trust a man with testicles', would go down with this crowd.

At five minutes to eight most of the men shuffled into the Big Room and took their places near – although not necessarily next to – their women. Jimmy looked anxiously round the room until he caught sight of Hattie.

'Alreet whey?' he asked her.

'Fine,' she said, smiling at him. He sat very close to her

on the banquette and she found herself curiously aroused by the way in which – when Auntie Mary and Dawn joined them – their bodies were pushed and squeezed together.

The lights dimmed as the master of ceremonies – a young man wearing a cheap, shiny dinner suit and bow tie – came up to the microphone to tell a couple of jokes Hattie couldn't quite hear, yet alone understand, and then proceeded to introduce the first act.

'Gi a warm welcome ta a reet canny act – Bill and Annie's Wild West Extravaganza,' he said as a middle-aged couple came on to the stage dressed as Annie Oakley and Wild Bill Hickok. She sang a verse from 'I Just Blew in from the Windy City' while he attached her to a piece of plyboard and then, to the gasps of the audience, theatrically threw a dozen sharp Sabatier knives around her.

Tom whispered something about how she looked as if she could do with a good 'skelping' and Auntie Mary laughed till the tears ran down her pancake-covered face. Wild Bill then produced a whip and, to the delight of the audience, prodded Annie Oakley into a weird dance routine that, Hattie thought, had distinct S & M overtones. As she watched she wondered what Arabella would make of this evening. And how she would write about it in her column.

At the end of the act Jimmy bought Hattie another glass of the cheap, sweet Hirondelle which she greedily drank.

Next on to the little stage was a man 'straight from Gateshead' who did 'voices'. It was difficult for Hattie to work out who he was imitating as his accent was so thick that she had to guess from the different hats he wore. But everyone else laughed like drains and screeched in recognition of his mimicry.

There was a small interval then, and the men and women began to dance beneath the spinning silver ball. Auntie Mary urged Jimmy to take Hattie on to the floor and the two of them, horribly embarrassed, shuffled around together, aware of the eyes of his family following them as they made their awkward progress through the crowd. It was clear that Jimmy's family – as her own had – assumed that the two of them were having a relationship.

'Alreet, hinny?' Jimmy whispered in her ear.

'Yes,' she said, although in truth she felt somehow diminished by the evening.

When they got back to their place on the banquette seating Hattie noticed an odd man in a white coat walking round the room with a tray of something indeterminate strapped round his neck. He looked rather like the cigarette girls that teetered round some of the big, smart London restaurants, except that he was overweight and balding, and the merchandise he was selling was entirely different.

'Moosells, crab sticks . . .' he said as he made his way over to them.

Dawn wanted some crab sticks (which looked to Hattie about as close to a real crab as a packet of pork scratchings was to a pig) and when Tom declined to buy her some they started to row, Tom berating Dawn for having drunk too much.

'She's tottin aboot all ower the place,' he said, pushing her drink out of her hand and onto the floor.

Dawn, who was now swaying in her seat, looked up at him fiercely but didn't say anything.

'She's elwis actin' horsell,' Tom said defensively to the crab stick man.

'Aa'd fettle hor,' he said.

At this Tom pulled Dawn roughly to her feet and began to push her out of the Big Room towards the front door of the club. Hattie was shocked that no one tried to stop him and, in the absence of any other intervention, stood up to follow them.

'What are yees gyeping at?' said Tom to Hattie, pushing

her out of his way and resuming his progress out of the club.

'Jimmy, do something,' Hattie said.

Jimmy followed them out, with Hattie and Auntie Mary hurrying behind him. Outside on the steps of the club Tom had begun to slap Dawn around the face.

'Gi ower, man!' shouted Jimmy, pushing himself between his mam and Tom.

'Ben canny, lad, or I'll towe ye,' Tom said, raising his hand to Jimmy.

'Gannon whey then,' said Jimmy

Hattie wasn't sure who struck the first blow but within a couple of minutes the two of them were grappling with each other in a vicious fight. Jimmy fell to the ground first and Tom, with an almost reflex action, kicked him in the chest. A spray of blood flew through the air.

Out of nowhere a crowd of ranting men formed round the couple fighting on the ground and Hattie could no longer make out what was happening although she could hear, through the shouting, the sounds of blows falling on flesh and the resulting grunts of pain. She had never felt so powerless in her life. The brute force of the men, and the braying macho posturing of the onlookers, frightened her and made her aware that as a woman she could do nothing to stop them, nothing to help Jimmy.

But she tried anyway, pushing her way past the awful throng of men and back into the club to get someone to do something. It was no use going in the Big Room because she could hear the sound of the next *turn* – an Elvis impersonator singing 'Only the Lonely' – and she began looking round the other rooms in search of someone sober enough to help.

There was no one in the snug so she had no option but to push open the door of the Men's Bar and walk in. A terrible hush fell over the room as the assembled men took in the sight of the small, dark, bonny lass standing in their midst.

'Eee, whey ye bugger mar!' exclaimed the barman.

Afterwards she thought that they had probably only followed her so that they could discipline her for breaking the centuries-old rule banning women from entering the Men's Bar in the West Allotment Working Men's Club. But at least they stopped the fight.

As they pulled the two bloodied men apart, Dawn, who had been sobbing in a heap on the steps, pulled herself up, cast a savage glance at Jimmy, and then went over to help Tom, taking the weight of him on her shoulder as she led him back into the club.

Jimmy and Hattie went back to Auntie Mary's two up, two down, a couple of streets away from the club, since it was clear Jimmy would not be welcome at home that night.

'Ya can sleep in the spare room, pet,' she said to Hattie gently, 'and Jimmy can lie down in the front room.'

She made them a pot of the strong orange tea, and then went to fetch some cotton wool and disinfectant and began to bathe Jimmy's bloodied face.

'I'll leave you two now, but no messing mind,' she said when she had finished. 'The privy's out the back, pet.'

Hattie sat down opposite Jimmy at the little kitchen table and reached out her hand to him.

'Is that how it always was with your mother and her men?'

'Aye, hinny.' he said sadly.

There had been a time, he told her, when his mother had worked tricks down at the Golden Fleece on the Fish Quay. His own father, he was certain, had been a paying customer. And all through his early childhood he had been aware of her bringing home men. At school, when he had attended, he had been teased and bullied because his mam 'were a slapper'. It was one of the reasons why she had fallen out with his nan. That and her drinking. The men who had stayed around for longer than a night had, he said, always ended up like Tom, beating her up. And, from time to time, turning their fists on him.

'Boot she's still me mam, like,' he said looking at Hattie.

She nodded, aware of her own grudging affection for – and loyalty to – the woman who, although she in no way fitted the usual definition of a doting mother, had given birth to her.

'I'm reet tired, hinny,' he said with a weary smile.

She helped him into the front room and covered him up with the blankets his Auntie Mary had left out for him. There was a bruise coming up along his left cheekbone and a little clot of blood had collected beneath his nose. He fell asleep almost immediately and she stood watching him for a while, bending down as she left the room to trace her finger tenderly across his beautiful, beaten face.

She went out to the back of the house and the little bathroom that was nothing much more than a lean-to shed. Even though it was summer it was cold and there was a strong smell of damp. She washed her face and rinsed out her mouth with her fingers dotted with a little of Auntie Mary's toothpaste. She had left her overnight bag at Jimmy's house and she felt uncomfortable without her own things.

Upstairs, in the little spare room with its rosebud wallpaper, she undressed down to her bra and pants and slipped between nylon sheets beneath a faded pink candlewick bedspread. The only other furniture in the room was a small bedside table on which stood a chipped ornament made of plaster, the kind of thing, she suspected, that you might win at a fair – a garishly painted figure of a little boy holding a puppy. But for all its cheap sentiment, she thought, it was more appealing than the precious art that surrounded her in her own home. It had more value, she decided, than one of Benedict Wright's pretentious and repulsive pieces. She lay in the bed unable to sleep, feeling, in her own way, as displaced as Jimmy must have done the first night he had slept on the foldaway futon in her flat.

If nothing else came from her visit here – if she failed to convince Jimmy to return to London with her – at least she had seen a little of his world. And realised it was as much a foreign country to her as her own world must have seemed to him.

That night, for the first time in her adult life, she had felt vulnerable and powerless. For the first time in her life she had come to a place were her wealth and her privilege – however much she might claim to disregard it – could not help her. A place where she had no more status, no more worth, than Jimmy. She finally fell asleep counting the rosebuds on the walls around her, dimly glimpsed in the orange streetlight that slipped through the thin curtains that hung at Auntie Mary's windows.

Hattie was woken by the smell of cooking. She pulled on her clothes, tidied the bed and made her way down the stairs to the kitchen. Jimmy was sitting at the table, his face sorely displaying the drama of the night before.

'Aye, there yourn are, pet,' said the genial Auntie Mary, pouring Hattie a big mug of tea. 'Sit doon and have tha brickfist.' She passed to her guest a plate on which sat several slabs of something dark brown and soggy.

Hattie looked to Jimmy with a puzzled expression on her face.

'Breedndreepin,' he said enthusiastically.

Hattie didn't normally eat breakfast – at home she would grab a cup of Earl Grey and a glass of freshly squeezed orange juice – but she didn't want to offend Auntie Mary. She was sharply reminded of Jimmy's first morning in her flat – his confusion at the food that filled the sheet steel cupboards of her beautiful kitchen, all those absurd French breads and pastries, all the expensive jams, all the ridiculous, affected herbal teas and infusions. 'Breedndreepin' was as foreign a delicacy to Hattie as pain au chocolat had been to him.

Gingerly lifting her knife and fork she cut a small piece and ate it. After a few moments – and three more mouthfuls that she thought might choke her – she put down her knife and fork.

'It's delicious but I really can't eat any more,' she said.

'Aye pet, no wonder thas so scrawny,' said Auntie Mary.

When they had finished their meal and Auntie Mary was getting ready to leave for work, she turned to each of them and hugged them.

'Yous better go and see ya mam now,' she said to Jimmy.

He nodded.

'Thank you so very much for having me,' Hattie said.

'Ye welcome, pet.'

They caught the bus back to Meadow Well a little before midday. If Jimmy was nervous of the scene that would greet him, he didn't show it. But then he wasn't really showing anything that morning. The confidences he had shared with Hattie the day, and the night, before – the talk about his criminal record and his relationship with his mother – were either forgotten or had been regretted and pushed aside.

Hattie sat next to him on the bus feeling that she might never reach him again. He had given her no indication whether or not he had forgiven her for the betrayal of the bet. Looking at his bruised profile, she felt as if he were almost unaware of her presence.

When they reached the house they found Rex tethered to the concrete base of a broken rotating clothesline. It looked as if he, too, had experienced some fallout from the rest of Jimmy's family. There was a livid scratch above his left eye.

'Tyson . . .' said Jimmy angrily, kneeling down to release his pet.

He knocked on the door and, several minutes later, a bleary-eyed Dawn answered.

'You coom for your stuff,' she said, indicating Hattie's bag, which sat by the door.

There was no sign of Tom or Jimmy's brothers. Hattie stood back, fearful of intruding on the scene between mother and son, but Jimmy pushed his way past Dawn and indicated that Hattie should follow.

'Coom with us while I pack,' he said, leading her up the dark stairway to a little back room containing two sets of bunks and, across the remaining scant floor space, a battered old mattress.

'Was this your bedroom?'

'It's where us all slept,' he said as he began to retrieve his few possessions from around the room.

'Are you coming back with me then, Jimmy?' she asked tentatively.

He shrugged his shoulders as if he still hadn't made up his mind. 'There's nowt for me here,' he said, picking up his holdall and case and looking sadly around him.

When they got downstairs his mother had gone out. The house was empty apart from the growling presence of Tyson.

If Jimmy was a little regretful about leaving his home behind, Rex was obviously relieved. With every step away from number 23 Avon Avenue the dog seemed to regain his confidence. They took the bus back to Newcastle in time to catch the two twenty-five train to London.

As they pulled out of Central Station Jimmy looked up at Hattie and smiled. She put her hand out to touch his, unable to find words that might express her reaction to the last twenty-four hours. She felt that they had achieved a new understanding and she was confident that once they had done the publishing deal Jimmy would finally be free of his past. But she could sense that the trip home had been painful for him, that instead of finding that he was back where he belonged, he was as displaced in North Shields as he had been in London. She felt even more strongly now that she must help him to find, not just happiness and financial security, but a sense of belonging. They sat in silence for many miles, watching the countryside changing as they journeyed South.

'I want ta get away from all that, hinny,' Jimmy said earnestly, eventually breaking the silence. 'I want to learn.'

'You are learning, Jimmy. I can't believe how fast your reading is coming on.'

'Not joost the reading, I want to learn *everything*,' he said eagerly. 'I'll win that bet; I'll show them . . .'

Chapter Eighteen

Claire and the literary agent Jay Hector were already seated at a corner table in The Ivy when Hattie and Jimmy arrived. Every head turned as they made their way through the restaurant. Not just because of Jimmy's brooding presence, Hattie thought, but also because of the big purple bruises that were the lingering legacy of his trip home.

She had spent a couple of hours that morning briefing him on how he should behave – not about which knife and fork to pick up – for once that wouldn't matter – but about the impression he should make. It was important, she had told him, that he conformed to Hector's idea of the stereotypical Geordie because it was the language of the North East that had attracted him to *The Final Whistle*. One of his greatest successes in recent years had been the discovery of a now very famous writer whose first – critically acclaimed – novel had been written, without a single punctuation mark (not one comma, full stop, capital letter or colon in the entire 200,000 word manuscript) in broad Scouse.

'So you have to be what he expects – raw, Northern man,' Hattie had explained, not mentioning, for fear of putting Jimmy off, Hector's predilection for big, beautiful men (raw or well done).

'How da ya mean, like?' he said.

'Oh, you know, a cross between Jimmy Nail and Gazza,' she said.

The great man rose on their arrival at the table, clearly overawed by Jimmy's appearance. Hattie supposed that

Jimmy – wearing his leather jacket, tight white T-shirt and button-fly jeans – probably represented Hector's idea of the perfect man. If there had been any doubt about his enthusiasm about the manuscript before he had set eyes on the author, there was none now.

'Jay, this is Jimmy Ryan,' Hattie said as they took their seats and Claire poured them both a glass of champagne from the bottle that already sat, half empty, on the table. Jay Hector was a notorious homosexual, although this was not necessarily immediately obvious since his style was more well-hard than limp-wristed (apart, that is, from his unfortunate inability to pronounce his Rs). His hair was cut into a number one, almost shaven really, and his clothes were morbidly macho – beautifully cut black suits uniformly worn with plain black T-shirts (it was said that Hector had over a hundred plain black T-shirts in his vast expensive wardrobe). He was one of the most important men in London. His prominence amongst the influential gay mafia of the new left had placed him in a powerful position within Blair's emergent political and social establishment. Hattie had met him with Toby at several New Labour conventions. She loathed him, found him pretentious, self-important, sly and manipulative, but he was probably the only man who could successfully launch Jimmy and ensure that he got the advance that would liberate him and win her and Claire their bet.

Claire did most of the talking for the first few minutes, giving Jay a carefully edited version of how they had come to meet the homeless Jimmy. Jay Hector must, they had decided, never know about the bet.

'He's always wanted to be a writer,' she said earnestly.

'Aye,' said Jimmy, winking broadly at Hattie and laying his accent on with a mell, a sledgehammer. 'I've aalwaa wanna reet . . .'

Jay Hector was a highly respected figure in the literary

world. His stable of writers included the cream of the literati. Among them were the wife of a prominent businessman and Labour Party activist who had founded a new genre of up-market erotic novels, a Kenyan dissident – Eggo Massif – who won the Booker Prize for a novel about his homeland, and the columnist-turned-novelist Brian Brute, who had turned his own navel-gazing into an innovative, much talked about new book, the cover of which featured a moody, black-and-white photographic study of his own excrement. What is more, Hector was a fanatical supporter of Chelsea and had played an important part in raising the status of the game. It was he who had discovered Billy Dean, whose study of tribalism in football, *Offuckinside*, had gained the sport a new respectability with the intelligentsia. Jimmy would not only fit perfectly with his client profile, he conformed utterly – Hattie could tell – to his sexual tastes.

'Well, Jimmy,' said Jay, unable to take his eyes from the face and form of his new author, '*The Final Whistle* is up for auction. As a matter of fact we've alweady had an offer. I think we're looking at about £150,000. Over two books, of course. You will be able to wite another book, won't you?' he said a little flirtatiously.

Oh God, Hattie thought, what's he going to say now?

'Awwaay the lads,' said Jimmy with a particularly vacuous look on his face.

It was at this point that Hattie realised that Jimmy had taken her advice so seriously that he was acting as if he were doing a *turn* at the West Allotment Working Men's Club. He had made himself into a Geordie caricature.

Curiously, though, Jay Hector didn't seem to notice. Indeed the more unintelligible Jimmy was, the more entranced Hector was. And, thankfully, Jimmy still hadn't seemed to pick up the sexual signals that the agent was throwing out at him.

When the waiter came over to take their order Hector

looked across at Jimmy and asked, in rather breathless tones, what he would like.

'Newkie,' Jimmy said.

'Pardon?' said Hector uncertainly.

'Newcasselbrown,' said Jimmy.

'Oh yes, what a good idea – Newcastle Bwown,' Hector said to the waiter.

'Make it 1998 Newcastle Brown,' said Claire, trying to make a joke of the waiter's confusion, 'a particularly good year.'

'And to eat?' said Hector, looking as if, frankly, he might pass on the food and instead consume Jimmy.

They picked up their menus. Hattie was frightened that Jimmy might lose his courage when faced with reading the various dishes and their pretentious descriptions (which, frankly, would have been difficult enough for someone with a degree in modern languages to decipher).

Luck was on his side that day, though, because Jay Hector had noticed that black pudding, which had become a chattering-class delicacy in the last couple of years, was on the menu.

'I think I'll have the black pudding. And you, Jimmy?'

Jimmy uttered a grunt of assent and put down the menu.

'Black pudding for all of us then,' said Jay. 'You know, Jimmy, *The Final Whistle* forcibly weminded me of that marvellous Dan Leno quote: "I see the world as a football, kicked about by the higher powers with me clinging on by my teeth and toenails to the laces"'.

'Haddaway and bowl yor gord, ya kite,' said Jimmy with a fixed smile on his face.

Hattie, who mentally translated this as 'go and fuck yourself, you fat git' nudged him beneath the table, fearful that any moment he would go too far. Or, worse, that he might have finally noticed Jay's sexuality. Gay men,

Hattie now knew, were regarded with horror and disgust in the North East. Lord knows what Jimmy might do if he realised that Jay Hector was physically attracted to him.

The maître d' had to send out for a six-pack of Newcastle Brown which he brought to the table sunk into a big silver ice bucket.

'Eeee, man . . .' said Jimmy, pulling off a tab and drinking from the can, not pausing until it was all gone. Then, leaning back, he let out a belch that could quite clearly be heard above the twittering from the surrounding tables.

'Aye, pardon . . .' he said to those fellow diners whose attention had now been drawn to their table. Then he took another can from the ice bucket, pulled off the tab and proceeded to empty that too, Jay watching his every move with growing fascination.

'Whey ye bugger mar! Thaas good,' Jimmy said, pulling off his leather jacket – to reveal the T-shirt that outlined his own remarkable six-pack (as Claire referred to his stomach muscles).

Hattie didn't even have to interpret for Jay, who acted as if he perfectly understood every grunt and obscure colloquialism that Jimmy could spit out.

'This book is in touch with the mood of the moment,' said Jay, his eyes moving restlessly across Jimmy's chest. 'This sense of wedundancy that so many young men are feeling. The loss of masculine pwide . . .'

It was, Hattie thought, probably Jimmy who needed an interpreter now. Jay's unfortunate speech impediment coupled with his awful pretentions made him as difficult to understand as Jimmy's mam.

'And then of course football is the new weligion,' said Jay, wondering if it would be too obvious to lay one of his manicured hands on Jimmy's muscular knee. 'The most moving moment for me was when you were told you would never be able to play football again. The cwuelty of fate . . .'

'Naaa, man, it werrant *cwuelty*,' Jimmy said, standing up, rolling up his jeans and pointing to the still florid scar on his left knee, 'I were crocked.'

Jay – and in fact most of the people on the surrounding tables – looked aghast at the sight of Jimmy's scarred but muscular leg.

'And was that an emotional moment?' asked Jay, trying desperately to regain his composure.

'I wept like a babby,' Jimmy said, doing an agonisingly awful imitation of Gazza weeping at Euro '92.

Hattie wasn't sure how they had managed to escape from the lunch. Jay Hector would have sat, spellbound, all day looking at Jimmy. There had been one or two moments – towards the end of the meal and the Newkie six-pack – when she thought things might turn nasty.

But even when it had finally dawned on Jimmy that Jay Hector was, as he said 'on the oother bus, like', he had managed to contain himself. Although he *had* rather obviously recoiled from Jay's attempt to kiss him on both cheeks as they left the restaurant (but then so had Claire and Hattie).

Claire pronounced the lunch a huge success and admitted, at least to Hattie, that she had orginally gone to Jay because she had been certain that once he saw Jimmy there would be no question of rejection.

In fact, such was the appeal of Jimmy that two contracts were biked round to Hattie's flat the next morning: one from Jay Hector himself and one from the publisher he had already lined up. Claire then put the PR machine in motion, leaking a story to the Peterborough column in the *Telegraph* which would, she felt certain, be followed up by all the tabloids.

Within hours of the item appearing, Jimmy's career took off. Within three days there had been pieces on Jimmy's book deal in the *Mail*, *The Times*, the *Mirror* and the *Express*. He even made that week's Pass Notes in the *Guardian*.

Jay Hector and Claire had drawn up a teasing PR strategy, feeding the papers and the publishing industry journals with little titbits about Jimmy. They were rushing through publication because, Hector reasoned, the time was right. He wanted to launch *The Final Whistle* within six months – sometime in the middle of the forthcoming football season.

He was also very keen to work on Jimmy's image. On the Thursday after the deal had been announced he was booked into one of the top fashion photographers for a series of portraits masterminded by Hector but carefully watched over by Hattie and Claire. It was the literary agent's intention that Jimmy should look 'wed-blooded and wugged', which was one of the reasons why, Hattie decided, he was so keen to attend the session himself.

In one of the pictures Jimmy was posed ripping the tab off a can of Newcastle Brown so that a spray of the ale was captured flying through the air and trickling down his naked torso.

In another he was pulling off the top of an Everton team strip, so that his thick blond hair was tousled by the action and the tattoos that ran across his left arm were exposed to the camera. In a third he was lying on a bed with a white sheet twisted round his body reading a copy of the *Big Issue* with a photograph of himself superimposed on the cover.

Perhaps the most dramatic, and the one which would appear on the glossy back cover of *The Final Whistle*, was of Jimmy sitting looking soulful in a doorway with Rex at his side. It was shot in black-and-white and intended to appear as if it were a genuine picture of Jimmy in his homeless days, the reader, of course, unaware that the Hilfiger jeans that he wore had been artfully ripped and distressed by a stylist or that, out of camera shot, a wind machine was blowing his hair around his moody face – which had been given just a hint of designer stubble by a make-up artist. In one hand he was holding out a copy of the *Big Issue*.

Nine days later, exactly ten weeks after Jon had first come up with the bet, two impressive-looking envelopes arrived at Hattie's flat addressed to Jimmy Ryan. The first contained a cheque for £50,000, which represented the initial payment on his two-book deal. And the second contained an embossed invitation card requesting the pleasure of Jimmy Ryan at the annual Carlisle Square Garden Party in three weeks' time.

'Jimmy!' Hattie screamed as she took the cream card from his hand. 'We've won, Jimmy!'

'Nearly, hinny,' he said, a note of caution entering his voice.

'You don't imagine you'll stumble at the last hurdle, do you, Jimmy? Keep up the show you put on for Jay Hector and you will be the toast of the party. Tony and Cherie will adore you, Portillo will embrace you, David Mellor will engage you about footie. My father and mother will fawn all over you. Lords, ladies, earls and countesses will bow to you, Jimmy . . .'

They had more than one reason to celebrate that night. They had all but won the bet, they had pulled off the publishing deal and, as Jimmy shyly confessed, it was his birthday. Moreover, the progress he had achieved in his education since he had decided, on the journey back from Newcastle, to apply himself, was astonishing. He wasn't just reading a range of contemporary classics, he was also forcing himself to read the *Independent* and the *Guardian* each day. It was time they recognised his hard work and his achievements.

Before Hattie left for work she rang Claire to tell her the good news.

'Let's go out to dinner,' Claire said, 'make a big show of it.'

'No, Jimmy wants the three of us to celebrate at home. I'll slip out of the office at some time and pick up some food. And some gifts, I suppose . . .'

Despite the fact that she had to catch up on a lot of dull paperwork, Hattie managed to get out at lunchtime. She bought helium balloons in the colours of Newcastle United, a cake shaped like a football pitch, some gifts and the food for a proper celebration meal. Claire was contributing a fridge full of champagne.

That afternoon Hattie had another long session with Lisa. They were fast approaching her trial date and Hattie felt it was important to continue meeting three times each week.

'Hello, Lisa,' Hattie greeted her as the little girl was brought into her office.

'Hello, Hattie.' Lisa gave her a bright, winning smile, smoothing down her dress as she took her seat.

They chatted a little about what she had been doing. She had a tutor at Linton House and although she was kept away from all the other children the conditions in which she was living were infinitely better than those at home. While at home she had been ruled by the wrath of God – as interpreted by her obsessive and domineering father – at Linton House she was offered, despite the general repulsion for her crime, a gentler and more encouraging environment. Moreover, she was allowed the books she loved, she had a television in her room and even a computer. Her response to the stimuli of this more normal life had been extraordinary and, as Hattie had guessed right from the start, she had made dramatic academic progress.

Not that the improved quality of her life, since she had been placed in custody, made her happy. Despite the cruel punishments her father had regularly inflicted on her, and regardless of the deprivations she had endured, Lisa longed to return to her family home.

'You know that we'll be going to court soon, Lisa?' Hattie said.

The child nodded.

'Are you worried about that?'

'No, I'm looking forward to it.'

'Are you, Lisa? You know a lot of people – lawyers, social workers, forensic scientists – are going to be talking about what you did?'

The child nodded again.

'It won't be like an ordinary courtroom. There will be people there to look after you, and there is a possibility that the press will be there. Your case may be reported in the papers.'

'I don't mind. I want to go to court.'

'Why is that, Lisa?' Hattie asked, curious about the girl's enthusiasm for what would be a dreadful ordeal.

'Because then I can go home,' she said with an eager smile.

Hattie couldn't find the words to tell her that she would probably remain in care for several years.

'Lisa, I don't think they'll let you go home—' she began softly.

'But you promised me. You said that you would help me. You can tell them I'm good. You can make them let me go home,' she said, tears streaming down her face.

Hattie was tired when she came home. The afternoon session with Lisa had depressed and distressed her, and

244

dampened her mood and her enthusiasm for the evening ahead.

Claire arrived at eight sharp, looking stunning, bearing the booze and some beautifully wrapped gifts: an elegant Mont Blanc fountain pen so that Jimmy could, she said, attend book signings with pride; a bottle of some new designer aftershave that would not, she felt, compromise Jimmy's strident masculinity, and an entire wardrobe of Calvin Klein underwear – buttoned Y-fronts, boxers, vests and little tight skimpy pants that would show off what was known, she told Hattie with a giggle, as his 'lunch box'.

'What do you mean, lunch box?' she asked.

'You know, Hattie, *lunch box* – as in Linford Christie in tight Lycra running shorts . . .' Claire explained to a blank Hattie.

'Ya mean a bait-box for ya dinner?' said Jimmy, as uncomprehending as Hattie.

'You mean you call it a bait box, like for your *tackle*,' screamed Claire. 'Well, these Y-fronts will reveal Jimmy's perfect lunch box.'

When he had examined all his presents – clearly pleased with them – Claire walked over to him and put her arms around him, embracing him, muttering something in his ear that Hattie couldn't quite hear. Hattie found Claire's increasingly coquettish behaviour with Jimmy irritating and inappropriate.

But even more disturbing, this evening, was the way in which he was responding – laughing with her, flirting with her and relishing every fawning compliment she threw at him. By contrast Hattie felt that she must seem – in Jimmy's eyes – dull and plain. She looked at the assortment of little gifts she had bought and realised that they perfectly illustrated the difference between her approach to Jimmy and that of her friend. Instead of picking presents that were overt symbols of his new success and status Hattie had picked a selection of things that were more relevant to the old Jimmy – an Everton duvet cover to replace the one he had left at his mam's house, a Newcastle United poster and a book she had found that was a pictorial history of old Newcastle. There was even a picture of the thriving Fish Quay at North Shields, taken in the seventies – near enough the way that Jimmy would remember it.

'And I've got something you'll never believe, Jimmy,' Hattie said, producing a Harrods carrier bag. 'Stottie-kyek! They sell it in the food halls.'

Jimmy looked blankly down at her presents and she realised how dramatically he had changed. He was no longer amused by those things that had once been so important to him. And he was becoming increasingly sensitive to being patronised and stereotyped.

'Whey ye bugger mar!' he said in a way, she realised, that was intended to be ironic. He was trying very hard not to use the expressions that she so loved but which he now seemed to find embarrassing. In fact, in the last two weeks there had been a noticeable softening of his accent; the wonderful sound of the Tyne was mutating into the kind of estuary English that was more common – and acceptable – in his new world.

Hattie was beginning to realise that Jimmy's attitude to everything that Claire and she had been trying to teach him had changed since their return from North Shields. He was now so much more focused on what Claire called his education. In truth he was more focused on Claire. There wasn't much Hattie could teach him now, she thought; he had no real need for her any more. It was Claire who could coach him in what he wanted to know. Claire who had taught him to eat – not just with the right knife and fork – but also with chopsticks. Claire who was able to introduce him to designer culture so that now he couldn't – thanks to Hattie and his own newly discovered facility to learn

– just read and write fluently, he could spell Dolce & Gabbana, Moschino, Versace. Claire who had encouraged him to know the difference between Cabernet Sauvignon and Chardonnay. Claire who had taught him how to eat asparagus, Claire who had shown him the way to reach an artichoke's heart and maybe – along the way – her own. Hattie felt rather foolish for having picked presents that, she should have realised, represented everything from which he now longed to escape.

'I did get you these as well, Jimmy. I hope you like them,' she said nervously, presenting him with a small selection of reference books that she had carefully chosen. She had realised in the last few days that she had been rather reluctant to allow him to progress. It was as if she was frightened that the more he absorbed – and it was now clear that he was even brighter than she had imagined – the less he would be the Jimmy she cherished. She desperately didn't want him to lose those things about him that had seemed so different – so pure and untainted – when they had first met.

'Thanks,' he said, examining the books with great interest, the mementoes of his old life pushed to one side.

They opened a bottle of champagne – Claire carefully tutoring Jimmy in the difficult art of removing a cork without causing an eruption of fizzing liquid – and then they toasted his future.

Hattie was rather quiet and withdrawn during the meal; watching and listening as Jimmy and Claire talked about some film they had seen together; smiling indulgently, but without any real enthusiasm, as they discussed the forthcoming party – who would be there, what they would wear.

'We're in the heart of the season now, Jimmy,' Claire said enthusiastically. 'You'll love it all – Ascot, Glyndebourne . . .'

Filled with horror at the thought of the homeless boy

they had first met – sleeping in a doorway within sight of the Royal Opera House – turning into someone who could bear to wear a dinner jacket to picnic from a Fortnum and Mason hamper during the interval of *Don Giovanni*, Hattie got up from the table and began to clear the plates. She decided against producing the birthday cake. It seemed to her now like the choice a mother might have made for a small boy, not something that was relevant to the sophisticated young man that Jimmy seemed determined to become. She fought against it, she tried hard to be bright and hopeful that evening but she couldn't throw off the feeling that this great victory was not so much hollow as shallow.

Chapter Nineteen

'You don't think the cream is a little – well – obvious?' said Hattie a few weeks later as Jimmy walked the length of the Harvey Nichols' menshop wearing a pale Armani suit.

'But he's got to look obvious, he's the star. He must stand out. And it's not as if he could ever look vulgar,' said Claire, remembering, a little poignantly, the first time she had taken him shopping in Paul Smith. 'And it does look good with his skin tone . . .'

'Aye,' said Jimmy to the assistant, 'I'll tyek it, man.'

'How will you be paying, sir?'

'Card,' said Jimmy confidently.

He had a bank account now and a credit card. He loved this credit card thing. All he had to do was produce the bit of plastic and sign his name. And then, like a magic Provy cheque, whatever he wanted was his.

Having secured Jimmy's outfit they went to the designer collections on the first floor, Claire taking one of his arms and Hattie the other. In the lift Claire glanced at their reflection in the polished mirror and smiled broadly. The great thing about Jimmy, she thought, wasn't that he was beautiful – causing a flurry of attention wherever they went – but that he was such fun.

It had been his idea to take them shopping that day. It was, he said, pay back time. And just as Claire had picked clothes for him on the first day of his transformation, so now he was going to select their outfits for the party. And pay for them with the card he called his plastic Provy cheque.

The extraordinary thing was that he seemed to know

what would suit them. He picked Claire a beige crocheted dress that made the most of her extraordinary figure, revealing the best bits and offering just enough cover to the rest of her.

When she emerged from the changing rooms dressed in the clothes he had selected, he applauded her and she bowed.

'Bonny, bonny . . .' he said.

'You don't think it might be better a size bigger,' said Hattie, unable to keep a note of envy from her voice. Claire always made her feel so *small*.

'No, she looks perfect,' said Jimmy, which only served to make Hattie feel even less confident.

'I love it, darling,' Claire said, rushing over to him and kissing him full on the lips.

'Now it's your turn, hinny,' Jimmy said, turning to Hattie.

'You know I hate shopping for clothes,' she said nervously. 'Toby used to take me off to places like this and force me into things I didn't like. I mean, Jimmy, I'd really be happiest if I could just wear my old black velvet dress . . .'

'Nay, hinny,' he said thoughtfully, appraising her in a way she found disconcerting. While Claire changed back into her day clothes Jimmy wandered round looking very carefully for the right outfit for Hattie.

In the end he chose a very feminine, full, flared silk taffeta skirt in the softest pale lilac tone which he matched with a very simple fitted N. Peal cashmere cardigan in exactly the same shade.

Hattie blushed when she came out of the dressing room because for once she knew she looked good. The combination of the tight cardigan and the full flirty skirt was perfect on her, waif-like yet glamorous, and falling at just the right length for her pretty, slender legs.

'Aye, pet,' said Jimmy when he saw her. 'Let your hair down now.'

Shyly she reached behind her head to undo the clip that held her black curls back from her pale face.

'That's it,' said Jimmy, producing his card and handing it to the assistant. 'Now I'm going to buy you lunch.'

It was the first time, Hattie noticed, that Jimmy had used the word lunch and it sounded odd.

'Actually, Jimmy, I've got to meet someone for lunch – in fact I'm late already.'

'You can take me, Jimmy,' said Claire, glancing triumphantly across at Hattie. 'We'll go somewhere *à deux*.'

As she left them, arm in arm marching off to the Fifth Floor Café, she reflected that it probably wouldn't be long before Jimmy's wonderful dialect was further eroded by the introduction of affected French phrases such as *à deux* or *billet-doux*. Or even, she thought darkly as she watched Claire caress Jimmy's arm, *soixante-neuf*.

Hattie had mixed feelings about meeting Toby for lunch. He had, since turning up at her flat a few weeks ago, contacted her from time to time, usually about some small financial detail of their previous lives that needed resolving, but occasionally to see how she was. She felt it was safe, now, to meet him because her work with Jimmy was all but over. It wouldn't be long before he would leave her home to pursue his own life again and although she didn't really want Toby back she owed it to him at least to talk about their relationship.

Her first mistake, she realised, was in being late. Her second was in lighting up as soon as she was seated at the corner table in the restaurant.

'Hattie – how long have you been smoking?' he said disapprovingly, clearly assuming it was another nasty habit she had picked up through her exposure to the homeless Jimmy.

'Since for ever really, Toby. I was too frightened to

smoke in front of you. I used to keep a packet in one of my drawers in the bedroom and sneak a cigarette when you were elsewhere. With the window open, of course, so that you wouldn't notice.'

She watched his face and wondered, quite dispassionately, how many similar small secrets he had kept from her during their years together.

'I had no idea,' he said. 'Why did you think I would stop you?'

'Because you despise cigarettes and smokers. Surely you haven't forgotten the scene you made every time one of our friends tried to light up after dinner?'

The waiter arrived and Toby ordered for them both in the manner of Hattie's father. He assumed that after all these years he knew exactly what she liked to eat. She didn't stop him but she was irritated by his arrogance.

'Anyway, how is the project going? I read something somewhere about Jimmy's book,' he said. 'Something about football – *The Final Whistle*, was it?'

'Well, despite your doubts, Toby, it's gone really well. The proofs on the book have just come through and he's been making a few corrections. What was it you said about Jimmy when he first arrived in our lives? Something about him being an "animal that was on the same evolutionary level as his dog"? Funnily enough both the man and the dog are now fully house-trained.'

'It never liked me, that dog,' said Toby.

'He didn't like me either at first. But funnily enough he's almost more my dog now than he is Jimmy's. He's loyal, funny and very good-natured.'

'And he doesn't talk back or nag?' said Toby with a cynical smile. 'Perhaps you should have replaced me with a dog years ago, Hattie.'

'We had some good times, Toby, didn't we?' She didn't

want to fall out with him here, and her tone was placatory.

'I thought so,' he said wistfully.

'How are things at work?' she said, realising she had rather ignored what was going on in his life.

'Good . . . very good actually. After we broke up I put everything into the job and then things started to move politically.'

'You put everything into the job and your politics long before we broke up,' she said quickly.

'Well, let's say I have been less distracted. And it's paid off. I'm up for selection in Southwark.'

'A safe seat? That's great. And emotionally? Is there anything other than New Labour and the law in your life?'

He looked at her for a moment, putting down his napkin. 'Well, yes, as a matter of fact there is. I suppose you could say that it's all connected.'

'You've met someone at work?'

'Chrissie actually,' he said a little sheepishly.

Chrissie had been his PA for the last two years and, suddenly, Hattie felt a pang of something that must be jealousy.

'Oh Chrissie, I remember her. She was pretty, and bright,' Hattie said, realising Chrissie was far closer to Toby's ideal woman than she herself could ever have been.

'As a matter of fact she's moved in with me,' he said tentatively.

'I'm pleased for you, Toby,' Hattie said although, deep down, she was rather upset. He hadn't wasted any time.

'And what about you? Is there someone else in your life – apart from Jimmy and that dog?'

'No, no, rather like you I'm very caught up in my work. But not romantically,' she said.

'You know I didn't want it to end, Hattie. I still don't . . .' He put his hand across the table to touch hers.

'What's Chrissie then, some fill-in, some stopgap fuck?' she said a little angrily.

'Well no, it's just that if you'd only have shown me that you needed me . . . I mean, if you needed me, if you wanted me now I would be there . . .'

'I don't know what I need, Toby,' she said uncertainly. 'Or what I want.'

They spent the rest of the meal carefully avoiding talking about their relationship, chatting instead about the party that Jon had chosen as the showdown for the big bet. When they parted, with the casual kiss to both cheeks that indicated – in their world – a distant affection, Hattie felt unaccountably sad.

Claire came round to Hattie's flat so that they could all get ready for the party together – the two women upstairs in Hattie's huge bedroom while, downstairs, Jimmy dressed alone.

'I can't wait to see Jon's face when the three of us walk in,' said Claire, adding yet more mascara to her lashes.

'I think he'll only have eyes for you, Claire,' Hattie said, feeling, as she glanced in the mirror at their joint reflections, that probably every man at the party would only have eyes for Claire. Especially Jimmy.

'Why? What makes you say that?' asked Claire.

'Oh, because every time I've seen him recently all he's talked about is you. I don't think he ever got over the break-up,' she said, watching Claire's face carefully for her reaction.

'Oh, spare me, Hattie. He got over me again and again with a hundred and one pretty, witless bimbos. He'd just like to drag me back to bed from time to time. Like a lot of other men I could name.' She paused, wondering whether to mention Toby's unwelcome interest in that area, but decided against it.

'I think it's more than that with Jon,' said Hattie, trying her hardest to encourage Claire to take more of an interest in her ex-lover and less of an interest in Jimmy.

'Jon would run a mile from a serious relationship. And you know, Hattie, what I want more than anything now is a serious relationship,' Claire said, admiring her reflection in the mirror.

'I think you're wrong about Jon. I really think he wants your relationship to be – oh, you know – one to one, emotional, total. He just doesn't know how to go about it. And he's terrified of your reaction,' Hattie said, although she sensed that Claire had stopped listening.

Claire continued to stare at herself in the mirror, twisting and turning to check every inch of her reflection.

'I think it's probably too late now. I am not sure Jon is my type any more,' she said meaningfully.

'And just who is your type?' said Hattie sharply.

'Hattie, aren't you going to put on some make-up?' asked Claire, changing the subject. Avoiding what they both knew. That Jimmy was Claire's type.

'I am not very good with make-up. I've got some lipstick somewhere but I'm not sure it will go with lilac,' Hattie said despondently.

'No it won't,' said Claire, bringing over her vast bag of cosmetics. 'Here, let me put a little bit of powder and blusher on you. Soft to match that outfit. And a pale pink lipstick, I think . . .'

When they were ready the difference between their reflections in the mirror was, Hattie thought, even more marked. Hattie thought Claire looked impossibly sexy in her short crocheted frock. She was so tall and so glamorous. Hattie felt dwarfed and drab standing next to her – even in the clothes that Jimmy had chosen that she had thought suited her.

Downstairs they opened a bottle of champagne and

toasted each other as they waited for Jimmy to come out of the bathroom.

They didn't realise that he was in the room until he coughed and then they turned simultaneously and saw him. He was breathtakingly beautiful. The late summer sun had tanned his skin and made his hair blonder than ever so that – in the cream suit – he seemed to give off a kind of glow that dazzled their eyes. He smiled at them, revealing teeth that Barry Driver might have made to match his gleaming white shirt which he wore, unbuttoned and without a tie, beneath the suit.

'Jimmy,' said Claire under her breath, 'a man of distinction . . .'

Claire had wanted to hire a big cream limousine to take them to the party but Hattie had, instead, ordered a rather more discreet Daimler that dropped them – at exactly eight thirty – in Carlisle Square.

It was, without doubt, the most important A-list party of the year. A crowd of paparazzi lined the pavement outside the entrance into the big marquee that had been erected in the centre of the garden square. The next morning's papers would feature selected snaps of the arriving guests beneath captions that would confirm, to the readers, who was in and who was out at that year's party.

Security was tight because as well as the Prime Minister and the Leader of the Opposition there were a number of royals within the canopied square. Hattie felt as nervous as she imagined Jimmy must be. There was no doubt that they were, she thought, the most striking group there and already a clutch of well-known people had appraised the face and figure of Jimmy and nodded in greeting. But she was, nevertheless, frightened that something would go wrong.

But nothing did. Jimmy was, exactly as Claire had

planned, the talk of the chattering classes. Even if they couldn't quite understand what he said.

Within minutes of their arrival Jay Hector had swept down on them, taking Jimmy off to meet those people that he regarded as essential to his future career – Melvyn Bragg, Alan Yentob – their host, David Frost – and, most importantly, Tony and Cherie Blair. In many ways, as he stood in the glittering crowd in his cream Armani suit, Jimmy represented the dream of New Labour. And no one understood this more than the eternally smiling Tony.

'Jimmy Ryan,' he said, shaking Jimmy's hand with rare enthusiasm. 'Jay sent me a proof copy of your book. It's a remarkable feat . . .'

'Eee, man,' Jimmy said bashfully, and the clamouring crowd of celebrities and politicians around him laughed. With him, not at him.

Claire and Hattie stood together and watched Jimmy's progression round the crowded interior of the marquee feeling a little like proud parents.

'We did it,' Claire breathed.

'We did, didn't we?' said Hattie, exchanging smiles of triumph with her friend.

'Don't look now but Jon is over there,' Claire said.

Jon – with one arm draped around a pretty blonde girl – was also watching Jimmy's progress.

'He's coming over,' said Claire excitedly. 'Go and get Jimmy, Hattie.'

Hattie set off to recapture their protégé, pushing her way through the now throbbing crowd to reach him, tucked in the corner having a conversation with Frank Skinner, David Baddiel and Brian Brute.

'Jimmy,' she hissed.

'Hi,' he said, grabbing her hand and pulling her across to his side.

'Jimmy, it's important that you come and see Jon now.

The bet . . .' she said, smiling apologetically and leading him away.

They made their way through the crowd to Claire, who had now been joined by Jon, the blonde no longer in tow.

'Jon,' Hattie said, tapping him on the shoulder, 'I'm not sure if you've met Jimmy Ryan . . .'

Jon turned round. 'Jimmy, nice to meet you again, and in such very different circumstances,' he said, shaking Jimmy's hand and making warm eye contact.

'I think you owe us,' said Claire with a smile, 'big time.'

'I'm a man of my word,' said Jon, not taking his eyes from Claire as he reached into his top pocket and removed an envelope addressed to Jimmy. 'Here you are . . .'

'You knew all along that we'd do it, didn't you?' said Hattie.

'No, not all along. But with all the publicity you have got for him in the last week I would be a fool not to have come prepared tonight,' he said. 'Let's just say that for all my bigotry that's probably the best £5000 I have ever spent.'

'And the best we have ever earned . . . I mean Jimmy earned.' said Hattie passing the envelope to Jimmy who put it into the pocket of his jacket.

'Look out,' Jon said quickly, 'the Persian Cat is on her way.'

For once Hattie was delighted to see her sister. Proving to Jon that Jimmy was a man of distinction felt good but proving it to her family would give her even more pleasure.

'Arabella!' she said with unusual enthusiasm as her sister sidled up to her.

'Hattie darling,' Arabella said through clenched teeth, 'and Jimmy! Daddy nearly choked on his champagne when he saw you in conversation with Tony Blair. Can I borrow him for a minute, darling? I thought I might have my picture taken with him for this week's column.'

Hattie was appalled at the idea but Claire, who realised the potential of such a picture, pushed Jimmy forward and Arabella led him off, stopping here and there in the big marquee in order to introduce him to her friends.

'It seems your young man has landed on his feet, Hattie,' said her father as he came up to her and appraised the disappearing figure of Jimmy.

'I keep telling you, Daddy, that he is not my young man,' Hattie replied, thinking that if he was anyone's young man he was now Claire's.

'Your mother and I didn't like him at all but he seems to be going down very well tonight,' he added, wandering away from her.

Hattie hated parties like this and was a little disturbed to note how much Jimmy seemed to be enjoying himself. Her initial pleasure at his success had begun to fade and she wondered if anyone would notice if she slipped away.

'He's out there on his own, and he's doing OK,' Claire said as if she were reading Hattie's thoughts.

'He's doing brilliantly. But then that's what we wanted, wasn't it?'

'At first maybe. But I think I enjoyed it when he was more dependent on us. And if I am honest I want to be central to his needs tonight,' she said, looking at Hattie as if she were seeking her approval.

'I have no doubt if that's what you want, that's what you'll get,' said Hattie a little snappily. She had a strong suspicion that Jimmy's needs had centred on Claire for quite a while.

She felt a little dizzy from the combined effects of the heat and the champagne. She made her way round the back of the marquee and out into the garden to get some air and some space.

'Hattie, why aren't you inside?' said Jon who, she realised

as her eyes got used to the dark, was standing alone in the garden.

'I hate parties like this,' she said.

'So do I,' he replied, 'but I think your Jimmy is enjoying himself.'

'That was the bet, wasn't it – to turn him into someone you could "pass off in polite society"?'

'And I think one of the other conditions was that he could conduct a "civilised conversation". I am not sure that this crowd is either polite or civilised,' he said.

'Where's your girlfriend?' Hattie said, suddenly remembering the blonde.

'Oh, she's not my girlfriend really, just someone I hang about with from time to time.'

'Like Claire?' asked Hattie.

'Nothing like Claire,' he said ruefully.

'Then why don't you tell her how you feel?' Hattie said.

'Do you think she'd listen? She's far more interested in Jimmy.'

'I know,' said Hattie sadly.

They made their way back inside the marquee. Claire was dancing with Jimmy, her arms clasped tightly round his waist.

'I think I'm superfluous to his needs now,' said Hattie dejectedly as Jon went off to get another drink.

She stood alone, judging the right moment to go. It was inevitable that Claire would make a move for Jimmy tonight, and that he would respond. Edging her way towards the exit she turned round to take a last regretful glance at her protégé.

'Hinny,' he said, detaching himself from Claire and rushing over to her. 'Where are ya going?'

'Jimmy, you did it. You're a star. Arabella is going to put you in her column, Tony Blair had his picture taken with you. Claire is mad about you. You don't need me any more. Enjoy yourself,' she said, smiling bravely.

'I'll always need you,' Jimmy said, reaching down and taking her hand in his.

His words, his husky voice, took her by surprise. She could not meet his eye.

'No, Jimmy, you won't. You've come so far and you can go so much further. Without me . . .' she insisted.

'Dance with me?' His voice was low and there was a new, seductive tone that for a moment took her aback.

She still shook her head. 'Claire's waiting for you . . . and anyway I can't dance.'

Ignoring her protests he led her over to the small dance floor and put his arms around her. It was quite different from the moments they had shared at the West Allotment Working Men's Club, and not just because of the vast social gulf between the two venues. For the first time they felt comfortable together in a public place.

'Let's go home, hinny,' Jimmy whispered after they'd danced for a minute or two.

'I'll go and get Claire,' she said, reluctant to leave his arms.

'No, just us,' he said urgently.

She looked up at him a little fearfully then, unsure what he was suggesting.

'Oh . . .' she said breathlessly. 'But I'd better say goodbye to her.'

She found Claire on the other side of the dance floor, with Jon hovering a few feet away from her.

'We've both won the bet. But you've won the man, Hattie,' said Claire with just a little bit of an edge in her voice.

'Don't be silly. I don't see Jimmy like that. It wouldn't be right. My feelings for him are different – maternal . . .' Hattie said.

'Nonsense, Hattie. That's absolute crap and deep down you know it. There is nothing remotely maternal about your feelings for Jimmy. You want him, perhaps even more than I do,' Claire said gently.

'Claire, really you're being silly,' said Hattie impatiently.

'No I'm not, you are. I suppose this is a classic case of the best woman winning. Or at any rate the nicest woman . . .' Claire tried to keep her disappointment out of her voice. She should have realised all along that Jimmy only had eyes for dull, drab, do-gooding Hattie.

'Nonsense, Claire, really that's nonsense. I never wanted anything like that,' Hattie admitting to herself, even as she said the words, that she was lying.

'Well, I did . . . more than anything,' said Claire with a defeated smile. 'Still, it looks as if I might have won the consolation prize.'

'What do you mean?'

'I think I've won the punter who lost the wager,' Claire whispered to Hattie, and then made her way over to Jon whose face, at the very sight of her, brightened into a dazzling smile.

Chapter Twenty

They walked, hand in hand, to the King's Road and then got a cab back to the flat. For once Jimmy didn't insist on sitting on one of the little pull-down seats and instead sat next to Hattie, not daring yet to kiss her.

They didn't talk in the cab, or touch each other. Rex leapt on them when they came in the flat, and Hattie leant to stroke his head. Jimmy went to the fridge and took a bottle of champagne and opened it apparently effortlessly. Another sign, she thought, of the way in which he was adapting to his new life. Then he brought two glasses over to the sofa, pushing aside a puzzled Rex, so that he could sit next to her.

He still didn't kiss her – just ran his hands through her hair and then pushed it back off her face and looked at her intently.

'You're beautiful, hinny,' he said, sinking his head into her thick, dark mane so that when she looked down all she could see was his pale blondness contrasted against the blackness of her own hair. Opposites, she thought, we are opposites.

On the Persian rug across the room Rex laid his head down and watched them, whining a little for attention.

Then Jimmy raised his head and found her mouth and kissed her with such passion that she thought she might die.

'Whey ya bugger mar!' he said, stopping for a second and fighting for breath.

'Whey ya bugger mar!' Hattie repeated and they both laughed.

Then he led her up the stairs to her bedroom and stood kissing her hungrily again. Rex leapt up and followed them, looking expectantly up at them. Jimmy drew her into the bedroom and closed the door on the dog.

She wanted him so much by then that she felt faint, as if she might collapse from the strain of waiting for him to find her, touch her, enter her.

Then, so slowly she thought she would scream from anticipation, he began to undo the buttons on her prim cashmere cardigan, fumbling over each button until he reached the point where, beneath the soft lilac wool, he could see and feel her breasts. He pulled the cardigan off her shoulders and released the catch on her bra so that now she was standing naked to the waist – wearing just her full silk taffeta skirt – looking like a wanton ballerina.

'Now you, now you,' she said, easing off his jacket and unbuttoning his shirt so that she could see all of him – the tattoos, the fading bruises from the fight, the scars of his past life.

Her hands fought to unbuckle the belt on his trousers and release the cream Armani trousers revealing, beneath them, his straining Calvin Klein briefs.

'Your bait-box, Jimmy,' she said between kisses.

'*Your* bait-box, hinny,' he said, pushing her back down on the bed and easing her out of her underwear but leaving on her black stockings and the full taffeta skirt.

He pinned her arms behind her head and entered her, his face lost in an expression of wonder as he pounded into her, aware only of the urgency of his desire and the sound, as he fucked her, of rustling taffeta.

'Hattie!' he shouted as he came, using her name she realised, for the first time.

Sometime later – maybe half an hour, maybe an hour – she

eased herself out from beneath him and sat looking down on his sleeping body.

'Jimmy,' she said, kissing him awake and feeling him stir again.

'Hattie,' he said, looking up at her, 'I love you . . .'

She held her breath and smiled at him. She had, of course, gone through the motions with Toby, panted and sighed and grunted through innumerable sexual acts, but she had never before felt as if she were participating in sex. With Jimmy it was different and it terrified her.

There was so much she didn't want to think about: his expertise, his assurance, his confidence as a lover and where that knowledge had been acquired. And her own reaction to it. She was a little drunk, she knew, but it wasn't just alcohol that had sparked this.

She leant down and kissed him. She didn't want to think of the future, or the past, she just wanted to make love to him again. She looked up into the mirror over the bed and saw her reflection – she was still wearing her stockings and suspenders and the full taffeta skirt. And for the first time in her life she was struck by how provocative she looked, which only served to make her want him more.

This time she took the lead. She began to kiss him more passionately, savagely, then she reached down and grabbed his cock and lowered herself on to him, looking up in the mirror to watch herself as she fucked him.

Even when he had come she wanted more. He rolled over so that he was on top of her, looking down.

'Hattie, Hattie, slow down . . .' he said, holding her tightly to him.

She didn't want to sleep. She felt more alive, more awake than she ever had before in her life. As if some magic elixir had been slipped in her drinks at the party. As if she could go on fucking and fucking for ever.

'I'm hungry, Jimmy,' she said smiling up at him, when they had paused to recover.

'Stay there, pet,' he said, getting out of the bed.

'Cover your bait-box, Jimmy,' she said, laughing, as he went down the stairs to the kitchen. He brought a feast back to bed: two of his giant sandwiches, a big bar of chocolate and another bottle of champagne.

They alternately fed and stroked each other, pausing between mouthfuls of chocolate to share a deep kiss. And when she spilled her drink he made her lick every drop off his body. She lost count of how many times they made love that night.

They must have slept, fitfully, for a few minutes now and then but for the major part of the night they explored each other's bodies with a ferocity that shocked Hattie. When she woke in the morning she thought she would die of embarrassment at the thought of last night's fevered activity. But she didn't. Instead she looked down at the mess of food, wine, and clothes that littered the bedroom floor and insisted on him fucking her again.

'Let's never leave here again, Jimmy,' she said, holding him to her because, she knew, that outside the bedroom all might be lost. She lay there, listening to the sound of Rex's bewildered whining on the landing, and wondered if it were possible for their love to survive in the real world.

Claire woke up feeling frightened, as if she had suddenly emerged from some kind of nightmare. And then she remembered what had happened the night before and she instinctively slipped back down beneath her duvet, wishing she could dissolve back into sleep. She couldn't have, she shouldn't have . . . what on earth had made her do it? All that new resolve. All that determination never to compromise again, never to allow herself to slip back into her old ways. That absolute belief that she had overcome her old behavioural pattern. Her resolution never to allow herself to be used by a man again.

And what had she done? She had danced with Jon till the early hours, she had walked with him all the way home and, in the first light of dawn, she had passively – no, in truth it was more passionate than passive – fallen into his arms.

She might not have been so weak, she thought regretfully, had Jimmy returned the passion she felt for him. What should have been a rapturous, victorious evening that reached its climax with Jimmy and herself walking off hand in hand into the sunrise, had turned into a dreadful moment of truth. Realising that Hattie was more than just a mother figure to him was shocking. Accepting that Jimmy apparently found the dutiful, selfless, awkward and otherworldly Hattie more attractive than herself had been a terrible blow to her self-esteem. She had tried to hide the jealousy she had felt when she had seen them dancing together. She had tried to be the good loser – urging Hattie on – but it had been like a knife thrown into a heart that was, in any case, already irreparably scarred from the slings and arrows of her own outrageous romantic misfortunes. She couldn't remember when she had wanted a man as much as she had wanted Jimmy.

And instead of slipping away with dignity, she had instead transferred all the sexual tension she was feeling – all that pent-up, erotic heat – onto the nearest available man, Jon.

She heard a noise beside the bed, a slight cough, and she surfaced from beneath the duvet. Jon was standing by the bed with a tray of breakfast in his arms: toast, tea, croissants, jams and to one side – like some prop from a Mills and Boon novel – a single red rose in a silver vase.

'Jon, you look like the Milk Tray man. Or at any rate the breakfast tray man,' she said, glancing up at him with a mixture of disbelief and wonder.

He sat down, precariously, on the edge of the bed and put the tray before her.

'You look beautiful first thing in the morning,' he said.

Jon was the one man whom, with painstaking self-restraint, she had managed to keep close to her. The one man with whom she had sworn – since they had broken up all those years ago – she would never have sex. He was the only man she really trusted and now she had probably blown it.

'Is this part of your normal morning-after-the-night-before routine, Jon? Is this why you score so highly with all those pretty, blank girlies you screw? I must say you've changed your style since we were together. I have no recollections of breakfast in bed. But perhaps you thought you had better put on a bit of a show for old times' sake,' she said, irritably.

He looked a little nonplussed. 'What happened last night wasn't for old times' sake, Claire. It was for real.'

'And what exactly does "it was for real" mean?' she said. 'It strikes me as a phrase that men use to make women feel better. We're meant to think that "it was for real" is another way of a man saying that what happened between then – even a one-night stand – was in some way special. When of course it's nothing of the sort. I mean, for God's sake what sexual act isn't *for real*? Of course it would be very convenient for you men if it wasn't real, if the woman they had just fucked could just dissolve away. What men would like is not sex that is *for real* but sex that is virtual reality – I fucked her, then I unplugged the machine and it was as if it didn't happen at all,' she said.

'If that's the way you want to see it . . .' He looked hurt.

'I keep this list, you know, Jon. I've been thinking of writing a concise man/woman dictionary so that we poor females don't keep misinterpreting what you bloody men say to us. I'd forgotten about that magical phrase "it was for real".'

'I've never lied to you, Claire.'

'There you go, another marvellous male cliché, "I've never lied to you." That one has a dual use. Men say it when a woman wants *commitment* and he wants *out*. In that case what he means by that pat phrase "I've never lied to you" is that he's never loved her. And then they say it when they get caught out cheating on you. In truth I can't think of a man that has ever, ever, told me the truth.'

'I have,' he said.

'Oh, spare me, Jon. What about that other neat little expression you used a couple of minutes ago: "You look beautiful in the morning"? Which, roughly translated into language a woman can understand means "How about another quickie before I go?" It might have worked once for me. I might have fallen for that line – oh, too many times to count – but I'm not falling for it again.'

'Then I suppose I'd better go,' he said, getting up from the bed. 'It's obvious that what happened last night meant something different to each of us.'

She looked up at his face then, and for the first time caught what she supposed must be a glint of sincerity in his untrustworthy brown eyes. Had she made a mistake? Was he, to coin a phrase, *for real*?

'Jon,' she said as he made to leave the room, 'can we still be friends . . . ?'

But before she could finish her sentence he had slammed the door and left.

Hattie didn't go to work that day. She just made love. In the big sandstone bath, on the marble floor beside the big sandstone bath, across the kitchen table, on the pure white sofa, on the hard wooden floor beside the pure white sofa, on the foldaway futon in what was Jimmy's bedroom, up against the wall in the hall, in the power shower, and, finally, on the Persian rug that Rex had made his own. The dog watched them all the while with what seemed to Hattie to be disapproval.

By five in the afternoon, sated and sore, they went back to bed to sleep.

She woke in the early hours of the morning and the doubts began. However much she loved him, wanted him, needed him, how could it ever work? He was nearly ten years younger than she. In just a few months he had made a giant journey of discovery and this passion with her was just a part of that. It wasn't, it couldn't be, true love.

She must, she thought, let him move on. She must not tie him to her for ever. She must not let this develop into anything more than a brief, passionate affair. All she would do, in giving in to her desires, would be to hold him back, keep him from moving forward.

She lay in the dim light of dawn, watching him sleep and wanting him. Some time later, in the clear light of morning, he made love to her again. She looked up into the mirror and imprinted the image she saw there – of his body in hers – on her brain like a snapshot that she would keep for ever.

She left him sleeping and went downstairs to make herself some tea – the thick orange brew she had come to prefer to her former Earl Grey. Her breakfast routine, now, was probably as unhealthy as it was possible to get. With the hot, sweet tea she smoked four cigarettes.

She cleared up the mess they had made the day before, throwing out half-eaten food, bottles and cans, and putting plates, glasses and cups into the dishwasher. Rex sat watching her. She sensed, although she knew it was ridiculous, that Rex was as concerned about the new element in her relationship with his master as she was. She stroked his head and he looked up at her with his sad eyes, and she wondered why she had thought him so unattractive when he had first arrived. He was, she thought now, beautiful.

She looked at her watch and judged that she had just about enough time to feed him and take him for a quick walk before she need leave for work.

When she got back she noticed that the answerphone was flashing in an alarming fashion and she supposed she should play back the messages left the day before, even though part of her still wanted to block out the rest of the world and hide away with Jimmy for the rest of her life. She stood with a pen and a Post-it pad and made notes as she played them back.

'Hattie, it's Claire. Where the hell are you? What goes on? Call me.'

'Hattie, it's Jean from the office. Just ringing to see if you're better. You sounded very poorly when you rang in this morning. Let me know if you are going to need a day or so more and I'll sort out your diary. 'Bye.'

'Hi, it's Toby. I was just calling to say well done with Jimmy. I saw Jon and he told me you won the bet. Anyway, take care . . .'

'Hattie/Jimmy, could you call Jay Hector's office as soon as possible? Many thanks.'

'Hattie, it's Arabella. Any chance of my borrowing Jimmy on Friday night? Strictly professional, of course. Ring me back ASAP.'

She ran herself a bath, washed her hair and dressed for work. When she went up to say goodbye Jimmy was still sleeping. She left him there, grabbed her jacket and made her way out of the flat, wondering, as she walked the few yards to the tube station, if she looked as different as she felt.

She was dazed and confused and emotionally battered. But

work, she decided, would keep her from dwelling on what she had done and what it all meant.

She was conscious that she had let her colleagues down by not turning up the previous day. She had, she knew, been rather distracted in the last few weeks and it was time she concentrated on her professional life again.

Jean gave her the case notes on a boy who had been taken into emergency care a week before. He was only seven. The biggest section of Hattie's patients were adolescents. And the majority of those were referrals from the juvenile courts – persistent offenders like Ben, with antisocial tendencies and attitudes that even at her most diligent she often found impenetrable.

Children under the age of ten were easier to reach but had the power to move her more. Perhaps that was because they were most often referred to her by the social services not because they had perpetrated some crime but because they were passive victims: children in care because of neglect, abuse or some dreadful tragedy within their family.

Cases such as Lisa's – which was about to come to court – where a young child had committed a serious crime were so rare that they had occurred only three or four times in Hattie's career.

The boy today – Josh – had been in and out of care since he was born, picked up and put down again by his alcoholic mother who, she understood from his notes, he none the less adored.

Hattie's older patients tended to dislike and sometimes detest their parents even if they had been raised with love and encouragement. The younger children, regardless of the horror of their circumstances and the treatment they had received, loved those that had hurt or neglected them unconditionally.

Normally Hattie would have taken longer to study the case notes and have done a great deal of background research before accepting a new patient – talked to the case workers and carers who knew him; tracked down relatives of friends who might be able to give her a clearer picture of the child. But there was no time and, having grasped as much as she could from the thick file in front of her, she buzzed Jean and said she would see Josh as soon as he arrived.

Josh was tall for his age, with white hair that would, she guessed, fade to a dark blond by the time that he was twelve or so. He was dressed like a million other children of his age, in a pair of tracksuit bottoms worn with trainers, and a T-shirt bearing the sponsored legend 'Action Man'. He had pale skin and shadows beneath his grey eyes. He was nervous and probably frightened, and he sat, fiddling with something in his left hand, looking at her.

'Hello, Josh,' Hattie said gently, moving from behind her desk to sit beside him. 'I'm Hattie.'

He nodded and moved his lips as if he were meaning to say hello back, but no sound came out.

'I think today we'll just get to know each other a little. Will that be all right with you?'

He shrugged.

'We could talk about things you like. You will talk to me, Josh?'

'If you like,' he said, his voice little more than a whisper.

They talked – or rather Hattie talked – about his step-sisters, his friends, his favourite television programmes. Then she showed him the toys she kept – the helicopter on a piece of wire that could be wound up and made to fly.

He listened mostly, occasionally responding to a question, all the time fiddling and picking at whatever it was he had hidden in his hand.

'Is that a toy you've got there, Josh?' she asked carefully. 'Will you show me?'

He opened his hand to reveal in his palm – dirt-stained and sweaty – a small piece of frayed yellow ribbon that, she guessed, was all that was left of his babyhood comforter.

'Mum doesn't like me having it all the time,' he said.

'Why do you think that is, Josh?'

'Because she says its babyish,' he said.

'Do you think she's right?'

'I suppose so . . .' He looked up at her with an expression of such despair on his face that she wanted to seize him and hold him.

'Do you have a name for it, Josh?'

He smiled coyly and nodded. 'It's my Bit.'

'And how does your Bit make you feel, Josh?'

'Safe,' he said.

'When your mum isn't around?' she asked.

'Even when she is,' he said.

By the end of the session she felt she had made a little progress. She could see that with patience and kindness she might penetrate his reserve, reach him and maybe help him to resolve some of the anger and pain he was feeling.

At lunchtime she made some calls, returning messages left on her answerphone the previous day. Claire was in the middle of a meeting so she couldn't really talk about what had happened with Jimmy or, indeed, what had happened with Claire and Jon. She told Arabella to call Jimmy at the flat and arrange whatever it was she wanted with him – some dreadful social function that her sister thought he would like, the opening of a themed restaurant devoted to football. She didn't tell Arabella that she and Jimmy were now together – an item, a couple, in love – it was all too soon and she was still too unsure.

In the afternoon she had several case meetings and a load of paperwork to do. She was used to compartmentalising her life, to pushing from her mind even the most haunting and disturbing of her patients. But she couldn't get Josh out of her mind. There had been something about him – perhaps just the blond hair – that had made her think of how Jimmy must have been as a child. All the agonies that he had endured as he grew up.

There had been no concerned social workers or clinical psychologists in Jimmy's childhood, no one to help him understand what was happening to him. In all his life, she thought, he had never had anyone really – apart from his nan – who had cared for him. His only experience in relationships was of betrayal, neglect and indifference. She put her head in her hands, aware of the burden that she had taken on in loving Jimmy, wondering if she hadn't made a terrible mistake.

Chapter Twenty-One

Hattie left the office quite late that evening, feeling a little nervous about going home and seeing Jimmy. By the time she got back it was nearly seven. Rex jumped up enthusiastically as she came through the door and she bent down, as was her custom now, and made a fuss of him.

Jimmy was waiting for her, the table laid for two, a bottle of wine open and, she suspected from the aroma, something other than Pot Noodles cooking.

'Ya late, Hattie,' he said a little tensely.

'I had a lot of work to catch up on,' she said, keeping her distance from him.

'What's wrong?' he asked, moving to put his arms round her.

'Oh, I don't know, Jimmy – I'm just so frightened . . .'

'Of what?' he said gently.

'Of this. Of us.'

'It was meant to happen,' he said, kissing her softly and then breaking off, suddenly more intent on whatever it was he had in the oven.

'I've got some good news,' he said. 'Come here, darling.'

'What news?' she said, thinking how odd the endearment 'darling' sounded coming from Jimmy's mouth. To her, 'darling' was a word couples used when their love for one another had become dull and routine – an automatic endearment, not something she expected to hear from the man with whom – just last night – she had shared such an extraordinary passion. But then Jimmy's language and his accent had been undergoing significant changes. Sometimes, she thought, it was as if he were trying so hard to put his past behind him that he was deliberately talking as he imagined all her friends did so that only the occasional word sounded anything like the Jimmy she had first encountered.

'The film rights, like, Jay has sold them,' said Jimmy, eager to share his news.

'That's great, Jimmy,' she said, genuinely pleased for him.

She sat down at the table and watched in amazement as he produced a big dish of pasta and another of salad that was covered in a French dressing and sprinkled with freshly shaved Parmesan cheese. She noted that there was no brown sauce on the table, or ketchup or Branston pickle. Instead they were back to Toby's extra virgin olive oil and black pepper.

'Claire told me how ta cook this, it's reet easy,' he said with pride as he served her a plate of carbonara

'Whey ye bugger mar!' she said, and he laughed.

It was delicious. When they had finished he took the plates away and stacked them in the dishwasher, and Hattie remembered how he had been when he had arrived – how he had peed in the sink that first night and how defensive he had been when she had tried to find out his life story. It was as if, she thought as she watched him confidently pouring himself another glass of the good white wine, he were a different person.

She reached down for her bag and retrieved a packet of cigarettes, lighting one and inhaling it gratefully.

'Hattie,' he said in a disapproving manner, 'I wish you wouldn't smoke in the flat ...' She was momentarily dumbfounded, wondering if he were joking. Then she realised she hadn't seen him lighting up indoors lately. She sat there, the ash building on her cigarette, unable to move or say anything. Then she stubbed it out, got up, walked over to the television and switched it on.

'Jimmy, we can just catch the second half of *Coronation Street*,' she called to him in the kitchen.

He came over and took the remote control from her hand. 'Claire says I've got to keep up with what's going on,' he said, switching over, to Hattie's horror, to Channel 4 News.

'But, Jimmy, I was watching that . . .' she protested.

'Eee, it's crap, Hattie,' he said.

She sat next to him, not loving him any less but aware that the changes that she had begun in him had now taken him so far from the man he used to be that he wasn't just different he was – well, he was turning into *Toby*.

When the news was over he took her face between his hands and kissed her, which was a very un-Toby-like thing to do and temporarily allayed her fears.

'Hattie . . .' he whispered.

'Jimmy . . .' she said.

Rex, clearly unsettled by the changes that were taking place around him, sauntered over to them and jumped up on the white sofa.

'Doon, Rex,' said Jimmy sharply.

'Oh, it doesn't matter. Let him sit there.'

But Rex had skulked away and was lying sulking on the Persian rug, his head between his two front paws.

'I had lunch with Claire today,' Jimmy began.

'Did you?' said Hattie, faintly concerned that perhaps her friend – whom she still hadn't managed to reach – had not yet given up on the idea of an intimate relationship with Jimmy. In fact, in Hattie's least confident moments in the last twenty-four hours, she had begun to wonder if it wasn't Claire who had taught Jimmy – not just to eat with chopsticks and appreciate Chardonnay – but how to make love so wonderfully.

'We're working on the book promotion,' he said, stroking her hair.

'Of course,' said Hattie.

'She's got all these things lined up,' he said.

'Such as?'

'Ascot, Polo, the opera, some dinner Jay has organised . . .'

Hattie felt, yet again, as if she were no longer part of the changes to Jimmy that were being orchestrated by Jay and Claire. As if their lives – away from the frenzied activities in the bed upstairs – were taking different courses.

'I've got to get up early tomorrow,' he said.

'Why?'

'Claire's taking me out.'

'Oh is she, where?'

'Smith's Lawn.'

He sounded as if he were a part of her sister, Arabella's, ghastly society column. Surely he wasn't really taken in by all this nonsense? She understood that he needed to promote the book but she couldn't see why he should have to go to charity polo matches or Ascot.

'Shall we have an early night then?' he said a little coyly, as if he too were uncertain of their relationship.

When they went upstairs to bed – Rex sternly told to stay downstairs – Hattie felt awkward again, as if all that had gone on between them in the previous forty-eight hours had not happened.

'Hattie,' Jimmy said, trying to recapture the way they had felt the night before.

She gave in, put her arms round him and sank her head in his chest feeling, as she did so, a surge of pure lust for him.

'Oh Jimmy . . .' she said as he began to undress her.

And now they were kissing as they had the first night. As if neither of them would let go until they had lost consciousness, their mouths more concerned with consuming one another than breathing.

When they finally broke away, she smiled at him properly for the first time that evening.

'I love you, Hattie,' he said when they lay naked beside each other.

'And I love you, Jimmy.'

'I've never loved anyone like this,' he said, kissing her again.

Then he entered her and she was gasping for breath again, as if she might die of pleasure.

Hattie woke up to the sound of a banging on the front door, accompanied by Rex's barking. She looked at the clock and realised they had forgotten to set the alarm. It was already eight thirty.

'Jimmy,' she said, shaking him awake, 'you've got to get up.'

He looked up at her, smiled and pulled her down to him and began to kiss her.

'Jimmy, no, listen there's someone at the door,' she gasped.

'It'll be Claire. She can wait,' he said.

'No she can't,' said Hattie, pushing him away and pulling herself up out of the bed, grabbing a white waffle robe and putting it on.

She was aware from her reflection in the mirror that she looked rather dishevelled – her wild dark hair full around her face, the robe tied loosely at her waist, her legs bare. But she didn't really care, she was just concerned to let Claire in.

Rex was leaping at the door when she got there, as was his habit when people knocked or rang the bell, and as she opened it she noticed how his paws had worn away the paint.

'Claire . . .' she said, suddenly feeling a little self-conscious.

'Hattie,' said Claire, looking her up and down as if she

were searching for physical signs of the sexual activity she had guessed had been taking place.

'I'll make some tea,' Hattie offered, going to the kitchen. 'Jimmy's just getting dressed.'

As usual Claire looked exquisite. She was wearing a light linen trouser suit in a shade somewhere between cream and primrose that worked brilliantly with her auburn hair. And her face was made up very subtly in a way that made Hattie feel, bare-faced and bare-bodied in her white robe, distinctly underdressed and inadequate.

Hattie made a pot of strong tea. Jimmy came leaping down the stairs just as she was pouring a mug for Claire.

'Hi,' he said, kissing Claire on both cheeks in a manner that Hattie found, so early in the morning, disconcerting.

He was wearing the particular Calvin Klein Y-fronts that Claire had said – God it seemed so long ago now – would show off his perfect lunch box.

'What should I wear?' he asked Claire.

'It's sort of smart casual. Those chinos we bought the other day, with the Ralph Lauren chambray shirt and the Gucci loafers,' said Claire as if she were making an order in a restaurant, clearly unperturbed by the sight of Jimmy in his underwear.

'Tea, Claire?' said Hattie, passing her a mug of the strong, dark liquid.

'Good God, what's this, Hattie?' She almost choked on her first mouthful.

'Tea, Claire, proper tea. Not that perfumed gnat's pee you drink,' said Hattie, passing Jimmy a mug too.

'I can't drink this,' he said, raising his eyebrows to Claire over her head. 'Can't you make a pot of Earl Grey?'

'No,' said Hattie, lighting herself a cigarette and sitting down with her own mug of her delicious tea. 'Make some yourself.'

Jimmy disappeared upstairs to get dressed and Claire filled the Alessi kettle and put it on the hob to boil.

'Well, things have certainly changed around here,' she said coldly to Hattie.

'As a matter of fact I'm about the only thing that hasn't changed around here,' said Hattie in equally cold tones.

'Oh, come on, girl, since when did you drink tea you could stand your spoon up in?' sniggered Claire. 'Camomile was more your thing.'

'Well, I may have adjusted a few of my, my tastes . . . but essentially I am the same Hattie who used to be your friend,' she said meaningfully.

'Things aren't going too well with Jimmy then?' said Claire as she made two mugs of Earl Grey tea.

'If you must know, Claire,' Hattie glanced up the stairs to check that Jimmy was out of earshot, 'we've been having spectacular sex since the night of the party.'

'But lousy conversation?' said Claire.

Hattie put her head in her hands. She needed to talk to someone about Jimmy but she was certain that Claire wasn't the right person.

'You know, Hattie, I don't want to be pessimistic but Jimmy – that is, the new Jimmy – is as far removed from you and your precious principles as Toby was.'

Hattie narrowed her eyes at her friend. 'What do you mean?'

'I mean he's caught the bug. Loves all the things you despise: social climbing, shopping – oh and sex . . . but then you know about *that* . . .'

Before Hattie could question Claire any further Jimmy came tripping down the stairs dressed like an extra from Jilly Cooper's *Polo*. She looked at him in astonishment, wondering at what point his personal style had so dramatically changed. It seemed like only yesterday that he had stood – where he was standing now – wearing that stinking lumberjack shirt and tracksuit bottoms. At what point had he discovered Ralph Lauren and Gucci and Harvey Nichols?

'Jimmy,' said Claire, standing up and looking at her watch, 'you look perfect. Let's go or we'll be late. We've got to pick up Arabella on the way.'

'Arabella?' said Hattie, aghast.

'Yes, Hattie. Why the surprise? Arabella's set the whole day up. Jimmy is guest of honour at Johnnie Elm's table,' said Claire. 'Shall we be off then, darling?'

Jimmy came over and kissed Hattie on the top of her dishevelled head. He smelt, she noticed, very strongly of Eau Sauvage.

'See you later, darling,' he said as he and Claire left.

Hattie lit another cigarette and poured herself another cup of her strong, reviving tea. As she sat there, wondering whether to laugh or cry, Rex came over and laid his big head in her lap.

'Oh Rex,' she said, stroking him gently, 'whatever has happened to our Jimmy?'

Hattie was getting distinctly nervous about the forthcoming court case with Lisa. She had written a comprehensive report on the child. She had, she felt, uncovered enough instances of brutality in Lisa's own childhood to offer – if not an excuse – then at least some explanation of her behaviour in the playground on that day.

She wanted to be able to influence the judgment. She wanted to be able to present to the court a picture of Lisa as something other than a psychopath. She wanted to evoke some spark of compassion for a little girl who had been raised by a cruel, unforgiving and misguided father. But she knew that the real compassion in the courtroom would be reserved for the parents of little Lindy who was, after all, the real victim. And she also knew that

Lisa's own childhood deprivation did not fit with what the judge and jury might expect. Her background, while not exactly middle class, was – at least on the surface – one of old-fashioned family values. The fact that her father had taken those Christian values to such extremes that his daughter had attempted murder – as she believed – for God, would not be easy for Hattie to put across in court. The abuse that Lisa had suffered, because it was part of her father's perverted religious beliefs, was not the kind that would win points with the people who would be judging the child. That morning – when she wasn't distractedly pondering what Jimmy, Claire and Arabella were up to – Hattie spent her time polishing her report, adding further instances – taken from her tapes of her talks with Lisa – of the extraordinary home life the little girl had led.

Hattie had told Jean to hold all her calls for her but mid-morning the phone on her desk rang. It was Jon.

'Hattie?'

'Jon, how are you?'

'Look, Hattie, I need to talk to you about Claire. Will you have lunch with me?'

She hesitated only for a moment. 'Yes, of course. Where shall we meet?'

'I'll come to you at about twelve forty-five.'

'Do you know where I am?'

'It's part of St Thomas's, isn't it?'

'Yes.'

She was surprised he was so well informed about her professional life. He had always been so critical of her work that she had generally avoided any mention of it during the years in which the two of them had been pushed together socially.

She was waiting in the shabby reception area when he arrived. They went to the same pub she and Jimmy had gone to on the day he had recorded the tapes that had been edited into *The Final Whistle*. Jon would have been happier in a restaurant but since Hattie only had an hour he reluctantly agreed to a pub lunch.

'What will you drink?' he asked

'Just mineral water. And a ploughman's.'

He brought the drinks and the food to the little round table in the snug that she had secured. It was crowded and noisy, and not at all the place in which he wanted to discuss his troubled emotional life but it would have to do.

'Has Claire spoken to you recently?' he began.

'I saw her this morning. She took Jimmy off to some polo match at Smith's Lawn,' Hattie said bleakly.

'Did she?' he said, looking, she thought, more mournful than she had ever seen him.

'What's wrong, Jon?'

'Oh, you know at the party that night, the night of the bet . . . ?'

'Yes.'

'Well, after you had walked off into the night with Jimmy, we danced. And then, you know, one thing led to another and it was like I wanted it to be . . .' He paused discreetly.

'You mean you made passionate love all night,' said Hattie.

'Something like that.'

'And?'

'And then in the morning I was like – I can't tell you, Hattie, I was just so happy. I got up before she was awake and I went out to the little shop round the corner and I bought all this stuff and I made her breakfast and took it up to her.' He stopped again.

'And?'

'She gave me all this crap about how all men are bastards and how I was no better than the worst of them.'

'So you left?'

'Well, everything I said just seemed to make it worse,' he said, looking down into his drink.

'And have you spoken to her since, sent her flowers, written to her?'

'I'm too frightened . . .'

Hattie couldn't think what to say. She didn't want to upset him further by revealing her own fears about Claire and her relationship with Jimmy.

'Well, I suppose that if you really love her, Jon – if you're really sure – you'll just have to convince her that even if you are a bastard, you're the right bastard for her,' she said with a weak smile.

'And how will I do that?'

'It would have to be something very bold, very unusual . . .'

'Like what?' he said eagerly.

Hattie sighed. She had rather hoped that she might be able to open her own heart to Jon but realised now that would be impossible. She couldn't tell him about Claire and Jimmy. Besides, she noted when she looked at her watch, she was due back in the office.

'I'm sure you'll think of something terribly clever, Jon. It's what you do, isn't it, think up ways of persuading people to buy into things? Well, this time think of yourself as the product and Claire as the sector of the market place you need to reach,' she said, getting up to leave.

'I might just do that Hattie . . .' he said, thoughtfully as they parted.

Hattie had half expected Jimmy to be home when she got back that evening. But there was only a desperate Rex to greet her.

'Oh God, Rex, you've been stuck in all day,' she said to him. 'Look, I'll just change into my jeans and we'll go to the park.'

She had rather neglected the dog recently. She supposed

that if he were going to be a permanent fixture in her life – and if Jimmy were out promoting his book all the time – she had probably better find a dog walker. He needed more exercise than he was getting.

She walked him all the way to the park and threw his ball for him for a full half-hour. Jimmy still wasn't back when they got home. It was now nine o'clock and she reckoned that when he did return he probably wouldn't want to eat. She made herself a big sandwich and opened a can of beer.

There was nothing interesting to watch on television and anyway she was feeling too restless and preoccupied to absorb anything. She began to tidy the flat. The cleaning lady had walked out sometime after Rex had walked in, so she got out the hoover and ran it across the wood floors and the Persian rugs. Then she began to collect up the last few things of Toby's that still littered the place – a few books, the fruit bowl that Rex had supped his Newkie from, some CDs. She put them all in a big bag and decided to store it out of sight behind the Japanese screens.

Jimmy's holdall was still there, still packed. He must have put it there when they had returned from North Shields. Having cleared out the last remnants of Toby's presence she thought she might replace them with a few of Jimmy's things. She took out the Blackpool snowstorm and the Junior Achievers Cup 1990 and placed them side by side on the coffee table by the television. Then she put the picture of his nan in the seashell frame on the big wooden shelf that ran beneath the window right across one side of the big open-plan room. In the kitchen, as she was carefully sticking up several of his Newcastle United posters, the phone rang.

'Hello?' she said.

'Hattie?' said Jimmy.

She could hardly hear him for the background noises

around him – people talking, music – and she guessed he must be in a restaurant or a pub.

'Where are you, Jimmy?' she shouted.

'The Met Bar,' he shouted back.

'That's a long way from the polo.'

'Pardon?' he said.

'You've gone a long way from Smith's Lawn,' she shouted.

'Arabella brought us here for a drink,' he said, but the noise around him was so intense that she couldn't make out what he said next. And then they seemed to be cut off.

She put the phone down, lit a cigarette and sat curled up with Rex in front of the television, flicking her way through the cable channels. Eventually she found one of those American true-life relationship dramas she had come to love on UK Living, a story about a couple – a rich woman and her apparently perfect husband – and the tragic disintegration of their relationship after their baby died. How pathetic she was, she thought, crying over such nonsense when real events in her life – and the events in the lives of some of her patients, particularly Lisa's – were so much more deserving of her tears.

She was tired as well as upset and in the end she gave up waiting for Jimmy and went up to bed, the dog following her.

She was woken by Jimmy coming into the bedroom and pushing Rex roughly off the duvet. She didn't say anything, pretending instead that she was asleep. He crawled in beside her and the smell of alcohol was so overwhelming that she turned over with her back to him.

He began to caress her but she didn't respond and eventually he stopped. She lay there marvelling at how far he had come in just under four months. From drinking Newkie in doorways with Mick to drinking champagne in the Met Bar with Arabella. Perhaps, she thought as he began to snore, that was Jimmy's definition of being a man of worth. Being able to get pissed alongside the posh, rather than the poor.

Chapter Twenty-Two

Hattie got up as soon as the alarm went off the next morning. The bed beside her was empty.

She pulled on her robe and went downstairs to find Jimmy standing in the kitchen drinking a cup of tea (Toby's Lapsang Souchong, she noted).

'I'm sorry, Hattie,' he said, offering her an apologetic smile.

'No need to be, Jimmy . . .' she said, although she didn't really mean it.

'It was Arabella's idea to go on last night. I just got carried away, like,' he said.

'Did you have a good time at the polo?'

'Yeah. And ya sister introduced me to all sorts of people at that place last night.'

'The Met Bar? I'm not surprised,' she said.

Someone had told her – Claire probably – that entrance to the place was strictly vetted. Only the most beautiful, famous or influential people were allowed to rub shoulders with one another within the minimal (and minimalist) bar. Jimmy began to list the famous people he had encountered the night before. It was a dreadful – at least to Hattie – litany of inconsequential and superficial names, few of which, apart from Chris Evans and Grant from *Eastenders*, she knew.

He broke off, aware that Hattie wasn't impressed. 'But I'd rather have been with you,' he said.

She didn't say 'Then why weren't you?' because she knew full well why he chose to be out with Arabella rather than here with her.

'I'm holding you back. You want all this – it's fun for you. I understand. It's just not what I want,' she said.

'Boot you made all this possible for us,' he said.

'Well, I helped, Jimmy. But all this – the season, the Met Bar, the shopping – well, you've gone further than I imagined you'd ever want to.'

'Claire and Jay say I've got to be seen as much as possible. With the book coming up in a couple of months and everything,' he said.

She nodded, aware that the launch – which would no doubt be masterminded by Claire – was looming closer in their lives. 'And where are you off to today?'

'Ascot,' he said sheepishly.

'Of course,' she said, watching him check his tie in the image of himself that bounced back from the big sheet steel cupboards. She glanced at her own reflection beside him and wondered how she could ever have really believed they were a match for each other. He would be far more suited, she thought, reflected alongside the tall, elegant Claire or the stunning Arabella.

'I almost wish I were coming with you,' she said, thinking of the day she would face in the office.

'Why don't you?' he said, his face lighting up.

'Because I have a lot of work to do. But have a good time. And give Claire my regards,' she said, kissing him lightly on both cheeks – as she had Toby the last time she had seen him – and then making her way upstairs to get ready for work.

It was to be Hattie's last meeting with Lisa before the trial. Her defence team had already tutored the child – as much as was possible – on how she should appear in court. She knew what to expect because, as happened in cases where the defendant was so young, she had been shown round the court in which she would be tried.

Lisa had come to terms – as far as she ever would – with the fact that she would not be allowed home. What she hadn't seemed to accept was that being parted from her family – at any rate from her father – might ultimately be the best thing that had ever happened to her.

When she arrived in Hattie's office that day she was quieter and more reserved than usual. It was as if finally she understood the enormity of what she must face the following day.

'I've written my report, Lisa,' Hattie said gently. 'The prosecution case is conclusive. All I can do is perhaps make the jury – and the judge – see the other side of you. Make them see a little bit of the Lisa I have come to know.'

The child nodded. Hattie didn't explain that this would involve revealing some of the more harrowing stories Lisa had related – in the privacy of Hattie's office – about her home life. She had a feeling that the girl would regard such intimate moments being mentioned in a courtroom as a betrayal, but it was a risk she had to take if she was to make any impression at all on the people who would decide the child's fate.

'Will you be there all the time?' Lisa asked.

'Some of the time. If you need me I'll be there for you at the end of each day.'

'And after? Will I see you then?'

'It's one of the recommendations I have put forward in my report. I think we should carry on with the work we have done. I have suggested that I come to see you at least once a week,' said Hattie. 'As long as you want me to.'

Lisa nodded.

They spent the rest of their time that day going through the new books that Hattie – aware of Lisa's hunger for new stories – had added to her collection. When it was time for her to go, the child came and laid her head on Hattie's shoulder and they clung to each other for a few moments.

'I'll see you tomorrow, Lisa,' Hattie said, aware that she might be the only person in the courtroom who could find it within her to feel compassion for this poor, disturbed child.

For the second night running she arrived home to an anxious Rex and an empty flat. For the second night running she took him for a walk, reckoning – since the last race at Ascot had finished three hours ago – that by the time they returned Jimmy would be there.

When she got back the phone was ringing.

'Hattie darling?'

'Claire . . .'

'Ascot was a huge success. Jimmy's going to be in Dempster tomorrow – we thought we'd celebrate and go out to dinner. Will you join us?'

Hattie was irritated and angry but she didn't want Claire to pick up on how she felt.

'Oh, Claire, I'm in court tomorrow. I thought I'd get an early night.'

'But we won't be late. Jimmy's insisting on your coming. But he's too frightened to ring you himself.' She gave a little laugh.

'I think you're exaggerating, Claire.' Hattie tried to keep the venom from her voice.

'Oh go on – don't always put such a damper on things. And anyway, it will do you good. Take you out of yourself,' Claire said.

It was the last thing that Hattie wanted but she thought she ought to make a bit of an effort, even if it did ultimately end – as she felt it would – in some sort of a showdown with Claire or Jimmy, or both of them.

She rushed upstairs to change. She had become more aware of her appearance lately. When she had been with Toby he had put up a constant battle to make her wear the kind of clothes he liked – short, tight, restricting things that she hated. But the clothes that Jimmy had picked for her to wear to the party had made her feel so good that they had prompted her to buy more.

She put on a beautiful, fitted, cream single-breasted jacket she had bought in Jigsaw a couple of days before together with a pair of plain black trousers. Underneath she wore nothing but a cream silk Wonderbra.

She had even bought some make-up that the girl in the shop had showed her how to use. She put on the eye pencil and the mascara and added some lipstick and then stood back to examine herself in the mirror over the bed. There was something not quite right about the effect and then she remembered her hair which she wore at work scrunched back from her face. She unclipped it, and shook it and then looked again. It was OK, she thought; she looked fine.

Curiously – or perhaps symbolically – they were having dinner at Vong, the very place where she and Claire had begun their wager to turn Jimmy into a man of worth. Not, of course, that they knew he was called Jimmy then. Or really that they cared who he was or what he might be called.

There was a crowd of them round the big table in the corner. Claire, Arabella, Jimmy, Jay Hector and a number of other people Hattie thought she should know. She was immediately aware that there wasn't a spare chair.

'Oh Hattie! God, there isn't a place for you . . .' said Claire.

Jimmy stood up and offered her his seat, kissing her on the top of her head as she sat down. The waiter brought along another chair and placed it between Hattie and Jay Hector.

'Well, what did you think of Ascot?' she said.

'It's not what it was . . .' said Claire. 'Hattie, the Editor of the *Sun* had the box next to ours, imagine!'

'And a lot of fookin' tarts in white stilettoes . . .' said Jimmy, laughing along with Claire. His Geordie accent and all his wonderful colloquialisms had all but disappeared now. In their place was this awful stilted laddish talk, presumably picked up in places like the Met Bar from people like the man sitting two places from Jimmy – the editor of a successful men's magazine that had made its name by pioneering cover shots of famous women in soft porn poses.

Indeed, the people that surrounded Jimmy this evening were almost entirely drawn from Jay Hector's Soccerati – as they were known – men distinguished in some way or another who had a common obsession with football: a Welsh cult comedian, a disgraced Tory politician who had made a secondary career as a football commentator, a senior television executive, a well-known cockney television presenter, a celebrity journalist, an actor from the *Street*.

No one made any attempt to introduce Hattie to anyone and since she was the only person there who hadn't consumed enormous quantities of champagne at Hector's expense at Blenheim, she felt even more the outsider. She couldn't even find solace in a cigarette since smoking was forbidden in the restaurant.

They had already ordered their food and Jimmy made a big show of calling over the waiter and ordering for Hattie. She should have protested – but she didn't want to seem to be putting Jimmy down in public. So, in rather the way she did when she lunched with her father, and when she had been with Toby, she just smiled submissively and accepted his choice.

She hadn't intended to drink any alcohol that evening – she was concerned about the trial the following morning – but she decided that it was the only way she could get through the meal.

It had been a mistake to come. She didn't really need

proof that her relationship with Jimmy – begun so passionately just a few days before – was doomed, but she got it that night.

Not just in the way in which he interacted with the flirtatious Claire – the private jokes, the secret asides, the touches – but also in the manner in which he reacted to the attention he was receiving from Arabella (who was, at least, more restrained than Claire) and from the clearly besotted Jay Hector.

Hattie supposed she had been a ridiculous idealist imagining that the man of worth that the homeless Jimmy had been transformed into would be just that – a man with values. She had been naïve to think that the shy, earnest boy that she had taken into her home would not be corrupted and irrevocably altered by money and his exposure to people like Jay Hector. And Claire, she thought, as she watched her friend and former collaborator run her hands through Jimmy's perfect blond hair. Why on earth had she expected anything else?

Jimmy was now relating an anecdote he had been told the night before in an accent that was closer to that of the Welsh comedian than his native Geordie. He was like some awful mimic – the man at the West Allotment Working Men's Club who had done the *turn* with all the different voices and hats. His story – a coarse joke about a prostitute and a midget – was punctuated again and again by words he would never have used previously, even when he had been at his most desperate, living on the streets and begging with Rex – but which here, in this smart restaurant, were deemed acceptable.

She could stand it no longer. She couldn't be a witness to what was happening to Jimmy. The man she had fallen in love with wasn't the creature sitting here entertaining what Claire no doubt thought of as *polite society*. This was someone else, someone other than her Jimmy.

'I'm terribly sorry,' she said, 'but I have to get up early tomorrow. I've got a difficult day . . .'

She got up then. She hadn't eaten a thing. But then no one had really. She walked to the door without even glancing behind her.

She stood for a moment outside the restaurant, not sure what to do next. And then Jimmy was beside her.

'Hattie,' he said sharply.

'Jimmy . . . ?' She was surprised that he had followed.

'Come back and finish the meal,' he said aggressively.

She shook her head.

'You can't stand it, can you?'

'What, Jimmy, what can't I stand?'

'You can't stand the fact that I am a success.'

'What do you mean?' she screamed.

'Everything was fine, wasn't it, as long as I was poor Jimmy? Little Jimmy in the gutter. The underdog. The boy you could pity, the boy you could control, the boy you could patronise . . . like one of your patients – like the girl you'll be defending tomorrow.'

She couldn't bear to listen. What if he was right? What if she could only love the old Jimmy, the one the world looked down on? Not the one she had helped create – who was on equal terms with everyone else inside that restaurant. What if the only thing that had really upset her in the last few days was the fact that he no longer needed her? She could feel the tears coming now and she turned away, saw a cab and hailed it.

'Don't run away when I'm talking to you,' he yelled.

She opened the door of the taxi and got in, but before she could close it he grabbed the door and climbed in too, pulling down one of the little seats he had sat on during the first cab journey they had taken together, just a few months ago.

But this time it wasn't because he got any childish

297

pleasure from it. He did it because he wanted to sit as far away from her as it was possible to get.

He gave the driver their address and then pushed the connecting window shut and turned his attention back to Hattie.

'What did you want from me?' he said.

'I don't know what you mean.' Hattie's tears blurred her view of him.

'I tried so hard to be good enough for you. I tried so hard to be what you wanted me to be.'

'I don't understand you, Jimmy.'

'But you understood me before, didn't you, hinny, when no one else could? When I talked the way you liked?'

They had reached the flat now. Jimmy paid the driver and then led Hattie, still crying, inside. Over the sound of her own sobbing she could hear Rex barking behind the front door.

'Did you sleep with me for the bet?' he said, pushing her through the door, across the room and onto the sofa. 'Did you fuck me to find out if I was a man of worth?'

'What do you mean?'

'Like Claire said . . . it had to be one or the other of you.'

'Claire said that?'

He nodded.

'That's not true, Jimmy. I slept with you because I thought I loved you. Not because of a bet, not because of anything other than the way I felt. You must believe that. But . . .'

'But?'

'But it would never have worked, would it? I mean tonight, with all those people, you were much happier than you ever would be with me. I said it before – you don't need me any more. You've moved on. We are as different now as we were at the beginning,' she said softly.

'You mean it wouldn't do to be with someone like me. What would people say? Fine to win some bet, have a quick fling, but not something you would seriously consider. Not you, not Hattie George. Not with me. Some boy from nowhere . . .'

He began to pace up and down the flat and then stopped, staring as if out of the window into the night.

'And you would never have let me forget, would you?' he shouted, moving forward and picking up the picture of his nan in the seashell frame that, Hattie had quite forgotten, she had put on the shelf by the window.

'Why do you want to forget so badly?'

'Why do you think, woman?'

Then he saw the Blackpool snowstorm on the table. He went over and picked it up and threw it across the room, smashing it against the wall, so that a trickle of liquid and artificial snowflakes slid into a little pool on the floor.

'Because I don't know who I am any more,' he said passionately. 'Because I don't fit in my world and I don't fit in yours.'

'Perhaps you fit in Claire's,' she shouted.

He looked at her with utter contempt, then turned and walked out.

A curious thing happened to Claire when she got home from the restaurant that night, something that quite put Jimmy and Hattie and the silly – maybe even wicked – game she had been playing out of her mind.

Someone had – somehow or other – got into her house. Lamps had been lit in every room, curtains had been pulled. But this was no ordinary thief, no ordinary break-in. For a start the whole place had been filled with flowers – the pink lilies that she loved because of their sweet smell. There must have been hundreds of them – in vases, in buckets, in bottles, in anything her mystery guest could find.

Then on the hi-fi the only piece of music in the world that could move her to tears was playing, although it had been years since she had heard it – something by Samuel Barber she remembered from some film she had seen.

She didn't know whether to go upstairs. But in the end she did. The bed was covered in thousands and thousands of fresh pink rose petals. Laid carefully on top of it was a beautiful La Perla négligé – in the same shade of pink. On the bedside table there was a bottle of Laurent Perrier champagne in a proper ice bucket and beside it a box of her favourite chocolates.

On a little card that had been laid on her pillow someone had written, in perfect italic script '. . . *and all because the lady loves bastards.*'

He was standing behind her, watching.

'You mean it *was for real*?' she said without turning round.

'I thought, if it would be all right with you, I would hang around and help you write that concise man/woman dictionary.'

'What are you trying to say, Jon?'

'You tell me. You're the expert.'

'That you are finally ready to *commit*. Not suicide, or murder, but to me . . .'

She wasn't entirely certain that committing to Jon was the right thing to do. It would probably ruin a beautiful friendship. But hey, it was the best offer she'd had in the seven years since they had split up.

Chapter Twenty-Three

Hattie reached Wood Green Crown Court early the following morning. She wanted to try to see Lisa, to offer some comfort, before the ordeal of her trial began. Already there was a small crowd queuing for places in the public gallery. She shouldn't have been surprised: a serious criminal charge involving a nine-year-old girl was bound to attract attention.

She noted, too, as she made her way through the building, several press photographers and a couple of seedy-looking journalists loitering in the lobby. Across from them she spotted Tina Brooks, the social worker who had been so enraged by Hattie's preliminary report.

'Tina,' Hattie called across the hall, 'can I have a few moments with Lisa?'

Tina Brooks cast a look of disdain at Hattie and shook her head. 'She's fine. It would probably be better if you spent a bit more time thinking through the evidence you are going to give,' she said, turning her back on Hattie and hurrying away.

Hattie was shown into the court room and allotted a seat alongside various other experts who would, in the days to come, be called on to give evidence.

Hattie noted the bent figure of Lisa's mother. There was no sign of her father, the man Hattie held responsible for the tragedy that had prompted this trial. He wasn't, Hattie decided, just a bully, he was a coward.

It took about half an hour for everyone to file into the court and when finally they were almost all there – the judge, the jury and the various lawyers and bewigged barristers – the defendant was called.

There was a sudden hush as Lisa was led, by two social workers, to her place. She was dressed, as she had been on every occasion that she had seen Hattie, in a neat, pretty, old-fashioned dress, her hair held back from her sweet, expressionless face by a pink plastic Alice band.

Hattie knew the details of Lisa's crime. She had read and reread those transcripts of her confession. What she hadn't heard, and what chilled her now, was the victim's halting and tearful evidence relayed to the court via a TV monitor.

It was late afternoon before they called Hattie to the witness stand and by then she had begun to lose her nerve. Her previous belief that it was her duty to somehow redeem Lisa in the eyes of the jury had been worn away not only by Lindy's sobbing description of the events of that day but also by the evidence of the old lady who had remembered seeing the smiling Lisa leading the smaller girl from the playground. And the policeman who had found Lindy and given her the kiss of life.

Moreover, Hattie was frightened now. She had, from time to time, been called upon to give evidence in court but never in a case such as this. She made her way to the witness box, hardly daring to look around her for fear of being struck dumb by the sight of so many people watching her.

But then she caught sight of Lisa. And for the first time that day an expression – actually a little smile – passed across the child's face. Hattie remembered, then, why she was here. How important it was to impress on this court room that it was the circumstances of Lisa's childhood that had prompted her to commit this crime. It was as if in this child – undoubtedly guilty – was the proof of all Hattie's theories. That nurture ruled over nature. That had this little girl received the care, the love, the attention and the encouragement that should be the right of all children, she would not be in this court today.

'Miss George,' began the rather pompous prosecuting barrister, 'you have, I believe, compiled a detailed psychiatric report on Lisa Price.'

Hattie nodded.

'Could you briefly tell us how you came to the conclusions set out here?'

'I spent over fifty hours with Lisa Price. And many more in considering the disclosures she made and in studying the recordings of our talks.'

A copy of the report was passed to the judge.

'It is your professional opinion, I believe, that the difficult circumstances of Lisa Price's home life might offer some insight into her actions on 16th November 1997.'

'It is,' said Hattie.

'But according to the reports of the social workers involved in the case Lisa comes from a close-knit, supportive family, with both parents and full siblings.'

'I think it would be foolish to assume that a child raised in a two-parent family is automatically assured of a childhood in which there is no cruelty, neglect or emotional deprivation,' said Hattie.

'And yet we have no previous evidence of abuse. Social reports on the other children in the family reveal them to be well-behaved, well-disciplined, well-adjusted,' the barrister countered.

'If you were to study my report you would see that I have concluded that it was the rigid application of that discipline – and the extraordinary fear that Lisa felt for her father – that was at the root of the child's disturbed behaviour,' she replied.

'But George Price brought up his children to believe in

God. To know the difference between right and wrong,' continued the barrister.

'It is my professional view that George Price's obsessional religious beliefs were misguided and ultimately damaging to his children,' Hattie explained. 'I do not believe that Lisa has natural psychopathic tendencies. She took no pleasure in what happened that day. She is not unduly fascinated by the macabre, by death, by torture or pain. She is a confused child whose absolute belief in her father's authority and example resulted in her mistaken belief that what she was doing she did for her father's God. She said to me – and you will find this quote on page 54 of my report – "I tried to tell her about God absolving her sins. I tried to baptise her to take away the sins. But she kept screaming and screaming".'

There was a faint muttering around the court room.

'And do you have any direct evidence of Mr Price's mistaken religious beliefs?'

'Lisa revealed to me that she was severely punished by her father. He would beat all the children with a belt for their sins, not their naughtiness. There is also a strong suggestion of sexual abuse – against the girls in particular.'

'A strong suggestion?' said the barrister sharply.

'Again I will have to refer you to my recordings of my sessions with Lisa. She told me – you will find this on page 44 – that her father was "the master" that he made the girls do "those things".'

'But I wasn't asking for allegations, Miss George, I was asking for supportive evidence of abuse. Could you please answer my question more clearly?'

'Well,' Hattie stuttered, 'there isn't any concrete supportive evidence at this stage . . .'

'Is there any evidence at *all* of the father's abuse of the child?' said the barrister, casting a cold eye first at Hattie and then at the jury.

'He absolutely adhered to the belief of "an eye for an eye, a tooth for a tooth". On one occasion, when Lisa had accidentally spilt a small amount of the tea she had made for her father, he poured boiling water over her arm.'

As Hattie related this, Lisa's mother stood up, shook her head and began muttering, 'No, no, no . . .'

The judge ordered her to sit down and directed Hattie to continue.

'And then there were a number of instances in which he used stories from the Bible to frighten his children. Lisa grew up being told stories that endorsed this feeling of her father's will being that of God. The story of Abraham being ordered to sacrifice his son; Josiah; the Walls of Jericho and so on.'

'The Bible, Miss George . . .' said the barrister, turning towards the jury and then adding, 'the Good Book. I'm only sorry that Mr Price is not able to be here in person to defend his name. It might be important for the court to know that Lisa's father is unable to be present today because of his ill-health.'

Hattie knew then that there was little point in continuing. It might have been possible to convince the court that Lisa was not a monster had her childhood terrors involved more modern forms of horror – exposure to drugs, alcohol, obscene material, video nasties – but none of these things was relevant in Lisa's case. And with her cowardly and cruel father absent from the proceedings she had little hope of arousing any pity for Lisa from the jury.

But the prosecution hadn't finished with her yet.

'Is it possible, Miss George,' the barrister began, 'that you yourself might have misinterpreted Lisa's father?'

'Lisa bears a scar from the incident I mentioned.'

'A scar that I think you will find has quite different origins. I have here a report – you were shown all the

305

medical reports on Lisa, Miss George – of an accident that occurred at Lisa's school.'

Hattie looked across at Lisa and realised, instantly, that not all the disclosures she had made during their many sessions had been truthful.

'If that is the case I will have to revise my report,' Hattie said, her face betraying her confusion.

'Mr Price's illness might also have a bearing on the revision of your report,' said the barrister contemptuously. 'He is in St Mary's Hospice in the last stages of a two-year fight against cancer of the oesophagus. That is all for now, Miss George. You may stand down.'

Afterwards Hattie wasn't sure how she had managed to get back to her seat. She had been certain that she had examined every scrap of paper – every dental record, every page in the GP's notes – that existed on Lisa. She felt unprofessional, let down, cheated and, when she glanced across again at Lisa, manipulated. Why hadn't she been more thorough, more mature? Why had she been so eager to believe in Lisa's suffering? And then she remembered Jimmy's words from the night before, his accusation that she had only been interested in him when he was the underdog, when she could pity and patronise him.

Would she, she wondered, have fought so hard to help Lisa Price – would she have listened so eagerly to her story of parental abuse – if she, too, were not a social outcast?

Jon and Claire had lain on the rose petals all that night, just talking, not making love. If she needed proof that this was *for real* – apart from the obvious evidence of this whole mad, romantic stunt – it was that in the hours since she had got home and found him here he hadn't attempted much more than a couple of long kisses.

She had known, really, the moment she had opened the front door, that it must be Jon. He was the only man –

she was rather ashamed to admit – that had ever been close enough to her to know that her favourite flower was the pink lily, that her favourite piece of music was Samuel Barber's *Adagio for Strings*, that La Perla was her favourite lingerie.

And the only man she supposed – thinking with just a hint of regret about Jimmy – who cared enough to find out.

What is more, she thought as she lay looking at his familiar face, he was the only man who could see through her brutal cynicism to the tender woman beneath.

'You never told me what prompted all this,' said Claire, throwing a handful of petals at him.

'Hattie,' Jon said.

'Hattie?'

'Yes. You see I had been talking to her for a while, since I seemed to have lost you to Jimmy. I had taken her on as my confidante. Besides, I couldn't talk to you about us.'

'It might have been cheaper if you had,' she said, sipping another glass of the Laurent Perrier.

'But you wouldn't have listened, would you? You would have given me more and more of that shit about men never meaning what they say.'

'They don't.'

'Shut up . . .' he said, but his eyes were laughing.

'At least very rarely,' she said with a smile.

'Anyway, I could see that you and Hattie had got pretty close over this thing you were doing with Jimmy. And, after all, she does know a thing or two about human behaviour and motivation. So I put my prejudices behind me and started confiding in her. I know it's odd because she always irritated me so. I have always found her ardent idealism, all that men-are-born-equal crap, so bloody, bloody, naïve. And she was so obstinate and humourless with it . . .' He paused. 'And then if I'm honest—'

'Oh no,' she interrupted, 'not more honesty.'

'If I'm honest – which of course I am and always will be – I also thought that her principles and her life of privilege sat rather awkwardly together. There was something hypocritical, I thought, about a woman – born into all that wealth, living in that flat and with a man like Toby – insisting in smart restaurants that all men are equal.'

'But?'

'But then once she'd kicked Toby into touch I realised she was probably all right,' he said.

'But Toby is your oldest friend, you shit.'

'You really don't know anything about men, do you?' Jon said wearily. 'I never liked him, never really talked to him, I'd just known him a long time.'

'So, finally, you talked to Hattie about me,' said Claire.

'Yes, and she was very sweet and listened and kept telling me to tell you how I felt.'

'But you didn't.'

'Have you completely forgotten the occasion on which I did?'

She laughed.

'Anyway a couple of days ago – when you and Jimmy were off at some polo match or shopping in Harvey Nicks or somewhere – I had lunch with her. I think by then she was convinced that you and Jimmy were an item, but she was too nice to tell me.'

'Oh God . . .' said Claire.

'She said to me that if I wanted you I would have to do something big, something dramatic. Said that I should imagine myself as a product and you as my ideal consumer. Which is what I did. I sold myself to you. I thought of all the things you liked best in the world, all the things I knew you would want, and then I hoped that you'd realise you wanted me too,' he added, looking at her a little smugly.

'And I did,' she said. 'Only . . .'

'Only?'

'Only I do feel a bit bad about Hattie.'

'Why?'

'Because I was so mean to her. Because I was so cross with her for having won Jimmy that I wouldn't give up.'

Jon's face fell. 'Do you still want Jimmy? Did you hope it was him that had done all that last night?'

'How could it have been? No, no I don't think I really wanted Jimmy. It's just that you know how competitive I am.'

'I do.'

'And I didn't want to be the loser. Not that winning Jimmy was such a big deal, really. I mean, he is beautiful but . . . if I'm honest—'

'Which of course you are. Unlike men, women are always honest,' he said cynically.

'If I'm honest I couldn't bear the fact that he had chosen her over me.'

'Bitch,' he said, kissing her.

'I'll have to put it right with her because she thinks that Jimmy and I had a thing going, I know she does . . . and we didn't, honestly . . .' She broke off then because his kissing was becoming more urgent and, really, it was about time they consummated their new relationship.

Hattie had begun to wonder if her relationship with Rex wasn't the most meaningful of her life. When she got back from the court – the judge had adjourned for the day at the end of her own cross-examination – Rex seemed to know what she needed.

He was, she had long since decided, a remarkable dog. She knew it sounded ridiculous – she had always been slightly contemptuous of people who started to attribute to their animals human characteristics – but it was almost as if he knew she had been through a terrible experience that day.

He didn't run to get his lead, as he normally did, nor did he jump at her. He just came over to her and leant against her. She stroked his back and he looked at her as if he knew it was she who needed, this evening, a gentle pat on the head.

When she thought about it, Rex had always been rather astute. Hadn't he, after all, driven Toby out of her life by ruining his best pair of Gucci loafers? And hadn't he – that night when Jimmy had brought his friends back to the flat and made the dog perform his loathsome trick with the Newkie – taken refuge in her bedroom with her? And wasn't it true that in the last couple of weeks – as the full effects of his new-found success had changed Jimmy – Rex had somehow switched his allegiance to her? She bent down to pick the mail off the mat and walked over to the kitchen, the dog following, deciding that she was in desperate need of a drink and a fag.

'And then, Rex, we'll go to the park.'

She took an open bottle of white wine from the fridge and poured herself a glass. Then she lit her cigarette and began to glance through the post.

There were a couple of bills and some sort of card in a handwritten envelope. It was an invitation to Toby's marriage to Christine Mary Baker. It didn't surprise or even upset her. Toby had told her he'd been chosen as the candidate at a forthcoming by-election and clearly the most important possession for a politician – even a non-sleaze New Labour one – was a wife. She laughed out loud then, stubbed out her cigarette, finished her wine and decided to take Rex out for his walk.

It was still quite warm and sunny and she sat on a bench in the park while he ran round interacting with other dogs. She didn't really want to go back to the flat. She felt like running away with Rex, somewhere that didn't remind her of Jimmy, or Claire or the terrible events of the day.

When she got back she fed and watered Rex and then made herself a sandwich. She hadn't eaten all day. Then she sat down on the sofa to watch *EastEnders*.

Rex began to bark before the doorbell rang, as if he sensed the presence of whoever it was outside the flat door – Claire, oddly enough. Hattie let her in and went straight back to her sandwich and the TV. Even Rex, once she was inside the flat, ignored her. Claire came over and turned the television off.

'Do you mind if I get myself a glass of wine?'

Hattie shrugged, leant over and put the TV back on.

Claire came back, put two glasses of wine on the table and then went over to the wall and pulled out the plug of the television.

'You'll have to talk to me now,' she said, passing Hattie a glass of the wine.

'I don't think I've got anything to say to you, Claire. I've had a dreadful day and the last thing I need right now is a girlie heart-to-heart with you.'

'I know I haven't behaved very well in the last couple of weeks,' said Claire. 'Over Jimmy, I mean . . .'

'I really don't want to talk about it, Claire. Except to say that when you get home you can give Jimmy a message from me.' Hattie looked coldly at Claire '*I'm keeping Rex.*'

As if on cue the dog jumped up beside her and laid his head on her lap.

'I don't know why you think I've got Jimmy at home. I rather thought he'd be here,' Claire said. 'He did follow you – a little like Rex – when you stormed out of the restaurant last night.'

Hattie thought about this for a moment. 'You mean he didn't come to you?'

'No. And I'm not sure I'd have noticed if he had. I was rather preoccupied.'

Hattie looked at her again, this time with a little more warmth. 'With what?'

'With Jon,' Claire said with a smile.

'How did he do it?' she asked, thawing still more.

'With flowers, champagne, chocolate, rose petals and a sense of humour.'

'And you, as it were, swallowed it?'

'Well, actually, Hattie, I'm rather concerned about it. No one has ever treated me that well before. And although I have always been a bit of a mug for a bastard I'm not quite sure how to handle someone whose intentions towards me are honourable. Someone who is sincere, sensitive, says what he means . . .'

'You're not really talking about Jon?'

'Look, I'm not so taken by all this that I expect it to last for ever. I mean, I do retain certain critical faculties about him – probably because he's being so nice – but heavens, I really think he cares.'

'Well, I suppose I'm pleased for you both.'

'But I didn't come here to talk about me.'

'That makes a change,' said Hattie with a weary smile.

'I came to apologise. You know I really, really wanted Jimmy.'

'But not as much as Jon?'

'Oh God, much more than I ever wanted Jon.'

'So that augers well then, for your future together.'

'Oh you know what I mean. It was like an obsession. I wasn't thinking straight.'

Hattie didn't say anything.

'You know, I was consumed with jealousy when the two of you got it together. I'm a fucking rotten loser.'

Hattie still didn't say anything.

'And if you must know I couldn't *believe* it when he waltzed off with you that night. I couldn't understand –

and this is going to sound awful – why on earth he would have picked you when he could have had me.'

'Do you know, Claire, I thought my self-esteem – after my ordeal in court today – was at rock bottom. But I was wrong . . .' And, horror of horrors, she began to cry.

'Heavens, Hattie, whatever is wrong?'

'Do I need to tell you? I'm unprofessional, I've just made the biggest cock-up of my career. I've won and lost Jimmy in the space of four days. Oh, and on top of that you've just confirmed what I have always thought: given the choice nine out of ten men would choose Claire.'

'What happened with Jimmy?'

'He told me a few home truths and I told him to go and fuck himself – or to be more accurate, to go and fuck you,' she said, wiping her face with her sleeve.

'I wonder where he went?' said Claire.

'I don't really think we should worry. All doors are open to Jimmy now. He might have gone to Arabella or Jay or any one of those ghastly people at that dinner last night.'

'I know he loves you.'

'No you don't. It was all – it was all a mirage. He said something, though, last night that made me want to kill you. He said that you'd claimed we had a side bet about who would get him into bed first.'

'Well, in a way we did.'

'What do you mean?'

'It was never said but right from the start – the moment he came out of your bathroom that day with the towel wrapped round his waist – I think we were competing for him.'

Hattie sniffed a little and thought about it. She was probably as much in denial about her real intentions with Jimmy as she was about everything else in her life. As she had been about the possibility that Lisa was – as all the evidence against her suggested – a cold-blooded, psychopathic attempted-murderer.

'Anyway, it's over.'

'Is it?'

'Oh yes, I told him it would never work. And he agreed.'

'I'm sorry, Hattie.'

'The thing is – to paraphrase his last words to me – I don't fit in his world any more and he doesn't fit in mine,' she said, tears streaming down her face.

Chapter Twenty-Four

Hattie rang the office the next day and asked if she could take some leave. Coming so soon after the three days she had taken without warning the previous month – and following the professional humiliation she had suffered the day before – it didn't go down too well.

But there was no question of her being called again at Lisa's trial. Her report had been excluded from the evidence. Nor was it likely that she would retain Lisa as a patient – in fact, she had already recommended that the child be reassigned to a colleague. And because she had cleared her diary for the ten days or so that it had been estimated the trial would last, she put her foot down and insisted that she needed to get away.

In fact she didn't so much need to get away as to go to ground. She locked herself away in her flat, took no calls, saw no one – apart from Rex – and began to turn her professional skills on herself; subjected her own behaviour to the kind of analysis that she usually reserved for her patients.

From time to time Claire or Arabella would leave a message on her answerphone but she didn't respond. After a couple of days, presumably alerted by Bella, even her mother rang expressing, in her high trilling voice, her concern about Hattie. Any moment now, Hattie thought, as she replayed her mother's message, her father would be called in. So she called her back.

'Hattie, how are you?' her mother said, in the familiar tones that Hattie always described as 'faux feeling'.

'Oh, I'm fine. I've just taken a few days' leave.' she said.

'We read about you in the *Telegraph*. Your father said that he had kept telling you it was the wrong profession for you,' she said

'You say all the right things, Mother.' Hattie was aware that her mother, even if she was listening, wouldn't have picked up the irony.

'Anyway, at least there is some good news in the family.'

'Oh really?' said Hattie, suddenly interested.

'Jontie . . .'

'What about her?' asked Hattie, thinking to herself that probably her mother regarded her dog as more part of the George family than her daughter.

'She's going to have pups. Sired by last year's Cruft's winner.'

'Well, that's marvellous. Any news from Arabella?' enquired Hattie, just saving herself from referring to her sister as 'your other bitch'.

She thought about Jimmy all the time, but she was convinced that she wouldn't hear from him again. She had received an invitation to his book launch which – on a somewhat grandiose scale, she thought – was being held in a little over a month's time at St James' Park, the home of Newcastle United Football Club. She supposed she had only been invited – and obviously at Claire's instigation – because with a venue that big they needed anyone they could get. She was certain that Jimmy wouldn't want her there so she didn't bother to reply.

Hattie fell back into some sort of routine. She went back to work and took on a number of new cases – amongst them the little boy, Josh, who had reminded her so forcefully of the young Jimmy.

The days passed in a monotonous haze. Work, home, walking Rex, TV, bed. At the weekends she did little more than sleep – she seemed to have an endless capacity for that. It became her only hobby. And along with the junk food she ate it was the only thing that sustained her.

She tried not to think about Jimmy – or indeed any of the events of the previous few months. But occasionally some image of him would penetrate her consciousness and she would be overcome with a kind of grief.

She neither heard nor spoke to any of her friends. Outside work she was, in fact, turning into something of a recluse. Occasionally someone would leave a message on the answerphone, but she never picked up the receiver and talked to anyone. Jon made the occasional stab at getting through to her, presumably because he held her in some way responsible for his reunion with Claire. Arabella left the odd high-pitched monosyllabic greeting. Once her father had barked out some stern concern for her future.

Two weeks after her return to work she received an urgent call in her office from her mother.

'Mother, what on earth is wrong?' Hattie was alarmed because her mother had never rung her at work before. In fact she was surprised her mother knew where to reach her.

'The most terrible thing has happened.'

'Not Daddy?' Hattie said.

'Oh God, no, nothing like that. No, it's Jontie. She gave birth to four puppies two days ago, a week early.'

'So what's the problem? Are they all right?'

'Yes, they're fine. It's just that it's quite clear the Cruft's champion isn't the father. She must have come into season earlier than we thought. She must have got out and encountered some stray mongrel.'

'Encountered?' said Hattie.

'Oh you know, some bloody stray must have impregnated her. They are the oddest little hybrids. I think there must be a bit of whippet in them, and a touch of Jack Russell . . .'

'Oh dear,' said Hattie, trying to stop herself from laughing.

'Of course, she's finished with the Kennel Club now,' said her mother, trying to impress on Hattie the gravity of the situation.

'How awful!' said Hattie in mock sympathy.

'But actually, Hattie, they're really rather sweet. Arabella wants one.'

'And me. I want one . . .'

'But you don't like dogs, Hattie.'

'Oh, but I like the sound of *these* dogs,' she said.

'Probably because they're mongrels,' said her mother sharply. 'You always liked underdogs.'

When Hattie got home that evening she congratulated Rex, remembering the only amusing thing that had happened on the day she and Jimmy went to Whitehaven – how they had walked together in the gardens and found Rex and Jontie. And then she began to remember other moments she had shared with Jimmy: the night they had watched the Toon thrash Spurs; their time together in North Shields; the magical evening of the party.

About a month after her return to work she began to encounter real, not remembered, images of Jimmy, first of all on the cover of the *Big Issue*. She was astonished by the amount of publicity he had got. She couldn't think of a book that had been published in the last few years that had received quite so much media hype. Not Jilly Cooper's *Appassionatta*, not Brian Brute's *Bollocks*, not Martin Amis's *The Information*, not Eggo Massif's *In the Horn of the Rhino* – no book she could remember had caused quite such a stir.

Why, not even Salman Rushdie's *Satanic Verses* could have received as much media attention and publicity as Jimmy Ryan's *The Final Whistle*.

It seemed as if everywhere she turned she saw Jimmy. The *Big Issue* cover had just been the start of his media exposure. He had subsequently featured in a variety of magazines and papers from *GQ* to *Gay News*. He had even found himself, surely not at Claire's suggestion, as a 'page seven fella' in the *Sun*.

The forthcoming publication of the book was backed up by a poster and newspaper ad campaign which featured two of Michael Roberts' portraits of Jimmy – the one in which he was removing a tab from a can of Newcastle Brown Ale and the one in which he was lying in bed draped in a white sheet reading a copy of the *Big Issue* with his own face on the cover.

He had, as well, become something of a broadcasting pundit, being wheeled out on all manner of programmes – Frank Skinner's chat show, of course; *TFI Friday*, *Room 101* as well as a number of programmes dealing with many of the contemporary issues raised in his book. He made an appearance on a *Kilroy* special on child abuse; he featured on an edition of *The Time The Place* devoted to the North/South divide and he was on the podium for Esther's look at dysfunctional families.

Then there were all the gossip column items. Jimmy, usually accompanied by Arabella, was at the most socially prestigious occasions in the run-up to the launch so that his beautiful face – and Bella's, of course – popped up in the People columns of *YOU*, *Hello!*, *Tatler*, *Harpers* and *Vogue*.

The evening before the launch – as Hattie was sitting slobbing with Rex in front of *Animal Hospital* (her taste for popular culture, born of her relationship with Jimmy was in danger of becoming an unhealthy addiction) the doorbell rang. Rex began his banshee barking but she didn't move. She had no intention of opening the door. But whoever it was refused to give up, kept his or her hand on the bell and began to shout through the letterbox. She pulled herself up and looked through the peephole she never usually bothered to use. It was Claire. She supposed she had better let her in, if only to silence Rex.

'Hattie, what on earth is wrong with you? You look dreadful.'

'According to you I always do,' snapped Hattie.

'Well, particularly dreadful,' said Claire.

'I just needed some time and some space,' she said. 'Do you want some tea?'

'No, thank you,' said Claire, glancing with distaste at the mess on the table in front of the television. 'I've come to persuade you to come to the launch of Jimmy's book.'

'I don't think I could bear it. Good choice of venue, though, if a little on the large side . . .'

'Actually it was a bit of a compromise. Jay wanted to hold the party on the Wembley pitch. It would, he said, be symbolic in all manner of ways, evoking images of victory, national pride and heroism, all of which had been denied Jimmy.'

'God, that man is full of crap,' said Hattie.

'Look, you've got to be there. After all we went through you can't not be there to see his moment of glory.'

'I'm quite sure Jimmy doesn't want me anywhere near his moment of glory.'

Claire went quiet then so Hattie knew that Jimmy hadn't sent her.

'The thing is, Hattie, that it was all my fault. If I hadn't meddled you wouldn't have broken up.'

'Do you know, he threw his precious Blackpool snow-storm at the wall? If you look carefully you can see where it chipped the paint,' Hattie said distractedly.

'Oh, for Christ's sake, pull yourself together, Hattie, and tell me what it is you want.'

'I don't know . . .'

'Well, I can't promise that Jimmy will come up to you with open arms but I think you should be there,' Claire said firmly.

Hattie shrugged. 'I suppose I would like to see how it all turns out for him,' she admitted.

'Well, if you do come,' Claire said as she prepared to leave, 'for fuck's sake do something about your appearance.'

It was Rex that made up Hattie's mind for her the next morning. Even if Jimmy rejected her he would want to see Rex. He hadn't come so far from his roots – the launch was in Newcastle after all – that he wouldn't want to see his dog.

But Claire was right about the way she looked: she was a mess. She would need to shop – buy something to wear, get something done with her hair. And there was so little time.

She went to Harvey Nichols and bought a short cream dress with a fitted waist and a slightly flared skirt. The assistant said she looked lovely and for once she allowed herself to believe her. Then, for the first time in she didn't know how long, she went to the hairdresser's and let the stylist trim her long curly hair and blow dry it straight and smooth so that it fell like a curtain across her face. There was a good chance, she thought as she looked in the mirror, that Jimmy wouldn't even recognise her.

She dashed back to the flat to fetch Rex and caught the last possible train out of King's Cross.

As soon as she was seated, the dog at her feet, she knew she had made a mistake – not just in deciding to go to the launch, but in picking the slow train. She was going to be late, so late she wouldn't be able to check into the hotel where Claire had booked her a room. She would have to change on the train and go straight to St James' Park.

She went into the loo and looked at herself in the awful yellow light, put on her little bits of make-up, undressed and changed into the silk dress, pulling on the sheer, shiny tights that the assistant had recommended and finally adding the ballet pumps that – at least in the shop – had seemed so right.

It was gone ten before the train pulled into Newcastle Central. She had to wait, in all her finery, for twenty minutes in a queue for a cab. And when finally she reached St James' Park, the place was packed.

Everyone you could think of was there, which was just as well with the amount of space that they had to fill – Chris Evans, Brian Brute, Melvyn Bragg, Gazza, Benedict Wright, Alan Yentob, Nick Hornby, Alan Shearer, Skinner and Baddiel. Jay Hector had, apparently, flown over two hundred people up from London.

Hattie took a drink from a tray being passed round by one of twenty or so nubile girls in football strip, and watched the spectacle with disbelieving eyes.

She wanted very much to be happy for Jimmy. But this was not quite how she had seen his future. He would say, of course, that she wanted him to have a future no different from his past. But that wasn't true – she knew that now. She didn't want less for him, she wanted more.

She remembered how much of an outsider Jimmy had been when she had first found him and thought that now it was *she* that was the outsider. She felt as if she had nothing at all to do with the product being peddled in *The Final Whistle*.

Curiously, she could see no sign of the man himself. She saw Arabella, and managed to duck out of sight before her sister registered her presence. And she thought

– fleetingly – that she saw Jon behind a Sky Sports camera crew.

It was Rex who gave her away. From the heart of the party she heard a familiar voice call his name.

'Rex . . . Hattie . . .' Claire shouted. 'You came!'

'Yes, well, I thought he might at least like to see Rex,' Hattie said awkwardly.

'Oh yes, I am sure he would,' Claire answered nervously. Something, Hattie could tell, was not running according to Claire's plan.

'Where is he?' she said.

'Well, that's a bit of a problem, actually,' Claire bit her lip and glanced round to ensure that no one else could hear. 'He was here at the beginning. But he got upset about something or other. Something to do with Jay. And he went.'

'Where?'

'If I knew that I'd drag him back,' she spat.

Hattie had a hunch where he might have gone. She remembered Jimmy telling her about how his grandfather used to take him to St James' Park to see matches and how, afterwards, they would go to the quayside and eat fish and chips. She abandoned her drink and led Rex out of the turnstiles down towards the Tyne.

It must have changed since Jimmy was a child. There were no fish and chip shops, just a lot of restaurants rather like the ones in London, with sleek interiors and expensive menus. And the big cranes had gone too. In their place were the kind of lavish developments – lofts, apartment blocks, hotels, shopping malls – that indicated the new prosperity of the city.

She recognised him from behind even though, she noted, he had cut his hair very short. He was standing by the river's edge, looking up at the vast, arched, illuminated Tyne Bridge.

'Jimmy,' she said.

He turned round and looked at her. 'You came, hinny.'

'Well, I had to bring Rex,' she said as the dog greeted his master.

He bent down to stroke the dog and she marvelled at how much better he looked with his hair cropped close around his face.

'You were right, hinny, it was all shite.'

'What?'

'All those people,' he said, pointing back towards St James' Park. 'All that crap they talk. All that coming on to you because of who you are, what you did, how much money you've got.'

'You won, Jimmy. It doesn't matter how.'

'You changed your hair,' he said, reaching out and touching it.

'And you . . .'

'You know what I was thinking? I was looking at this place and remembering what it was like when I was a kid and I thought – it's like me. They've taken away the cranes, and the workers and the fish 'n' chip shops and they've made it all look like something else. It's like what's happened to me.'

'You're not the only one who's been changed,' she said.

He looked at her tenderly, ignoring her comment, and continued, 'I only did it for you, to be good enough for you . . .'

'You were good enough for me at the beginning. I knew right from that first night you were a man of worth. You didn't need to change, but I'm glad you did because you made me change too. You were good enough for me from the start, am I good enough for you now?'

'I love you, Hattie,' he said

'And I love you, Jimmy.'

Although the day had been warmer than was seasonal, there was a real chill in the air now and she shivered. He put his arm around her and they walked along the quayside, marvelling at the changes, Rex running ahead of them.

'Look, Jimmy,' she said, pointing to the last remnant of the old quayside: a small old-fashioned fish and chip shop positioned a little way from the Pitcher and Piano. They bought fish and chips and sat on a bench feeding each other and Rex, looking out across the Tyne.

'Will you be with me, hinny?' he said

She nodded.

'Always?'

She nodded again.

'For richer or poorer?' he said, feeding her another chip.

'In a castle,' she said, 'or a shop doorway . . .'